The
WINDS *of* COURAGE

Best Wishes!

Marilyn
Kun

Books by Marilyn King

The Winds of Love
The Winds of Grace
The Winds of Courage

Hearts of Home
Isabel's Song

The
WINDS *of* COURAGE

Book Two

MARILYN KING

CROWN LEAF PUBLISHING

ISBN: 13: 978-0-9967258-0-4 Trade paperback
ISBN: 10: 0996725806
Library of Congress Catalog Card Number:

Cover design by Karri Ross
Cover artwork copyright ©2015 by Karri Ross

Printed in the United States of America
2015–First Edition

THIS BOOK IS dedicated to my four children,
Janine, Rick, Andy, and Sam for the encouragement
you've given me. You make my heart smile.
I love you a bushel and a peck.

ACKNOWLEDGMENTS

MY SINCEREST THANKS to my critique groups, The Romancers: Roberta Smith, Anne Fowler, Holly LaPat and Liz Pye, and the Wordsmiths: Molly Jo Realy, Therese Moore and Mary Ruth Hughes, Mary Langer Thompson, Richard Zone, Loralie Pallotta, John Garner, Willard and Suzanne Holbrook. You all helped keep my facts, points of view, storyline and tenses straight. My peers are great friends who helped me every step of the way.

Special thanks to my sisters, Verdean Palmer and Theresa LeRoy who took the time to look at my work and give me advice. I appreciate all the hours you spent on the story.

Also, a special thanks to my brother, Robert LeRoy whose talent with photography is unsurpassed. He managed to get my character just right for the cover of this book.

Many thanks to my editors, Jenny Margotta and Gloria Graham. Your insights were both educational and invaluable. I couldn't have produced such a fine piece of work without you.

My love and gratitude go out to my husband, Bob, who has been my backbone, advisor, and ear throughout the building of this book. His willingness to research and edit the book is much appreciated.

NOTE TO THE READER

The Jamaican slave revolt–which lasted from 1831 to 1838 brought turbulent years that irrevocably changed the lives of slaves and plantation owners along the Caribbean Coast. Old traditions crumbled and the philosophy that had kept everyone–prominent, poor white, and servant–in their places vanished.

In the effort to accurately portray the era in which this historical fiction is set, I have used certain terms in this work that are offensive to me personally and which are no longer prevalent in today's speech and attitudes. This is true in regard to the men and women held in slavery on the plantations described in this novel as it moves to the South in early America. Please know that when terms like *darky, blackie, coloreds,* and *Negro* are used, they are reflective of this time frame and not meant as any offense to the African-American people. Terms that referred to slaves that were also common in the period, but which were the most offensive, are not used in this novel.

Though I find the period in which I wrote this story fascinating, I find the treatment of human beings as slaves repellant, and I believe God created all men as equal in His eyes. May the day come when humans treat each other with grace and see each other for who we are and not by the color of our skin. For I believe this is what God intended.

In His Grip,
Marilyn King

PROLOGUE

Riverbend, Jamaica
14 January, 1831

TIA HARGRAVE STEPPED down from the wagon and picked up her skirts as she threaded her way past a throng of sailors who lingered on the wharf. A balmy breeze washed over her as she smelled the loamy scent of the sea purling against the hull of the ships. Walking swiftly, she ignored the row of harbor buildings, warehouses and pubs on her right, and glanced instead at the bow of each vessel, searching for the craggy old ship, the *Caribbean Dragon*.

She came upon a spanking new brig that bobbed gently in the inky waters. To her right, a street lantern lit up the dark road, its rays casting a yellow glow on the name of the vessel, *Caribbean King*. Her lips curved upward. Had he finally done it?

"Good evening," a man's voice boomed above her. "Come on up."

She searched the ship's railing to see Jule Spade standing overhead, peering down at her. Tia picked up her skirts and walked toward him. In no time she stood on the main deck and stepped into the arms of her new lover and business partner.

Jule's eyes were tawny and piercing, and just now they raked over her face. He grinned appreciatively.

"As you see, I received your message." She brushed a kiss on his cheek.

This wasn't the first time they'd met in the still of the night. Tia felt it was time to join forces with Jule Spade. The man was not tall and broad, but he had a commanding presence, a worldliness about him gained from his experience on the seas, and from working with rough-edged slavers who bargained for a fair deal on the trade. Jule was of the same cloth and haggled with the worst of the worst plantation owners to get the most money he could for the captives in his ship's hold.

He was also a man who wielded a whip. He was fond of the long leather strap and preferred it to a pistol any day. Yet Tia felt safe with him. She was determined to escape this miserable island of Jamaica and disappear to the island of Tobago with Jule.

"I want you to see every inch of this vessel." Jule dropped his hand from Tia's waist and led the way. The crewmen watched as she glided past them. Several sailors held ropes in their hands as if they should be working, but instead, they stopped and stared at her. She could tell they were curious that the captain held company with a black woman. Other than the gentle lap of waves against the hull, an odd silence lay suspended on the main deck. Tia felt eyes bore into her back as she followed their captain.

After escorting Tia on a grand tour of his new ship, Jule asked, "So what do you think?"

"I'm impressed. What have you done with the *Caribbean Dragon?*"

"I sold the miserable piece of scrap to a sailor up the coast."

"Good. You did well."

"Come to my cabin. We must celebrate." Jule escorted Tia to the Captain's quarters. Once inside, he broke out a bottle of rum and they clinked glasses to his great success. One bottle led to another, and though she tilted the glass to her lips, she hid from him that she was drinking little of the rum.

"I have to admit," he slurred an hour later, "buying this ship didn't all happen with the selling of slaves." Jule opened a drawer beside his bed and pulled out a brown leather bag. He fished out an emerald from the small pouch.

"Where did you get that?" Tia asked in a bored voice, feigning disinterest.

"Never mind where I got it." He staggered sideways. "There's a whole bag of those fine gems and just *one* of them helped me purchase this ship." He waved his arms wide and smiled as he dropped the emerald in her open palm. "Take a look."

And look she did. Tia held the sparkling stone up to the lantern swinging above the bed. "But Jule . . ."

"Give it back to me." His hand was already stretched toward her.

She reluctantly gave up the small jewel into his outstretched hand. Her mind was racing a hundred different ways. She watched as he pulled the leather pouch open and deposited the stone inside. When he drew the strings closed, the pouch fairly bulged. Judging from its size, there could be at least a hundred gems in the small bag. She watched him return his treasure to the drawer, then close it, taking note of the fact that there was no lock.

When he came back to her side, she wrapped her arms around his neck and grazed his rough cheek with a kiss. "I'm so proud of you," she whispered.

"That's what I wanted to hear, my love. Soon the two of us will sail away from this island."

"We can't leave soon enough for me." She stroked the back of his head and neck and leaned in seductively.

"Enough talk for now." He pulled Tia over to the bunk side of the cabin. But before he could act upon his impulses, he slumped to the floor, his back against the side of the bed, and passed out.

Tia smiled, a wicked plan forming in her mind. "Goodnight, Jule." She gave him a shove with her foot, and he slid sideways until his head thumped against the plank floor.

She glanced at the drawer on the other side of the bed, back to Jule, and shook her head. *Not now*, she thought, *another time*.

A week later, the *Caribbean King* came into port at night. Garbed in dark clothing and counting on her ebony skin to help her pass unnoticed, Tia had been skulking around the wharf every day, anxiously awaiting its arrival. Now she hid behind a wall of crates, watching as Spade and several of his shipmates strode down the gang plank on their way to town.

She held her breath as Jule walked by her, waiting until the men disappeared into a tavern up the road. Then she quickly crept up the gangplank and into his cabin.

It was dark, but she didn't need a light. She'd have to be quick or risk getting caught as two of Jule's men walked the deck guarding the ship.

Stealthily, once inside the captain's quarters she inched her way to the other side of the bed and opened the drawer. At first her fingers did not find the leather pouch. Disappointment shot through her. But as she dug deeper her fingers found what she wanted. Heart pounding, she clutched the small leather bag to her chest and closed the drawer.

She could hardly breathe; her heart pounded harder. *Flee!* her every instinct screamed.

And flee she did. Pulling the thick wooden door of the cabin open a crack, Tia hid the pouch inside the pocket of her dress and glanced toward the steps leading up to the deck. No one was in sight. The creaking of the hull as it rubbed against the dock disguised the sound as she slipped out and quietly pulled the door shut behind her.

Before she could climb the companionway stairs to the deck, however, she heard footsteps above. She quickly pressed herself against the wall, holding her breath until the sound of boots faded away, then she threaded her way between barrels and crates and hurried down the gangway. Across the road was the wharf's warehouse. She ran to the building feeling as if there were eyes everywhere watching her.

What now?

As Tia debated her next move, Captain Drew Harding and a few men descended from the *Savannah Rose*. The vessel was moored two ships over from the *Caribbean King*. Tia was familiar with the *Savannah Rose*. It once belonged to Phillip Cooper, her master, before he passed. Captain Harding frequented Cooper's Landing when he was in town. The vessel now belonged to him, a gift from Phillip Cooper.

She waited a moment, trying to spot any crew members standing watch on his ship. She saw no one. Emboldened by the apparently unguarded deck, Tia took the risk of hurrying up the gangway pausing at the top to look around. Clouds slowly slid apart and the moon beamed down brightly. She was in its spotlight. Quickly she ran down the companionway below the quarterdeck.

Earlier that evening, Scoot Sweeny had watched Tia board the *Caribbean King*. A crewman on the ship, Sweeny knew Tia by sight and knew she trafficked in the slave trade. He also knew she didn't belong aboard the *Savannah Rose*. Her dark clothing and furtive manner caught his attention and he was curious as to what she was about. So he followed her.

Careful to stay in the shadows, he crept down the companionway in Tia's wake and watched as she disappeared into the first cabin. Creeping quietly down the passageway, he could hear the rough scrape of something in the room and he moved to peer through the partially open door. Moonlight streamed through a small port window and Sweeny could see Tia kneeling beside the bed, a drawer pulled from beneath the bunk. As he watched, she took something from her pocket, leaned forward and tucked it into the space created by the removal of the drawer. She then returned the drawer to its original position.

As Tia rose, Sweeny moved away from the door, slipped down the hall and stood in the dark shadows. Soon, Tia came out and firmly shut the door. She stopped and glanced his way. Did she see him? He stood stock-still, afraid to breathe lest she see his movement.

Shaking her head, Tia moved up the stairs and opened the door leading to the main deck. When she closed it, Sweeny let out a breath. He waited. Five . . . ten minutes. She didn't return. Sweeny crept toward the cabin and opened the door. He crossed the floor and pulled out the drawer. He felt around on the rough-planked floor until his fingers encountered a small leather bag. Sweeny loosened the tight string and lifting it up to the stream of light that poured in from the porthole, he peered into the pouch. His heart nearly stopped. Emeralds! He pulled the strings, closing the pouch. Clutching it in his fist, he dashed out of the room, forgetting to put the drawer back in place.

A sly smile spread across his face. He felt certain the gems belonged to Jule Spade and that Tia had moved them without Spade's knowledge. He shoved the pouch inside his shirt and made his way out onto the main deck. A cool breeze whipped at his face as he breathed in the salty air. Glancing about to make sure no one had seen him, he stealthily moved down the gangplank and back to his cabin aboard the *Caribbean King*.

Sweeny would have to hide the jewels for a while. If he did anything with them now, Spade would know he had stolen them, albeit from Jule's mistress. The ship captain was too free with his whip. Many a man was scarred for life from a run-in with the lethal weapon. No, he wouldn't do anything with the jewels just yet. He'd hide them far from here, on the island of Tobago where he stored his other treasures. He'd kept a map of where he had buried a tiny chest of goods. A few gold coins and a couple of ivory pieces . . . also taken from his captain, Captain Jule Spade. Now he would add to his collection. He'd wait yet another year before digging it up, then sailing across the ocean to America. No one would know him there. He would start over a wealthy man.

Spade planned to stay in the harbor for the night, but first he had business to attend to, then he'd find Tia. He still remembered the look on her face when he'd given her a tour of his new ship. Those crystal blue eyes had lit like he'd never seen before. When he showed her the emeralds, the stunned pleasure had played in her eyes again. He planned to see that look more often. She could have the world if she wanted it. Spade went into town eager to be done with his responsibilities. Then he'd see his ebony woman.

Hours passed, but Tia did not come. Something was wrong. Spade peered out over the inky waters toward the dimly lit wharf. Her wagon should have rolled up alongside the dark warehouse where a longboat waited at the dock.

He paced the main deck of the *Caribbean King,* his fingers sliding over the leather whip in his hand. The hour had grown too late. Dread crept up his back. Where was she? Spade pulled his wide-brimmed hat off and ran his fingers through his hair. "She's not coming," he grumbled. He strode to his cabin and slammed the door shut. Yanking off his boots, he dropped onto the side of the bed. Head in hand he stared at the drawer where the emeralds lay.

"Curse me for the lovesick idiot I am," he said aloud. He should have known better than to count on any woman, especially one as self-centered and scheming as he knew Tia to be. But even as he berated himself, he knew her resolution was part of her very nature. She wouldn't avoid him for long. Not with riches within her reach. A sly smile replaced his frown. He leaned back against the pillow, bringing his feet up onto the bed. Whatever had delayed her from coming tonight, he'd find out later. He'd see her the following week, but for now, his ship would be sailing in the early hours. Sleep claimed him.

It wasn't until the *Caribbean King* was out to sea that he discovered the jewels were gone. What a fool he'd been! He shouldn't have kept the emeralds hidden in the drawer by his bed. He wanted to believe that the she-cat hadn't taken them, but she was the only one who knew they were there. As soon as he delivered this cargo of slaves to Brazil, he'd turn the vessel around and find Tia. Those were his jewels! He'd get them back. Maybe it was time she learned a lesson.

He'd been too soft on her. That would have to change. He eyed his whip lying on the round table in his cabin.

ONE

Cooper's Landing, Jamaica
20 January 1831

TIA SLAPPED KINDRA, leaving an ugly red handprint on her daughter's honey-colored skin. "I'm not going to be a part of such a ridiculous fiasco."

Kindra staggered back as her hand flew to her burning cheek. Tears swam before her eyes as she shook her head. "Mother–"

"Stop it!" Tia walked out to the veranda.

"But I . . ."

"No!" Tia's voice rang harsh. "First I lose *my* sister Minerva to the vile sea because of that hateful woman you call *your* sister, Grace Cooper. And now I'll lose you to that idiot overseer, Denzel Talmaze. You're throwing yourself away on that no-account colored."

"Mother, please . . ."

Tia swung around, her crystal blue eyes blazing shards of fire. "You're not thinking how society will view your marriage, Kindra. You have money now. You have a plantation of your own. You have the ability to make a name for yourself. You don't have to marry this poor excuse for a man. You can have your pick of just about any respectable white man on the Caribbean coast. And what do you do?"

Tia turned back to the French doors overlooking the sugar plantation. "I'm colored, too, Mother. You seem to forget that."

"You're only half colored, Kindra. You were fortunate to be born with light skin. You have a much better chance of having a bright future than I ever had."

"You can't tell me you never suspected that I'd marry Denzel. I've never had eyes for any other man." Kindra crossed to where her mother stood gazing out at the open grounds, the sugar cane fields, and the sea beyond. She laid a hand on her mother's ebony shoulder, tentatively, hoping to subdue her mother's outrage.

"Don't." Tia brushed Kindra's hand away. "I will not be a part of your self-destructive foolishness. And just whose idea was it to bring in that old broom from the slave quarters?"

It was Kindra's turn to bristle. "That was my idea, Mother. I want a traditional wedding."

Tia's eyes bored into hers. "Really Kindra, have you gone *completely* mad?"

❦

Denzel stood alone in the bedroom and told himself to breathe deeply. He had the window wide open, letting in the tropical sea breeze, but still felt as if he were going to suffocate. This was his wedding day. He'd waited a long time for this day to come. As an overseer for Cooper's Landing, he'd gained respect from the Great House and his master and he'd been treated like a brother to the master's adopted son, Cameron Bartholomew. The two had been raised together from childhood.

Today he'd marry the headmistress' daughter, despite the fact that Tia hated him. He didn't feel apprehension for marrying "up," for marrying above his station; he had no uncertainty about being able to live up to what now would be expected of him. But the headmistress hated him, he knew, and the feeling was mutual–he despised the way Tia talked to her daughter.

Resplendent in his formal attire, he looked taller and broader than ever, and self-assured. But in truth, he was sick inside. Standing outside Tia's chamber door, he listened to Kindra and her mother argue. For a moment he feared the woman would convince Kindra not to marry. It wasn't long, though, before he heard what he wanted to hear. Kindra remained steadfast. Nothing Tia could say would change

Kindra's mind. The whole day was beginning to feel like a dream. He moved away from the door to check his suit one last time before going downstairs to wait for his bride.

Kindra stepped from the room, she closed the door soundly behind her to escape her mother's wrath. Once outside she squared her shoulders to compose herself before she descended the stairs to join Denzel and the small gathering of people who were waiting.

This was the second time within a month and a half that friends and family of Cooper's Landing sat in the ballroom for a wedding. The first was the union of Cameron and Grace, whose lavish wedding was put together with much fanfare. It seemed all of Riverbend had showed up for the nuptials and many of their father's merchant friends had traveled from far-lying ports, as well.

But Kindra's situation differed from that of her half-sister. When Phillip Cooper died a few months earlier, his powerful protection that had sheltered Kindra all her life had died with him. Kindra reluctantly acknowledged the truth in her mother's words. Many of the elite gentlemen and exquisitely gowned ladies who had attended Grace's wedding would not be present today. She didn't care. Her love for Denzel was strong enough to face whatever might be in store. Straightening her spine she gazed below.

Every facet of the many crystal chandeliers shone like prisms. Every potted plant still glistened from a coat of oil. Furniture glowed with rubbed-down wax; marble floors shone. All the French doors leading to the verandas were swung open to admit a fresh tropical breeze.

Out front, lined against the fence rails, were polished carriages and buggies, their drivers tending to the horses. The coachmen smoked their pipes and shared the news of the day.

Grace had begged Kindra to join in a double ceremony. But Kindra wouldn't hear of it. She wanted Grace to have her day in the sun at the side of the man she'd cherish for the rest of her life.

Besides, Kindra had spent two years hiding her feelings for Denzel from her mother and the world. Once they were married, Tia would not be able to stop them from seeing each other anymore.

Kindra's father had left her more than the plantation in Barbados. Her inheritnce had given her a way out from hiding her love for Denzel, a way for her to have somewhere to go, where they could be together to share that love. She would finally stand hand-in-hand with the man she wanted to be with, for all the world to see.

The tiny buttons on her lavish gown were just about to burst with the joy she felt. She was only minutes away from becoming Mrs. Denzel Talmaze. No more hiding. No more threats. So much had changed in the past few months that at times she nearly had to pinch herself to see if all that had transpired was really true. Not only was she about to become a bride, she could hardly wait to move to Barbados and claim her new home. She and Denzel would save their honeymoon for that voyage.

There was much to be done after this day was over. Much to look forward to.

Kindra stilled her heart and, peeking over the mahogany railing, saw Cameron, dressed in a dark suit jacket and black pants, waiting below to escort her to the altar. He looked up and raised his brows. A starched white collar with a black bow tie set off the sun-bronzed color of his skin.

She shook her head slightly, letting him know that Tia would not be joining her, and then raised her chin as she began her descent. As she glided down the marble staircase, it was all she could do to brush off the hurt of her mother's words.

She decided to focus on Denzel, her beloved, and her heart began to beat a little faster. In moments the two would become one. She was ready.

There was a hush, a pause in the music, as Cameron and Kindra appeared at the wide entrance to the ballroom. Denzel waited at the altar. *She's beautiful,* he thought. So beautiful—especially with her black silky hair piled high and kept in place by a little bouquet of daisies. Like an angel, her white gown floated around her. She wasn't dark like the rest of the coloreds on Cooper's Landing. Her skin had a honey glow, and her eyes were as green as emeralds just like her father's. With a faint smile on her face, she gathered her voluminous white skirt, let go of Cameron's arm and moved to stand beside him.

Grace stood to their left as Kindra's matron of honor. She quickly moved around to straighten the back of Kindra's long gown, then with a slight smile on her lips, she stepped back.

" . . . in the presence of these witnesses and with the power invested in me by God, I now pronounce you man and wife," the minister said.

Cheers and applause resounded through the ballroom as Denzel and Kindra looked at each other and grinned. They held hands and jumped the broom, indicating they were entering the land of matrimony. Having been married by a minister, it wasn't necessary for the bride and groom to perform this ritual, but Kindra had dreamed of doing this since she was a child.

Her mother had never married her father; slaves were not afforded the legal right of marriage. But her ancestors on her mother's side had maintained the symbolic tradition of "jumping the broom" for as long as anyone could remember. A broom was believed to sweep away past wrongs and ward off evil spirits. The couple jumped the broom to ensure a happy and fruitful life together. The slaves then celebrated in whatever meager way they could. The people sang and danced into the night. The women scrounged together a special meal. Then the couple slept together under the same roof. The people in the colored town honored the ritual of jumping the broom. The men in their community knew that the woman who jumped the broom with her man was off limits.

Denzel drew Kindra into his arms and kissed her long. Murmurs grew as it seemed he would never let her go, but he finally pulled back and Kindra laughed softly. He turned his new bride around to face the small group. Again, cheers went out as well as laughter.

For many years Denzel had worked side by side with the servants and field hands who now sat across the ballroom from the Jamaican elites. For some of the slaves it was their first time setting foot inside the Great House. Their eyes grew round at the impressiveness of the home. Kindra could see they tried to keep their gaze on the newlyweds rather than allow their eyes to stray to the walls and ceilings to take in the richness of it all.

The nuptials had just come to an end when the culinary servants and cooks filed into the ballroom with roasted meats and a fine line of food on polished silver trays. The women wore black and white parlor maid uniforms, while the men wore stark white. The band in the corner began to play softly, the sway of music filled the air.

"Congratulations!" Grace was the first to hug Kindra.

"We did it!" Kindra whispered in Grace's ear. She looked up, as if she could see through the ceiling to her mother's room, and then back to Grace.

"Yes, and you make a beautiful bride." Grace kissed Kindra on the cheek, and they hugged once more.

As anticipated, the line wasn't long. Her wedding guests were far fewer than those of Cameron and Grace. Those that mattered were here to celebrate with Kindra and her new husband. She was ready to get on with the party. Kindra glanced around for Denzel and found he had wandered a few feet away to talk to some of his friends. One of them, a big man named Mingo looked her way and smiled. Kindra lifted a hand and waved at him. The ebony man was Cooper's Landing second overseer and would likely move up to becoming the main overseer once she and Denzel set sail for Barbados.

The room buzzed as the party began. Kindra felt as if she were going to wilt in all the layers of her gown, while Denzel looked as if he would be willing to discard his suit jacket if given the word. She watched him for a moment, her heart hammering in her chest. He was her *husband*. And in a few short hours they would finally be alone in her chamber where he would claim her once and for all.

Interrupting her thoughts, Kindra noticed a couple of servants come in from outside, heads together, whispering. They headed straight for Cameron. The room quieted until only a soft stir remained. Some of the guests looked toward the portico entrance as the sound of horses clopping down the palmetto-lined drive filled the air. People moved to the wide doors and looked out in alarm. Kindra could hear the muffled voices of the guests as they looked on in curiosity.

"What is it?" Kindra followed Denzel to the portico and looked out over the expanse of lawn. A procession of troops dressed in the traditional British uniform—red coats, black hats, white breeches and black knee-high boots moved up the circular drive and stopped before the Great House. The cavalry regiment waited as the head officer dismounted and removed a document from inside his coat pocket.

Kindra moved out to the lawn in front of the house and noted that behind all the fine horses and men in red coats, a crude wagon waited. It pulled up at the rear of the regiment.

Kindra grasped Grace's arm, a feeling of dread tugging at her heart.

"Why are they here?" Kindra whispered. She glanced over her shoulder to see Cameron standing before the porch steps.

"I don't know," Grace said. She squeezed Kindra's hand. They watched as the officer walked up to Cameron.

"I'm looking for Cameron Bartholomew."

"You're speaking to him."

The officer looked Cameron over, then glanced past him at the house.

"What is the meaning of this?" Cameron waved his hand at the cavalry waiting behind the officer.

"I'm here to arrest Tajairah Hargrave for dealing in illegal slave trade. It's been brought to our attention—and verified—that she has been kidnaping and selling slaves from plantations on the island. She's been smuggling them to slave traders on the Caribbean coast." The officer appeared grave as he lifted his arm and handed Cameron the documents.

Cameron frowned and stared at the man. He opened the envelope and read for a moment. Then he folded the paper, raised his shoulders, and dropped them in response to the news.

"She's inside. If you'll just give me a moment, I'll bring her out."

"That won't be necessary, Cameron," came Tia's harsh voice. She stepped out onto the front porch.

Two soldiers left rank and pushed forward, each climbing the porch steps and taking hold of Tia's arms.

"Get your hands off me!" Tia jerked to get out of the soldiers' grip.

The men paid no attention to her demands. They pulled her to where the officer waited.

"Mother!" Kindra started toward where her mother struggled to free herself.

"Stand back." The officer gave Kindra a stern look. "She's in our custody now."

"But you can't take her." Kindra looked wildly behind her. "Denzel, tell them!"

Denzel strode to his bride's side. "Hush. There's nothing we can do. We knew it was only a matter of time before the law caught up with her."

"No!" Kindra pulled free from his hold. "Mother!"

Tia turned her eyes on her daughter with a look of hatred. "Leave me be. You've got what you wanted." Kindra stopped as her mother's words ripped at the lining of her heart.

The redcoats prepared to leave as the two men dragged Tia to the waiting buckboard. They shoved her hands together and clamped shackles on her wrists. Once Tia was seated, she looked away from the group of people who stood waiting on the lawn. Kindra held her breath as she watched her mother sit straight as a board, chin up, a cold terrifying glare in her blue eyes.

As he turned to mount his horse, the officer said to Cameron, "These are document copies of our records. You may keep them."

"Wait!" Kindra pulled from Denzel. "Where are you taking her?"

"She'll be at the prison in Princeton Harbor." The officer did nothing to disguise the contempt in his voice. Ignoring Kindra, he addressed Cameron. "If you wish to visit the prisoner that's where you'll find her." He reined his horse to the front of the regiment and rode out stiffly. The horsemen followed him two-by-two, the wagon centered between them. The sound of horses' hooves clopping down the long drive slowly died away.

Kindra watched her mother go. She had prayed this day would never come. She knew her mother had been involved in smuggling slaves. And Denzel was right, it had been only a matter of time before the law caught up with her. Still, Tia was her mother. Kindra had never known a time she could please her hateful mother. And truth be known, she had grown tired of trying. Nevertheless, she brushed at the lone tear that trailed down her cheek.

Denzel drew her to his muscled chest. "Come in the house, Kindra."

She felt Denzel's strong hand move under her elbow as he guided her toward the house. His touch brought a surge of strength. She lifted her quivering chin. She'd get through this.

"How could this happen on my wedding day?" Kindra swallowed, fighting welling tears.

"Shhh." Denzel said. "She'll be all right. Your mother be a strong woman."

Kindra basked in Denzel's embrace, in his assurance that Tia would be fine. In truth, she knew her mother would be in control no matter where she was. She wiped her eyes with the back of her hand. Denzel kissed the top of her head.

Kindra pushed away from him and brushed the wrinkles from her wedding gown. She steadied her voice as she prepared to face the group of people who stood on the lawn gaping at them. "Please join my husband and me for the wedding supper."

A murmur ran through the crowd. Holding her head high, Kindra moved past the throng and down the side of the portico to the entrance of the ballroom. There, she found her chair at the table set up for the bride and groom.

Three of the house servants, Dinah, Gemma and Penny stood at the serving table, their eyes wide as saucers. Behind her, she heard scattered footsteps as guests came back into the ballroom.

Wasn't it just like her mother to steal the attention of the day? Well, today was *her* wedding day and she'd not let her mother spoil it. Tomorrow she would deal with what to do about her.

Denzel came to the table. She patted the chair beside her. "Come sit, Denzel. We must celebrate. I won't let Mother take that from us."

Looking around the half-empty room, Kindra realized that she had been given a priceless gift. She now knew who her real friends were. A chill ran down her spine and she said a silent prayer. *Please God. Don't let this be a forewarning of what our life is to be.*

Grace touched Cameron's arm, stopping him from following the guests into the ballroom. "This is terrible timing. Did you know the British officer would come today?"

Cameron's dark brows rose as if in apology. "No. They didn't give me any indication which day they would come out to the Landing. They only said it would be soon, but it's only been a couple days. I expected them to arrive next week." Cameron combed the sides of his black hair with his fingers. "But I don't apologize for the woman being removed from the premises." He stepped back and pulled Grace to the side wall of the portico.

"I just wish it hadn't happened so soon," Grace said softly. "I wanted Tia gone, too. But not at the expense of being hauled off on Kindra's special day."

"That's unfortunate, but she'll be all right." Cameron pulled Grace to his chest and kissed her forehead. "It did make a nice wedding gift, don't you think? Now they'll be able to start their new life together without Tia's interference."

"I hear music," Grace said, pushing away. "We should get back to the party."

"All right." But instead of moving, Cameron pulled Grace tightly into his arms.

"Cameron . . ." Grace started to say more, but stopped when she looked up.

His lips claimed hers before she could speak. When they came up for air, he crooked his arm. "Care to dance Mrs. Bartholomew?" His voice was low and husky.

"I'd love to," she said, sliding her hand onto his proffered arm.

When Grace entered the ballroom she heard the pleasant din of voices and laughter, the tinkle of glasses, the music playing in the background, and the swish of gowns as beautiful women danced about the floor with their partners. Grace's eyes panned the room looking for Kindra and Denzel. She spotted them in the middle of the dance floor, Denzel holding her sister close for all the world to see. It was what Kindra had wanted forever.

Grace felt joy for Kindra. At least for the moment. Tomorrow was another day.

TWO

DENZEL WATCHED AS Kindra shifted, and her eyes fluttered open. The trade winds blew in from the bay and danced playfully through her jet-black hair then drifted over her nightdress. She moved ever so slightly, creating waves of shimmering silk in the moonlight. As Denzel gazed at the way her feminine curves filled out the silky fabric, he was beginning to think that the gift Grace gave her sister was more of a gift to him than it was for Kindra. He smiled and then breathed in huskily at his approval; he watched her cheeks redden under his perusal. It was their first night together in her bedchamber and he found it alluring that he could make his bride blush with only a look.

Kindra stirred and drew his gaze to her face. "What are you thinking, my love?" she asked, lifting a palm to caress his chest.

"I'm thinking I never want this evening to end. I'm thinkin I could crush you in my arms if I wouldn't break your delicate bones." He kissed her full lips. "I'm thinking I'm the luckiest man in the world, Mrs. Talmaze, and that I don't deserve such a beautiful woman in my bed." He grazed her cheek with his thumb.

Soft fingers touched his arm, drawing him toward her. "Enough talk, my husband," she whispered as she pulled him down and kissed him with such desire that it awakened a strong sense of need to crush her delicate body to his. Yet he touched her gently, patiently wanting the evening to last.

A salty breeze awakened Kindra the following morning. Remembering the warmth of Denzel's touch the night before, she smiled. She rolled over to place a hand on his chest only to find he wasn't there. He must have dressed and gone out to the sugarcane fields. He was her husband, but he was also an overseer for Cooper's Landing. Unfortunately, the business of the Landing did not stop for them.

She smiled again and rolled back to face the sunlight streaming into the room. She had never felt happier than she did at this moment. She was Denzel's wife. They would leave for Barbados in the coming weeks and start their new life together at their new plantation. It all seemed like a dream. She considered pinching herself to see if she was real.

She heard noises beyond the veranda and left her bed to gaze down at the workers in the kitchen garden. The Landing teemed with life. She needed to get dressed and join the others downstairs.

Kindra pulled on the bell cord in the corner of her room then turned to the washstand to freshen up. When the door opened, she expected to find Rhea, her chambermaid.

"Rhea," she said without turning, "pick out a dress for me. I must hurry downstairs. Breakfast is likely getting cold."

When Rhea didn't respond, Kindra turned to find Denzel standing tall and muscular in the doorway.

"I came to see if you were awake." His eyes roved over her as the breeze played with her silken gown.

"You should have awakened me. I'd have gotten up with you."

"You were sleeping so soundly, I didn't want to disturb you." He moved to where she stood. "Now that you're up," he nuzzled her neck and pulled her close, "I suggest we go back to bed." He kissed her forehead, her cheek, and then her mouth. His lips lingered there.

Only too soon a small rap at the door interrupted them.

"Miz Kindra, you rang the bell?" Rhea peeked her head in the door and her eyes grew round.

"Never mind, Rhea." Kindra waved her away.

"I be a-wonderin'." Rhea chuckled and shut the door.

Kindra could hear the servant's voice as she moved farther down the hall. "Seems like alla you gettin' up late this fine mornin'!"

An hour later, Kindra and Denzel entered the dining room. It seemed Cameron and Grace, sitting at the table waiting for their breakfast, had arrived only moments before.

At the other end of the table, Aunt Katy and Josie were just finishing their meal, each holding a china cup of coffee, their eyes gleaming. The two had come to Cooper's Landing to chaperone Grace after her father died. Aunt Katy, her mother's sister had promised to look after Grace before her mother died. When Grace learned her father was in Jamaica, no one could talk her out of traveling to meet him for the first time. Aunt Katy had warned Grace not to make the trip. What if her father didn't accept her? What if he wasn't alive anymore? Her aunt tried everything to keep Grace from making the trip, to no avail.

Josie, Grace's cousin was the closet thing to a sister Grace had ever known. The two were inseparable. When Grace's father died leaving her alone at the Great House with the plantation's foreman, Cameron Bartholomew, Grace sent a letter requesting her aunt and cousin come and chaperone her. This way, she could stay at the Landing, and close to the man she loved. Now that she and Cameron were married, Aunt Katy and Josie could relax and enjoy their time on the island.

"Well, it's about time you lovebirds got up," Aunt Katy teased. "I was beginning to think the cooks were going to have to serve you lunch instead."

"Good morning, everyone," Kindra sang. She waited as Denzel pulled out her chair.

"Good morning." Grace smiled mischievously, her cheeks tinged a deep red. She glanced at Cameron who had a silly grin on his rugged face.

Kindra didn't miss that Grace kicked his ankle under the table. The house was full of newlyweds and their routines were out of kilter.

Cameron cleared his throat. "The cooks will bring out the food momentarily." He no sooner spoke than the servants came through the kitchen's swinging door, laden with bowls and dishes: platters of scrambled eggs and salt fish, bacon and biscuits, fruits and jams.

"Now that you've tied the knot," Aunt Katy said, glancing at Kindra, "I expect you've got big plans."

Kindra pulled her gaze from Aunt Katy and looked at Grace, a deep ache dug a hole in her heart. She would miss Grace. She would miss her sister's tender touch and understanding. But now that she'd said her vows and married her beloved, she could walk away from all the pain her mother had caused throughout the years. *Just leave . . .* She wished she was able to do just that . . . but she couldn't.

Tia believed in the black magic of the village people. Kindra had tried to show her that nothing good could come from the evil spirits. Tia wouldn't hear it. Her mother was a lost soul, but Kindra couldn't turn her back on the woman now, not when she had been sent to prison. Torn between leaving her mother stranded in prison and starting her new life, Kindra swallowed.

It was quiet for a few moments before Cameron broke the silence. "I expect she'll be wanting to go to Princeton Harbor to see Tia." He looked at Kindra, who in turn dropped her eyes and dabbed at her mouth with her napkin.

"I want to." She leaned into Denzel. "I think we should try to see her before we leave for Barbados."

Denzel pushed his food around his plate. He chewed for a moment, and then gave Kindra a sidelong glance. "Think she'll see you?"

Kindra lifted her shoulders. "I won't know if I don't try."

"I don't think she will. But if you have your heart set on it, I'll make arrangements with Captain Kincade to sail to the other side of the island. We'd reach Princeton Harbor much faster sailing than going by land and it would give us a chance to check out the ship. How does that sound?" He raised a thick brow.

Kindra grabbed his arm and squeezed it, leaning her chin on his shoulder. "Thank you. It would mean a lot to me." She grinned at the others at the table. "And yes, that would give us an excuse to board the *Sea Baron*. I'd like to tour the ship before we sail to Barbados."

"That's settled then. I'll ride out to the dock and make arrangements with the captain to sail tomorrow morning."

Kindra picked up her fork and scooped a bite of scrambled eggs with renewed energy. She couldn't keep the smile from her face.

"Would you like us to come along?" Cameron asked. "It may make it easier to get into the prison."

"That won't be necessary, Camp," Kindra said, using his nickname. "You've got things you need to do. Besides, this can be an outing for Denzel and me."

"I agree." Cameron dropped his napkin on his plate and glanced at Denzel. "To change the subject, I ran into Captain Drew Harding yesterday."

"How's he doing?" Denzel asked.

"Fine for the most part."

Denzel held his fork poised above his plate. "What's up?"

"Drew said he came upon an odd situation in one of the guest cabins on his ship." Cameron lifted toast off a center plate and continued, "Seems someone entered the first cabin and ransacked the room."

Denzel's brows rose. "Why would anyone want to do that?"

"That's what's got him puzzled. There wasn't anything for anyone to take. The room was empty. But a drawer was pulled out from under the bunk and thrown across the floor. Drew thought maybe there was something someone was looking for under it."

"Was there?" Kindra asked, her eyes round.

"He didn't find anything. He checked the floor under the bed. Nothing there."

"Hmmm," Grace said. "That *is* unusual. I hope he finds who did that." She brushed a curl over her shoulder. "That's the room I stayed in."

Josephine glanced at her mother and nudged her elbow.

"I have an announcement to make," Aunt Katy said. All eyes turned to her. "It's obvious we're not needed as chaperones at Cooper's Landing anymore. And I've been gone five weeks. I've an apothecary shop to run back home. And your grandfather Unruh is surely needing Josephine to get back to the account books." She took a deep breath and said, "I'm thinking it's time we bid you goodbye and go home."

"Oh, Aunt Katy," Grace said, "you'll be missed." But in truth she knew her aunt was eager to get back to Charleston, South Carolina. They had remained so that she could stay at Cooper's Landing after her father died. She never dreamed she would have fallen helplessly in love with Cameron, the foreman, who also lived in the Great House. Grace couldn't have stayed on at the plantation without a chaperone. Aunt Katy and Josie traveled across the Atlantic as soon as they got her letter pleading for them to come.

"Oh, go on!" the older woman chuckled. "You've all got your hands full with your new lives. We really should board the *Savannah Rose* and sail home." She took a sip of coffee.

Before Grace could answer, Cameron cleared his throat again. "I was hoping to have a moment when we'd all be together. I want to address a few matters that involve all of us here.

"We've come to a crossroad . . . things are changing." He nodded toward Kindra. "The two of you want to get on to Barbados, and rightfully so. But, before you go, I suggest we talk to our attorney, Desmond Rothschild." He held his fork above his plate and pointed it at Denzel. "You'll need to sign papers to show you own Kindra Hall."

Denzel leaned back and frowned. "Glad you mentioned it. We can't show up at the house without proof."

"Exactly," Cameron said. "With Phillip's passing . . . and having left the two of you your inheritance, names need to be changed. It'll take Desmond time to write up the papers. The same goes for the *Sea Baron*, too."

Kindra listened, her heart racing. She'd never dreamed she'd own a plantation or a merchant ship. She was glad Denzel had worked the sugarcane fields as an overseer all these years. He had a way with the field hands and he knew how to run the plantation. He'd learned every job from the ground up: tilling the ground and planting the seeds, harvesting the tall green stalks and processing the cane through the shredding mill, then transferring the pulp to the boiling house for crystallization into refined sugar.

Kindra Hall was a tobacco plantation. It would take time for Denzel to get the drift of how to produce this kind of crop. But her man was smart. Kindra had every confidence he'd learn the trade in record time.

Denzel had confided in her that he was eager to learn the merchant trade on the high seas. He had confessed that he envied the times that Grace and Kindra's father, Phillip, had left the Landing to sail to far lands. Once he got a handle on the tobacco trade, he intended to sail the Caribbean Coast.

Cameron was right, they had come to new crossroads in their lives, everything was changing. Kindra returned her attention to the conversation to hear what else Cameron had to say.

"I suggest we plan a day this week to go into Riverbend and have Desmond prepare the necessary documents. Grace and I have papers that need to be drawn up as well."

"I agree," Aunt Katy said. "After all the problems your uncles created over the deed to Cooper's Landing, you'll need to get those papers drawn up right away."

Grace's back stiffened at mention of her uncles. Her father was barely cold in his grave when his brothers showed up to claim Cooper's Landing as their own. After months of searching for the deed and proof that the Landing belonged to Cameron and Grace they found the documents. And with their attorney's help, proof sent the two men back to England for good.

Grace smiled at her aunt and then at Kindra. "There's never a dull moment around here. That's for sure."

The kitchen door swung open and Penny and Dinah circled the table removing empty plates and filling coffee cups. "Can I bring you anything else?" asked Dinah.

"No, thank you." Cameron looked to the others.

The rest of them shook their heads. "The food was good as always," said Kindra. She glanced at Denzel.

"Can't say I ever had food as good as this," he said and grinned at Dinah. Before this morning, he'd taken his meals with the field hands out by the barn. They had separate kitchens where the food was prepared.

"Is there anything else you'd like to bring up?" Grace asked her husband.

Everyone at the table stared at Cameron and quieted again. The kitchen door swung shut as the servants left to allow them some privacy.

"I intended to broach the subject with you in private," Cameron said, eyeing Grace, "but now that we know Aunt Katy and Josie are planning to go home, maybe this is a good time to speak up."

Grace set her napkin down and paled as if she sensed something ill to come.

Cameron reached for her hand and held it firmly in his. "Over the past year there's been plenty of talk about a slave revolt on the island. We've learned firsthand that some of the slaves have been discontented and have disappeared. The last one to come up missing was Cuffee. He was one of our strongest field hands. I believed he was a loyal worker.

It's difficult to understand how he could up and leave his family. The last time I saw his wife, Tabitha, she looked as if she was going to have their baby any day now. This would make their sixth child their oldest is a daughter who is twelve years old and the youngest is a two-year-old son. And still, Cuffee ran away."

"Excuse me, Camp, but how would you know the ages of his children?" Aunt Katy asked. "I've walked the premises and there are too many children to count."

"I keep a log of everything that goes on here. I've been doing it for a lot of years. Pip wanted an accounting of every slave, animal, and implement here at Cooper's Landing. I've grown accustomed to knowing such things, which is why I know when a slave is missing."

Cameron leaned back and folded his hands in his lap. "Needless to say, word has it that Jamaica may be in for a rebellion such as hasn't been seen on this island in two hundred years. There's an undercurrent of turmoil brewing. I've talked to other plantation owners and they feel it, too."

"What are you trying to say, Cameron?" Grace paled. "Do you think our own field hands would turn on us?" Her emerald eyes grew wide.

"I'm saying that I think it's time we leave this island and move back to the States." He looked at Grace who stared at him in disbelief.

"Move back to South Carolina?"

"Yes. Somewhere in the Charleston area."

"That's one of the best things I've heard in a long while!" Aunt Katy cut in.

"But what about Cooper's Landing?" Grace asked, looking at Kindra and Aunt Katy, then back to Cameron.

"It'll keep. We'll have field hands who'll still work the sugarcane fields. I'll leave an overseer to keep an eye on the plantation. What I won't do is jeopardize my wife's future for the sake of fond memories of this place." The look on Cameron's face was stern, unshakable.

"How soon are you planning to move?" Grace asked. She picked up the napkin and dabbed at the perspiration on her forehead.

"Before the end of this year. The reason I brought this up now is because of Aunt Katy's decision to go home. I don't want to leave you here at the Landing alone while I search for another piece of land to build a plantation."

"You're just going to go gallivanting to Charleston, and buy a piece of property? What'll we do there? Have you thought it through?" By now, Grace had scooted her chair back, and was tapping one foot on the floor.

"Grace." Cameron stood and pulled her to her feet. "Trust me. I *have* thought it through. Sugar sales have declined the past six months. We can't compete with the machinery that has been invented in the States. They can produce and export sugar much faster than we can."

Grace dabbed at her lips with her napkin.

"The talk on the coast is Carolina Gold."

"Rice?"

"Yes, rice. The field is wide open to growing it and making a profit. The Lowlands along the rivers in South Carolina are conducive to growing rice. If we get in on it now, we'll be in on the ground floor."

Grace's shoulders relaxed. "You *have* thought it through."

"Yes, I have. I wouldn't spring a wild-haired idea on you. I don't work that way."

Grace laid a hand on Cameron's forearm. "I should have known." She swallowed and looked over the table to her aunt. "Can you stay a little longer?"

Aunt Katy glanced at Josie and the two nodded. "If it means bringing you back home, I'm certainly open to staying a little longer. I'll need to send a post to my employee. He was expecting us to be home by now. And Peter, he's keeping an eye on the house."

"Thank you, Aunt Katy. I'm hoping to leave within the week. The sooner I go, the sooner I can come back and move Grace to South Carolina, too," Cameron said.

"You're leaving so soon?" Grace paled again.

"If you don't mind, I need to talk to my wife alone." Cameron picked up his wide-brimmed straw hat and placed it on his head. He took her hand and escorted her out the front door.

The rest of them sat and stared at each other. Denzel was the first to speak. "Cameron's right. We *have* come to a crossroad in our lives."

The following morning, Denzel and Kindra rode the carriage to the docks in Riverbend. Denzel wore his day clothes, black breeches and a beige muslin shirt.

Kindra, however, had been warned not to visit the city of Princeton Harbor in the day dresses she typically wore at the Landing. "I'd wear a working dress if I were you," Grace had said. "The people in Riverbend are accustomed to seeing you in your fine gowns, but truth to tell, when I first met you, I was taken aback by a darky wearing lavish gowns."

Kindra's hand flew to her mouth as her brows puckered. "I offended you?"

"At the time, yes, but not anymore. Now I don't care what you wear." Grace touched Kindra's hand. "I'm just saying, a stranger will not look upon you as we do. They'll show hostility, I'm sure of it."

"All right. Then help me pick out a dress."

Together, she and Grace climbed the marble stairs to her bedchamber and combed through the clothes in Kindra's armoire.

"Goodness," Grace remarked. "You've not too many plain gowns to look at."

"Mother always looked for the finest gowns she could find in Godey's catalog. Heaven knows I've told Denzel a dozen times, I'd settle for the slave clothes the women wear out in the fields, just to have a simple life. I wanted to spend time with the slaves, but mother wouldn't have it. We have family in the slave quarters, did you know that?"

"Yes. I helped your aunt with her baby one day. The baby had a fever. Tia was none too happy that I tended to someone in a shanty." Grace frowned. "You'd rather wear a black cotton skirt and a white muslin blouse than these fine gowns?" She raised a brow.

"Yes." Kindra giggled. "Maybe not that extreme, but I'm not opposed to the idea."

"Well, let's look some more. Surely you have something in here you can wear." After shuffling the dresses to the side on their wooden hangers, Grace pulled out a blue dress with a wide white-laced collar held together by a large blue button. The gown was trimmed in a darker shade of blue ribbon. She held it up to Kindra's neck, pulled the sleeves away from the gown and nodded. "This will have to do."

Kindra rode beside Denzel wearing the blue day-dress and a charcoal-colored jacket, with a tiny hat trimmed with ribbon rosettes.

Her heart skipped as they neared the docks. For years, she and Penny had driven the Landing's wagon to the dock and watched as ships pulled into port, but Kindra had never set foot on the deck of any ship, much less her own.

The carriage pulled up alongside the *Sea Baron*. Denzel helped her down and grinned. "My fine lady, you look like a child about to rob a candy store."

The wharf bustled with seamen loading crates of merchandise. Sweat glistened on muscled bodies as they heaved hogsheads of the island sugar up the gangplanks. There were bales of cotton and barrels of rum going up and down the gangways. Stevedores lifted heavy kegs and dropped them onto the back of drays waiting on the dirt roads. Horses and mules shied at the activity. Roustabouts shrilled whistles, signaling another crate coming down one of the wooden ramps.

Kindra breathed in the mixture of ocean water and salt air. The breeze rustled her curls. She was ready to go up the gangplank leading to the *Sea Baron*, ready for an adventure on the sea, yet she dreaded the confrontation she'd meet on the other side of the island. She shoved the thought aside as Denzel's hand touched her back and guided her to their ship.

Captain Austin Kincade met them on the deck. His thick, unruly bleached-blond hair skimmed the top of the collar of his navy-blue cotton shirt. His thin mustache, close-cut beard, and eyebrows were bleached by the sun as well. The blue of his eyes stood out in his sun-bronzed face.

He reached out and shook Denzel's hand. Kindra noted at once that the captain had a ready-made smile. Seeing this relieved some of the tension she felt in her stomach.

"Good to see you again," Austin said to Denzel. His eyes shifted to Kindra.

"This is my lovely wife, Kindra Talmaze. We've only been married two days." Denzel's white teeth shone in his broad smile.

"Congratulations. It's an honor to meet you," Austin said to Kindra, nodding his head.

"Cap'n!" came a booming voice across the deck. "You 'bout ready to sail?"

"Yes, Barnabas, but before we do, come here."

Dressed in a tattered pale shirt that barely covered his bulging muscles, and blue overalls with straps that buckled to a bib in front of his chest, a shiny, bald-headed man lumbered across the deck to where the three of them stood. He towered like a giant in their midst. His size could have been intimidating, if it weren't for the kindest chocolate eyes looking down on them.

"Barnabas, I want you to meet the new owners of the *Sea Baron*," the captain said.

The giant man stared at them with obvious confusion. "Pardon me if I seem out o' line, but I nevah heard of such a thing as a darky owning a merchant ship like this." He waved his big hands at the vessel. "It does my big ole heart good to hear it!" A smile spread across his face. The man chuckled and stretched out a large hand. "Your name?"

"Denzel Talmaze, and this is my wife, Kindra."

Barnabas bowed to Kindra, his shiny head level with hers.

"We'll be taking them to Princeton Harbor this morning, instead of leaving for San Martin. Get the crew ready to sail," said Captain Kincade.

"Yassir!" Barnabas eyes shone as he turned back to the center of the main deck and boomed instructions to leave the port.

"I'll be happy to give you a tour of the ship just as soon as this vessel is out to sea. It won't take us long to travel to the other side of the island."

"Thank you," Kindra said, and clamped her hands on Denzel's strong arm. Already the merchant ship crept away from the mooring and moved out to sea.

"Are you ready?" Denzel asked, looking down at her with love in his eyes.

"As ready as I'll ever be." She tugged on his arm to stand at the wooden rail. This would be a first, looking down at the people on the dock's landing.

Please give me the strength I'll need to see my mother today, dear Lord. Don't let her spoil our new beginning, Kindra prayed as the people on the wharf grew smaller, appearing like ants running to and fro. She felt Denzel's protective arm around her shoulder. She was ready for whatever today would bring.

THREE

KINDRA SQUINTED AGAINST the shimmering sunlight. The tropical breeze ruffled the jade waters of the Caribbean, as the salt air touched her skin and softly billowed the hem of her blue dress. She lifted a hand to shade her eyes from the glaring sun. The *Sea Baron* sliced through the waters nearing Princeton Harbor, where she could see through masts and rigging of ships at anchor. Beyond, the Blue Mountains rose above the small city and dominated the horizon.

Kindra's heart began to pound against her chest. Apprehension at visiting the unknown city added to the excitement of the journey. She'd never been beyond the confines of Cooper's Landing and the small bay town of Riverbend. People knew her there. She was used to the familiar sights of the buildings, the busy streets, and the wharf that teemed with stevedores unloading or loading crates. She and her longtime friend Penny had sought any excuse to travel into town, just to observe the people coming and going from places they'd only heard about. She had always wished for the day she could board a ship and sail to an unknown port and visit new places. Now that she was doing just that, she felt like turning around and going back home.

The *Sea Baron* slid into the harbor and the crew busied themselves securing the vessel to the dock's mooring. Denzel strode to where Kindra leaned against the wooden rail and pulled her against him, his strong arm reassuring her she was not alone in this new adventure.

"Busy city."

"Yes, I was just thinking that I've never set foot beyond our side of the island." She took a deep breath, trying to calm the frantic beating of her heart.

"You're not alone, Kindra. I'm here." Amusement played in his dark eyes. "You're trembling."

"Silly of me, I know. Maybe it's more than visiting a new location."

"Your mother?"

"I suppose. I've tried not to think about her until now." Kindra dabbed at her forehead with her handkerchief.

"Like I said," Denzel squeezed her shoulder against his hard chest, "I'm right here. You'll be fine."

The sun beat down on them as the ship's gangplank lowered to the wooden planks of the dock. The colors of Princeton Harbor were bright, vibrant and alive. The crew wasted no time going ashore where peddlers and merchants greeted them with their wares.

Captain Kincade's boots echoed behind them. "The prison is over there on that low rise." He pointed. "It's about a ten-minute walk from the wharf."

Looking above the buildings, Kindra spotted a tall square tower. "Thank you," she said. "We shouldn't be long."

"Take your time. Our crew enjoy the sights of this city. I'm sure they'll take respite in one of the taverns along the street. Sun's already bearing down."

Denzel guided Kindra down the gangplank, and they started up the road toward the prison. They would have to cut through town and come out the other side. It wasn't long before Kindra was aware that curious eyes followed them. She was glad for the warning Grace had given her to pick a simpler dress for the outing.

Fancy carriages and buggies swept past them with gentlemen and ladies frowning at her and Denzel. Kindra glanced toward Denzel, who held her hand tight. She hoisted her parasol, hoping for some relief from the sun's heat.

Jamaican natives swarmed the street, some in a hurry and bumping into her and Denzel as they wove in and out among the pedestrians. Other natives leaned against the buildings watching them pass, their eyes round as Kindra and Denzel trudged up the cobbled road.

It wasn't long before Kindra felt out of place. "Why must they stare at us?" she asked.

"Because you're one fine-looking colored woman, wearing your fancy dress and holding that fancy parasol." His lips thinned. "Look around. You see any other colored folks dressed like you?" His hand was behind her back nudging her up the street. "I'm not so sure this was a good idea. We should've borrowed one of the slave women's clothes for this outing."

Kindra heard the tension in his voice.

"Who she think she be, a-wearin' white people clothes?" asked a darky in the crowd.

"Out of the way!" came a disdainful cry. A buggy narrowly missed Kindra's shoulder as its driver sneered down at her.

Fear squeezed Kindra's heart as she observed the insolent, angry looks sent her way. It didn't seem to matter whether the people were dark or light, the harsh stares were the same. Sweat trickled down her back as the prison came into view. They only had another hundred yards to walk before the town would be behind them.

A fine-looking carriage passed them with four women riding in the back. Two of the women stared out the window at Kindra. One woman spat at her, but missed. Kindra halted in time to keep the spittle from hitting her dress, but she could hear the words '*uppity colored*' as the carriage rolled on. It turned left and rode up a hill toward imposing mansions.

"Keep walking," he said. The more they walked, the more rankled Denzel became.

Kindra's heart was in her throat, making it difficult to breathe. She'd never felt so low in all of her life. She wanted to strip off the gown, yet she could do nothing about it now. She had to keep going, battling the urge to run back to the ship and hide from the scrutiny of mean stares.

The wagon lane stretched on, but at last they came to a large wooden door. The bulky structure was several hundred yards wide in either direction. A round iron ring hung from the door with a hatch door above it.

Denzel grasped the ring to clang it against a metal plate. He glanced down at his wife and shook his head, as if he wasn't sure they were doing the right thing.

Kindra clung to his arm, not so sure herself. It seemed a long wait before the small hatch door opened and a gruff-looking guard peeked out at them. His eyes grew round as he peered first at Denzel and then Kindra.

"Whatcha doin' here?" he barked.

"We are here to see Tia Hargrave, sir. She was brought here three days ago," Denzel said.

"I know who she be and when she be arrivin." Frowning, the guard looked past them as if expecting someone else to be there. "Where's your master? Don't you know you can't come to the prison 'less you be with your master or you gots a pass from him." He turned sideways and spat tobacco.

"We don't need a pass, sir. We don't have a master. We're free folks from Cooper's Landing on the other side of the island."

"Free or not, you-uns needs a pass from a white man 'fore you can come inside the prison." The guard studied them. "A lot of rebellion goin' on these days. Can't trust any of you darkies."

"We're not part of the rebellion . . ."

"So you say. From what I heard, the blackie you're here to see led the rebellion. Why should I believe the likes of you?"

Kindra's heart sank. What the guard said made perfect sense. "Tia Hargrave is my mother," she tried. "I just want to see her, make sure she is going to be all right." Denzel put his hand on her back for support.

The guard leaned closer to the opening. His eyes raked Kindra from head to toe assessing her status as free or a runaway slave. "How come you wearin' a dress like that? Don't you know you could be whipped for stealin' yer mistress's clothes?"

"This is my own dress. My father, Phillip Cooper, a white man, bought it for me." It was all she could do to keep from turning and running. A tremor ran through her at the mention of a whipping. She wasn't a slave, never had been.

"I thought you said you don't have a master?"

"My father is dead." Kindra hated saying that. She still wasn't used to his being gone.

"Come to think of it, your mammy arrived in a gown fit to kill. Worked up a lot of folks inside these walls. The prisoners don't have a need for clothes like that." He spat again. "Don't matter. It'll be rags in no time." A sneer spread across his face. "In case you ain't heard, the prisoners don't come here to party."

"Her mother was arrested on our wedding day. The soldiers came in the middle of the celebration," Denzel said.

Kindra frowned. What Denzel said was true. What he didn't disclose was that her mother never attended the wedding. She hadn't shown her face until the British soldiers came to the plantation.

The heat from the sun beat down on them. Kindra could feel the back of her dress sticking to her damp skin.

The guard glanced back at the iron gate behind him, then at her. "She won't look so fancy for long. Things go on behind bars that we ain't got no control over."

Kindra's heart jumped into her throat. She elbowed her way in front of Denzel, her hands splayed on the rough-hewn wooden door. "Don't hurt her!"

The guard jerked the thick door open and stood before them, a whip in hand. "It won't be me layin' a hand on 'er. It be them what's inside," he crowed, "that'll take a toll on her fer sure. Mark my words." He spat a wad of dark tobacco juice at their feet.

Both Kindra and Denzel stepped back. She felt Denzel's hand draw into a fist at her back and knew she had to think fast. It wouldn't do if Denzel lost his temper. She stepped away from her husband.

"May I see my mother? We won't stay long."

The guard swept a glance along her skirts and shrugged his narrow shoulders. "I don't usually do bidding for blackies."

"Please?" She cupped her hands together at her chest.

He turned and shut the slab-door behind him with a loud thud.

Denzel pulled Kindra toward him. She laid her head on his chest, heard his heart pounding a quick rhythm in her ear.

Time wore on. Had the prison guard forgotten about them? They shuffled their feet and gazed out toward the open field between the city and the brick walls of the prison. Neither spoke. Words weren't needed.

At long last, the heavy door scraped open and the scrawny guard leered at them. "You may as well scoot on home. Yer mammy won't be seein' you."

"But . . ."

"That uppity blackie be sayin' she won't be seein' the likes of you. Ain't nothin' I can do 'bout that." He paused. "Said to tell you don't come back. So you best be movin' down the road." He stepped back and slammed the door shut.

Kindra jumped at the sound of finality. "How long will she be here?" Kindra cried out.

"Ten years." The guard yelled back from behind the door. "That be what the warden say."

"But she hasn't even had a trial. How can you keep her ten years?"Kindra asked.

"You forgettin' she be a Negro. She don't get no trial."

Kindra's knees buckled. "Ten years?" Denzel rushed to her elbows and held her up. Tears pooled in her eyes. "Now what?"

"We go home." Denzel pulled Kindra into his arms and rubbed her back. "You can't make your mother do anything she doesn't want to do." He stepped back and ran a thumb below her eyes, wiping the tears away. "Come on." He gripped her hand and pulled her along the wagon road toward town. After a few minutes of walking, he tenderly asked her, "Are you hungry?"

She swallowed and shook her head. "My stomach's in knots." She brushed a tear away.

"I don't mean to sound cold at a time like this." He glanced down at her.

Kindra looked up. "Go on."

"We've never been anywhere together outside of Cooper's Landing, much less a thriving city like Princeton Harbor. I'd hate to waste an opportunity to take you to a food-house to eat."

The proprietor looked them up and down and scowled. "Coloreds aren't welcome here!" He pushed Denzel's chest with a thick, stubby hand. "You gotta go down the road to your own people." He gave an extra shove and Denzel nearly tripped over his own feet as he stepped back.

The proprietor wiped his hands on his dirty apron and turned back inside the eatery.

"Let's go back to the ship. Surely Captain Kincade has food there," Kindra said.

"No. We're going to sit down and dine at a respectable place."

Kindra swallowed as they wove through the crowd of pedestrians pushing along the busy street. Up ahead, she saw three black men standing outside a building, talking. The smell of food wafted along the sidewalk.

Denzel squeezed her hand. "Here we go." He opened the door, nodding toward the men staring at them.

Kindra didn't miss that the trio gaped at her before she and Denzel disappeared inside the establishment. Once inside, her mouth began to water at the savory smells filling the air.

A short, squat woman with a colorful bandana tied over her head clucked her tongue as she led them to a table. "May I be askin' where you folks come from?" She ogled Kindra's dress and her parasol as Kindra folded it and set it beside her chair.

"We're from the other side of the island," Kindra said, smiling.

"Well, we seed you walkin' by earlier. It be all the folks been talkin' 'bout, wonderin' who you be and watcha doin' here?"

Kindra stalled for an answer, then said, "We came to town to visit my mother." She left it at that.

"Well, gone be a lotta folks talkin' 'bout that fine darky woman traipsin' through the streets of Princeton Harbor, long aftah you be sailin' outta heah."

"We're hungry," Denzel cut in.

"Of course you be starved near half to death aftah that long walk out in that scorchin' heat." The woman leaned her head back and chuckled. "Whatcha wanna eat?"

"What do you have?" Kindra poked her head past Denzel's chair to see a plate of chicken and rice at a customer's table behind him. "I'll have the same dish as his," she said, pointing at the table behind Denzel. A man bent toward his food was eating away.

"You gone have that too?" she asked Denzel.

"Looks good. That'll do."

"I'll be right back." The woman left, chuckling and shaking her head, rambling something about, "fixin' dem uppity folks a fine meal."

After ordering, Kindra looked at Denzel. He just sat there, his eyes on her.

She folded her hands in her lap. "Now what?"

"Your mother needs time to adjust. I didn't expect her to see you."

"Ten years." Kindra said.

"That's a long time to be sure."

"She's strong, Denzel, but I don't think she can handle ten years."

"She don't have a choice."

The woman returned to their table laden with two large plates. "Here you go," she said as she set their food before them. "I'll be back with your fruit punch."

Kindra inhaled the spicy fragrance; her eyes welled with tears.

"What?" Denzel reached across the table to take her hand. "We're out here eating this good food. Kindra. We can't go through life regretting every move we make. Your mother put herself in prison. She was warned."

"Warned? You warned her this could happen?"

"Yes. We had our differences, but I didn't want to see you hurt."

"Thank you." Kindra picked up her fork and looked out the window. Beyond the building she saw the sun dipping to the mountains. "We'd better eat and get home."

"Are you ready to sail to Barbados?" Denzel asked.

"Yes. Before today, I had my doubts. But now, I'm ready."

Forty-five minutes later, Kindra saw a familiar figure lumbering along the road as if he were looking for someone.

"Is that Barnabas?" Kindra asked.

Denzel rose from his chair and stepped outside into the street. She watched the two men talking and pointing and nodding their heads. When Denzel came back to the table, he said, "Time to go. Captain thinks a storm is rolling in."

Denzel paid for their meal and the two of them hurried out onto the sidewalk.

Kindra saw the people's scowls, but didn't have time to dwell on them. Denzel tugged her hand to keep both of them at a steady pace walking toward the *Sea Baron*.

When they reached the gangplank, he abruptly came to a halt.

"What is it?" she asked. Her eyes followed his to the vessel neighboring their ship. In bold print the words, *Bloody Mary,* were inscribed on the bow.

"That's Morgan Blissmore's ship. What's he doing here?"

"I can't imagine." She glanced at the frigate with a skull imprinted on the flag flying on the masts. She remembered hearing her father and Cameron talk about the sea captain who'd kept the skull as an insignia on his ship. Privateers still roamed the sea, but Morgan Blissmore was a slaver. There was no mistaking the man posed a threat to anyone who stood in his way.

Denzel's jawline tightened. "He's here to see your mother."

Kindra's hand went to her mouth. "I'd hoped we'd seen the last of him. It's because of Blissmore that mother got involved in smuggling the slaves. Where are the constables when you need them?"

Denzel let out a deep breath. "Apparently not at the prison." Walking ahead a few steps, his neck craned to get a better look at Morgan's ship. "Is that Cuffee?" He strode up the gangway and moved to the foredeck.

Picking up her skirts, Kindra scurried after Denzel, coming to rest by his side as he watched the men on the deck of the neighboring ship through a spyglass.

"Is it?" Kindra asked.

"Yes. He's shackled to a pole on the main deck."

"Are you sure it's Cuffee? He helped Mother deliver the slaves to Blissmore's ship. That doesn't make sense." Kindra said.

"It's him all right." Denzel handed her the spyglass. "See for yourself."

Kindra closed one eye and peered through the lens with the other. Cuffee's head was tilted forward, his chin nearly touching his chest. Red stains soaked through the cloth of his shirt at the shoulders. Sweat ran down his brow and trickled down his ebony cheeks; his face was drawn, as though he were in pain. His arms were constrained behind him, his wrists shackled to a post. She lowered the telescope with a gasp. "But why is he in chains?"

"Maybe he had a change of heart. Maybe he tried to get back to the Landing, and Blissmore found out." Denzel shrugged. "If Cuffee backed out of helping them smuggle slaves, it could seriously interfere with Blissmore's sales."

"Shouldn't we try to rescue him . . . take him back to the Landing?"

"I wouldn't attempt such a thing with you on the ship. It's too risky."

"Cameron needs to know Cuffee's a prisoner on Morgan's ship," Kindra said. "Someone needs to go after him." Kindra glanced at the *Bloody Mary*, feeling helpless to save their fieldhand.

The gangplank was pulled away from the dock, stowed on deck, and the *Sea Baron* moved out to sea.

"Word gets around fast." Denzel changed the subject. "I'm thinking Blissmore was at the prison when we arrived."

"How did we miss seeing his ship when we first got here?" Kindra asked.

"I don't know. We weren't paying attention. We were focused on seeing your mother."

"Blissmore's the last thing Mother needs," Kindra said. A spark of anger ignited through her. Tia had refused to see her own daughter, and yet the probability of Morgan Blissmore sitting within the prison walls visiting with her mother was real. It irked her to no end.

"Have it your way, Mother," Kindra whispered into the wind. "I'm going to move on."

FOUR

FIVE DAYS LATER, Cameron stood on the starboard side of the main deck with Butler Wilder, the captain. He hadn't been on board the merchant vessel *Valiant,* until today.

"This is a first for you," Butler said, squinting into the morning sunlight. Around them, the crew prepared the frigate for sea.

"Yes. I'm *still* reeling from the fact that not only do we own this merchant ship, but nine more."

"Phillip was a wise man. He had a business head on his shoulders and he sure knew how to fatten his bank account." Butler ran the back of his hand over his forehead.

Cameron gripped the rigging as the ship ploughed through the choppy sea, but the captain rode the waves with ease, as if his boots were bolted to the deck.

"You did good marrying Phillip's daughter, a catch worth fishing for."

"It wasn't for the goods in Pip's coffer," Cameron's back stiffened at the suggestion that he married Grace for her father's money. "I'd have married her if she were a pauper."

Butler slapped a hand on Cameron's shoulder. "Just funnin' you, my man. If you hadn't taken a liking to the woman, I may have tried my hand for her myself. I've heard she is a remarkable lady. She takes after her father."

"Yeah, well, she's taken." Cameron grinned at the ruddy-faced captain, mentally sizing him up. The man was a natural leader and used to being in command. Just looking at him, Cameron could see the captain would take no guff from anyone. He was taller than most of his crew. His auburn hair was slicked back and tied with a thin leather thong. His rust-colored, close-cropped beard and mustache gave him a clean-cut look. He didn't wear a wide-brimmed hat like most sea captains, thus his face was bronzed by the sun. His clothes were dark. A baldric worn over his right shoulder supported a sword by his left hip. A pistol tilted from a wide belt at his waist. The man looked ready for battle.

"You always wear weapons while you're out to sea?" Cameron asked, curious that there would be a need for them.

"I've been sailing the seas for twenty years. Been taken by surprise enough times that I've learned to be prepared for the unexpected. Gives me a sense of security." Butler patted the hilt of the sword. "And the men show a little more respect."

Just then a tall, bald-headed colored man walked up. He looked young and strong, with a ready smile.

"Kasper, meet the new owner of the *Valiant*," Butler said.

"Good to meet you, sir," Kasper said. His dark brown eyes seemed curious as he nodded before turning to the captain. "There's a couple o' crewmen missin', Cap'n. Didn't realize it 'til we be out to sea."

"Who?" Butler's brows knitted together.

"Dun 'n Skeeter."

"Just as well we left them behind," the captain said. "Both of those men have been falling short on the job and drinking too much. Put Jeb and Trenton on their posts. We'll be all right."

"Yassir." Kasper scooted off hollering for the two men to change duties.

"Is there a problem?" Cameron asked.

"No." Butler frowned. "I've been tempted to throw both those men overboard a few times. They just saved me the trouble. Now, if you'll excuse me, I'll check on the crew." The captain strode toward the quarter deck.

Cameron remained on the main deck. He leaned against the rigging, arms folded, and smiled with confidence. The *Valiant* had a good crew, and better yet, a good captain. His heart pounded in his chest in anticipation of reaching the port in Charleston.

He'd felt for some time now that the unrest and probable slave revolt in Jamaica was knocking on their front door. He wanted to get Grace to safer ground, so he needed to find a secure place for them to live. Once he accomplished that, he'd get home and pull her back in his embrace. Problem was—he'd only been gone half the morning and already he missed holding her in his arms. Cameron's thoughts lingered on Grace and he chided himself for being a hopeless love-sick man. He breathed in the salt air to clear his head. He wanted to enjoy the voyage; if he were going to achieve that he would have to put his pretty little bride in the back of his mind for now.

Three weeks later, Captain Butler strolled up to Cameron. "We'll be docking soon. You can check with the harbor master for information on renting a horse or hiring a carriage."

"I'll do that. Any recommendations for a good hotel?"

"I usually stay aboard the ship at night, but I recommend the King's Inn on the river front. They have superb accommodations and the best food around." The captain left Cameron standing on the main deck and went back to work.

Cameron stood near the railing, his eyes intent on the shoreline. It was the middle of February, twenty-four years since he'd seen Charleston. The last time he'd stepped foot in this port, he was a nine-year-old boy. Memories flooded his mind like a sledgehammer. He had run away from his grief-stricken, drunken father and stowed away on the *Savannah Rose*, Phillip Cooper's merchant ship. Once found, Phillip took him under his wing and treated him like a son. He sailed to Jamaica, which became his new home.

Now, he stood looking out over the water, a grown man. The ship had sailed into port late that morning, enabling them to move up the Cooper River without delay. The *Valiant* had a reserved berth at the harbor; it sailed here often enough to rent a permanent space.

As the vessel approached the harbor, Cameron noticed Charleston had changed a great deal in the past twenty-four years. There were more solid-built buildings along the wharf. The cobbled street that stretched along the river front was busier than ever with people bustling about and wagons and drays swerving in and out of the hectic crowd.

Cameron left the railing and went down the companionway to his cabin to collect his belongings. He grabbed his satchel and shoved on his black wide-brimmed hat. Before long, he stood in line to descend the gangway. People moved at a snail's pace. His stomach rumbled. The thought of a good meal on land made him eager to secure a room, unload his gear, and then find a café.

Feeling closed in on every side, Cameron was impatient to break free of the crowd. As soon as he found a gap, he edged forward and slipped past a group of elderly men. Eying the signs on the buildings along the river front, he soon found what he was looking for. An oblong billboard read: The King's Inn. He stepped off the boardwalk and opened the door to the lodge. The bustling noise of the pedestrians outside quieted once inside.

The mahogany paneled lobby was spacious and clean. A large arch in the wall revealed an entrance to the dining room adjoined to the hotel, making it convenient to settle into his room and then find a table. Smells wafting in from the dining room made Cameron's stomach rumble.

"May I help you, sir?" the desk clerk asked. He eyed Cameron over his narrow spectacles.

"Yes. I need a room for a few days."

"Three days, sir?" the gray-haired man's lips thinned.

"Make it seven. If I decide to leave before then, I'll let you know."

"Very well." The clerk set about jotting the room information in the guest register, then turned it toward Cameron. "Sign here."

Cameron signed his name with the quill pen, then turned the book back to the clerk. "You'll be upstairs in room nine." He gave Cameron a key. "Down the long hall in the east wing."

"Thank you, sir." Cameron reached for his satchel, but a blond bellboy, who looked to be in his early teens, snatched it and led Cameron up the stairs.

After Cameron unlocked his door the bellboy slipped past him to set the satchel by the four-poster bed. The boy turned around, held out his hand, palm side up. Cameron's brows rose along with the corners of his lips. "Here you go." He dropped two coins in the boy's hand and watched him leave.

"Thanks, mister!" The boy walked happily into the hallway and stopped. "I'll be bringing you the morning paper, too."

"If I'm not here, just slip it under the door." Cameron winked. "I'll catch up with you later."

"Yes, sir!" The boy disappeared down the hall.

Cameron's sparkling clean room was simply furnished: bed, dresser, chair and washstand. He went to the window, brushed the green linen curtains aside, and peered down at the busy street. It occurred to him that after he'd finished his business in town, he ought to look up the old home place where he was born. Having left Charleston at a young age, he wondered if his father's house was still standing. Were any of his brothers or sisters living in the city? Would he recognize any of them?

The aroma of pork roast drifted up into his room, and he salivated. He dropped the curtains in place and headed for the door.

Downstairs, the dining room was bursting at the seams with diners. It was noon, obviously a bad time to hope to be quickly seated. Cameron panned the room for a spare chair, when he saw a middle-aged man beckon him over to his table. Not sure if he was the object of the man's gestures, Cameron pointed at himself with brows raised. The man nodded and waved him to come. Cameron cleared his throat and threaded his way between patrons and chairs to the man's table in the middle of the dining room.

"Join me," the man said, then scooted his chair back and reached out a hand. "Sid Sparrow."

Cameron grinned and took his hand. "Cameron Bartholomew. Busy place."

The dining room buzzed with the hum of patrons talking and waitresses skittering from table to table taking orders or bringing food.

"Are you new in town?" Sid asked.

"Just came into port." Cameron said.

"What brings you to Charleston?"

"I'm looking for land . . . rice plantation land."

"I know of some prime property that's for sale," Sid said. "It's between here and Beaufort, about twelve miles up the road. The owner is asking a steep price, but truth to tell, it's worth double or triple what he's asking."

"Do you know the owner?" Cameron asked.

"William Chastain, a prominent businessman in these parts."

A waitress scurried past their table and Sid called out, "Can a man get a meal in this house?"

"I'll be right there, sir." She set a plate down at a table and came to his side. "Have you looked at the menu?"

"I don't need to. I want the house special."

"Pork roast, mashed potatoes and vegetables?" she asked.

"That'll do. And I'll have some of that cherry pie for dessert."

She scribbled his order on a pad. "And you, sir?"

"I'll have the same," Cameron said.

The waitress hurried toward the kitchen, slipping the pad in her apron pocket.

"Why is Mr. Chastain selling?" Cameron leaned in for the answer.

"His wife is sick. Doctor says she needs a drier climate. Her lungs are bad. Word has it that William is eager to get her out of here. They're moving out west."

"Hmm. You say the property is about twelve miles from here?" Cameron asked.

"It's a great piece of land up by Fields Landing, right off Taney River, prime property for rice growing," Sid replied. "I have a plantation upriver from Mr. Chastain's land."

When the waitress brought their food, Sid dove in to eat while Cameron bowed his head and said a silent prayer of thanks to the Almighty for his food.

"There's just one word of caution about the land," Sid said, after swallowing a bite.

"Uh oh, here it comes." Cameron laid down his fork. "What is it?"

"There's a man by the name of Wendell Seward, a prominent businessman near Beaufort. He's got his sights on it. He's already got a rice plantation that's bringing him good profits."

"Go on." Cameron swallowed.

"Well, he's already made an offer on Chastain's land. But last I heard they hadn't exchanged any money or drawn up the necessary paperwork for the deed."

"Why would I want to spend my time looking at property that's just as good as sold?" Cameron's hopes plunged to the ground.

"Because word has it that William Chastain isn't in a hurry to sell it to Wendell Seward."

"Why's that?" Cameron asked.

"The man's as uncouth as they come. I've never met a man more boorish and crude. He thinks his money gives him the right to treat people with disrespect. Not too many folks around here trust the man. Word has it that Wendell's trying to buy up as much rice land as he can." Sid leaned forward. "I'd bet my merchant ship that William would be willing to sell the land to you if you've got the funds to buy it, just to spite Seward."

Cameron felt uneasy about the whole thing. But he'd come to buy good land, and Sid had said it was prime property.

"I can introduce Mr. Chastain to you in the morning. Just say the word."

"All right. Where do you want to meet?" Cameron asked.

"We'll meet here," Sid said. "You won't regret it." The two men stood, shook hands, and went their separate ways.

Cameron watched Sidney Sparrow stride away in the direction of the shipyard. Could he be lucky enough to find land so soon? Prized land at that? If this thing happened as he hoped it would, luck wouldn't have anything to do with it. He'd given this trip to God. If everything fell into place without a hitch, he'd be thanking the good Lord for it.

FIVE

WATCHING PEDESTRIANS IN the early morning sun from his dining room table near the window, Cameron saw Sid Sparrow and an older gentleman walk past and enter the hotel. He stood and waved the two men to his table.

"Good morning." Sid shook Cameron's hand. "This is Mister William Chastain."

Cameron turned to the silver-haired man dressed in a gray tweed suit. The man was medium height and on the portly side.

"Have a seat, gentlemen," Cameron said.

The elderly man came right to the point. "I understand you're interested in my land."

"Yes. I'm looking for property conducive to growing rice. I understand you haven't sold your land yet."

"No, I haven't. And if you've got the money and find you want the land, I'd be far happier selling the property to you than to that Wendell Seward. He's too full of himself." William's chin wobbled when he shook his head.

Sid Sparrow stood. "I'll leave the two of you to talk. I've business to attend to." He shook hands with them and walked out.

Three hours later, Cameron found himself traveling up the Taney River on the *River Belle* steamboat. He and Mr. Chastain had boarded the steamer in Fields Landing, bringing along a couple of horses they'd rented. The steamer stopped in front of a narrow dock and let off the two men and their horses.

"I built this dock myself," Mr. Chastain said. "We'll take the horses up the road."

Cameron looked at the suit the man was wearing and thought he was overdressed for an excursion like this. But then, maybe the man always wore a suit.

They rode up a lane from the river, covering a vast amount of acreage that took hours to travel. The greenery was suited for rice, and much of the Lowcountry had already produced the grain. Canals had been dug and trunks divided the sections that needed to be watered and drained. Slave shanties, built along this stretch of land, were a sorry sight. Cameron mused that he'd want something better for his workers.

"The larger shack to the left belonged to the overseer. I didn't stay on the land. I left it up to him to monitor the slaves and get the work done. I paid him well enough."

"None of the workers are here now?" Cameron asked.

"No. I sold them all a month ago."

Little rivulets veined in from the Taney. Cameron's mind was running a mile a minute. He could picture where the other rice fields would be, where the slave quarters needed to be built. It was always best to have the workers' habitations close to the work at hand. There was enough property to have pastureland for cows, pigs, and sheep.

They rode from the central property through a small forest that opened up to the beach at the Atlantic Ocean. The water pulsated from the sea to the rivulets of fresh Taney River water inland for the rice crops.

After hours of riding and combing the area, there wasn't time to look at any more land, but Cameron knew in his heart this was what he wanted. He could picture Grace here and raising a family.

The two horses stopped side by side as the men eyed the waves crashing onto shore.

"What do you think?" asked William Chastain.

"I'm not a man to make rash decisions. But I will say, a man would be a fool not to see the potential of this land," Cameron said.

"You've not seen all of it, but the day is nearly gone. We should head back. The *River Belle* will be along soon."

They talked as they made their way back to the river. "Sid Sparrow tells me that Wendell Seward made you an offer," Cameron said.

"I told him the offer was too low," William said.

"I like the land, but there's a lot of work to be done to get the rice fields ready before planting season." Cameron rode on, his mind already set. "What is your asking price?"

Mr. Chastain gave him an amount, eyeing Cameron with a level gaze.

"Mr. Seward couldn't meet your demand?"

"No, sir."

"I'll meet it, Mister Chastain." He reached out and the two men shook hands.

"Good. Good." William Chastain took in a deep satisfied breath.

"But if Wendell Seward should change his mind and raise the money—"

"No! I never did want to sell my land to the likes of him. In good time you'll understand why."

"All right. Meet me in the morning and we'll go to the bank."

They heard the whistle of the steamboat as they neared the river. The two men were quiet on the trip back to Charleston, each lost in his own thoughts.

The next day, standing at the rail of the *River Belle*, Cameron watched a large water bug skitter across the water. Seconds later, a gray pelican swooped into the murky river and came up with a small fish. Flapping its wings, the pelican tipped his head back and swallowed its prey, then drifted as if he hadn't a care in the world before he took flight.

As the steamer picked up speed, Cameron leaned forward and rested his elbows on the polished wood. A few more passengers appeared on deck. Cameron nodded, hello, and turned back to the river. He watched the formation of the ripples in the water as the paddle-boat churned its way through the Taney River. He felt the rumbling of the boat underfoot, and he swayed every so often as the steamer pushed forward. A mist filled the air, giving off a refreshing scent. The banks were a deep green with bright yellow jessamine drifting over their edges. Graced along the river were two-hundred-year-old oaks whose low-hanging moss draped and blew in the cool breeze.

Every once in a while, a plantation, teeming with life, appeared through a break in the landscape. People, black and white, roamed the grounds. Horses, cattle and peacocks moved over the land. Periodically, the steamboat rounded one of the many bends in the river, creating a swirling mass of bubbles in its wake.

Cameron's interest held as each new landscape appeared and the steamer pushed on. It wouldn't be long before he reached his new property. As expected, within a few minutes, the whistle blew and the boat stopped at the rickety dock. Cameron led his rented horse down the gangplank with a brief wave to the captain. "Three hours!" he called out. The river captain tooted the whistle and the paddleboat went up the river.

Cameron mounted the roan and headed out across the fields. There before him lay hundreds of acres waiting to be ploughed, waiting for the first rice crop to be planted. He rode slowly in the Lowlands. In some areas it looked as if someone had tried to grow a crop other than rice. There were rows of tilled ground with dried vegetation.

Riding up-land, following the river, he scouted out the sections of land that would be put to use, maybe provisions fields, if not, he'd put stock on them. He traveled the grounds a good two hours. Satisfied, he nudged the horse into a canter and rode back toward the far side of the land near the forest. If he sat very still, he could hear the sea pounding on the shoreline. The horse snorted as if he heard it too. "Come on." Cameron reined the horse to the east. "Let's take a look."

Horse and rider followed the rivulets that in time met the pounding surf. Cameron squinted as he glanced down the shoreline some three hundred yards. A small group of men stood on the beach as if surveying the property around them.

A man waved. Cameron waved back. His heart lurched for several beats. Was he looking to buy this property–his property?

The man broke away from the group, stepped up into the saddle of a horse tethered nearby. He pulled on the reins, turning his horse toward Cameron. Within moments his horse trotted up in front of Cameron.

"Good day, Mister . . . ?"

"Bartholomew, Cameron Bartholomew."

"My name's Wendell Seward. Most folks in these parts call me Dell."

Cameron touched the brim of his hat and waited.

"You're riding on private property," Seward said. "This land's as good as mine come tomorrow."

Cameron pushed his hat off his forehead. "I beg to differ. It'd be you who are trespassing on my land."

"Excuse me?" Color drained from Wendell's face. He shifted in his saddle. His eyes wide. "You must be mistaken."

"Mister Chastain sold the land to me yesterday morning." Cameron fixed his gaze on Wendell Seward.

"I'll see about that!" Wendell nudged his horse up next to Cameron's. "Chastain and I had an agreement. A man's only as good as his word."

Cameron worked his jaw but said nothing.

"If I were you, mister, I'd be looking for land elsewhere. I've had my eyes on this land for some time."

"I've already purchased the land. I'm not looking any further." Cameron kept his gaze level.

"You haven't seen the last of me, Bartholomew." Wendell reined his horse away and rode back toward the group standing on the shore.

"Come on fellas," he called over his shoulder to the men. "It'll be dark soon. I've got to pay that no-good Chastain a visit."

Cameron watched the sand kick up as the men galloped away. "I think I just bought a boatload of trouble along with this beautiful land," he said to the horse, then reined the animal back toward the river.

Cameron came to an area where oak trees, covered with moss dangling like long crocheted shawls, densely lined two sides of a dirt lane. He slowed his steed and rode under the large branches that arched over the road. The sun peeked through and speckled the ground before him. The horse slowly clopped along the path toward the end of the tunnel. Cameron pulled on the reins while staring ahead to a clearing on a rise. Rusty stakes were driven into the ground marking the four corners of a large square. Cameron slid off his horse and walked to the center of the square. Whoever had driven the stakes into the ground had picked the perfect place to build the Great House. Having come from the river, he now stood in the center of what would be the new home's location, Cameron grinned. *"River Oak,"* he said under his breath. That would be the new plantation's name.

Back in Charleston that evening, while Cameron shared a meal with Sid Sparrow, the men talked of nothing but rice. In these parts rice was considered Carolina Gold. As Sparrow had informed him earlier, he owned a plantation upriver from the property Cameron had just purchased. Sparrow seemed more than happy to help Cameron with information to get him started on his new enterprise.

Parting company with his new friend after dinner, Cameron returned to his room, made an inventory of the supplies he'd need to plant a rice crop, and wrote a second list of building materials for the house. He would visit the land office in the morning to get names of two contractors known for building some of the finest mansions in the area. That would be his next stop. He thought of Grace. She would have the loveliest home in the Lowlands.

Men needed work. He would hire them to build bridges over the ponds and a large ferry landing big enough to stack hundreds of gunnysacks of his Carolina Gold rice next to the riverbank. It was February. He had plenty of time to seed the rice fields. It wouldn't be long before river barges would be stopping at River Oak to load the rice barrels and large rice sacks that would be transported to the merchant ships.

The more he planned, the more excited he became to get the projects up and running. He'd need to hire men to build the slave district first. The field hands would need a place to sleep. On and on the thoughts ran through his mind. He scratched all his ideas on paper.

Sid had reminded him that April is rice planting month. The ditches needed to be dug and the canals readied for the fresh water to flow from the river to flood the fields after the rice was planted. "To start with," Sid had said, "you'll need seventy-five to a hundred slaves to plant the crop. By the time the harvest comes around, you'll need upward of three hundred and seventy-five slaves to make the rice operation run smooth."

It was nearing midnight before Cameron set aside his lists and stretched out on the bed, he couldn't will himself to sleep. A man of action, he lay listening to the sounds of the street below as plans swirled through his mind. He visualized the rice fields being planted and the mansion being built.

A woman's voice floated through his second story window from the street below, breaking into his thoughts. The feminine sound made him think of Grace. He missed her . . . he missed the smell of lavender in her auburn hair, her soft skin against his. He had accomplished what he came to do. It was time to go home.

SIX

Cooper's Landing

THE FIRST OF March found Kindra with a million and one things to do. With so much to accomplish she lost track of the time and before she knew it the days had soared. The *Sea Baron* was in port and this time she and Denzel would be on it when it sailed.

In preparation, Kindra spent the cool hours of early morning going from her wardrobe to the bed, arms filled with gowns and day dresses. She looked at the heaping pile of garments, dresses of every imaginable color and fabric. *How am I going to fit these in my trunks?* She gazed at the open containers waiting to be filled. One by one, she folded the gowns in half. She pushed, shoved and tucked until she was able to close and latch the first trunk lid.

When she stood, a wave of nausea gripped her. She lowered her body to sit on her rose-colored chair and massaged her stomach, not for the first time in the past few days.

What's wrong with me? Was she so excited to sail to Barbados that she'd worked herself into a case of nerves? *Surely it will pass once I'm on the vessel and out to sea.* In that moment, the aroma of fried bacon reached her nostrils. She gagged. She covered her mouth and ran to her private bath. Moments later, her head swimming, she sat to get her bearings.

A rap came at the door. "Miz Kindra," Rhea peeked into the room. "Breakfast be ready."

"I'll be down momentarily."

"Yes'm." Rhea shut the door.

Kindra stood and ran her hand over her stomach, then down her skirts to straighten out the wrinkles. She glanced at the cluttered room and shrugged. "This can wait," she murmured.

Descending the stairs another wave of nausea hit her. *Maybe I need to go back to bed.*

Denzel came through the front door as Kindra's feet landed on the polished floor of the foyer. She smiled weakly at him. "Morning."

"Morning, my love." He kissed her forehead, then leaned back eyeing her. "Are you all right?"

When Kindra's smile faded, she wiped her brow. "Yes, of course. I'm just feeling a bit hot and tired. I've been packing."

"Don't overdo. You have Rhea to help get the job done."

"I know. I just wanted to do this myself."

"Come on, let's eat."

Grace sat at the head of the table flanked by Aunt Katy and Josie. Cameron wouldn't be back from his trip to Charleston for another two to three weeks.

"Good morning, Kindra, did you sleep well?" asked Aunt Katy.

"Yes, thank you."

When Kindra and Denzel sat down, Kindra saw that Grace looked as green as Kindra felt. "Are you all right, Grace?" she asked.

Grace took a deep breath and fanned her face with her hand. "I don't understand it. This is the second time this morning I've felt I was going to be sick."

Kindra noticed a grin on Dinah's face, but she ignored it.

"Really? I've been nauseated all morning, too. I wonder if something is going around that we haven't heard about just yet."

Grace glanced at Denzel, sweat beads on her forehead. "Could you ask Doctor Moses if we've a virus at the plantation?"

"Well, I'll be." Aunt Katy clucked her tongue. "Could be something else." Her eyes twinkled when she glanced at Josie.

Dinah began to chuckle and all eyes turned to the cook.

"What's so funny?" Grace asked, dabbing her forehead with a table napkin.

"The only virus I 'spect goin' on at Cooper's Landing is little bitty babies cookin' in the ovens." She laughed, her belly jiggled. "I can see it written all over your faces." Dinah set down a large bowl of scrambled eggs, then she placed her chubby fists on her hips.

Kindra and Grace stared at each other.

When Kindra glanced at Denzel, she found him smiling as wide as a cat who'd caught a mouse. "Why are you grinning?" She ribbed him with her elbow.

He leaned away, but his eyes lit up. "I believe Dinah is onto something. You may be in the family way." He pulled Kindra into an embrace. "You make me a happy man."

"Not so fast. We don't know if that's true."

Kindra looked up at Grace, who had blanched.

"A baby?" Grace pushed her plate away. "I still think we should send for Doctor Moses. It's the only way we'll know for sure."

"No, Grace," Denzel said with a comical smile.

"No?"

"No."

"Why not?" She looked confused and glanced at Kindra.

"He don't tend to women when it comes to babies," Denzel said firmly.

"Then who does?"

"Laulie," Kindra said.

Now it was Grace's turn to smile. "You'll have to forgive me. I'd completely forgotten that she's the midwife and nanny on the plantation."

Just then, Gemma appeared at the dining room entrance with Laulie in tow.

"I be hearin' you be needin' my services," Laulie beamed.

Before the morning was over, Laulie confirmed that the two new brides were in the family way. At two months along, Kindra would have to convince Denzel that she was fit to sail as planned. She'd not wait another several months to make the journey.

While Rhea finished up the packing, Kindra walked out to the fenced-in graveyard to see her father's tombstone. She knelt in the high grass and stared at the gray rock etched with her father's name.

"Goodbye, Father. I'll always miss you. I believe somewhere in your heart you always cared for me. You just didn't know how to show it. This home I'm going to will be a reminder that you never forgot me. Somewhere in the back of your mind—you loved me." At the foot of the headstone, Kindra placed a clump of white magnolia blossoms. "I just learned you're going to be a grandfather. I hope my child will be your first. Thank you for all you've done for me." She stood and touched the warm gray rock.

"Miz Kindra," Rhea said, "Your trunks be packed. Amos and Cato done loaded them in the wagon."

"Thank you, Rhea. Follow me." She led Rhea to Tia's bedchamber where several trunks were scattered about the room. A breeze drifting through the open French doors made Kindra feel better. The scent of jasmine lingered in the air. Tia had always kept a spray of jasmine in a vase in her room. And though she was gone, the maids continued the tradition.

"I want you to pack Mother's clothes while I set about getting her personal belongings together."

"Yes'm, Miz Kindra. I be doin' that right away."

It seemed to Kindra that Rhea set about her task with a little more enthusiasm than she had earlier that morning. Of course, it wasn't news that most of the servants disliked her mother. Tia had been a hard task-mistress and had shown little remorse for her actions. Kindra wouldn't be surprised if Rhea were ready to say "good riddance" to anything attached to Tia.

Despite their many differences over the years, Kindra had every intention of bringing her mother to Kindra Hall. She couldn't imagine her mother wanting to return to Cooper's Landing. Kindra would have to occasionally keep in touch with the prison to check on Tia's release. She hoped her mother wouldn't serve the full ten year's sentence and be released earlier than expected. When that day arrived, Kindra planned to be at the prison gates to take her mother home.

Rhea hummed as she worked and Kindra went from the bedside tables to her mother's desk looking for anything she felt her mother would need when she cames to live in Barbados. It would be a good many years before that day would arrive, but Kindra wanted to be prepared to give her mother her personal things.

When Kindra opened a bottom drawer to the desk, she found a hard-bound journal that had been tucked behind papers and paraphernalia.

"What's this?" she half whispered. The cover of the journal was plain and gray. Thumbing through the pages she realized it was her mother's diary and immediately recognized the story she knew by heart. It began when Tia had met Phillip Cooper and soon learned she was with child.

At first Tia had been troubled, the journal said, but after turning several pages, Kindra read that her mother had begun to express joy at being brought into the Great House, and though there hadn't been a marriage between her and the master, she had been given the duty of domestic headmistress at Cooper's Landing.

Surprised and pleased to have a written record of her birth, Kindra determined she would read every word once they were aboard the *Sea Baron*.

Flipping the pages to the middle of the journal, Kindra noted that much of the diary notes had changed to information about slavery. Her stomach twisted when she realized her mother had documented every slave she had smuggled. Why would she keep records of her crime? Didn't she know this book could incriminate her and the penalty would be the gallows rather than a few years in prison? They'd taken Tia on hearsay more than proof, she was sure of it. Kindra had heard of men hanged for stealing a horse. If that were so, stealing slaves and smuggling them onto Blissmore's ship would be a far greater offense.

A hand touched Kindra's shoulder and she jumped.

"Miz Kindra," Rhea said.

Kindra slammed the journal shut and let out a deep breath. "Sorry, Rhea. I forgot you were in the room." Kindra slid the journal between the folds of her skirts as she turned around.

"I be done packin' your mothah's gowns. Do you need me to be packin' anything else?"

"No. That will be all. You may leave and set about your other duties."

Kindra watched Rhea leave the room, shutting the door behind her. She let out another deep breath. "Oh, Mother. I should burn this book!"

Kindra took the diary out to the veranda where she had better light. Filled with apprehension, but driven to see what more was in the journal, she turned a few more pages: *I hate the little brat that has shown up at Pip's front door. She claims to be Phillip's daughter. How can that be? I will do everything I can to prove she's an imposte,r after Phillip's money. He only has one daughter and that's Kindra. How dare the wench come begging for Kindra's inheritance. She won't be here for long. I'll see to that.*

A small paragraph stood alone on a page: *Phillip is sick. He won't last much longer. I fear what will become of me after he's gone. Will I have a home on Cooper's Landing?*

A few more pages and there were more records of smuggling. This time she mentioned Cuffee: *Cuffee is willing to leave his family and the island for freedom. Fool. He'll never know freedom. Morgan Blissmore says I can make double the money for Cuffee. He's strong and muscular with no scars on his back from whippings. A slave this clean could possibly bring triple the money.*

Kindra cleared her throat, and her skin crawled as she read the journal penned by her mother. She leaned against the rail on the veranda as she continued: *I have had enough of Phillip's distrust. I don't need him. Jule Spade has convinced Jesse into believing the Caribbean Dragon will be his when it's paid in full. But Jule has no intention of selling the ship to Jesse. He'll take the money and sail away!*

And a few pages later: *Jule Spade is the man I want. We're two of a kind. He has promised to take me to the island of Tobago. I'm ready to flee this place and leave them all behind.*

Kindra lowered the book and turned her gaze to the sparkling sea beyond the plantation. "You always cast your spell on men," she murmured. *But what good did all this do for you? You're in prison. Father, Jesse and Minerva are dead. And who is Jule Spade? I've never heard of him.*

The next entry sent tingles up Kindra's arms: *I have the jewels that belonged to Jule Spade. I hid them where he would least expect it. Jule is the man of my dreams, and maybe he would have shared his booty with me. But that was a chance I could not take. He can only surmise that I took the jewels . . . but never be sure of it.*

Kindra stared at the page, disbelieving the words written in her mother's hand. *Jewels? Mother stole jewels?* Her eyes left the page as she glanced over the veranda's bannister to gaze at the sparkling sea. Again she wondered, *who is this Jule Spade? Why have I never heard of him? And, Mother . . . did I ever really know you?*

Voices floated up to the veranda from below where she saw Denzel and Cato walking toward the stables. Moments later they emerged holding the reins to Angel, Kindra's white Arabian horse.

"Angel!" Kindra said excitedly and leaned over the rail to wave. "I'm nearly ready. I'll be right down."

She went back into Tia's bedchamber, threw the journal into her satchel and carried it to her personal luggage.

When she closed her mother's door, she shut a part of the past behind her; she was moving forward with hopes for a brighter future.

Early the next morning, the Cooper carriage rattled and swayed as it traveled over cobblestone streets to the wharf. Kindra, Denzel and Grace rode in silence. Kindra mentally completed a checklist of everything she had wanted to take.

Denzel touched her arm. "Did you remember to bring the documents with the deed to Kindra Hall?"

"Yes." Kindra laughed nervously. "I packed them in my valise." Of all the things they'd need when they arrived at Barbados, it would be the document proving she and Denzel were the new owners of the plantation. She was grateful that Desmond Rothschild had sent notification to the foreman of Kindra Hall telling him they were coming.

As they rode through town, Kindra and Grace stared at each other from time to time. Kindra could see that Grace was doing everything in her power to keep her emotions in check. Kindra wasn't so sure it was working. It certainly wasn't for her. She could barely swallow for the sob stuck in her throat. It was easier not to look at Grace. She was leaving her sister, the only person other than Denzel that she cared for with all her heart.

There was a time she had resented Grace. She resented her for showing up at Cooper's Landing and winning her father's love. Everybody had loved her, while Kindra felt invisible. And then one day, Grace admitted she knew they were sisters. That day they put their differences behind them, along with the color of their skin. That's when everything changed. Grace began inviting Kindra along to everything she did. And every day since then they had grown closer to each other.

Now the Caribbean Sea would lie between them. She'd miss Grace. She'd miss her smile and gentle touch.

The carriage pulled up and stopped in front of the *Sea Baron*. Out the window, Kindra watched a crewman lead Angel up the gangway. Trunks and crates were being carried up the long plank.

"We're here," Grace said softly, as she stood to step down from the carriage.

Kindra followed close behind. She looked past Grace at the stevedores coming and going not only from their ship, but to and from other vessels along the wharf. Sweat glistened on their muscled bodies as they heaved crates of merchandise and barrels of sugar and rum. A number of trunks were going up the gangway on crude carts, but some of the men hefted their heavy load on their shoulders and muscled their way through the crowd.

"This is it," Grace said. Her voice sounded strange, as if she struggled to gain control of her emotions. Her face flushed and a tear streamed down her face. "Come here."

Kindra stepped into Grace's embrace. She hugged her tight. "I'm going to miss you terribly!"

"Me, too," said Grace. Kindra could hear the tremor in her voice.

"Write me," Kindra demanded.

"Every day." Grace laughed softly with a catch in her voice. She kissed Kindra's cheek.

Denzel stood back as he watched the two women say their goodbyes. A bell tolled from the *Sea Baron*.

"Goodbye!" Kindra cried out.

"I'll be waiting for a letter!" Grace said.

Needing his support, Kindra held Denzel's hand. She felt weak-kneed going up the gangplank. When they reached the top she went to the ship's rail and leaned over to wave goodbye. Grace waved and blew her a kiss.

"I love you, too," Kindra whispered. She waved and waved.

She felt Denzel's strong arm around her waist, and tears ran down her cheeks as the ship crept away from the wharf. The farther they slipped away, the smaller Grace became.

"I wish I could've said goodbye to Camp," Denzel said in a husky voice.

"We'll see them again." Kindra wrapped her arms around his waist.

"You're right about that. And when we do there'll be three of us." His eyes lit. He pulled her away from the rail. "Let's find our cabin. I don't want you out in the cold air too long."

"The air might do me good, but I do want to see the cabin."

On Tuesday the following week, the waters were choppy from a new storm. Denzel found Kindra, with a white-knuckled grip, sitting on a bench on the foredeck. She appeared to be fighting another bout of seasickness . . . or was it because of her delicate condition? He turned to the bow and called out to Captain Kincade, "How much longer will we ride in this tempest?"

The captain came and stood before Kindra. "Are you ill, Mrs. Talmaze?" He turned to one of his men. "Bring her some hot tea!"

Kindra looked up, her face green. "I suppose I'm still getting used to the sea."

The captain nodded sympathetically. "It takes a bit of an adjustment."

Denzel cleared his throat. "My wife is in the family way. I'm sure she's more ill than she'd be otherwise."

The captain jerked his head to face Kindra. The sails caught a strong wind; black clouds raced overhead. "I want you below deck, ma'am. This is no place for a woman in your condition."

"I can barely breathe in the cabin, which is why I came topside."

"Still, the storm is picking up. It's better if you go below to your quarters." He looked at Denzel. "Get her below."

"Yes, sir." Denzel helped Kindra to their cabin. He could feel her shaking and hoped the crewman would be along with her tea.

"I'd lie down, but the swaying of the ship makes it intolerable."

"I reckon that's so, but I'm thinking you'd be better off if you'd take to the bed."

"Oh, Denzel. I didn't want to wait months to make this trip, but now, I don't know." Kindra crawled into bed.

"If it's any consolation we'll be going ashore in Bridgetown in another week." He rubbed her arms and brushed the hair off her brow.

"We're almost there." She smiled weakly.

A rap at the door interrupted them. Denzel opened it and took from a crewman two mugs and a pot of hot tea before the man quickly disappeared.

"Thank goodness for hot tea. It's the one thing I can keep down," Kindra murmured.

Seven days later, the *Sea Baron* had cleared the rough, windward, wave-tossed coast of Barbados and was headed through the calm leeward waters to Bridgetown.

Kindra shaded her eyes to watch longboats being rowed across the jade waters to the docks. It was the twenty-sixth of March when she stood on the deck and gained her first view of Bridgetown. They had come late in the day and hit high tide, enabling them to move up the bay without delay. Unbeknownst to her, she would have little time to adjust to the changes about to overtake her.

Slowly the ship sliced through the warm waters of passage. The *Sea Baron* was taking them to a home in a land Kindra had never seen. Her heart skipped a beat. They were coming into unknown territory, but she was ready to claim that which was hers–the home her father had built and prepared for her future. In the back of her mind, she quoted part of a familiar Bible verse: *I will fear no evil, for Thou art with me; Thy rod and Thy staff, they comfort me.* "Lord, I'm ready," she whispered into the wind.

SEVEN

GRACE STEPPED OUT onto the front porch of the Great House wearing her mother's blue-flowered day dress. With Cameron in Charleston, and Kindra and Denzel having left a few weeks ago for their new life in Barbados, she had awakened feeling melancholy.

She ran a hand over her abdomen. It was flat. Still, she was fully aware of the life growing inside and the wonder of it all. It would be another month or two before a bump would show a child was on its way into their lives. Would Cameron arrive home today? She couldn't wait to tell him they were in the family way.

Grace raised a hand to shelter her eyes as she gazed out at the scenery before her. She watched the sun come up over the horizon as tall palms gently swayed in the cool morning breeze. The sight of twinkling leaves reflecting the sun never ceased to send a thrill through her. The effect made both the carriage drive that led to the plantation house and the circular drive in front of the house a welcoming sight. The flowers interspersed among the plants gave off a fragrance that enhanced the early morning air.

As she stood there, breathing in the tropical scents, she heard a soft meow at her feet. Her cat, Smitty, appeared next to her. He ran his head against the bottom of her skirts, stepping over one foot and leaning into her.

"And good morning to you," Grace said, picking up her orange and white cat. She held him away from her to look at him. Smitty blinked nonchalantly and closed his green eyes. Grace snuggled him to her chest. "At least *you* haven't left me."

Smitty started purring and she felt the vibration of his body through her fingertips. After scratching behind his ears she set him down on the porch. He strolled away, his tail lifted high as he found shade under a wicker chair. Grace picked up her parasol. A walk around the lane behind the house would do her good.

She skipped down the porch steps and moved out toward the sugar mill, stopping to stand beside a fenced yard and study the workers. A lane led from the cane fields to the building. As she watched, field hands guided donkey carts full of chopped cane stalks to the mill house. Workers grabbed arm loads of the thick, green sugar cane and carried them to the side of the long structure, where they dropped their load onto the growing pile.

A second set of men and women shoved the sugar cane through a chute on the side of the building. A loud grinding noise sounded from inside the mill house. Behind the building a windmill loomed high overhead with paddles that turned round and round. Grace observed the colored men and women, while here and again a field hand glanced her way. Was it her imagination, or did they really scowl at her?

Grace decided it was her imagination since there was no reason for the workers to be upset. She waved, then held her umbrella high as she walked down a narrow dirt road that led toward the slave district. There were rows and rows of small, wooden houses, fenced in, dirt walkways leading to each one.

Early mornings found older women sitting in doorways watching small children playing in the dirt yards. The children's mothers would already be out in the fields working, either hauling piles of cane stalks to waiting wagons in the fields or hoeing in the provisions fields farther behind the main buildings. The provisions fields fed everybody on the plantation with their variety of vegetables. It seemed the slaves' jobs were never-ending since the fields first needed to be seeded, then came the weeding, and later the harvest.

Grace had made a habit of walking around the narrow lane behind the Great House from the first day she had arrived at Cooper's Landing. She loved getting out and seeing the plantation teeming with life. After nearly a year of living here, the workers were used to seeing her make the rounds. Sometimes she stopped and visited with one of the women in the shanties. She wanted to know more about them, and she wanted them to trust her. After she walked around the lane, she often stopped at the stable to give her horse, Dandy, an apple. Today would be one of those days. She felt for the piece of fruit in her pocket.

Grace lifted a hand to wave at one of the women sitting on a top step, holding a large wooden bowl on her lap. The woman did not, however, so much as look Grace's way. Instead, she stood and went inside the dark shanty.

"Hmm," Grace said to herself. *Have I done something to offend her?*

She'd gone out of her way to prove to the people that she, like her father, was not a hard taskmaster. Unlike the custom at most plantations on the island, Grace abhorred threatening a slave with a whip. But on Cooper's Landing, when the slaves didn't follow the rules, another way was found to discipline them—solitary confinement. She had learned, however, by her father's sheer mercy to the workers, that by showing them respect as human beings, they got more done. Cooper's Landing had a reputation for being one of the largest, and most prosperous sugar plantations on the island. Grace was sure that handling their slaves with respect had much to do with their success.

Yet today, she felt shunned by the old woman. She knew she shouldn't let it bother her and decided to brush the offense aside. After all, she *was* the mistress of this plantation. And surely what the slave women thought of her didn't matter. *Did it?*

As she moved away from the colored district a thought occurred to her. She'd heard women who were in the family way became overly emotional. Breathing a sigh of relief, Grace smiled to herself. Was she being a bit testy lately?

As she rounded the lane, she came upon a group of field hands sitting on bales of hay behind the barn. They faced the provisions field, unaware that she was there. Grace abruptly stopped walking. Why were the men sitting around instead of working in the cane fields? She backed up so that she was hidden behind the wall. Where was Mingo? Grace studied the profile of each man, but none of them was the overseer. As she stepped back behind the side of the barn, she tilted her head to listen to their excited tones.

The wind was still blowing and she missed much of what they said. Still, she caught a few words that floated her way. "Tia gone" came across clearly, but then in their broken English other words came across faintly . . . "we get away" . . . "in a fortnight" . . . "wait for others coming this way."

She felt a chill lick up her spine and settle at the nape of her neck. It wasn't her imagination after all. The atmosphere in the slave district had changed. What she dismissed as her own emotions was true: eyes were watching her with animosity.

Grace had heard enough. She slipped away from the side of the barn and strode determinedly to the stable where she pulled the apple from her pocket and gave it to Dandy before she stopped to talk to Nate, their stableman.

He brushed straw from his breeches as he stepped out from a stall. His salt and peppered head came up to greet her. "Mornin', Missus. You be up and about a bit early this fine day."

"Yes, well, it's a good thing that I am up," she said, eyeing him to see how he responded to her.

"You sho' be all fired up, I'm thinkin'. What be wrong?"

"Nate, what's going on around here?"

"I sho' don't be knowin' what you be talkin' about." He raised his brows and his lips thinned.

Grace placed her hands on her hips and tapped her foot on the dirt floor. "You've not heard anything suspicious around here? The field hands haven't talked to you about being unhappy here at the Landing?"

"Well, now that you mention it, it seem some of the field hands and their women be riled up some, but they don't be sharin' their thoughts with old Nate. I be thinkin' they look at me and the house servants a different way."

"I noticed the women seem angry, but I thought it was just me until I came across a group of field hands talking behind the barn. Where's Mingo, by the way?"

"I ain't seen Mingo this morning. A few of the field hands come down with the stomach flu. Might be the overseer sick, too."

"I don't know what to make of it, Nate."

"I be gettin' the looks as well, Miz Grace. Been feelin' I best be watchin' my back." He peered toward the stable door. "When Camp due home?"

"Any day now."

"Good. I be feelin' a whole lot better when he sets foot on Coopah's Landin'."

"Me too." She touched the old man's arm. "Keep this between you and me. I don't want to alarm the house servants."

"Yes'm, Miz Grace." He nodded his speckled head.

"Brush Dandy. I want to take her out for a ride later this morning. I think it's high time I find Mingo and see what he's up to."

"Sho' nuff, Miz Grace."

When Grace continued her walk to the Great House, she paid particular heed to the workers in the kitchen garden. Guarded glances turned her way. With her back up, Grace's mind swirled with thoughts of the past year. How quickly these people had forgotten she had stood side by side with them in the middle of the night fighting the barn fire. She had stood in line and heaved bucket after bucket of water at the relentless blaze. She had taken the colored women under her wing, had helped them with their babies and opened up a school for their children.

Feeling grumpy and out of sorts, she ventured to the front of the house where she found Aunt Katy and Josie sitting on the porch.

"You're up and about mighty early this morning," said Aunt Katy.

Grace collapsed her umbrella and set it against the porch rail. "Yes, I am. A good thing, too."

"Why is that?" Katy asked.

"With Cameron and Denzel both gone, I felt I needed to see that things are running smoothly." Grace found an empty chair and sat down, a bit stiff.

"Uh oh. What's going on?" Aunt Katy asked, giving Grace her full attention.

"Well, for one thing, I didn't see Mingo anywhere. Then I found a bunch of field hands sitting behind the barn doing nothing but talking. But that's only the half of it." Grace let out a deep sigh and frowned.

"Well, don't stop now," Aunt Katy urged. "What'd they do?"

"It sounds like they're up to something. I couldn't hear them very well, but it sounds like they're planning something."

"Like what?" asked Josie. She leaned forward to hear.

"I heard them say Tia's name, and then they said something about going away, maybe in a fortnight."

"That kind of talk has got to stop." Aunt Katy sat close enough to pat Grace's hand. "I'm thinking Cameron expected some of the men to slack off from their duties with him and Denzel gone. But running off from the plantation–that's nonsense."

"What am I going to do Aunt Katy?"

"Don't fret about it, Grace. You need to keep a good attitude for you and the baby."

"I don't think Cameron expected Mingo to shirk his duties. He's a good overseer. It just doesn't make sense."

"Cameron's going to be home soon. He'll take care of it," Aunt Katy said.

Grace glanced over at Josie. Her cousin's knitting needles were clacking away.

"What are you making?" Grace asked.

Josie held up several rows of yellow yarn knitted in an elegant design. "A baby blanket. I'm hoping to get this done before we leave."

Grace smiled and ran her hand over her midriff, something she found herself doing often these days. "You're a gem, Josie. I shall cherish that blanket."

The door creaked open and Dinah poked her head out the door. "You best be comin' inside. Your breakfast be getting cold!"

Grace's stomach growled just then. She glanced down and thought, *I better keep this little one fed!*

Three days later, Grace stepped outside in time to see a trail of dust flying behind Jimmy Downs' cart. The horse was trotting at a good clip, and the winds had kicked up. She shaded her eyes and saw that Cameron was Jimmy's passenger.

"Camp!" she cried as she ran down the steps. The cart rolled to a stop in front of the house. Cameron jumped down and strode over to Grace, whose heart was thumping in her chest.

"Grace . . ." was all he said as he pulled her into his arms. Before she knew it his lips claimed hers, all the while holding her tight. He finally released her and stepped back. "You sure look good to a tired man's eyes."

Jimmy Downs set Cameron's bags on the ground beside them. When Grace looked his way, Jimmy smiled and nodded.

Cameron reached into his pocket and fished out a couple of coins. "Thank you, Jimmy."

"My pleasure, Master Camp!" He stepped back into the small cart and shook the reins. The horse took off at a trot.

Cameron's hands went around Grace's waist as he gazed down at her, his blue eyes shining. "I've missed you."

A thrill shot through Grace. She was standing right where she wanted to be, in Cameron's arms, when she told him her surprise.

"I've got news for you, Mister Bartholomew."

"Can it wait?" He leaned forward as if to kiss her again.

She pushed him back with the tip of her forefinger.

"Hmm. News? From the mischievous look in those beautiful eyes, I'm not sure I want to hear it."

"You want to hear it, all right."

He kissed her nose. "What is it?"

She felt his warm breath on her face and smiled. "You're going to be a father."

Cameron stiffened for a moment, then his eyes opened wide. "Wh . . . what?"

She giggled. "You heard me."

Cameron swooped her up and swung her around. "I'm going to be a father," he laughed and set her on her feet. His hands quickly went to her shoulders when she stumbled ever so slightly.

"I shouldn't have done that," he said, his large hands holding her steady. "Are you all right?"

"Yes, I'm fine." She laid a hand on her stomach and his eyes followed her hand.

"When is the baby due?"

"Laulie thinks it will be October."

"Seven months? There's so much that needs to be done in that time." His brows furrowed for only a moment.

"Come inside. I want to hear about your trip." She tugged on his arm and lead the way to the sitting room off their bedchamber.

"Grace, we're going to be rice plantation owners." He stopped and pulled her back into his arms. "Everything can wait for just one more minute." He groaned huskily as he planted a kiss on her lips.

When they came up for air she said, "I've missed you too, Camp. There's so much to tell you."

An hour later, the two of them sat in silence. Grace had just told him about the field hands' conspiracy, relieved to finally be able to tell him what she'd heard.

"This isn't good, Grace." Cameron was clearly disturbed by her news.

"I didn't think it was. What are we going to do?"

"I wish Denzel was here. He had a way with them. They respected him as being one of their own."

"But they respect you too," Grace said. "I've seen them around you."

"Times are changing. Your father and I talked long and hard about the possibility of a revolt. We knew the slaves were getting restless up the coast. I'm going to have to speak to Mingo. We've got to put an end to this kind of foolish talk."

Grace shuddered. She wanted to change the subject. "Tell me about the trip. Did you find a place for us to live?"

Cameron told her all about the property in Field's Landing.

"It seems our lives are changing in the blink of an eye," she said, leaning into the crook of his arm and feeling safe now that Cameron was with her. They snuggled on the sofa before the French doors of the veranda.

"Yes. Maybe it's time for things to change. Your father's gone and so are the others. It's just us."

She knew he referred to her sister, Kindra, and Denzel, not to mention Tia.

"You're going to love the land, Grace. It's beautiful. And I've already got contractors starting on the Great House."

"I want to be in on the plans," Grace said, raising her head.

"Of course. I wouldn't have it any other way. The house won't be ready for your touch for some time, though. It's going to take several months to get it built. Then it will need your personal attention. I want you right in the middle of all the decorating."

The thought of planning the colors for walls and fabric and curtains, not to mention the furnishings of the house, felt like a monumental project to Grace. She'd never done anything like that in her life. "I can't wait to get started. But you said it's going to take most of this year. Does that mean we'll be separated for the time being?"

"Yes and no. I'll come and go. As much as I dislike you being here with the unrest going on, I have to be on hand in Fields Landing to see that everything gets done as planned. I need to be there to supervise the planting of the new rice fields. There's no one else to oversee it. The slave quarters are being built as we speak. But Grace, I've decided I cannot have you out of my sight for long."

"What are you saying?"

"I'm saying, I'll get you out of here as soon as I can. I'll have a small cottage built so I can have you there with me. And that way you can be on hand to help with all the decisions."

Grace let out a relieved sigh. "Good. I want you near when the baby comes."

Cameron frowned. "That's the problem. You can't travel the seas in your condition. As much as I want you there, you'll have to wait the first seven months. I'll plan my trips so that I'll be here when the time comes."

"But—"

"It's only seven months. You should be safe that long. Don't forget how protective the servants and slaves have been to all of us. They may want their freedom, but I don't believe for a minute that they'd want to harm us. When the baby is born, then you and the child can come to River Oak."

"River Oak?"

"You will understand why I chose the name when you see the land. We have to travel to our plantation by river. And when we get off the steamboat at the dock, and go up to the house, it is lined with old oak trees that look as if they have been there forever." He stopped and gazed into her eyes. "River Oak came to me when I stood where the house will be built. It will be the perfect name for our new home."

"River Oak." She tasted the name of her new home on her lips. "I can't wait to see it."

"You will have the grandest home in all of South Carolina, my sweets."

"I'd be happy to live in a shanty just to have you by my side." She snuggled in a little closer.

"But you will have a home fit for a queen." He kissed the top of her head. "And maybe a little prince?"

They both sat in contemplative silence again before Cameron said, "I just hope this business of the slave uprising can be prevented. We've got to find a way to keep them from leaving the plantation."

Grace thought to herself, *can we get away before it's too late?*

EIGHT

AFTER TWO MONTHS in prison, Tia stood in a long line with other female prisoners waiting for the guard to open the door to the filthy cells below. The sun bore down, hot and scorching, on her inky, stringy hair, adding heat to her scalp. Humidity, thick as a blanket, clung to her skin. Sweat trickled from her forehead, temples and neck and seeped into her gown.

Exhausted, Tia stood in line with the other scraggly-looking women, who waited to get out from under the fiery sky and into the humid cell. It wouldn't be any better in the prison once she settled in, except for the relief from the intense heat of the sun making her head feel as if it were on fire. Her black hair, like a magnet, drew rays that blistered her scalp.

Tonight, she would tear a large piece of material from the hem of her tattered gown. Then she would tie it over her head for protection. The white material should deflect the sun rays. Her scalp, tender and damaged, would still feel the heat after hours in the field, but she should feel some relief.

At long last, the metal door scraped open. The ragged line of women moved forward into the oppressive hole as if it were eating them up as they stepped through. Tia was far back in the line of women. She'd have to wait a bit longer before she could escape the blazing sun.

Most of the women who had depleted their strength, didn't have much to say and Tia was long past the mood for listening to those who did. All she wanted was to get out of her miserable shoes and find a place to sit.

Shuffling forward, she eyed the guard who shoved the women through the entrance to the dungeon. The man, if she could call him that, was of medium height with a big gut and broad hands. His face was flushed and his beard and mustache were sparse. When he sneered, brown teeth shone from between purplish lips. His bulbous nose, red and veined, was a sure sign he spent his spare time with the bottle. He smelled foul, as if he lived in the cells with the rats just like the prisoners.

"Move along," he ordered the short gray-haired woman in front of Tia. The woman hunched and stumbled when he pushed her forward. "Watch your step." It was Tia's turn. She braced herself. She hated the man's touch. "Move along," he said, gazing at her face.

Tia's shoulders rose as she leaned forward and peered into the dark cell, but she kept walking. When she was certain the guard's hand would push her, she took another brisk step to miss it. She felt a light brush on her back, but escaped being pushed into the black hole.

Once inside, the women stumbled down steps to a cellar-type hold. Each grabbed a space, slid down the wall to sit for the rest of the evening. Tia, though, shuffled forward until the woman in front of her stopped and found a place, then Tia turned, collapsed against the wall and slowly sank to the floor.

The finely woven fabric, once white with a jungle animal print splashed throughout the material, was the gown Tia had favored most among the dresses in her armoire. Now as she leaned against the partician the delicate fabric snagged as the silky threads scraped against the rough stone wall. Each time it happened, Tia clenched her teeth. The gown was ruined and no longer fit for anything except the trash barrel across the yard where hot coals burned the day's debris.

Two guards entered the cell and began to make their rounds. Tia squeezed her eyes closed, shutting out the sight of the other women also lined up against the walls. They would be shackled, as would she.

She listened to the clank of iron as the keepers went from one prisoner to the next and locked manacles around their wrists and ankles, attaching the chains to hooks.

She opened her eyes and glanced to the right. A shaft of light shone from a window set high on the far wall. For the first couple of hours they would be able to see what was around them. But after two months, Tia knew that when the sun went down, the dungeon would be black as hades. Down here, in the dank darkness, the rats would come out.

The disgusting guard loomed in front of her, wrapped his large hand around her right ankle as he clamped the manacle shut, inserted a key to lock it. His gray eyes brightened as he leered at her.

"Gimme yer hands, woman!"

Tia stretched her arms forward until the clamps secured both wrists. The man stroked her arm. She flinched. Some men preferred black women, this she knew. Her skin crawled at his touch. She refused to look at him, gazing instead at the light that shone through the window.

"You be full of yourself now," the guard sneered, "but you'll change in time." He made a sweeping gesture that encompassed the dismal cell. "You all do." He slapped her thigh and moved on to the next woman, roughly clasping the manacles to her wrists and ankles.

Tia gazed at the room full of women. They were all a sorry sight. A stench permeated the air like spoiled raw fish. Tia hadn't had a bath since the day she arrived. She was certain none of the others had either. She deplored how they smelled, but was sickened even more with the knowledge that she reeked with the same stench.

Again, she closed her eyes, partly because she was spent from the day's work out in the field, but also because she didn't care to have eye contact with the other prisoners. She never asked any of them what they'd done to deserve time in prison, and didn't want anyone getting nosy enough to ask why she was there. The keepers were still making their rounds, locking each prisoner to the wall as if anyone could get out. Once the iron door shut, she would listen to the sound of the key that locked them in. A sound she was sure she would never get used to.

They'd eat in another hour. Not that it mattered. The food wasn't fit for a dog.

If she forced herself to escape the scene around her, she could easily allow her mind to transport her to Cooper's Landing, where tall palm trees waved in the breeze and lined the long drive to the house. She envisioned the Great House and the sugar mill and the colored quarters beyond. Behind the fields of sugar cane was the ocean, its water rippling with the reflection of the sun, sparkling like millions of diamonds twinkling and bright.

The plantation she had lived on for the past twenty years was a paradise. Life there was easy. Food was good and she could do whatever she wanted, whenever she wanted. Pip had been good to her and her daughter—his daughter, Kindra. He had never demanded anything of her and had set her up in a lovely bedchamber with a soft bed and beautiful furniture, all handmade from Europe. Her armoire was full of exotic gowns and the simplest of her dresses was costly. Pip had always gifted her with the best. But all of that was so far out of reach now, it seemed like a dream.

And yet, she had grown to hate Cooper's Landing. She hated that little brat who sailed into their life from America. The day Grace Cooper knocked on the door of the Great House was the day it all started to come to a crashing end for Tia. She could read the writing on the wall, as it were, that Pip's heart would change. His attention would be swept away from Tia, and sail toward this mysterious daughter he'd never known.

She hated watching Pip's eyes light up when Grace walked into the room. Fury began to burn in her. Would he reward the brat with his riches after all the years he had denied their daughter, Kindra, even so much as an endearing glance?

For nineteen years, she had waited and hoped the day would come when Pip would acknowledge the child from their union. But not once, never a day, not a moment, did he give Kindra a smile, a kiss on the cheek, a tender touch—some form of acceptance that she was his daughter.

Tia dreamed of the day he would declare Kindra his child. But that was not to be. When Grace Cooper stepped into their lives, Tia felt molten coals overtake her soul. She wanted Grace gone from Cooper's Landing. Yet things had already changed for Pip and her long before Grace showed up. He took longer trips out to sea to lands he never spoke of. She began to resent that he didn't share his voyages with her. When he returned, instead of telling her all about his travels, he would invite Camp into the library and talk well into the night.

When Pip sailed away from Jamaica, Tia would go down to the wharf and watch the ships come and go. And over time, she came to know Morgan Blissmore, a ship captain and slaver. He transported slaves from Africa, primarily to Brazil and America.

When the two of them became friends, she figured she could make money of her own if she worked with the slave ships. And in time, she found she enjoyed the challenge of encouraging slaves on the island to accept the fabricated story that they'd find freedom in America if they boarded Morgan Blissmore's ship, the *Bloody Mary*.

It was too easy. Once she concocted the tale that America was a land of freedom for the slaves, the news spread like a wildfire. The slaves began sharing the good news from plantation to plantation. Thus began the nightly runs to pick up slaves on the road and deliver them to Blissmore. He would hand her a pouch full of gold coins and both of them were happy.

Other slavers learned of Tia and sought her out. That was when she met Jule Spade. He owned *Caribbean Dragon*, a beaten down scrap of a vessel that looked as if it was on its last departure every time it left the port. He made most of his stops in Brazil. Finding slaves who were *willing* to leave Jamaica at half the cost was any slave trader's dream. In short order he convinced Tia to let him in on the deal.

Before long, she found herself attracted to Jule Spade. They made a good team. And, unlike Blissmore, who had goals that did not include Tia, Jule started making plans for the two of them. He promised they would leave Jamaica and go to the small island of Tobago and build their own villa.

Tia was only too happy to leave Cooper's Landing and begin a new life away from Pip and his spoiled daughter. Tia often wondered if Pip knew she was stealing slaves from his plantation. She had come to the conclusion that he did. When he denied her even a scrap of his inheritance, she knew the underlying message confirmed that he knew. There were spies on Cooper's Landing, people who hated her and wanted nothing more than to cause her trouble. She felt it. She came to believe the only things she was good at were smuggling slaves . . . and stealing jewels.

True, she had been the headmistress at the plantation prior to getting involved in the slave trade. And she was good at keeping the Great House in good working order. But now, with her hatred for Pip who was dead and gone, and Grace, who was his pride and joy, her perspective had changed. Smuggling and stealing were now her only talents, her only way out of a life she had grown to loathe.

Tia's eyes snapped open and she mentally groaned. She was still in the dungeon. Her mind played over her arrest. She remembered the conversation that day—she should never have mentioned Jule's name to the British soldiers who came to arrest her. Had she given him away? Would he serve time in prison too?

"Who told you about me?" Tia asked a soldier.

He didn't respond.

"Was it Jule Spade?"

The soldier glanced at her, but still he said nothing.

"He wanted to get even with me, I'm sure of it." She glared at the soldier. "Keep your mouth shut if you will. But I'm not alone in this. Who do you think I sold the slaves to?"

Finally the soldier gazed at her. "Jule Spade."

She didn't answer. After all, her heart was pounding in her chest. What if it hadn't been him who'd turned her in? Yet, she was sure Spade was angry enough to send her to the lion's den when he discovered his jewels were gone. She would be his first suspect. But then, no matter how hard he tried to find the emeralds, he wouldn't. No one would.

Tia rubbed her forehead and shuddered. She had stolen the jewels only days before the British soldiers came for her. She hadn't heard a word from Jule before her arrest, and now, having been in prison two months, she found it hard to believe he wasn't responsible for her imprisonment. Was it his way of getting even with her? Did he suspect she had stolen the jewels?

Better that she spend ten years in the cell than to encounter his whip. The man was ruthless. Man or woman, he didn't care.

Shadows lurked all around in the cell. She looked up at the window. She hadn't noticed it had grown dark outside. Her back ached from sitting against the rough stone and her stomach rumbled.

Then she felt it. Tiny feet skittered up her arm and dropped down onto her lap.

"Get off of me you wretched—" She swung her hands to slap the furry rat off her skirts and onto the dank floor. Tiny red eyes looked at her in the pitch dark. It would be another restless night.

Jule Spade stood in the front room of a small hut in the village on the island of Tobago. A loud rap on the door broke the silence. He crossed the floor and swung the door open.

Three British soldiers stood on the stoop.

"What can I do for you?" Spade asked, his heart tripping over itself.

"You are under arrest for slave smuggling."

Two soldiers grabbed hold of Spade's arms, while the third man clamped iron cuffs around his wrists.

"You're mistaken." Spade struggled against the men. "I've done nothing wrong."

The soldiers escorted him out to the waiting wagon on the dirt road.

"I've done nothing wrong!"

The men remained silent as they shoved him onto the wooden bench.

Hours later, when an iron door clanged behind him, a guard asked, "Do you happen to know a black panther by the name of Tia Hargrave?"

A chill ran down Spade's back. "I do."

"You might ask her what yer doin' here."

Bile began to sour Spade's stomach. "What are you talking about?"

"She be locked away just like you. The two of you will have plenty of time to think about your wrong doin's," the guard said. "Ten years be a mighty long time."

"Ten years!"

"Yup, ten years." The guard walked away.

"I have a right to a trial!"

"You'll get one."

"Is she here—at this prison?"

"Nay. She's over down the coast. Conditions not so good over there."

"I'm not the only one who's worked with her. There's—"

"Listen mister, I've got other prisoners to tend to." He nodded toward the cot against the wall. "Make yourself at home."

Hey!" Spade hollered as the guard walked away. He eyed the grungy cement walls and the slim cot under the barred window. Reluctantly, he lay down on the hard cot, his body stiff with resignation. He covered his eyes with the back of his hand, his elbow leaning against the rough wall. How had he gotten here? He knew the answer. It all started with that trip to Tobago.

With pent-up frustration, he let his mind trail back to that fateful day just months ago when he sailed to the village on his wretched ship, *Caribbean Dragon . . .*

The sun beat down as Jule shoved the brim of his hat off his forehead to look out over the white sandy beach far off in the distance. The *Caribbean Dragon* swayed in the bay, but Spade paid little attention to its movement. Leaning against the rail on starboard side, he picked up his spyglass and squinted through the instrument at the scenery on shore.

To the left, a row of huts stood before a wall of tropical greenery. Bushes and palms made it impossible to see the village he knew was hidden behind them. To the right, a small road led to the marketplace.

Spade swerved until the telescope moved to the crest of a hill where a large structure came into view. It was there he was building the fortress for himself and Tia. Every couple of weeks, he brought his ship into the bay and anchored. He and a couple of his shipmates would climb down the rope ladder to a waiting longboat and row to the beautiful shore of Tobago. Coming here was a much-needed respite from the arduous task of buying and selling slaves.

Much of Spade's time was spent on the Atlantic with bawling slaves in the hold, delivering them to Brazil and America. Brazil was closer and the money was good.

But what good was money if you didn't spend it on your heart's desire? The time had come to build his dream, a fortress that would look out over the calm turquoise waters, a fortress with high walls to protect him from his enemies. A veranda would wrap around the twostory structure with cane chairs placed to look out over the bay and enjoy the view.

"Are you comin', Cap'n?" one of the shipmates asked.

Spade handed the spyglass to a crewman. "Yes."

He climbed over the railing and began his descent. When he reached the boat, he stepped over and sat on a wooden bench. The morning was cool and a light breeze washed over him. Several minutes later, the longboat reached the sandy shore.

"I'll only be an hour," he said to his crewmen. "Maybe less."

Trudging through the sand, he glanced about him. Fishermen were dumping nets of fish into barrels, then lifting the casks onto small carts pulled by donkeys.

One fisherman glanced over his shoulder, "You be back so soon?"

"That's right, Quanto. I'm going up the hill to check on the fortress, and then sailing over to deliver a cargo of slaves. Want to come along?"

Quanto shook his head. "Go on ahead. I have to get these smelly fish to the market or my wife will have my hide."

"Suit yourself." Spade lifted his hand and waved.

"Fetch me on your way back from the big house. I'll sail with you down the coast."

Spade nodded.

"But you must bring me back tonight. My woman no like it when I stay gone too long." By now, Quanto's voice had risen as Spade kept walking. Spade made no reply, but again he lifted his hand.

An hour later, having checked on the progress of the construction, Spade made his way to the colorful district that was Tobago's marketplace. He walked up the street until he came to Diego's Fish Market.

He pulled off his wide-brimmed hat as he ducked into the smelly building. It took a moment for his eyes to adjust to the dimness.

"What you doing here!" Maria Diego rushed up to Spade, shaking her forefinger. "I told you to leave my Quanto alone. He not available today."

Spade gave her a sly grin. "Hello, Maria. Nice to see you as well."

"You go away!" She shoved Spade's chest with an open hand. "You not welcome!"

Quanto entered the market from the back room. "What are you doing, Maria?" He pulled his wife back. "That's no way to treat a customer."

"He not a customer, he . . . he . . . make him leave!"

Quanto shot Spade a look of apology. "Maria."

"Did he come to get you?" She glared at Spade and then Quanto.

Quanto's shoulder's slumped. "Yes, Maria. We are going up the coast."

"No!" She picked up a basket of crackers and slammed it on the wooden table. The crispy bread popped up and spilled over the table and onto the floor.

"I will pay your husband a good day's wage for his time away," Spade picked up a few cracker chips from the table and shoved them into his mouth.

"We don't want your money."

"Why not?"

"Because you disobey my orders to leave my Quanto alone. You keep him all night long and then you bring him back a drunken lizard. Then he is good for nothing the next day. I cannot run a market without fish. He no work for whole day after you bring him back!"

"I'll double his wage this time. How about that?"

"Oh, go on!" Maria pushed Quanto's chest. "You going to do what you want anyway."

"He said he'll double my wage, Maria."

"Leave . . . and don't come back!" Maria's fists landed on her slim hips and she glared at her husband.

Quanto stepped over to where she stood and leaned in for a smooch. "I'll be back tonight."

"Go!" Maria swerved away from him and disappeared behind a green curtain that led to the back room.

"Come on," Spade said. "I told the crewmen we'd be back in an hour. We're late."

That night, having delivered slaves to Tibble Monroe, a Brazilian emerald mine owner, he and Quanto were invited to spend the evening at the rich man's home. The two men rode up the red crusty road in a rattling wagon, while gritty wind blew over them. In moments, they stood in the doorway of Monroe's house. Inside they found more than a dozen men sitting around the long dining room table. Most of them, Spade didn't know. There was, however one man he knew. Scoot Sweeny, one of his own crewmen from the *Caribbean Dragon*.

"What are you doing here?" Spade asked, irritated that the crewman had come to shore without permission.

"Sir, I was checking on my village hut when one of Monroe's men came by and asked me to join them. I couldn't very well insult the man and say no." He had a glass of rum in hand and was already beginning to look a bit loopy.

"I suppose not,"

Spade said, glancing at the rest of the men. "You will, however, report back to the ship within the next hour. And that's an order."

"Yes, sir." Sweeney said with a lop-sided grin.

Spade soon realized the men gathered at the table were involved in mining for emeralds as that was the main topic as the evening wore on. The table was loaded with good food and the women of the house had retired for the evening, leaving the men to carry on without them.

As the hours passed, the men became rowdy and obnoxious. Spade kept a smile on his face and a drink in his hand, but he had no intention of losing his control over the sweet rum. If the men turned nasty, he'd hold his own.

Quanto, on the other hand had let loose. He liked his liquor and became drunk early on. As the heat of conversation rose, it seemed the men became less aware of their loose talk and of the losses they'd made from slaves who'd been driven too hard in the hot sun. Bringing in more darkies was a constant turn-around. Stronger men were needed to replace the tired and depleted men who had been pushed to the limit, sometimes to death.

Tibble Monroe drank far too many glasses of rum, and it seemed that the later the hour, the louder his voice rose above his guest's voices. Monroe seemed to have lost control of his bearings, slopping rum on his expensive maroon vest and nearly knocking over a decanter of liquor. Wild-eyed, he became braggadocio, preening about his assets, and his emerald mine, and his horses.

Just when Spade was sure he'd had enough of the evening, Monroe raised his brows and cocked his head toward him. "Follow me," he requested.

Spade glanced at the table where most of the men had slumped, besotted and intoxicated. Some of the men were talking low, their speech unintelligible. A couple of them had dropped their heads on the table and were sleeping.

Scoot Sweeny's face was flushed and his eyes drooped. But he still sat upright, elbows on the table while he held a short crystal glass that looked as if it would slip from his fingers at any moment.

Spade didn't like the man, didn't trust him. Why he employed the sailor as a crewman on his ship he didn't know. He'd felt for some time that the black-haired man had been watching his every move. Why? What was he up to? It was as if Sweeny were spying on him, which was a switch. That was Spade's job. He spent too much of his time spying on others. Truth was, Sweeny was a good sailor on the ship. As much as he disliked the man, he could leave the ship in his hands and know that it would fare well in his absence. Sweeny would keep the slave business going as well as keep the crew working the ship as if Spade were standing there watching them.

Spade narrowed his gaze and watched Sweeny as he let the glass slip a little more, before he jerked his head up and set the glass down. He eyed Spade and gave him a crooked grin. He pulled the decanter over and poured another glass of rum then leaned back.

Interrupting the silent exchange between Spade and Sweeny, Monroe grabbed Spade's arm. "Come on," he insisted.

Eight

The two men left the dining room and went down a narrow hallway lit by fading candles on wall sconces. Monroe put a finger to his lips. "Shhh." He opened a door at the right into a room that was black at first. The moon shone through a slit in the airy curtain giving enough light to make their way without having to light a lantern to avoid bumping into any furniture.

Monroe winked and crossed the floor, tiptoeing in exaggeration to make a point of how quiet he wanted Spade to be. He cocked his head toward the library shelf on the left side of the room and knelt down near a lower cabinet. Opening the door, he grinned.

"See what I have here!" He whispered loudly. "Even my woman knows nothing of this."

Monroe opened the cabinet door. Inside was empty. He leaned toward the casing and lifted a floorboard in the cabinet. He reached down, and pulled out a small leather bag. Grinning widely, he held the pouch into the stream of moonlight.

"Come here." His mouth moved into a lopsided grin. He chose a streak of light on the floor and tilted the bag in the pale glow. Slowly, small emeralds slid out of the bag and rolled onto the polished wood, glistening in the shimmery light. Sparkles emanated from more than a hundred small jewels. The foolish man looked up and grinned. "I have a fortune here. Enough to buy an island if I want to."

Monroe scooped the sparkling jewels into the leather pouch. One emerald rolled a foot away and Spade reached for it, coveting the man's fortune.

Monroe shoved Spade's hand away and fumbled until he picked up the last jewel, dropped it into the bag and pulled the string ties shut. He squeezed the pouch in his plump hands. "This . . . is from many years working the emerald mine. I'm done here in Brazil. I plan to leave this place within a fortnight and relax for the rest of my life."

Monroe reopened the cabinet door and deposited the jewels inside. "Come, the others will be wondering where we are." He opened the library door and the two men stepped out. Monroe's chest swelled as he led them back to the dining area where the other men had become sullen from liquor.

Spade glanced at Sweeny who sat with his head against the tall chair, his jaw slack from sleep. The evening had been long and Jule wanted to get back to his ship. And he needed to get Quanto back to Tobago. But not before he accomplished one more thing.

He elbowed Quanto. "Let's have another sip before we head back to the ship."

"Señor, I can't." He rubbed his face with both hands as if to wake himself up.

"I can." Spade reached for the decanter and noisily scraped the bottle across the table to where he sat. He filled his crystal glass with the amber rum.

The others roused themselves and a new round of rum was had by all. The evening wore on. Another hour, and the majority of the men left, staggering out the door. Sacrificing another hour of his time, finally there were only Quanto, Spade, and their host, Tibble Monroe left at the table.

"I best be getting back to the island," Quanto said, apologetically. "My Maria . . . she will lock me out of the house."

"I agree," Spade said. "It's late." The two men bid goodbye to Monroe and left the house saying little as they rode the buckboard back toward town.

After they had gone a ways, Spade snapped his finger. "I left something at Monroe's house. Go on and take the wagon back to the shore. I'll be there shortly."

"I can ride back with you."

"No, I'd rather you told the crewmen to get the longboat ready to row back to the ship. I won't be long."

Quanto stopped. "You sure?"

"Yes. Go on."

Spade heard dogs barking as Quanto headed back through town. He picked up his pace to nearly a run as he worked his way back to Monroe's home.

A small glow lit the dining room window when Spade looked in. Monroe hadn't moved an inch. He slouched in his chair with his head tipped back and was snoring raucously. Space could hear the man from where he stood, even with the night sounds of insects chirring around him.

Spade went around to the front of the house and quietly crept in. He peered once more into the dining room to see Monroe sleeping, his mouth slack. He listened for sounds upstairs, but heard none.

With stealthy steps, Spade crept down the hall to the library. He turned the knob ever so carefully. The door squeaked loudly and he stopped in his tracks. He listened for Monroe, but all he heard was loud snoring. Spade wasted no time in crossing the room and opening the small cabinet. He pressed one end of the false floorboard and lifted the other side. Grabbing the wood and setting it aside, he leaned in and reached down into the hole. He felt the leather pouch and grabbed it firmly, lifting it out. He quickly he stuffed the bag inside his shirt and carefully replaced the floorboard. Shutting the cabinet door, he stopped. A sound came from somewhere behind him. The hairs on his arms rose.

Was that a floorboard squeaking in the hallway? His heart hammered in his chest. He leaned against the cabinet, keeping his body out of the rays of moonlight streaming across the room, holding his breath he rolled to his knees and crawled to the right where he could be hidden by the desk if someone should open the door. He waited. Time seemed to stand still. Every nerve in his body tensed. Several minutes passed, but no one opened the door.

Quietly he stood and inched his way toward the door. He listened. No sound. He opened the door a crack and moved to the entrance. The dining room beamed like the beacon of a lighthouse. The sound of

Monroe's snoring was still steady. Quickly, he slipped out of the room and out of the house.

He had stolen the jewels from Tibble Monroe, and now they were his.

Spade shook himself from his reveries as the cold and discomfort of his prison cell pulled him back to the present. Shifting in an attempt to find a more comfortable position, he promised himself he'd get even with the wicked woman. Tia had stolen the emeralds. He had no doubt. What a fool he'd been for showing her the jewels. He'd tempted the cat. But to steal them, and then turn on him, was more than he could stomach. *Ten years.* He would count the days until he got out of this stinking hole. Then her day of reckoning would come. He wouldn't rest until she got her just due. *She would pay!*

NINE

Barbados Bay, aboard the **Sea Baron**
26 March, 1831

TODAY WAS THE day she'd been waiting for. She would get her first glimpse of her new home before the sun set that night.

"Thank you, Rhea." Kindra got a glimpse of herself in the vanity mirror. The maid had just swept up Kindra's hair, allowing a few dark tendrils to curl about her forehead and ears, then she placed a fanciful green hat at a jaunty angle on her mistress' head and stepped out of the way.

Viewing herself in full regalia for the first time, Kindra liked what she saw. The green summer suit brought out the emerald of her eyes and flattered her figure. The skirt and cuffs were accented with bold, black-floral embroidery, and the high-necked, buttoned bodice was topped with a black and blue bow. The hat was the topping on the cake. Decorated with a small white bird nestled in a bed of blue flowers with a spray of black feathers, it matched the color of her outfit. The soft airiness of the hat contrasted with the stark lines of her suit.

But now she paused, wondering if it was unwise to wear such stylish clothing. She didn't want to attract undue attention.

She draped a black-fringed, multicolored shawl over her outstretched arm and let it trail down her side. "What do you think?"

"You sho'nuf be looking like white folks, Miz Kindra." Rhea wiped her forehead with the back of her hand. Sweat beads flowed back as fast as she could sweep them away.

"Is the hat too much?"

"You gone put your shawl on, Miz Kindra?" Rhea said by way of answer.

"For heaven's sake, no." Kindra waved a hand over her face. "If it's as hot and humid outside as it is in here, I believe I shall surely wilt before we get to shore."

"It gone get hotter before a breeze picks up."

"I know." Kindra took one last look in the mirror before she turned toward the door. "I'm ready to join Denzel."

Kindra climbed the companionway stairs to the main deck. When her feet were firmly planted on the wooden deck, she brushed her hand down the skirt of her fine clothes, knowing she would likely meet the foreman and his wife when they arrived at the plantation. It was imperative that she look her best. When she glanced up she saw Denzel standing at the ship's rail. He didn't turn. His mind appeared to be a million miles away.

"There you are," she said, breaking into his train of thought. "You look very nice." She brushed at a sleeve of his handsome linen suit.

Denzel gazed at her and grinned. "Thank you." She watched him scan her apparel and nod. "You look lovely." His brows creased. "Maybe a bit too aristocratic, but lovely just the same."

Kindra felt slighted, yet she understood his point. "I thought for today we should look like the new owners of a tobacco plantation." She felt her stomach clench.

She had wanted and dreaded this day at the same time. In less than an hour they would be riding up to the front steps of their new home. How would the foreman and his wife react when they found their master and mistress were black? Part of her felt she should dress down so as not to surprise or insult them. On the other hand, she thought she should set the stage for her position in the house. In the end she had decided it would be best to hold her head high to face whatever lay before them.

"Will we be landing at the dock or will we have to take the longboat?" Kindra asked.

"I don't know." Denzel still seemed deep in thought.

"Are you nervous?" she asked.

"I suppose I am. And you?"

A half hour later the *Sea Baron* moored against the dock. The gangplank was lowered and for the first time in her life, Kindra looked out onto the colorful island of Barbados. She held a parasol above her head as Denzel guided her down the gangway. Upon entering the bustling street, the two of them waited for a carriage.

Glancing about the settlement, Kindra tried to take in the scenery and the smells to familiarize herself with this region of the world.

Out of nowhere a tall, burly man sidled up to her. "Well, what've we got here? Maple sugar?" His voice was low and grating as he drew her against his side which reeked of sweat and foul-smelling clothes. The man glanced down the front of her and smiled, his teeth stained and brown.

Kindra struggled against him, looking wildly about for Denzel.

All at once a strong, muscled arm came between the stout man and Kindra. Denzel gently pushed her aside while in the next instant landed a blow to the man's gut.

"Oooff!" The scalawag stumbled backward trying to gain his footing. A look of surprise flashed across his face.

"Why you!" The man lunged for Denzel, shoved him onto a tipped-over barrel. He scrambled to his feet, regained the advantage. He drew his arm back and hit the stranger full force on the jaw.

Kindra gasped. She watched Denzel thrown to the ground while the crowd watched.

Denzel a muscular man, had always held his own. But the beefy rogue stood a good two inches over Denzel's tall frame. From Kindra's line of sight, the man was as thick as a mule. She nibbled her bottom lip as the fight went on.

By now a large crowd had formed to watch the fight. Kindra felt helpless as she watched her husband thrown to the ground. Each time he recovered he gave his opponent a thunderous blow. Suddenly, a band of stevedores headed toward them.

"Run!" Denzel called to Kindra.

Her feet were glued to the ground. She couldn't think nor move. All she knew was in that instant, her husband was surrounded by a crowd of men with fists flying.

"Somebody help him!" she cried.

Someone jerked her elbow, pulling her away from the scene. "This way!" One of the sailors from her vessel urged Kindra away from the crowd and led her to the waiting carriage. When she looked back she saw Barnabas lumbering toward the cluster of men. He picked off the men as if they were rats and flung them out to the middle of the road. She heard his terrible growl as he fended them off until he finally was able to pull Denzel to his feet.

Kindra was heartsick when she got a glimpse of her man—blood ran down his temple. His linen suit jacket was ripped at the shoulder—revealing a stained shirt underneath.

Barnabas stood in the center of the crowd daring the men to come toward him or Denzel. The other men brushed off their breeches and one by one staggered away. The man who had caused the ruckus turned toward Kindra and grinned wickedly at her.

Denzel limped to the open carriage, Barnabas close behind. "Thank you," Denzel said as he stretched out a hand.

Barnabas took it. "You best get on out to your place straightaway, Sir."

"We will." Denzel climbed into the seat and the carriage driver flapped the reins. The driver glanced over his shoulder, an uncertain look on his face. "Where to?"

"Kindra Hall," Denzel said.

"Oh, Denzel!" Kindra wailed. "With that swollen eye, you look more like a ruffian than the owner of a tobacco plantation."

Denzel pulled his arms out of the ruined jacket and laid the coat on his lap. They rode in silence.

"This is *not* how it was supposed to be," Kindra said, exasperated. It was all she could do to hold back the sobs that filled her throat. "How are we supposed to meet the foreman and his wife with you looking like this?" She felt a movement in her abdomen reminding her that there was more to her emotional behavior than what met the eye.

Denzel sobered. "I'd do it again in a second if I saw a man touching my woman."

She saw his brown eyes grow black with anger and she grabbed his large hand in hers. "I know you would." She leaned against his shoulder and heard a soft moan. "I'm sorry." She started to pull away from him.

Denzel pulled her back. "Stay right there."

"All right." She leaned into him feeling love for her husband deepen even more.

They were soon traveling through Bridgetown and out toward their plantation. What the town looked like, she didn't know. Her mind was flooded with the memory of what had just happened and the anxiety of arriving at their destination. But she didn't have long to wait; soon the carriage turned off the dusty road and onto a long narrow lane leading to a big white two-story house.

Kindra lifted her eyes beyond the carriage just as their tobacco plantation came into view. Large-leafed plants lined the lane, and a row of oak trees, thick with low-hanging Spanish moss stood on either side. The dark green foliage contrasted with yellow and fiery-red begonias that lit up the walkway leading to the Great House, which emerged large and impressive as the carriage came to a stop.

In the distance, colored men worked the tobacco fields; a few heads turned their way.

Denzel stepped down, reaching for her hand. But Kindra couldn't move just yet. Dumbstruck, she gazed at the large two-story structure before her. It was the most beautiful home she'd ever seen. The house was white with green shutters at every window. The second story had a veranda that looked out over the plantation and the red-bricked steps leading to the front porch were wide and welcoming. Two gables overlooked the roof, a black chimney behind each.

Kindra looked down at Denzel, feeling giddy. "I suppose I ought to quit gawking at our new home and go inside."

"There must be a shortage of servants," Denzel said, glancing at the porch. "No one has come to greet us." He pulled their luggage from the back of the carriage and fished a coin from his pocket. "Here you go," he told the driver.

"You're short a coin," said the man.

"I think not. If you had helped my lady from the carriage, and brought our luggage to the porch, I would have given you your fair share." Denzel scowled at the coachman.

"Good day!" The driver cracked the whip and the carriage jerked out of the circular drive.

Kindra started to pick up a small satchel, but Denzel said, "Leave it. I'll have one of the servants bring the luggage in."

Nothing was as it should be and Kindra gave a shake of her head. "Very well."

With growing unease, she gathered her skirts and climbed the six steps leading to the front porch. Two ferns flanked the front door. Kindra glanced about the spacious porch, wondering if they should just walk in or if they should knock. *Knock, of course.* A small grin played on her lips as she waited for Denzel to do the honors.

With a leather briefcase tucked under his left arm, Denzel lifted his right hand and knocked. The two of them waited. She knew they looked a sight, she in her aristocratic attire and he with a fresh shiner.

Moments later, a butler opened the front door, a tall black man with a bald head and well-groomed salt and pepper beard and mustache.

"May I help you?" he asked, glancing beyond them to the circular drive.

"Yes," said Denzel. "We'd like to meet the foreman of the plantation."

"Do come in." The butler ushered them in and stood aside. "The foreman, he be out in the fields. But Miz Bernard be heah. If you'd kindly wait, I'll fetch her." The man disappeared down a long hall.

Denzel and Kindra stood waiting, glancing curiously about them. A mixture of emotions ran through Kindra as she observed how beautiful her new home and furnishings were. It felt odd standing, waiting for permission to move about her own home.

It wasn't long before they heard the sound of footsteps coming down the hallway and looked up in time to see a middle-aged woman following the butler. Kindra felt trapped in the entryway of the mansion. Before her stood the foreman's wife, the woman she knew to be Ava Bernard. She was a slender woman with gold-blonde hair pulled back and pinned into a knot at the nape of her neck.

"Thank you, Boaz," she said waving him away. She clamped her hands in front of her and asked, "What business has brought you here?" She first glanced at Kindra and firmly clenched her jaw, then she looked toward Denzel and took a step back.

The front door stood open letting in a soft breeze. Kindra was thankful for the brief reprieve as she could feel sweat trickling down her neck. The few butterflies that had congregated in her stomach earlier had multiplied. Her knees felt weak.

Ava Bernard peered out the front door, then back to them. "Where is your master or mistress?"

Kindra looked out the door knowing full well there was no one there and back to the woman standing before them.

"Speak up, I haven't all day!" the woman blurted.

Her hostile stance let Kindra know the woman didn't want them there and nothing would change that unless Kindra immediately took the upper hand. She stepped forward, her fan in her palm. "I believe you must be Ava Bernard, the foreman's wife?"

Ava gave Kindra the once over. "I am. And who might you be?" Before she gave Kindra a chance to answer she continued, "How dare you come into this house pretending to be a woman of substance, wearing such English attire and refinery." Ava's eyes glared in distaste.

She quickly flashed her eyes to Denzel, seeming to observe the bruises on his face.

She turned her gaze back to Kindra. "How you got past the beating you surely deserved for your insolence in dressing as you are is beyond me."

Again, Ava glanced out at the driveway. "How is it you have arrived before your master?"

Kindra clenched the fan in her hand. "You are the one guilty of insolence, Mrs. Bernard. However, I shall reserve judgment about any beating I may decide to have administered to correct your faulty judgment. My name is Kindra Talmaze, and this is my husband, Denzel Talmaze. We are the owners of Kindra Hall. We have come to take our rightful place as heirs of Phillip Cooper, my father."

Kindra's chin lifted and her glance swerved to Denzel who shut the front door before returning to stand by his wife's side.

Ava took a giant step backward while a frantic look came into her eyes. "There must be a terrible mistake. Mr. Cooper never told us he had a daughter, much less a darky . . ." She stopped abruptly and took another step back, wringing the handkerchief in her hands.

Just then the sound of feet came clomping from farther in the house. Three children burst into the dining room from what must be the kitchen. Before the swinging door closed, Kindra caught a glimpse of a couple of colored women staring through the crack of the door.

Two boys, looking to be somewhere around eight and ten years old, and a small blonde girl, slid to a stop on the polished hardwood floor in front of Denzel and Kindra. The children stared at them, their eyes bugging out as if shocked by the appearance of the two newcomers. They looked at each other before they pinned their gaze back to the visitors.

It appeared that the children could not stop looking at Kindra. She watched their eyes flit over her. The older boy's gaze swept from the top of Kindra's fancy-feathered hat to the black shiny high-heeled boots. Just as quickly he looked at Ava questioningly.

Kindra cleared her throat.

"We're hungry," the little girl whined.

"Out of here! All of you!" Ava brushed her hand in the air. "Clara will get you something to eat."

The three children wheeled about and fled through the kitchen door, leaving it swinging back and forth.

Ava called out as if in second thought, "Chad!"

Wide-eyed, the older boy reappeared, and skidded to a stop.

"Before you eat, go out to the fields and fetch your father. Tell him to stop what he's doing and to come to the house at once!"

"Yes, Mother." The boy glanced one more time at Kindra and Denzel, then disappeared through the kitchen door.

"It's been a long day. We'll rest in the sitting room while we wait for Mr. Bernard." Denzel said.

Kindra's stiff shoulders relaxed at the sound of Denzel's authoritative voice. She was not alone. Her husband would take control of the situation here.

Ava glanced nervously about her. It was obvious that she did not want these people in any room of the house. But Denzel pressed his hand on Kindra's back and moved her forward, leaving Ava no choice but to lead them to the sitting room.

Kindra was pleasantly surprised at how airy the room was. Two large windows offered a vast view of the grounds and long flowered drapes framed the windows. She crossed the floor to one of the armchairs whose fabric matched the draperies. She picked up the brocade pillow that lay in the chair and gratefully sat, placing the pillow behind her back. A cream-colored sofa stretched along the window, with an armchair that matched her own across the floor. After Denzel claimed that chair, he leaned back and crossed an ankle over his knee.

Ava stood rigidly by the entrance, looking thoroughly out of sorts. "Um . . . ah . . . my husband should be in shortly." She made a swift exit.

Kindra gazed across the floor at her weary husband. "Well . . . we're here." She took that moment to pull the pins out of her hat, lift it off her curls, place it on her lap, then absently pick at the posies.

"We've got our work cut out for us."

"Shhh! They might hear you," she said.

"I don't mind if they do." Denzel straightened in his seat.

A servant woman entered the room. "Miz Ava say we have guests. Can I get you somethin' to drink?"

Kindra glanced at the slim colored woman dressed in a parlor maid uniform. The woman held a calm composure, her chin up.

"What is your name?" Kindra asked.

"My given name be Netty."

"My husband and I would like iced lemonade if you have it."

"We do." She stared at Kindra a moment longer than necessary, then turned and left the room.

No sooner had Netty disappeared down the hall than Kindra heard boots clomping on the hardwood floor. A tall, broad-shouldered man looking to be in his mid-forties marched into the sitting room. He swiftly glanced at the two of them. "What is the meaning of this?" He raised one arm toward the entrance. "I want the two of you out of my house at once!"

Denzel sprang to his feet and spread his palms outward. "You don't have the authority to remove us from our home, Mr. Bernard. I am assuming you are Stanley Bernard?"

Stanley stepped forward, a finger pointed at Denzel. "Do you have documented proof that you are Phillip Cooper's heirs? Because if not . . . I'll boot the two of you out on your rumps faster than a pack of rats."

Denzel picked up a leather valise sitting by the side of his chair. He opened the case and withdrew the paperwork. "Our attorney, Desmond Rothschild, has assured us that he mailed you copies of the deed of ownership. You should recognize these papers and his signature." He held out the documents to Bernard.

Stanley snatched the papers from Denzel's hand and silently scanned each page. The silence in the room roared.

Kindra's heart beat fast. She could not take her eyes off the ruggedly handsome man, not for his looks, but for his reaction. She didn't have long to wait. The color drained from the man's face as he passed the papers back to Denzel and his lips thinned.

"I have known Phillip Cooper a good many years. We have spent many hours in each other's company in this house." He brushed a shaky hand over his copper-brown hair. "Not once did he speak of having children, nor did he indicate that he had an heir to Kindra Hall."

Kindra could sit no longer . . . nor stay quiet. "But he does have two daughters . . ."

". . . Are they both darkies?" interrupted Bernard.

Denzel straightened and put out a hand to hold Kindra back. "There's no need for that kind of talk, Mr. Bernard."

"No," Kindra said through clenched teeth. "My sister, Grace, is white."

"Oh, I see. You were the product of . . ."

"Choose your words carefully if you intend to continue as foreman on our plantation," Denzel warned.

Stanley let out a deep sigh and paced the floor. He wheeled around and stared at the two of them. "What now?"

"For the moment, Mr. Bernard, we would like to be shown our quarters. After that, please see that we are served a meal. It has been a long day and I'm sure my wife not only needs to freshen up, but must be famished." Denzel's voice was that of sheer authority.

"That's not what I meant, but I will see that you are settled in," Stanley said.

"Thank you." Kindra finally let out a breath and smiled guardedly.

"After we have freshened up, I want the servants brought to the living room. They should be apprised that their new masters have arrived." Denzel said.

Stanley's eyes grew dark and his mouth twitched. "Of course."

"You and I can sit down after supper and discuss how we are going to proceed from here." Denzel tucked the document back into his satchel and buttoned it.

Just then, Netty appeared at the entrance with a silver tray in her hands. "Your refreshments, sir."

Stanley crossed the room to where Netty stood. "Tell Cook we have guest . . . er . . . to set the table for two more." He glanced over his shoulder. "Dinner is at six o'clock." With that he left the room.

Silently, Netty placed the tray on a table in front of the settee and started to leave as well.

"Netty," Denzel said.

"Yes, sir."

"Please tell the butler our bags are on the front lawn. Ask him to bring them to our chamber."

"Yes, sir." Netty's features pinched with a look of concern. She glanced at them for only a second before she shrugged her thin shoulders and exited the room.

TEN

BEFORE SUPPER, AVA led Kindra to a small guest room on the second floor. "This used to be the room Phillip Cooper slept in when he came to visit." She stepped into the room and stood at the foot of a narrow bed. "You and your husband may take this room."

May? Kindra looked around the masculine decor. Not only was the chamber small, but it seemed more suited for a man. "I'd like to look at the other rooms." She turned back to the hallway and asked, "Are all the rooms taken on the east wing?"

Ava hesitated. "No. None of the rooms are used."

"Let's have a look at them." Kindra did not wait to see if Ava followed. She walked down the hall and opened the last door to the right. When she stepped in, she came upon a large master chamber with a bath and sitting room. It looked much the same in arrangement as the room at Cooper's Landing: spacious, with tall windows overlooking the front of the house. The polished furniture was a rich mahogany. It, too, had a masculine feel, but with a few changes, she could make the bedchamber work for both her and Denzel.

"We'll take this room. Have the servants bring our trunks here." Kindra looked Ava in the eye. It wouldn't be too soon to set the record straight. The owner of the house had arrived. She would make that known right away.

Like her father, Kindra intended to be a good task-master, but she wouldn't tolerate anyone running over her. Smiling, Kindra placed her reticule on the large bed. "Let's look at the other rooms. I want to be acquainted with the layout of the second floor. And besides," she touched her abdomen, "We have a little one on the way. We'll need a nursery."

Ava paled. She pulled her shoulders back and worked her jaw. "Right this way."

As the servants filed into the living room, Kindra remembered the day Grace arrived at Cooper's Landing. They had done precisely the same thing. Each of the servants had lined up in front of her to be introduced to Phillip Cooper's long lost daughter. Now, the irony of tonight's event was surreal. History had a way of repeating itself.

Tonight, the servants of Kindra Hall would introduce themselves to Denzel and Kindra. The difference was that this was not a glad occasion for the foreman and his wife.

Kindra glanced at Denzel. "Shall I officiate this evening?"

"Please do. I will spend plenty of time learning the names of the field hands in the days to come."

Two lines were formed. All of the women were colored and all wore parlor maid uniforms. The butler wore a suit and a young man wore a plain shirt and breeches. The Bernards stood stone-faced as the servants waited.

Kindra pointed to the first woman on her left and said, "Your name and position, please."

"I be Clara, jist Clara, and I be the first cook." She frowned at Kindra.

"And you?" Kindra pointed to the woman standing next to Clara.

"I be Louiza. I be the second cook."

Kindra stood before an older woman, but not *old* by any means. Perhaps the woman was in her mid forties. She wore a colorful bandana over her head and her eyes were bright and kind. "Your name?"

"Corrie, ma'am."

"And what do you do?"

"I be the nanny and midwife at Kindra Hall, ma'am."

Kindra smiled. "We'll talk later."

"Yes, ma'am."

Within ten minutes all the servants introduced themselves. Most of them seemed to look down their nose at Kindra as if they thought the colored mistress was acting too high and mighty for a black woman. It was clear they would find it hard to serve someone they thought should know better than to be a slave owner. Little did they know that Kindra struggled with the same idea.

Though Abner was a stableman, he was brought into the house for the introductions since he was also the carriage driver. The black man was elderly with dark freckles on his face, short cropped white hair, and kind eyes. Kindra knew at once they would get along just fine.

Next, Kindra stepped up to a young servant woman who had declared she was a cleaning maid. "You said your name is Mayme?"

"Yes, ma'am. You pronounce it like the word, '*came*.'"

"Have you ever combed and prepared a woman's hair before?"

"Yes, ma'am. I fill in for Hagar sometimes."

"That is Ava's chambermaid?"

"Yes, ma'am."

Kindra stepped over to Hagar who stood gazing at Denzel with a pleased look on her face. She seemed not to notice that Kindra stood before her.

"Hagar."

The servant woman dragged her eyes from her new master and gazed at Kindra with a smirk on her face. "Yes, ma'am," she said lazily.

"Would you recommend Mayme as a chambermaid?"

"No, ma'am." Her eyes flickered.

"Hmm." Kindra went back to Mayme. The girl seemed pleasant with a ready smile. Not like the others who looked down their noses at her. She needed someone with a good temperament around her right now, especially with a baby on the way.

"Mayme . . . you're going to fill in tomorrow morning for my chambermaid. You'll keep the task as cleaning maid, but first thing in the morning, you'll report to me."

"Yes, ma'am." Mayme hung her head so that the others did not see the small smile that lit her face.

"That's all for now." Kindra said. "I hope we will all grow to know and respect one another, as we did our servants in our last home." She sought out Hagar's eyes, but the woman was already gazing at Denzel again with an intense look of interest. When she caught Kindra's eyes, she lowered her own.

The room stirred as the servants filed out of the living room. When all but the last woman had disappeared, Kindra touched her shoulder.

"Corrie." Kindra said softly.

"Yes, ma'am." The tall dark woman waited for Kindra.

"I'm sure it's been a while since a baby has been born in this house. But I will need your services soon. We'll be choosing a room for the nursery. I'll want your room set up next to it."

Corrie's mouth curved into a smile, and a row of white teeth gleamed. "Sho' gonna be good to have a little one in the house again."

"Did you deliver Ava's children?"

"Just Pauline, ma'am. The boys be born before they set foot in this house. But I deliver most the babies in the colored district. I know what to do."

"Very well. That's settled. We'll talk more about this later."

When Corrie left the room she didn't look at the Bernards on her way out.

Kindra sank into a chair and addressed the foreman and his wife. "Well, it's been a busy evening. With this out of the way, we can get to know each other better. Ava, I will expect your cooperation in learning how I want things to be done in the house. And I'm sure Denzel will want to start the day tomorrow with you, Mr. Bernard."

Kindra noticed that Stanley had paled earlier that evening. His color had not returned. The poor man surely was taking this hard.

After supper, the children were sent upstairs while the Bernards remained at the table, glancing at each other warily and sipping coffee.

"It's been a long day. My wife and I are going to retire. Good night." Denzel rose. "I'll want to go over the books with you first thing in the morning," he told Bernard. Pulling out Kindra's chair, Denzel escorted her from the room. Once the two of them were in their new bedchamber, they stood inside the door and stared at each other.

Denzel opened his arms and Kindra stepped into his embrace. Right now, she was where she needed to be, in the arms of her lover, her husband, her security. She thanked God for this man. "If it weren't for you, I would surely have felt at a loss with all that has occurred this day."

"You were equally strong," Denzel said, pulling her closer. "You showed the servants that you are now the mistress of this house. You not only showed authority, but you showed them kindness. They will not forget that."

"Which reminds me," Kindra said.

"What now?"

"You must be careful when we are in town. White people don't like us coloreds showing too much confidence around them," she said.

"You think I'm coming on too strong?"

"Yes. It could get you into trouble. Here at Kindra Hall you have the authority to speak up and be the master of this plantation. But in town . . . be careful, Denzel."

He drew his wife into his arms. "You're right. I guess you know I don't feel as confident as I put on."

"I know, however, you need to be more than confident here," Kindra said.

"I plan to do just that."

"Good." She pulled his head down and kissed him longingly.

Denzel led her to the four-poster bed. "Come."

Kindra pulled the bedcovers back. Her new chambermaid would do this tomorrow. Tonight she just wanted to be alone with her man.

As they lay snuggled together, the moon slipped in through a crack in the curtains. *Are you looking at the moon, Grace?* Kindra closed her eyes, her cheek nestled against Denzel's muscled chest. Tomorrow would come fast.

Ava stood by the veranda as Stanley paced their bedchamber.

"Nobody told us Phillip had a child much less a darky!" Stanley's jaw dropped as his stomach roiled. A vile taste rose in his throat. "I'll not allow this," he hissed, his voice cold. "No darky's going to become the master of Kindra Hall. What a slap in the face! Did you see the insolent way the two of them took over?"

"I did."

"I'd rather see this house burn to the ground than turn it over to those no-good beggars."

"I don't see how we have a choice."

"So you agree with me?"

"Of course. I can never trust a darky. I'll never be able to treat that woman as if she were an equal in this house."

"So what are you going to do?"

"I don't know. It's going to be confusing for the servants to serve two masters. They won't know who to listen to."

"That goes for the field hands." Stanley ran a hand over his head. "How did this happen? This has turned into my worst nightmare."

"We have to do something, that's obvious. But there's nothing we can do about it tonight, so come to bed, Stanley. It's late."

As the two of them lay restlessly trying to find sleep, Stanley's mind raced for answers. He hadn't told Ava that he had been secretly selling portions of the tobacco yields on the side–exporting some of the crop through illegal trade. Besides the appointed funds they earned for managing the grounds, he had deposited yields that did not belong to them. He split the money with a ship's crewman by the name of Scoot

Sweeny. Now that he'd likely be removed from overseeing the selling and exporting of the tobacco, he stood to lose a tremendous amount of money. He wasn't willing to do that. He *wouldn't* do that. He'd get those blackies off *his* plantation.

Resolved to find a way to stay put, Stanley closed his eyes. He wasn't going anywhere. *If that good-for-nothing thinks he can stop me . . . I'll give him another black eye!*

ELEVEN

River Oak, Fields Landing
May 5, 1831

"GOOD MORNING," SID Sparrow said, eyeing the line of slaves disembarking from the *River Belle.*

Cameron stepped off the swaying gangplank onto the rickety dock, extending a hand to his new friend. He squinted in the bright sunlight and pulled his wide-brimmed hat lower over his forehead. "I'm surprised to see you here. I was told you were out on a merchant run."

"Yeah," Sparrow said. "I'm home a day early. Trade winds were good to us this trip. I ran into Captain Wilder off the *Valiant* on the docks. He told me you were on your way down the Taney River. Folks are already talking about the shipload of slaves you bought at the auction."

Cameron watched the black men, women, and children form a single line, walk off the *River Belle,* and move up the path carrying crates, barrels, rakes, metal containers, and more.

"Looks like you're getting ready to build your house." Sparrow gazed up the slope of lawn.

Cameron followed his gaze to the location where the new mansion would be built. Off to the right were several piles of lumber stacked high. In the days to come, men would begin the process of excavating the cellar.

"I hired a contractor to build it, Gilbert Griggs. Do you know him?"

"Can't say that I do. New contractors have been pouring into the area, it seems daily," Sparrow said.

"Land Development gave him high recommendations. He'll build the Great House. I hired another company to start on the cottage Grace and I will live in while the house is being built. I plan on bringing her here this Fall after the baby is born."

Sparrow smiled broadly and extended his hand again. "Congratulations. Is this your first?"

"Yes, it is." Cameron couldn't keep the grin from forming on his lips. "We've only been married five months. She surprised me with the news on my last trip home. I meant to bring her to River Oak sooner, but now she'll have to wait another four months."

"How so?"

"I won't risk her sailing on the high seas in her delicate condition."

"Understandable." Sparrow reached down and plucked a long, thin blade of grass from the ground. He slipped it in his mouth to chew.

"Any of these slaves from back home?" He stepped aside as two colored men passed with a large heavy trunk.

"No. Bought them all in Charleston. I purchased seventy-five men, and if they had wives, I bought them, too. Most had children. After an hour of dickering over the price, I got most of the children at half price."

"The young bucks too?" Sparrow's eyes narrowed.

"No. The older boys cost more than the men."

"That's the way of it these days," Sparrow said. "You'll get more work and more years out of them. Looks like a healthy bunch."

"Spent all of yesterday at auction. Couldn't have been a more sorry lot coming off the ship. I hate seeing these people being half-starved before they get to dry land." Cameron scratched his head. "But I think I got the cream of the crop."

"I missed the sale. I got in too late in the afternoon," Sparrow said. "These must have cost you quite a tidy sum," he added.

"Yeah, well, I'll put that investment into the slaves working for me. The men and boys are going to build the new colored district near the rice fields as soon as we get these people settled into a semblance of living arrangements in the old shanties. The original shacks are falling apart. Once they build the new cabins, we'll use the old shanties for work sheds and chicken coops."

Just then, a string of men and boys passed them with lumber on their shoulders. Some of the men pulled wooden carts with metal buckets full of nails and hammers. Every so often, their eyes glanced toward Sparrow and Cameron. If they made eye contact, the new slaves would nod, as if to show acknowledgment.

Another group of men led donkeys with packs on their backs. Cameron tilted his head toward the men who pulled the stubborn animals that balked and brayed.

"I've got another load of supplies coming this afternoon. I spent a week buying them before the slave ship came in. I knew they'd need food and provisions. I bought beds, tables and cooking utensils, too. It's all in a storage warehouse in Fields Landing waiting to be picked up."

"How long have you been in town?" Sparrow asked.

"A week. I brought a list of supplies and wanted all that done before the cargo of slaves came into port." Cameron cracked a sheepish smile.

"What?" Sparrow smiled, too, though Cameron knew his friend would likely laugh when he admitted what else he bought while waiting for the slave ship to arrive.

"I bought chickens, too." His eyes crinkled from the sun's rays, but also from the humor of it all. He never thought he'd find himself purchasing a brood of chickens. Hands on hips, he watched the men, women and children continue up the path.

"Chickens?"

"Couldn't pass up a good deal. I found a man at the market square who had a wagon-load at a good price. Truth is, we'll need them. Like

I said, after the cabins are built, I'll have the men repair the shanties for chicken coops. That'll give us eggs and poultry. Can't go wrong with that."

"Hmmm." Sparrow smiled.

"I never did believe in starving my workers. I hope to be as good a master to our slaves as my father, Pip. I plan on keeping the families together and giving them more than just the bare necessities to live on. I also hope that in return, the slaves will become loyal to us."

"Your views with slaves are a bit unconventional, I daresay," said Sparrow.

"So were my father's with his slaves in Jamaica. It worked for him. I'm counting on it working for me too."

"Seems like you've thought it through." Sparrow straightened and spit a wad of green on the ground. "I'll expect to come by for an omelet some morning." He reached out a hand. "Better get on up to my place. My wife's expecting me home before the in-laws arrive. We'll be having company for the next three weeks. If things get too testy, I may show up to give you a hand setting things up."

"Appreciate it, Sparrow. You're welcome anytime. By the way, what's the name of your plantation, in case I need a break and want to take a gander up the river?"

"Cherry Hill. I'll be looking for you." Sid Sparrow wove his way to the mossy bank where a paddle boat was tied to the opposite side of the small dock. He climbed in, sat at the back, and pushed at the shore with one end of an oar. The boat eased out into the lazy water. He waved goodbye, and then rowed up to the bend and disappeared.

After three weeks of non-stop labor, the rice was planted. As Cameron stood in a field, a weight lifted from his shoulders. He thanked the good Lord that much of the hard work had been done by the former owner, Mr. Chastain.

A slight breeze wafted over the land, gently pushing the fresh scent of the new rice shoots into the air. He took in the damp, strong smell of the creek that wound its way toward the sea and to the muddy banks thick with flowers hanging lazily over the slow-moving river. The canals had been dug and the trunks that let the water in, or kept it out, were in place, but Cameron's field hands still had their work cut out for them

He watched each step and logged the progress in a journal. After the grounds had been plowed anew and the canals and trunks inspected, then it was ready for the water to flow through the fields, or hold it back to let the fields dry out. If there was any need for repair, the carpenters took responsibility.

After the slaves sowed the seeds, they immediately flooded the area, keeping it wet until the seeds germinated. This step usually took two to fourteen days. Then they drained the fields. The slaves hoed for weeds and kept the land dry until the young shoots visably formed rows across the track.

The fields were then flooded again with a series of water flows that gave the rice protection from choking weeds and provided the moisture needed to grow strong.

Satisfied that the rice was growing well, Cameron turned his attention toward the slave district. Today was moving day, not only for the slaves, but for him, too.

When he walked back to the slave's village, he found the people buzzing about like bees. He wove through the crowd and stopped in front of the cabin nearest the road that led to what would eventually be the Great House. From the cabin he could keep an eye on the development of the rice fields, as well as the construction of the mansion.

He stepped into his dark cabin, allowing his eyes to adjust to the dimness before he looked around at the fifteen-by-fifteen foot room. He already had a couple of men bring his belongings from the old shanty. He nodded. The room had what he needed for comfort: a bed, a table with two chairs, and a wall with three shelves centered between the two windows looking out onto the land. Now, he propped his valise on the cot and stepped out of the house to watch the slaves settle into their dwellings.

Standing nearby was Tungo, the tall, broad-shouldered black man that Cameron had chosen two days earlier to be the overseer. Tungo stood back and watched the new dwellers as well. Twice, he looked over his shoulder at Cameron. It was as if he was waiting for instructions.

Cameron stepped outside his door and strode over to Tungo. "Do you have a family?"

"A woman and small son," Tungo said, his eyes searching the busy crowd.

"Bring them to the second cabin. You will live there," Cameron told him.

"Tungo think it best to be in the middle of the village." He held himself rigid.

"No. Follow me." Cameron led Tungo to the second building. "It's best if you are set apart from the people. Since your cabin will be next to mine, the people will respect you more."

Tungo carried a whip under his left arm. Cameron hadn't seen him use it, but he pointed at the leather weapon. "You won't need that."

"But—"

"Give it to me."

Fire glowed in the dark man's eyes. He lifted his elbow and the whip dropped to the ground. He didn't look down, but kept his gaze fixed on Cameron.

"Pick it up."

Tungo's jaw tensed.

"I won't tell you twice."

Tungo's eyes stayed on Cameron as he bent his knees and reached for the whip. He jerked his arm forward, still holding Cameron's gaze.

"I may have to rethink giving you the job of overseer." Cameron pulled the whip from the man's hand.

"Tungo good overseer."

"You'll have to prove it. What I say, goes. If you can't live with that, you'll be replaced, which, by the way, will happen not too far into the future. You're only a temporary overseer until my man comes from Jamaica. If you prove yourself valuable, I'll put you second in command."

"Tungo prove he be first in command."

"We'll see."

The belligerent black man said nothing. His eyes moved to the people carrying crates and bedding to the small square houses. As he watched, an argument ensued between two colored women. He looked as if he wanted to leave Cameron's side and tend to them.

"One more thing, Tungo."

Tungo dragged his eyes from the fighting women to look at Cameron.

"Do you know any of these people?"

"Most of them."

"Can you suggest a good cook?"

For the first time, Tungo's shoulders relaxed and white teeth shone as he smiled. "Mama Jezelee," he said. "She best cook of them all."

"She'll be making my meals then. I don't want to keep making trips down river to get a good meal. Send her to my cabin with supper tonight."

"Yes, Mastah Cameron. I do that."

"Call me Camp. I prefer my nickname."

"Yes, Mastah Camp."

"Good. Now get back to work."

Tungo wasted no time threading his way through the crowd to the two women with lashing tongues. He spread his arms out wide and stood between them. Although Cameron couldn't hear what was being said, it was apparent the overseer was taking care of the problem, as the women quickly turned and hurried their separate ways.

Eleven

"Good," Cameron said to himself as he tucked the whip under his arm, and strode to his cabin. He lifted the lid of his large trunk and placed the whip inside, then he let the lid slam firmly in place. *No need in starting off on the wrong foot.*

TWELVE

TWO WEEKS LATER, Cameron met Sid Sparrow at the wharf and walked to the King's Inn on the riverfront. Since most of the overflow of customers had eaten and gone, the two men eased into the pleasant dining room and found a seat. After the young waitress brought their water, Sid asked, "How's it going at River Oak?"

"Steady. Better than I hoped. Not knowing the first thing about growing rice, it's been an experience learning the method."

"You got your fields plowed and the canals dug?"

"Better than that. The crop's in and has been flooded a few times already."

"I'm impressed." Sparrow drank his water to the last drop, then set his empty glass down. "Uh oh," he said.

Cameron cut his gaze across the room but didn't see anyone he knew.

"I see your friend Wendell Seward is here," Sparrow said.

Cameron panned the tables again until his eyes focused on the man who'd lost the bid for River Oak. He eyed the copper-haired man who seemed intent on conversation with his lunch partner, until he turned to see Cameron glancing his way.

At first Seward didn't show recognition. But a second look from Cameron brought him to his feet. His green eyes grew dark and his lips thinned. Seward bent and whispered something to his friend and then crossed the floor.

"I see you're back in town." He glared down at Cameron.

"Been back," Cameron said. "I've already planted the rice fields."

"I don't suppose you've heard that in these parts there's a county-wide competition to see who yields the most crops. After all the crops have been harvested and the numbers are in at market, there's a celebration right here in Charleston. Quite an event." Seward's eyes moved to Sparrow. "You've been to the event."

"Yes. Every year," Sparrow said.

"And who usually wins?" Seward asked.

Seeming to ignore Wendell Seward's question, Sparrow held his glass to the waitress as she passed by with a pitcher of ice water.

"I've won the trophy the past eight years," Seward said. "I expect to win it this year as well." He smiled sardonically at Cameron.

"I wouldn't be surprised if you do, Seward. I'm just getting started. But I like a healthy competition. You may find yourself running neck-and-neck in the next year or two."

"Doubt it. I've got the planting down to a system. I've brought in more 'Carolina Gold' than anyone else in these parts. No one could have come close in the future, either, had I won the land you stole from me."

"I bought the land fair and square, Seward."

"That land was meant to be mine. It *will* be mine when you get tired of trying to make a living off the rice fields. It's funny how things go wrong in these parts. And no one seems to know how they happen." He winked.

"Are you threatening to ruin my land, Seward?" Cameron was ready to stand toe-to-toe with the obstinate man.

"Of course not, Mr. Bartholomew. I never *personally* dirty my hands in other people's business." He gave a salute and went back to his table.

"Dirty scoundrel," Sparrow said. "You better watch your back."

"I'm not afraid of him." Cameron's jaw worked as he stared past Sparrow's shoulder. He started to make another remark just as a stranger walked into the café and scanned the room for a table.

Cameron blinked and leaned forward a tad.

"What now?" Sparrow looked back at the entrance.

"Do you know that man who just stepped into the dining room?"

"Oh, him? That's Newton Bartholomew. He's a boat repairman down at the shipyard—"

Sparrow glanced back at the man again, then to Cameron and stuttered, "Is . . . is that . . ." He stopped. "Are you related to him?" He thumbed his finger at the man.

"By gum, I am!" Cameron stood and stepped away from the table. The man looked his way, and then peered around the room as if searching for someone else.

Cameron moved toward him, feeling as if the room were spinning out of control. When he reached the man wearing rough work clothes, he stretched out a hand. "Newton?"

The man stared at him for a second before recognition showed in his eyes. "Cameron?"

"That's me." The two men shook hands, eyes taking in the other as if in a dream. Then they threw their arms around each other clapping the other's back and laughing. At long last, they drew apart. "I've been looking for you. Every time I'm in town, I've asked about you and Timmy, but I never got a lead on finding you. Now here you are."

"Where have you been?" Newton asked and studied the table where Cameron had come from.

"Join us. There's room for you. I believe you know my friend, Sid Sparrow." He led his older brother to the table, not wanting to take his eyes off him.

Sid stood and slapped Newton on the back. "It never dawned on me the two of you were related. Sit down, my friend."

Newton sat, but he seemed tongue-tied. He licked his lips and asked again, "Where have you been?"

The three waited while the waitress came by their table, set a glass of water before Newton, took their order, and walked away.

"Now, to answer your question," Cameron laughed softly, "I've been in Jamaica."

Newton looked stunned. "Jamaica? How in the world did you get to Jamaica?"

"It's a long story, but to keep it short, I stowed away in a ship. The ship's owner, Phillip Cooper, took me under his wing and took me to his place. He raised me there."

Newton shook his head in bewilderment. "All this time, since you were a child, you've been living in Jamaica?"

"Yes, brother, I have."

"We thought someone came to town and kidnapped you. We hoped you could break away and come home, but you never did." Newton stared at Cameron as if he still couldn't believe his eyes. "And here you are." He drank his water. "So what brought you back?"

"I've purchased land in Fields Landing up the Taney River. I'm building a home. I'm a rice plantation owner now."

"Well, I . . . I don't know what to say–" Newton was clearly at a loss for words. "You leave here a puny kid, poor as dirt, and come back a wealthy man." He grinned.

"Sparrow tells me you work for the shipyard as a boat repairman," Cameron said.

"That's true. It doesn't bring in any fancy kind of money, but I've been doing it for a good twenty years. I have a wife and children, too. What about you? Are you married? Do you have children?"

"I'm married to a wonderful woman by the name of Grace. And we have our first child on the way." Cameron smiled proudly.

"So is she here? We should get our families together, introduce our wives to each other. And I know Father will want to see you."

"Dad's still alive?"

"Yes. After we lost you, he quit drinking and sobered up. Your disappearance made him see the ill of his ways. He changed. He stopped feeling sorry for himself. Over time he found a good-paying job and he recently remarried."

Cameron couldn't speak. The news that his father had changed slammed him in the chest. He had run from Charleston as a small child, because his father was an abusive drunk. He'd treated all his children poorly after his wife died. Cameron wanted to believe his father had had a change of heart, but he was cautious in his optimism, so the only comment he made was, "It will be good to see him." After a pause, he continued. "My wife is still in Jamaica. She won't be able to travel until the baby is born."

"You left her there?" Newton looked incredulous.

"She's in good hands with her Aunt Kate and Cousin Josie. And there are servants who look after her."

"You have servants?"

"Ah, yes." Cameron leaned back as the waitress placed his dinner before him.

"You must be doing rather well, Cameron." Newton stared at him.

"My father . . . my adoptive father . . . left his estate to us." Cameron cleared his throat. He didn't want to talk about his financial matters with his brother. He didn't want to appear uppity. It was clear Newton worked hard for every nickel and dime he made at the shipyards.

"Are the others here, Timmy . . . Karen . . . Tina?" he asked, changing the subject.

Newton nodded. "They're all here in Charleston, as is Father. None of us left town." He drank from his glass and stared at Cameron. "They're not going to believe it when I tell them I've found our missing brother." He pinned his gaze on Cameron. "Why did you never try to get in touch with us when you came to town?"

"I looked for you. When I didn't find you, I figured that since I left town, you did too."

"Well, we didn't." Newton leaned forward. "You're here now. That's all that matters. It does my heart good to be looking at you."

Cameron let out the breath he'd been holding. "Tell me about the family. I want to hear everything." He and Newt left the café with the promise to get together. Newton gave him his address. In the next few days, Cameron planned to meet the rest of the family.

That evening, Cameron sat in his cabin feeling overwhelmed at the knowledge that after twenty-five years, his older brother walked back into his life. Savory smells of food wafted over the air. He opened his cabin door to step out and almost ran into an older, heavy-set colored woman with a plate of food in her hand.

"Oh! You nearly lost your supper, Mastah!"

"You must be Mama Jezelee?"

"Sho' nuff, that who I be. Tungo say you want me to fix your meals." She glanced past Cameron into his cabin. "You gonna eat out here or in your house?"

Cameron stepped aside and the black woman scooted past him to set the plate on a small table. She stood back, plump fists on her rounded hips. "I be droppin' off your breakfast first thing in the mornin', before first light."

"Thank you, Jezelee. I'll be awake."

"Mama Jezelee," she said. "Everybody call me Mama Jezelee."

"All right. Thank you, Mama Jezelee."

She started for the door and stopped. "Where your woman, Masta? You be here all alone?"

"My wife will be here shortly." He didn't feel he owed her an explanation.

"You need company 'til she come?" Her black brows went up to the red bandana tied over her head. White eyes rolled to the ceiling, and big dimples indented her plump cheeks.

"No. I don't need company, Mama Jezelee. I'm fine waiting for my wife."

"It ain't me who gonna take care of you." She laughed until her midriff jiggled. "There be plenty of pretty girls who'd be happy to do that."

"No, thank you." He opened the door indicating it was time for Mama Jezelee to leave.

"See you first thing tomorrow mornin', then." Mama stepped out.

"That'll be fine. Good night." He closed the door and stared at the food then sat down and bowed his head. He silently thanked God for the pleasant-smelling meal. When he said, "Amen," his mind went to the woman he missed with all his heart. *Grace, how I long to hold you in my arms.*

Bang!

Cameron jumped up. There was no mistaking the sound. He burst out the door looking for where the musket shot had come from. Slaves were running toward the riverbank, pushing against each other to get a look at something beyond his view.

Cameron pushed through the crowd and came to the river's edge. One of the slave men dragged an alligator to higher ground. The other men were talking fast and gesturing toward the water.

"Who shot the alligator?" Cameron asked.

"I did, Mastah." A short stout man stood up, his chest barreling with pride.

"What's your name?"

"Jonah, suh."

"Who gave you permission to shoot the gator?"

"Why, nobody." He looked warily at his catch.

"I don't want you shooting the alligators unless they're a threat to the village, you hear?"

"That be just it. This gator done climbed up the bank. The chilluns tell us. I shoot him."

"All right. What are you going to do with it?"

Jonah smiled wide. "I'm gonna skin him and put him in the fire. Make us a fine meal fo' sho'."

Cameron eyed the rifle in Jonah's hand. "Where'd you get that rifle?"

Jonah looked as if he were ready to run. "I found it up along the river. It be layin' there for the takin'."

"Give it to me." Cameron held out his hand.

Jonah placed the rifle in Cameron's hand.

Cameron inspected the weapon. It was fairly new. He stared at the black man. "Who taught you to shoot?"

"My pappy, suh. He was a guard for the prison and brought his musket home."

"You don't say!"

"Yes, suh."

"Who would have left the musket out there by the river bank?"

"Don't know. It be leanin' up against a tree. I don't see's anybody, so's I took it."

This troubled Cameron. Who was out there crawling around his property? He made a mental note to keep a watch out on the boundaries of his land.

The crowd lingered around them, some standing by the dead alligator, some watching Jonah and his master. "Take the alligator, Jonah," Cameron said, keeping the rifle in his grip. "After supper, I want you to show me where you found this rifle."

"Yes, suh."

While the crowd moved away, Cameron returned to the cabin for his supper, but when he stepped through the doorway, he found a large raccoon busily eating his meal.

"No!" Cameron rushed the table and the raccoon flew into the air. He landed on the floor running. Cameron hardly got a glimpse of the tip of his striped tail before he disappeared out the door.

Cameron went back to the table, stared at the mess, and angrily ran his fingers through his hair. He went to the door and looked out toward the crowd who were getting fed. He went back to the table, scooped up his plate, he stormed out to where Mama Jezelee was dishing out rice and beans. She glanced up at Cameron. "You want more?"

"Yes, thank you. Give me a new plate." Cameron didn't tell the cook–or anyone else for that matter–that his dinner had been stolen by a raccoon!

THIRTEEN

Kindra Hall, Barbados

DAWN BROKE CLEAR after the morning's ritual storm. The clouds rolled in to drop enough rain to wet the land, and then retreated out to sea where they dissipated for another day. A warm west wind blew through the open window. A scent of tangy sweetness filled the air coming from the tobacco curing barns. That scent awakened Denzel, reminding him that today he wanted to check the fencing on the boundary lines. He slid out of bed, careful not to wake Kindra, and stepped into his breeches. Within minutes, he was out the door.

Denzel spent the morning surveying the tobacco fields and inspecting the outbuildings on the plantation. Though the day was young, the air was already hot and humid. Steam rose from the still damp fields.

Kindra Hall awoke to a symphony of life orchestrated by an unseen hand. Men, women, and children came out of their shanties in the colored district and moved to their appointed work stations. The cook stoked a fire outside of one barn and soon the aroma of fried pork strips and porridge filled the air.

Men carried garden tools over their shoulders and headed to the acres of land they would hoe. Young children helped carry spades and rakes and bounced alongside the older men toward the provisions fields. Roads ran between the fields, and donkey carts waited to be filled with large tobacco leaves stripped from the thick stalks.

Jasper trotted out to where Denzel stood. "Mornin, suh."

"Good morning, Jasper. Walk with me." Denzel turned down the dirt road that led to the acres of crops. Up ahead a donkey cart stood at the side of a field. Several workers had dumped large basket loads of green tobacco leaves into the cart, but now they stood back warily. On the ground lay a large basket with the contents spilled onto the ground.

"No! Don't whip me!"

Snap!

"Ooow!"

Snap!

"Sorry, Massa! Please stop!"

Snap!

Denzel couldn't see where the voice and the sound of the whip came from, but he picked up his pace, Jasper close behind. The donkey cart piled high with green tobacco leaves blocked his view as he stormed forward. An overseer held a whip above his head ready to lick the leather strip across the back of a male slave who knelt behind the cart, his hands stretched over his head to protect his face.

"Stop that at once!" Denzel commanded in a loud and powerful voice, as he strode to the overseer and snatched the whip out of his hand.

"What's the meaning of this?" The man lurched forward to retrieve his whip, a vile expression on his face. "Give me that whip. It belongs to me!"

"Not any longer it don't." Denzel stood his ground and stared at the tall, bony man with a face like a hawk, then turned to examine the abused slave whose shirt was shredded in thin lines, blood oozing onto the material and sticking to his skin. "What has this man done to deserve such abuse?"

"You have eyes, have you not?" the overseer growled.

"What's your name?" Denzel asked the slave as he gently pushed the man's shoulder back, and grabbed an elbow so that the man stood to face him.

"Jones, be my name." The man appeared confused that Denzel, a black man himself had come to his rescue.

"Get your foul hands off my slave!" The overseer rushed at Denzel and shoved him back with his left hand, pushing Jones to the ground with his right.

Denzel felt the powerful force of Mr. Hawkface's shove, but he quickly recovered. He grabbed a handful of the overseer's shirt and shoulder and pushed him away from Jones.

"Enough! You have overstepped your boundaries." Although Denzel's words were controlled, an unmistakable blade of authority cut through his voice and gave his words a razor edge.

The overseer's eyes strayed to Jasper. "Who is this darky that he thinks he can come out to my fields and make demands?"

Jasper squared his shoulders and stepped forward. "He be your new boss, suh."

"What? I'll have no Negro telling me what to do! There isn't room enough on this plantation for two overseers!"

Jasper opened his mouth to speak, but Denzel's hand went up to silence him, and his eyes pierced those of the hawk-faced man. "You misunderstood the young man. I'm not one of the help on this plantation. I own this estate." He breathed heavily and looked beyond the overseer to the men and women standing at the edge of the fields, closing in to see and hear all that was going on. It was plain to see he had taken them all by surprise with his announcement.

"You all listen up," Denzel's voice boomed out over the fields. "You heard what I said. I'm the new owner of Kindra Hall. My name is Denzel Talmaze. My wife be Kindra. I'll have no whipping going on here." He paused, "That's not to say that I will tolerate any of you slacking off on your job. Later this evening, after the day's work is done, we will hold a meeting in the clearing in front of the barn. Until then, you all get back to work."

The field hands looked down at the ground. A moment later, one by one they looked up, hope in their eyes.

Denzel's eyes traveled back to the hostile man and asked, "What's your name?"

The man's eyes blazed and Denzel could see he didn't want to give a reply. Instead the man asked, "Where's Bernard?"

"I haven't any idea, but I asked your name."

"I'm not answering to a stinkin' blackie. I want to see Mr. Bernard." The overseer spit on the ground then tried to brush past Denzel.

Denzel's hand went up to stop the man, but the overseer stepped away. "Don't touch me!" He kicked a rock on the dirt road, and sent it sailing. He strode away at a fast clip.

Denzel watched as the overseer stepped off the road and disappeared behind the building. He glanced at Jasper. "What's his name?"

"Lee, suh. Mistah Zane Lee"

"Thanks, I'll deal with him later." He tucked the whip under his left arm and walked over to where Jones stood. "Go on back to the barn. Have someone tend to your back."

Jones stared at Denzel. "Is it true? You be our new massa?"

"It's true, Jones. Now go on. Do as I say. Find someone to put some ointment on your back."

"Yes, suh." Jones shuffled down the dirt road toward the outbuildings. He looked back once, but kept walking.

"Jasper."

"Yes, suh."

"I'll send someone out with water for the field hands. Keep them working after they have a drink, though."

"Yes, suh."

"I'll be back."

"Yes, suh." Jasper eyed the slaves and signaled them to get back to work. The men and women went back to stripping the large tobacco leaves from the thick stalks, filling their baskets as they kicked them along the rows.

Denzel walked back toward the main buildings wondering where he might find Bernard. He hadn't seen him all morning. When he reached the tall curing barn, the scent of dried tobacco filled the air. He stepped into the wooden structure and stopped. He needed a moment to let his eyes adjust to the dimness. When they did, he found that the rafters in the barn had long rows of thin poles with tobacco leaves draped over them to dry and cure.

The barn was full of slaves hanging the green leaves. Denzel gave a nod of approval as he watched the rhythm in which the men and women worked. Curious eyes looked his way, but they didn't stop their work to stare. Their hands and feet kept moving.

"How can I help you?" came a deep voice from behind.

Denzel turned to see a tall black man in a gauzy white shirt standing behind him.

"I'm Denzel Talmaze." He reached out his hand.

The man took it, as he glanced up and down at Denzel, then stared questioningly.

"I'm the new owner of Kindra Hall," Denzel offered.

"What about Mr. Bernard?" the wary man asked.

"He's still the foreman at the moment."

The man looked out the wide entrance of the barn as if he expected Mr. Bernard to make an appearance. "You be my new boss?"

"That's right."

A smile cracked his serious veneer and the man's white teeth shone bright. "But you be a darkie like me?"

"That's right," Denzel said again. "What's your name?"

"Ebenezer." He stared at Denzel as if trying to take it all in. "You sure you be my boss?"

"I'm sure."

"Mr. Bernard dun say nuthin' 'bout that."

"Have you seen him this morning?"

"Ain't seen him all mo'nin'. Come ta think of it, his carriage been gone since daybreak."

The workers kept moving and hanging the tobacco leaves, but Denzel sensed ears had perked up to listen to the conversation between him and Ebenezer.

"Are you the overseer for the curing process?"

"No, suh." Ebenezer's eyes stared at the wide opening to the barn again. "Mr. Lee be the overseer over all the grounds."

"I see. Well, why don't you show me what's in the other outbuildings."

"Yessuh." Ebenezer nodded. "Come this way. The carriage house be over heah."

When the two men stepped out of the barn they looked up in time to see four wagons coming up the long drive. Denzel turned to Ebenezer. "You'll have to give me a tour later. Our supplies have just arrived."

Kindra awoke to the sound of Mayme's footsteps as she entered the room. She looked up in time to see the servant quietly shut the door with her elbow, a wooden tray in her hands.

"Mornin', Miz Kindra." Mayme moved to the side of the bed waiting as Kindra scooted up to lean her back against the mahogany headboard. "Clara done said I ought to bring your breakfast since you sleepin' in."

"What time is it?" Kindra glanced at the window and realized the early hour had sailed on without her. The sun had risen high enough to be mid-morning.

"It be ten o'clock, ma'am."

"I can't believe I slept so late. I wanted to be up with the rest of the household." Kindra glanced at the tray. A plate of scrambled eggs, bacon, and sweet biscuits sat next to a porcelain tea pot designed in red and pink roses and a matching cup and saucer.

"Here," Mayme said, "let me pour your tea for you."

The young woman tilted the China teapot and hot liquid poured into the dainty cup.

"It's not often I eat in bed," Kindra admitted, her lips curved into a contented smile. "At home, we all meet in the dining chamber."

"Most mornin's Miz Ava eats in her room. She send the children down to eat, but she likes to take her breakfast alone. I s'pose cook thought you'd like to do the same."

"I will enjoy it this morning. But tomorrow, if I'm still sleeping past eight o'clock, I'd like for you to wake me. For that matter, Rhea should be here. She is my chambermaid. She knows I prefer to start the day early."

"You be sleepin' in 'cause you with child."

"I suppose that's true. I must say I rather like this. I could get spoiled quickly if I'm not careful."

While she ate, Mayme saw to her bath. Kindra hadn't freshened up the day before. With the humidity so thick, a fresh bath sounded wonderful. And it might put her in better spirits. The morning sickness had eased to some degree on the voyage to the island, but some days it threatened to linger.

Mayme left the room to call the men servants to bring up buckets of steaming water. While Kindra waited, she ate her meal, finding she had a more ravenous appetite than she'd realized. The sweet biscuits were scrumptious, and having finished the second one, she wished for another. The food had been rather bland on the ship.

Mayme appeared with fresh towels over her arm and two male servants behind her, carrying pails of steaming water in each hand. Kindra heard the water slosh in the tub and the men left for more.

"Our supplies and belongings should come this morning," Kindra said between sips of tea. "Have the captain and his men arrived yet?"

"No, ma'am."

Kindra nibbled the bacon while she watched Mayme move about the room picking up clothes and folding them or hanging them in the wardrobe.

"If you don't mind me askin', Miz Kindra, where you come from?"

"Jamaica. I was born and raised there on my father's sugar plantation."

"And then you come here," Mayme nodded, and glanced at the door.

"My father, Phillip Cooper, built this house for me. As a matter of fact, he named the estate after me."

"I figured as much. I remember your fathah. He seemed like a real nice man." Mayme put a finger up. "I best check on Bates and Duncan. They's suppose to bring up your water and they's only half through."

FOURTEEN

BATHED AND REFRESHED for the day, Kindra wandered into the kitchen an hour later. The morning flurry was over and the cooks were starting on the noon meal. Clara and Louiza stopped talking when Kindra stepped into the room. Their brows went up and the two looked at each other.

"Can we be gettin' you anythin,' Miz?" Louiza asked.

"No. I'm just exploring the house and acquainting myself with the run of things."

Clara asked, "Did those boys bring your hot watah for your bath?"

"They did, thank you."

"Them boys do sluff off sometimes. We have to keep on 'em." Clara glanced at Louiza and smiled. "They's good workers most times."

Kindra remembered watching the two servants. They weren't boys, they were men, strong and muscular, with broad shoulders. They seemed hard put to keep their eyes straight ahead as they carried the pails of steaming water past her bed to the bath room. She understood their curiosity in seeing the new mistress in the house. She had taken advantage of their multiple trips to observe *them*. They would be useful around Kindra Hall, she decided.

Kindra nodded acknowledgment to Clara and asked, "Has Ava come down yet?"

"No, ma'am. She don't be comin' down 'fore the noon meal."

"Is that so? Good. I want to explore the rest of the house before she makes her appearance."

"You got plenty o' time for that." Louiza rolled her eyes. "Dinner won't be served 'fore an hour."

Kindra went back to the hallway and up the stairs. The west wing was set apart for the Bernards. Rather than take a chance in running into Ava, Kindra walked down the east wing opening doors and inspecting the rooms. It wouldn't be long before she would need to set up a nursery. She came upon a rather large room that would make a grand guest room should Grace and Cameron come for a visit.

She walked to the window, pulled back the draperies to look out onto the front lawn, and blinked at the strong sunshine pouring in. She shifted her stance in order to glance down, and at the end of the drive saw a cloud of dust rumbling toward the estate from the south. A gust of wind picked up and blew it away, revealing four wagons rolling up the long drive. Angel, her Arabian horse, was tied to the back of one wagon, and trotted in rhythm with the others. "Good, they're here," Kindra whispered to herself. The wagons stopped in front of the house. When Barnabas looked up at the second story, she waved "hello" and dropped the curtain in place.

Kindra picked up her skirts and descended the stairs. When she came to the porch, she called out, "Welcome, Captain Kincade!" She skipped down the steps in time to see Denzel coming to the house.

He bounded up to the first wagon and said, "Welcome to our plantation, Captain."

When Kindra walked up, Denzel slipped his arm around her shoulder. She watched as the crewmen jumped off the wagon seats to stand on the ground.

Feeling eyes on her, she glanced up to find Ava Bernard standing behind a west wing window, her small daughter, Pauline, at her side. The two of them peered down at the activity in the circular drive.

Denzel followed her gaze. "I'm surprised she's up." Kindra told him. "The servants say she doesn't attend the rest of the household before noon."

"What does she do before then?" he asked.

"No one knows. But I'm glad. That will give me time and liberty to tour the house and acquaint myself with each of the household staff." Kindra caught a glimpse of her chambermaid. "Rhea," she called, leaving Denzel's side and quickly stepping to the third wagon. "How was your trip?"

"It be a fine ride, Miz Kindra." The chambermaid looked out beyond the wagon to the Great House and the buildings and fields beyond. Her dark brown eyes held a slight filmy haze, as if she couldn't focus as well as she normally did. "Lordy, Miz Kindra. This be a fine place. I believe you two gone have your work cut out for you."

"Yes, we will."

The butler, Boaz, and the house servants filed out of the house and congregated on the wide porch, some already moving down the steps to unload trunks and crates. Denzel was giving orders and Duncan lifted a crate to his shoulder following directions on where to take it.

Abner, the stableman, joined the commotion. A smile spread across his dark, freckled face when he walked to where Angel stomped nervously behind the second wagon.

"You sho' a pretty little lady, I do declare." Abner stroked her white mane and turned to Kindra. "I'll be takin' this fine horse of yours to the stable and brush her down." He glanced up to the second story of the house toward the west wing, then turned to untie the horse. Leading the mare away from the wagons, Abner smiled broadly. "Come on, little missy. I've got some fine oats for you in the stable."

Kindra watched the old man lead Angel away, happiness in her heart. It was evident that at least Angel would get the best of care.

"How things gone since you arrived, Miz Kindra?" Rhea's eyes traveled over the servants on the porch and in the driveway.

Kindra watched Rhea take in the people. She, too, would get to know all of them in good time. "To tell the truth, it's not been easy. But then, I'll tell you all about it when we're alone in my bedchamber."

"Heh, heh, heh." Rhea's shoulders bobbed up and down as she laughed. "I'm sho' to get an earful. Now tell me where you want this box?" She held up a large round hat box that was made of thin material. "I be thinkin' I best carry this on my lap. You know how men are. It woulda been crumpled fo' sho'." She pulled a simple handkerchief from her dress pocket and wiped her brow. When she shoved the hanky back in her pocket, she heaved a deep breath, that filmy haze still clouding her eyes.

Mayme stood beside Kindra. "Mayme, show Rhea my bedchamber. And, oh, let me introduce you two right now. Mayme has been taking care of me in your absence. This is Rhea, my chambermaid. Rhea, this is Mayme."

The two colored servants nodded, Mayme a bit on the shy side, Rhea showing more authority. "Lead the way. I best be seein' to the mistress's room right away."

Kindra giggled under her breath. She had no doubt the two women would become fast friends.

Kindra made her way back to where Denzel and Captain Kincade stood just in time to hear Denzel say, "You'll spend the night here before you sail, won't you, Captain?"

"I hadn't planned on it, but a day off the ship sounds enjoyable. You can give me a tour of the grounds." Captain Kincade slipped his hands in his pockets and rocked on the heels of his boots. "What about the other men?"

"Send them all back to the ship with Barnabas. My driver can get you back tomorrow after the noon meal."

"Good enough. Now if you don't mind, I'll supervise the unloading."

The next hour the front drive was a hive of activity. It wasn't long before the Bernards' three children stood on the side of the lawn, eyes suspicious. Kindra overheard Chad, the older boy say, "I don't know why them Negroes got all this stuff going into the house. Father said they wouldn't be staying long." He pulled on the shoulder of the younger boy standing next to him. "Come on, Harold. Let's go find him. He'll put a stop to this."

The two boys ran off toward the outbuildings, leaving the little blonde girl, Pauline to stand by herself. Her eyes wide, she looked up at Kindra. She stared for half a second before she stuck her tongue out and ran back into the house.

"Goodness," Kindra sighed. She looked up at the sky and saw that the hot sun had risen to the noon hour. Fanning her face with her hand, she went back into the house and headed for the kitchen.

Louiza and Clara stood at the dining room window watching the fanfare going on. At Kindra's appearance, Louiza dropped the white curtain into place. The two cooks folded their hands before them at attention.

"Our personal belongings have arrived as you see."

"Yes'm." The two chimed together.

"We'll have company for dinner. Add an extra plate for the captain."

"Yes, Miz Kindra," Clara said.

Kindra heard footsteps behind her and the cook's eyes peered over her shoulder. She turned to see Ava Bernard standing in the entrance, a vile look on her face.

"Good morning . . . or . . . should I say afternoon, Ava."

"What's so good about it?" She tore her eyes from Kindra and blasted out, "Move! You heard what she said. Get into the kitchen and stay put. There's nothing of interest out front that should concern you."

The cooks turned toward the kitchen rolling their eyes.

Ava stepped up to Kindra. "I don't know what all this commotion is about. You won't be staying long. Stanley will see to that." Her eyes traveled over Kindra's simple blue gown. "Enjoy it while you can. The two of you will be booted out of here faster than you can blink an eye."

"Ava . . . I'll not stand here and put up with your nonsense. If *you* want to continue to stay here at Kindra Hall, *you'll* have to curb your tongue. We are not going anywhere." Annoyance bristled up Kindra's spine and her hard-eyed stare never wavered.

"Stanley has gone to see our attorney. He'll come back with orders for the two of you to be removed from these premises at once. So don't give me your uppity attitude, you little snippit."

Ava brushed past Kindra, her gown rustling as she went. When she opened the kitchen door she poked her head in and said, "Send a tray to my room. I'll not watch the charade down here."

Kindra watched Ava flee up the stairs. *Oh, dear. I'll certainly have a crop of news to write Grace.* She went back to the porch just in time to see Mr. Lee storming up the drive, his hackles up.

"What's the meaning of this?" He glared at Denzel and then the crewmen. "Have you permission from Mr. Bernard to invade these premises?"

Barnabas stepped out from behind a wagon, his black frame a head taller than the rest of the men. "You got a problem with the Massa. You got a problem with me. Now what was you askin'?"

The rumble of carriage wheels and the trotting of horses' hooves sounded from behind the crowd. Stanley Bernard rolled the carriage into the circular drive and pulled the reins tight. He stood in the open carriage before he stepped down, observing the crewmen and servants moving up and down the porch steps, luggage or crates on their shoulders. He hung his head and stepped down walking past Denzel, the captain, and the sizzling man.

All eyes went to the foreman, waiting to see what he would do next. To their surprise the man brushed past the crowd and Kindra and went into the house, slamming the door behind him.

Kindra shot Denzel a look before she wheeled around and opened the front door for the workers, and to hear what the foreman had to say.

When she stepped into the front entry, she found Stanley Bernard standing at the foot of the stairs looking up at Ava who waited to hear the news.

"Well?" she asked.

Stanley shook his head dejectedly. "It appears Phillip Cooper informed our attorney of his daughter's rights to the estate. He had a copy of the deed. It was signed by their lawyer. It has all been witnessed and documented to belong to those Negroes. We haven't a say in any of it."

It was apparent that Mr. Bernard was unaware that Kindra stood behind him. She listened to the wonderful news wanting to leap and shout and clap her hands, yet for the sake of Ava glaring down at her she stood quietly, her demeanor calmly taking it all in.

Ava descended a step toward her husband. "So what now?"

"I continue as the foreman of this plantation until we can figure out a way to get these darkies off this land. I didn't spend the past six years of my life putting all of this together to hand it over to them. I've shed blood, sweat and tears for this land, and by God, I mean to keep it!"

Ava glanced past her husband, and for the first time he realized they were not alone. He spun around and glared at Kindra, color rising up his neck and into his face.

"How long have you been standing there?" he bellowed.

"Long enough to hear all of your explanation to your wife . . . and to know you mean to steal my land if you have your way about it." She stared at him and felt calm for the first time since she'd arrived at the estate. "We'll discuss all of this at supper tonight. Until then, there's a tobacco plantation to run. You might check with Denzel what is to transpire today."

Stanley Bernard shot Kindra an exasperated glance and for the second time today, he brushed past her in the opposite direction, this time headed back outside. "We'll see about this!" He stormed down the steps and crossed the yard to the group of men.

"I'd watch my back if I were you." Ava spun around and headed back up the stairs. "You'll see!"

FIFTEEN

THE SUN SLIPPED through the small slit in the curtains and shone across the mahogany bed. Kindra rolled to her left where the single ray slanted across her eyes. She squinted and rolled back, but soon realized her body ached from too many hours in that same position. Finally, she lay on her back and stared at the cream-colored ceiling. A new agitation bore down as her bladder insisted she get up and get moving.

Throwing aside the coverlets, she swung her feet over the side of the bed and sat on its edge long enough to steady herself for the first trip of the day to the water closet. A moment later she stood by the window. The sun was high enough that she shouldn't have lingered and slept this late in the morning. *Where's Rhea?* Her chambermaid should have awakened her long before now. The brass nightstand clock told her it was nearly nine o'clock.

Running a hand over her stomach, she felt a small nudge and smiled. She threw a robe over her nightdress. It wasn't like Rhea to shirk her duties. She should've been to the bedchamber by now, to dress Kindra and style her hair. Glancing in her vanity mirror, she tried to smooth the wild tresses that stuck out every which way from sleep. Then she crossed the floor and pulled the thick tapestry cord in the corner of the room and waited. More than ten minutes passed. No Rhea.

"Something isn't right." Kindra crossed the hardwood floor to the chamber door. Then she glanced down at herself. She looked bedraggled and couldn't go traipsing through the house in her nightdress and robe. Again, she pulled the tapestry cord and waited. Moments later, Mayme tapped on the door and entered.

"Mayme?"

"You rang twice, Miz Kindra. I came to see if you need my assistance."

"I suppose I do since Rhea hasn't shown up this morning. Have you seen her about the house?"

"No, ma'am. Shall I get you dressed?"

"Yes. You know what to do. When you're done, we must find out what has delayed Rhea."

"Yes, Miz Kindra." Mayme set about laying out a day dress for her mistress, along with fresh petticoats and under things. Before long, Kindra was dressed and Mayme had pulled her thick, lush hair behind her head and tied it in a ribbon to match the maroon day dress.

"Lordy, Miz Kindra, it be quite a task buttoning your dress at your waist. I be thinkin' today be your last day wearing it until your little one be born."

Kindra stood in front of the long mirror and said, "Hmmm. I believe you're right. I can hardly breathe. I'm certain to be in trouble if I should sneeze." She giggled and turned to Mayme.

"Oh, Miz Kindra." Mayme couldn't laugh at what she said. "You sure not like any mistress I ever serve. 'Specially Miz Ava. She never be funnin' herself."

"That's too bad. We all need to learn how to laugh at ourselves."

Mayme eyed Kindra with wonder. "Why you be talkin' to me like that?"

"Like what?"

"Like we be friends." Mayme stepped away as she spoke.

Kindra stared at the colored woman. She *had* spoken to her like a friend, hadn't she? Until now, she hadn't realized she needed a woman to talk to. True, Mayme was only a servant girl, but she was young like herself. Could she truly expect to find a friend in a servant?

Kindra crossed the floor to where Mayme stood wide-eyed. "Don't let my carrying on scare you." She held out her hand and Mayme took it. "Since I've arrived to this house not one servant has shown me kindness. Respect yes. Kindness no . . . except you. I believe you can do your job and still be a friend. Am I right?"

"In truth, Miz Kindra, you be the most delightful mistress I have ever known."

"Thank you, Mayme. Now let's find Rhea." It calmed Kindra to have someone to talk to in this troubled house where eyes of the foreman and his wife sneered at her every time they met.

When Kindra and Mayme reached the servant quarters below the first floor, they found Rhea's room and knocked. Rapping lightly at first, they waited. But after a moment, Kindra turned the doorknob and stepped into the dark room. Mayme found a candle and a box of matches and lit the wick. Holding the fluttering candle high, the light flickered over the small room, dancing on the walls and catching a lone figure huddled in her bed. Rhea lay in a deep sleep.

"Rhea," Kindra said softly as she tapped the chambermaid's shoulder. Rhea rolled onto her back and blinked into the candlelight. She stared at Kindra as if she didn't recognize her at first, and then she gasped. "Oh, Miz Kindra. Is it morning already?" she asked in a slow raspy voice. "What have I gone and done? You be up and dressed and here I lay sleepin' the day away."

Though Rhea spoke she hadn't risen from the bed covers. Her left hand went to her forehead and she heaved a long sigh.

"Are you all right?" Kindra glanced at Mayme, brows raised, and then back at Rhea.

Rhea groaned ever so slightly. "I don' think I weathered well on the voyage. I try to feel bettah. But these old bones don' want to keep me movin', Miz Kindra."

"How long have you been sick?"

"Since before we get to dry land."

"We've been here two months. You never said a word about it."

"No, ma'am. You be such a mess ever since we be gettin' here that I don't want to set your nerves on edge some more."

Kindra laid the back of her hand on Rhea's forehead and pulled back quickly. "You're burning up! You need to see a doctor." Kindra touched Rhea's shoulder softly. "Get some rest. You're not to get up until you feel better. And the doctor will be the judge of that."

"You don't have to do a thing like that. I be on my feet 'fore too long." Rhea closed her eyes as if a heavy weight pulled on her lids. In less than a minute, her breathing became steady.

"Mayme, stay with her. I'm going after the doctor." Just the other day, Denzel had informed her they had a doctor on the grounds.

"Yes, ma'am. You'll find his building back behind the wash room a ways."

Kindra climbed the stairs to the main floor of the house and marched out to the back porch, shielding her eyes as she gazed toward the outbuildings. Duncan, the all-around house servant, rounded the corner, a pail of water in each hand.

"Good morning, Duncan. Where are you going with that water?"

"Miz Ava's chamber, ma'am."

"Set the buckets down and go for the doctor. Tell him my chambermaid is sick and needs his services at once." Kindra wrung her hands as she spoke.

"Yes'm." Duncan set the pails near the porch steps and trotted off toward the outbuildings.

When the doctor returned several hours later and she asked him what was wrong with her chambermaid, he didn't have a direct answer. "It's hard to say, ma'am," he began. "Having come on the ship only recently, it could be anything. She may have contracted a virus from one of the other passengers. And I must say, Miz Kindra, you probably shouldn't be in this room since we don't know what brought this on." He wiped his hands on a clean towel. "I would prefer you let one of the servants bathe her fevered skin. Staying could jeopardize the health of your unborn child."

When Doctor Coby left the small room, Kindra gave his warning some thought. Perhaps he was right. What if Rhea had a virus that was contagious? But when the elderly woman moaned and tossed violently again, Kindra dipped the hot cloth into the cool water and wrung it out then gently dabbed the cool cloth over Rhea's forehead.

An hour later, Kindra made her way to the sitting room where a dainty cherry wood desk stood. She picked up a sheet of parchment paper, a letter from Grace, and read it once more. Having been at Kindra Hall nearly two months, she had a host of news to tell her sister. She sat down and pulled a crisp piece of paper from a narrow drawer, ready to answer Grace's many questions. She dipped a quill pen in the black ink well, and with a flourish she penned,

My dearest Grace.

A half hour later she stood, blowing the ink to dry it. She folded the paper in thirds and slipped it into a waiting envelope. The next time the *Sea Baron* came into port, she would send a messenger to deliver the letter to Captain Kincade. She trusted her letter would make it to Jamaica and to Cooper's Landing where Grace waited for a response.

When she stood, she felt the uncomfortable pull of her tight day dress. She had just gone back to her bedchamber to ring for Mayme to help her change when Denzel silently walked into their room.

"There you are," he said, crossing the floor to where she stood gazing at the multitude of gowns in the wardrobe. "What are you doing?"

"I can't breathe," Kindra said, her hands embracing her tummy.

Denzel stood back and stared at her midriff that was growing rounder every day. "You may need a trip to town to visit a seamstress." He came and stood behind her and wrapped his arms around her. His large hands cupped her abdomen while he nuzzled her neck.

"I believe you're right." Kindra let herself lean against her husband's hard chest, her head resting just below his chin. She placed her hands on top of his. "I'm fat." She grinned, seeing the two of them reflected in the mirror.

"You're beautiful, that's what you are." He kissed the top of her head.

"Thank you, my love." She turned and traced the line of his face with her forefinger. "How are things going?" she asked.

"As well as can be expected. The last two months have been rough. Not just on me, but the field hands too. They're bearing the brunt of things since we've arrived. There's a tug of war going on. And the only one who can win is me."

"Oh, Denzel. Be careful."

"I can handle it. One of the field hands and I spent the morning riding the horses out to all four corners of the grounds." He smiled. "You have quite an estate, Mrs. Talmaze."

"You've already done that. Why the second ride?"

"I want to make sure the fence lines are secure. And I wanted Ebenezer to make the rounds with me."

"Ebenezer?"

"He works the curing process in the large barn out there. A good man. I trust him."

Kindra slipped out of Denzel's hold and turned back to the wardrobe closet. She pulled out a pale green day dress and held it up to examine it. "I think I'll put this on instead." She glanced at her man with his large clumsy hands. "Unbutton me."

"Be glad to." He gave her a sly grin. "I came up to tell you dinner's nearly ready, but maybe that can wait," he said in a low voice, as he fumbled with the tiny buttons.

"Help me get dressed and then you have to skedaddle. I'll not have the house whispering about us." Kindra sounded bossy, but the dimple in her cheek indented a bit deeper as she smiled.

SIXTEEN

THE AFTERNOON MEAL looked more like a state dinner than a casual noon meal. Stanley and Ava Bernard sat at the head of the table, stiff-necked, having reached the table before Denzel and Kindra. The Bernard children flanked the east side of the table, their hands on their laps. Three pairs of eyes wandered from their parents to Denzel and Kindra and back to their parents as if waiting for an announcement.

Denzel sat at the end of the table near the kitchen door with Kindra at his right. Before today Stanley had rarely made an appearance for the noon meal, and Ava had continued to take her dinner in her room. So why had they made their appearance today? Kindra wondered. Was there a reason they decided to eat together or was it just a coincidence?

Kindra glanced at Denzel, glad that he was sitting tall, formidable and assured, reminding her that he rarely let anything ruffle his feathers.

The kitchen door swung open as Clara and Louiza breezed into the dining room, their hands filled with platters of food.

"You may begin by serving here," Stanley said. His eyes held the cook as if challenging her to do otherwise.

Clara stalled a fraction of a second when she eyed the full table. She glanced first at the foreman and then Denzel. A terrified look crossed her face as she obviously was at a loss as to whom she should serve first.

Denzel cleared his throat and smiled at the cook. "Smells good," he said, leaning back so that Clara could lean in to slip a steaming cut of smoked cod onto his plate. She immediately moved over to Kindra and did the same. From there, she moved to the head of the table and served the Bernards.

Louiza followed Clara's lead and set a small plate of salad greens before Denzel and moved on around the table.

Stanley snapped his napkin open, spread it on his lap and cleared his throat as the cooks brought out the rolls and jams.

"You shoulda served my father first," Chad said to Clara, his brows puckered together.

"Hush, son," Stanley said.

For the next few minutes the only sound that echoed through the dining chamber was the scraping of utensils on china plates. Stanley finished first. He wiped his mouth with the linen napkin and threw it on the table just past his plate. He stood and eyed Denzel before he took his leave.

Kinda dressed down as much as she could while attending to the mundane tasks of the estate, but most of the gowns she brought with her had been purchased by her mother. She hadn't too many dresses that were plain.

Her outer beauty served her well, but it was her inner person that overrode her outer appearance. Many women who were lovely to look at had little inner beauty. But with Kindra, this wasn't so. She went about Kindra Hall with a lightheartedness that grew on the servants. Those who had feared her when she first arrived had learned to relax when they were able to get to know the new mistress.

Ava, on the other hand, a beauty as well, with golden curls and an ivory complexion, spoke with a sharp tongue. She rarely had a good word for the servants. It wasn't long before the allegiance to the foreman's wife had switched to the mistress of the estate.

Ava missed none of this. The few times she and Kindra had occasion to be in each other's company, Ava looked down at Kindra as though she were one of the slaves. Not once had Ava called Kindra by her given name. And now the foreman's wife was jealous that the black woman had stolen her place. The tension in the Great House heightened.

Kindra hadn't known what it was like to feel black at Cooper's Landing. Having lived in the Great House there, she had been treated with as much respect as any of the white residents on the plantation.

Kindra loved hearing the story of her mother coming to Cooper's Landing and she never tired of hearing it during her growing years. Knowing she had African blood from her ancestors, she was grateful that fate had landed her on one of the most prosperous plantations in the Caribbean. Now sitting in the warm sun of the gentle Caribbean day, Kindra once again recalled the details of the story her mother, Tia, had so often told.

Tia knew what it was like being a darkie and a slave from the days before she was brought to Cooper's Landing. Her former master was known for his horrid treatment of the slaves because they were simply property to him, not human beings. If it hadn't been for the deadly plague that had killed far too many field hands who worked his crops, Tia would still be there.

Her owner couldn't keep up with the demands of producing sugar cane for export to pay the mortgage, feed the slaves, and manage the cost of supplies to run his plantation. He soon had to auction off his slaves to keep from losing everything.

One day Phillip Cooper drove up to that dreadful place with a long line of wagons. He appeared to be a prominent man of high society and wealth. He stepped from the carriage that held the Cooper coat of arms on each side, with *grandeur*. Walking over to her cruel master he said, "I've come to purchase your slaves. I will buy them all."

The man nearly tripped over himself when Master Cooper announced that he'd buy the whole lot that stood before the auction block–some, naked–bedraggled and bearing the scars of frequent beatings. They were a sorry-looking lot, at best.

Beside Master Cooper stood a young boy who climbed down from the grand carriage to watch. Phillip Cooper put his hand on the boy's shoulder and guided him toward the slaves as he eyed them, measuring their worth.

The confident man walked up to the slaves and smiled kindly. He squinted in the bright sunlight and walked among the black men and women, nodding here and again, sometimes lifting a gentle hand to the shoulder of a black man saying, "You'll do just fine."

When Phillip walked up to Tia, he looked down at her bare breasts, removed his vest and covered her. Their eyes held for only a moment before he moved on, but Tia knew at that moment life was going to change for the better.

The young white boy left Master Cooper's side and wandered among the colored children, his eyes wide. He came to a black boy who appeared to be his age. The two boys stared at each other, their eyes lighting up. The black boy smiled and showed a row of white even teeth. Before long the two boys giggled.

Master Cooper strode up to them. "What are you doing, son?" he asked the boy who'd come with him.

The boy raised his shoulders, then dropped them.

"Get back into the coach and stay there," said Master Cooper.

"Can he come with me?" The young boy stopped next to the slave boy.

"You know you don't play with slave children."

"But I don't have anyone to play with." The young boy hung his head.

Master Cooper stood gaping at the two boys. He shook his head but said, "Come," to the black boy. "You can sit in the carriage with Camp."

The young slave seemed unsure as he moved away from his people, and the other children watched with curious stares.

"What's your name, child?" Phillip Cooper asked.

"Denzel."

Master Cooper nodded toward the small white boy. "This is Cameron. We call him 'Camp.'"

The boys grinned and giggled again.

"In you go." Master Cooper helped the boys into the coach, then walked back to the former slave master. The plantation owner was given his money and the slaves were loaded onto the wagons.

The ride to Cooper's Landing was bumpy as the wagons rattled on the uneven roads for the next three hours. When Cooper's Landing came into view it was like a dream to Tia. The plantation was fresh and new, with hundreds of acres of raw land waiting to be planted with sugar cane and other crops.

Piles of canvas lay to one side of the property. The new master told the men and women to set to work making tents for them to live in until their shanties were built. The slave quarters would be set to the east of the Great House.

After months of setting up the shanties and planting the crops, the construction of the Great House was finally finished and a new mistress was brought to the home. Olivia Cooper stayed for several months, but the longer she stayed, the duller her countenance grew. She couldn't tolerate the heat and humidity. The beautiful woman was also bored within an inch of her life.

Philip Cooper had constructed the grandest home on the island of Jamaica, yet his wife was unhappy. Bound to the land to make it prosper, he seemed not to notice. Life couldn't have been more wonderful for him with his bride in the Great House, the crops growing lush and green on the hundreds of acres. There was a bounce to his step as he went about the business of overseeing the sugar cane plantation.

Young Cameron followed him like a shadow. But the mistress was often found in her bed moping, and soon her features paled. She was sick half the day before she roused herself from bed.

Then one day Olivia Cooper was gone. She sailed back to Charleston, South Carolina on one of the master's ships, never to be seen again.

Some of the slaves detested their new master. They wanted nothing more than to go back to their native land in Africa. It didn't matter that he had nothing to do with their captivity before coming to Jamaica. They were not free. They worked long, back-breaking days cultivating the fields and planting the sugar cane. And though they lived a better lifestyle than before, still they hated him.

On the other hand, there were many who had come to respect Phillip Cooper like none other. They did what they could to please him in return for the grace and mercy he extended to their people. When his countenance fell in confusion and hurt after the mistress fled, they did what they could to make his day brighter. They worked harder in the fields, the cooks went out of their way to make fancier meals, and the darkies lifted their eyes and smiled whenever he passed by. But nothing could make their master happy.

After the mistress fled the island, Phillip Cooper sailed away on his merchant ship. He was gone for long periods at a time. When he was home Tia encouraged him to visit her shanty. He had taken special notice of her and had asked where she got her beautiful crystal blue eyes.

But the truth was, Tia didn't know where she got them. She was sold from her native land at a very young age and separated from her family. She didn't know who her father was and her mother never said. She was young but not naive. She knew she could lure the master to her shanty. And she knew how to take the cares of the world from him for just a while.

He would come for a few evenings then he would sail away again. While he was gone the plantation seemed to lie in wait for the master to return, the same as the sugar cane waited for the sun after a long rain storm.

"And that's how you got me!" Kindra remembered saying the first time she heard the story as a child.

"Yes," her mother had replied "That's how you came to be." Tia had pulled a young Kindra into her arms. "And the master brought us into the big fancy house to live forever after that."

Although there had been a definite distinction between the black servants of the house and her mother, who became the domestic headmistress, Kindra had noticed something about herself while growing up. She had been treated just the same as white people. She had worn English clothes and English hair styles. Even though her hair was tightly curled like many of the colored girls her age, the chambermaid took the hot iron to make it long and straight.

Still, something had been lacking over the years. Her father had rarely made eye contact with her and her mother often made her keep quiet and out of sight when her father had been home. And then one day, after she was grown, her father died leaving behind a void in her life.

Now, standing in this house here in Barbados, grand and beautiful, Kindra knew he had loved her.

Now, if only she could walk from room to room without Ava's eyes boring into hers, ever threatening, ever hateful.

Stepping into the foyer, Kindra heard voices on the front porch. Thinking nothing of it, she moved toward the door to join in, thinking it was Denzel and Stanley speaking. She jerked her head back when she saw a stranger standing to the side, Stanley leaning close to the man in a conspiratorial way. Their voices lowered and Kindra tilted her head, straining to listen.

"What's that you say?" asked the stranger.

"You heard me. Darkies have come to rob me of my rights to this plantation. I mean to set things straight."

"What's come over you, Stanley? You and I both know darkies can't own a plantation. Kick both of their backsides off of this land. You aren't the one to go."

"That's just it. They have legal documentation proving they own this land. The prissy little black gal is the daughter of the man who built this estate. Now will you help me or not?"

The stranger rubbed his chin and glanced about him. "You say you got another drop of tobacco 'bout ready for the shipyards?"

"That's right. I've got to figure out a way to get the shipment ready without the new owner finding out some of it needs to be shipped out on another merchant boat. From what I understand, he has his own ship as well."

"What? He owns a ship, too? How can that be?" The stranger scratched the back of his neck and looked disgusted.

"Her father not only left the estate to her, he gave her a merchant ship, too. When I found that out, I knew I was sunk."

"How long before your next load be ready?"

"Two, maybe three days." It got deathly quiet as the two men stood staring at each other.

"All right, listen up," the man said, and he glanced toward the house.

Kindra continued to listen, but edged away from the door a little more. She stood to one side, her heart pounding. Was Mr. Bernard exporting tobacco for his own profit?

"I'll see what I can do," the man said.

"Good. Don't send word to the estate. I know how to reach you. Good day."

The stranger descended the steps and mounted his horse. Stanley stood for a moment, waiting. Then he, too, descended the steps and rounded the house to the outbuildings behind.

Kindra watched as the stranger trotted down the long lane away from her home. *Good Lord,* she thought, *I've got to find Denzel.*

SEVENTEEN

5 June, 1831

LIKE OIL AND water, the two families could not run Kindra Hall and the tobacco plantation effectively. The time had come to tell the Bernards they would have to go. Denzel knew there was no delicate way to make this known. He knew in his mind and heart, that today was the day.

Denzel strode out to the curing barn and found Ebenezer carrying an armload of tobacco leaves to a work bench. He set them down for the workers to thread together before they hung them in the rafters. Turning, Ebenezer stopped and stared at Denzel.

"Good morning, Eb." Denzel waved him away from the bench. When the two men stepped outside the barn in the shade of the tamarind trees, Denzel put his hand on Ebenezer's shoulder.

"Things are going to change today," Denzel said.

Ebenezer raised his thick black brows. "How so?"

"I'm appointing you as the new overseer."

Ebenezer pushed his straw hat off his short black hair and gazed at Denzel. "All right." Both his hands went to his hips and he glanced about their surroundings. "Whut 'bout Mr. Lee?"

"He goes. I'm talking to him next."

"You sho' this is gonna work?" Ebenezer licked his lips. Denzel saw a trace of nervousness tinge his eyes.

"Ebenezer," Denzel said, "You can do it. I've watched you. You have what it takes to oversee these people. I wouldn't have appointed you for the job if I didn't think you could do it."

"I ain't doubtin' that, suh." Ebenezer glanced at the curing barn then out to the fields. "But, I sho' don' think you can make Mister Lee leave this place. He been overseer since the tobacco fields wuz first planted."

Denzel's smile was easy. "Watch me."

"You best be watchin' yer back, Massa. He's a mean, evil man who don' take nuthin' off nobody. Be more slaves on this plantation with his mark on their backs than not."

"And you? Do you have a mark on your back?" Denzel asked.

"Yessuh. He dun whup me when I first come to Kindra Hall. I learned ta work fast and don' be droppin' nuthin' when he be 'round."

"Dirty scoundrel! There won't be any more of that kind of abuse on this plantation. You can count on it." Denzel pulled a handkerchief from his pocket and wiped the sweat off his face. The air was hot and humid, so hot that the parrots and popinjays in the trees had ceased their squawking.

"By the way," Denzel swung around to gaze out to the fields where the slaves bent under the hot sun, "I'm putting Jasper as your second in command." Denzel clapped Ebenezer's shoulder then pulled his straw hat down over his sweaty forehead and went in search of Mr. Lee.

When Denzel turned the corner of the stable, he found the hawk-faced Lee behind the building, a bottle of rum in his hand. His thin frame leaned at an angle, his shoulder pressed against the wooden barn while his long legs stretched out as if he were holding up the structure. From the look on his face, it was obvious Denzel had caught him off guard. He had just taken a swig and was wiping drool from his mouth.

Mr. Lee held out the bottle to Denzel. "The day is stinkin' hot," he slurred. "Have a drink."

Denzel took the glass bottle and tossed it to the ground.

"Hey, what'd you do that for?" Zane Lee pushed away from the building and bent to pick up what was left of the bottle.

"Leave it." Denzel nudged the bottle away with the toe of his boot. "You've got other pressing matters to deal with right now."

Mr. Lee, still bent over, looked up at Denzel. "I'm really sick and tired of you telling me what to do, you dirty blackie!" In a flash he straightened and lunged toward Denzel, his face contorted.

Denzel stepped aside in time to dodge Lee. The overseer stumbled past him and swerved around, swaying like a willow in the wind.

"Today's your lucky day, Mister Lee," Denzel said, standing tall and sturdy.

"What do you mean by that?" Lee straightened as best he could.

"You're fired. Pack up your things and hit the road."

"You can't tell me what to do!" Lee's face screwed. He spat at Denzel's feet.

"This is my land, mister. I don't want the likes of you crawling around on it. Now move it. Pack your stuff and get off my land."

Lee kicked the glass bottle and it whizzed past Denzel's side, then thudded against a building behind him. "I'm sick of this place. And I'm sick of you!" He raised a fist. When he drew near, Denzel's hand flew up. He grasped Lee's hand and twisted it up behind his back. He held it there while Lee groaned.

Denzel shoved him. "I meant what I said. Git!"

Lee swaggered away, taking off his straw hat. He beat it against his pant leg. Then he disappeared beyond the building. Ten minutes later, Lee rode out on a horse, a pack on its back. Denzel watched the horse's hooves kick up dust as it picked up speed.

"One down, five to go," Denzel murmured. He glanced at the house and then the tobacco field. Stanley Bernard and his bunch were next.

The confrontation with the belligerent overseer gave Denzel the determination he needed to keep going. Before the day was out, he wanted to walk this land without looking over his shoulder. Denzel marched out to the main drive and asked Jasper, "Where's the foreman?"

"Out to de fields, last time I see him, suh. He prob'ly comin' back in 'fore too long."

"Thanks. Lee's gone. You'll be working with Ebenezer. He's the new overseer. You'll help by keeping an eye on the workers in the tobacco fields."

Jasper's dark brows went up. He pointed at himself. "Me, an overseer?"

"That's right. Second in command. Ebenezer's in charge of the tobacco process now."

A wide grin spread across the young man's face, his eyes shining bright.

"Go on," Denzel said, clapping the man's back.

"Yes, suh!" Jasper walked out toward the tobacco fields, a jaunt in his step.

In the distance, Denzel could see dust rising from Stanley Bernard's horse. He took a deep breath and strode forward.

Moments later, the foreman rode up to where Denzel stood.

"I need to talk to you," Denzel said, signaling for the man to get off his horse.

Bernard dismounted and shoved his hat off his forehead. "What's on your mind, Talmaze?"

"I don't think it's any surprise that our two families can't live under the same roof."

"I was expecting you to say something before too long." He chewed his bottom lip. "So what're you saying?"

"I'm saying it's high time you find a job elsewhere. You've done good by Phillip Cooper. But now that his daughter has come to claim her rightful inheritance, it's time for you folks to move on."

"Now you just wait a minute." Bernard lifted his shoulders in defense, his eyes growing dark. "You can't make us leave."

"There's been a rift between our wives from the day we arrived. This is my wife's home. There can only be one mistress of the house."

What Denzel didn't say was that Kindra had overheard Bernard and a stranger talking on the front porch of the Great House. He'd been suspicious of Bernard from the first day he arrived. He didn't need a foreman who was bold enough to steal their crop and make a profit behind their backs. He knew now that Bernard's interest in the tobacco export wasn't just in ensuring that Phillip Cooper's investment would see good gains. It hit closer to home. Bernard was taking a cut out of the tobacco exports for himself. Denzel couldn't prove it yet, but his gut told him he'd find out the truth.

"I've been here since day one," Bernard said. "It was me who was responsible for the success of this land. I'm the one who foresaw all the angles it would take to make Phillip Cooper proud of this place. And if he was alive, he'd not stand back and let a darkie kick me off this plantation!"

"Think what you like. It's time for you to call it quits." Denzel stood his ground, teeth clenched, hands on his hips. "When I first arrived on the island, I had plans to write up a recommendation for you. You would have had something to take with you when you applied for work elsewhere." Denzel glared at the man. "But I've had second thoughts. Pack up your brood and get off my land."

Bernard spat on the ground. "I would never accept a recommendation from a blackie."

"Well then, you've got your notice. Get off this plantation and don't look back."

Stanley Bernard hung his head as if a storm were brewing. At long last he let out a deep breath. "Give me time to find a place to live," he finally said. "I don't know how soon I can accomplish that. It could take a month." His eyes smoldered.

"You've got three days. No longer."

Bernard's eyes flashed with anger as he brushed past Denzel. "You'll be sorry you ever set foot on this land," he threatened as he stormed to the house.

When Denzel glanced at the curing barn, where the workers were standing like statues in the humid heat. When they realized Denzel was watching them, they jumped back to their duties. He didn't miss the surprised look on some of the workers faces, nor the flash of white teeth as other slaves grinned. Only their eyes moved as they watched the foreman stride away.

He also hadn't missed the scowls on the slaves who hadn't shown him respect from the first day he arrived. These men held a hatred for him. He felt it daily. And he knew why. How could a black man own slaves? They'd never heard of such a thing. Yet Denzel had heard that black men owned large plantations in the South, in America. Some of those black men had more slaves than white plantation owners. Yet here, it was unspeakable.

Denzel didn't think for a minute that all his troubles were over. He knew little about the men who worked the plantation, even less about their families. He'd take it slow. That he was a black man who owned this estate was a twist of fate for many of these men. Did they believe he could run this plantation without a white man telling him what to do? Only time would tell. One thing was for certain, though. He wasn't a white man. Owning people for material gain grated on him. He had never liked the fact that he wasn't his own man. Marrying Kindra had changed all that. He was his own man now. There had to be a way to give the people he owned self-respect. He'd check on their living conditions and make sure they had what they needed. He'd set his course working on that.

Pulling himself away from his thoughts, he glanced at the house. He'd better get in there. No sense leaving Kindra to bear the brunt of the Bernards discontent. Things were sure to get worse before they got better. Three days. That's all he'd given the Bernards. After that he'd kick their carcasses out on the road.

EIGHTEEN

A HUSH FELL over the crowd. Denzel had their attention. "This is the eve of a new beginning." His eyes roved over the vast assembly. Inside the barn, workers sat on the dirt floor, on bales of hay, and in the rafters. Some were slaves, others were indentured servants. They were a mix of men and women, young and old. Those who couldn't fit inside the barn stood or sat on the ground outside the wide double doors listening to the new owner speak.

"Mister and Missus Bernard no longer live on the grounds of Kindra Hall. Mister Lee is gone as well." Denzel heard a low rumble among the people—exhaling a sigh of relief, knowing the dreaded overseers were out of their lives for good. Heads bobbed, necks craned, some eyes lit in response while others wore a mask—as if suspicious of the turn of events.

"Ebenezer is now the new overseer, and I've appointed Jasper as his second in command. You'll answer to Ebenezer. Do you understand?" Heads nodded in agreement. "Other than that, nothing else has changed. You'll continue to work the jobs you've been assigned in the past. If you do have questions, take them to Ebenezer, and he'll bring them to me." Denzel wondered if his voice captured respect.

A low hum reverberated up to the rafters and out to the clearing where workers waited for more, some grumbling in protest that things hadn't really changed so much. They were still slaves weren't they?

"I am not a man given to beating slaves with a whip. For those of you who have scars on your backs, trust me when I tell you that beatings are now a thing of the past."

Men hooted and women squealed in delight. The dull eyes of some of the slaves focused more clearly now.

"That is not to say, however, that I will tolerate indifference to your jobs. You do your work and you will be treated fairly. There *will be* discipline should you falter or create a spirit of rebellion. Is that understood?"

The barn rumbled with the hum of voices. The air was hot and humid, and Denzel had no plans to detain the workers any longer than needed.

"Are there any questions?"

"Yes, Massa," came a voice high in the rafters.

"Let me hear it."

"How come you bein' a black man, you hab de right to own dis here plantation and be a massa?" It seemed this man had voiced a question that had gone through the grapevine of all the slaves on the grounds of Kindra Hall. Restlessness stirred throughout the crowd, both those inside and those standing outside the double doors.

"That's a good question." Denzel paused until the low hum came to a stop.

"My father-in-law was the late Master Phillip Cooper. I know that many of you saw him from time to time when he came to inspect the progress of the tobacco yields. He was a white man and owned this plantation. His daughter, Kindra, in whose honor this estate was named, became my wife."

"But she be black too!" shouted someone deep in the crowd.

"That she is. Still, she *is* Phillip Cooper's daughter."

"Then, Massa Coopah no better than the other plantation owners who help themselves to our women," shouted another.

"The conversation stops here!" Denzel bellowed. "Phillip Cooper was a good man and I'll not listen to anything different. He did right by his slaves when other plantation owners did not. He loved Kindra's mother and he did right by her. I witnessed that with my very own eyes. I won't listen to anyone who intends to taint his honor. That will be all. You're dismissed."

Denzel strode out of the barn, clapping a few workers on the shoulders as he skirted the crowd to head back to the house. Glad this was behind him, Denzel was ready to relax for the evening. Still, the tension edged his nerves. He found himself wondering how long he could hold back those slaves who might rebel. They didn't like having a black man owning the plantation. They'd made that loud and clear in the looks they sent his way. He hoped things would simmer down in the next few days. The last thing he needed was an angry mob on his hands.

Just then Ebenezer strode up from behind and said, "Don' pay no mind to those men."

"I don't," Denzel said. "I expected as much. But it's behind us now."

"We be loadin' the wagons in the mo'nin' and takin' tobacco to the harbor."

"I'll ride out with you. We'll load this shipment on the *Sea Baron*."

"Yessuh."

"Good night, Ebenezer."

"Good night, suh."

Secrets were not an option on Barbados. What happened at Kindra Hall was soon known in every establishment throughout Bridgetown, every home of high society, and every lowly hovel on the island. What occurred when Denzel, a black plantation owner, kicked two white men off his tobacco plantation, would become common knowledge all over town. It wouldn't be long before the people shouted or whispered their disdain.

Stevedores began loading the ship with Kindra Hall's top quality tobacco. While bales of tobacco went up the gangplank, cotton bales came down, bound for looms and weavers in warehouses in Bridgetown. Shouts and calls echoed from the hold in the ship as the aromatic tobacco was hauled below deck and stored.

The wharf was alive with wagons and carriages clattering on the road. At one point, Denzel thought he spied Stanley Bernard hanging about, watching the commotion on the dock. Though annoyed that the man could not bear to stay away, Denzel had no say in the matter of the man's comings or goings.

The narrow road along the wharf was crammed with an assortment of wagons and donkey carts hauling supplies, their drivers calling out for people to get out of the way. Dogs barked and ran between wheels, dodging pedestrians and sniffing crates of smelly fish. Civilians and dock loaders alike called out to each other, the noise building. Plantation owners congregated before the alehouse as they watched their goods being loaded for export.

Ebenezer came and stood beside Denzel. "Mr. Bernard be heah."

"I saw him."

"He be wishin' he was in charge."

"I know."

"He be losin' money today."

Denzel shot Ebenezer a glance. "You knew he was stealing money from Kindra Hall?"

"I knew. But it weren't fer me to say. He'da sic Mista Lee and his whip on mah scarred back."

"Which one of these ships had a hand in his operation?"

"It be that one over there." Ebenezer pointed to a vessel named the *Caribbean King*.

"Captain Jule Spade's vessel." Denzel let out a deep breath. "Well, Bernard's thieving days are over. You make sure every bale be loaded onto the *Sea Baron*. He won't be skimming off our crop anymore."

"Sho' nuff, boss." Ebenezer gazed at the group of men standing in front of the tavern.

Denzel followed his gaze.

"Them be yer competition," Ebenezer lifted his chin toward the men.

"Do you know any of them?"

"Not person'ly." He looked away and eyed the bales of tobacco going up the gangplank and then looked back to Denzel. "There be a convention next week fer all the tobacco plantation owners. All the rich folks gather and talk about their yields."

"Oh?" Denzel eyed the men out of curiosity. "Where's it held?"

"It be held at one of them uppity men's estate, Massa Shelton Rumball. He got a big house. Big nuff it hold jist 'bout all the people of Bridgetown and the country folks too. They bring in the fiddles an' banjos an' party all night."

"So is this by invitation?" Denzel shoved his hands in his pockets and rocked on his heels.

"Don' know 'bout that. All I be knowin' is Massa Bernard an' his missus always 'tend the party each year. Don' know 'bout this year."

"Hmm." Denzel eyed the men again.

"Course, tobacca buyers didn't come lookin' and smellin' yer tobacca this week."

"What are you talking about?"

"This be the season fer buyers interested in purchasin' tobacca from suppliers, come out to the plantations an' check out yer blend. Iffen they want it, they draw up a contract and you ship to them. Buyers usually stay on the island fer a week, sometimes two, combin' the tobacca plantations on the island. Massa Bernard gen'rally make contracts with new buyers every year, increase the demand fer more work outta the people."

"And . . . now he won't have a hand in that either," Denzel said, more to himself than Ebenezer.

"Thing is," Ebenezer said, "ain't nobody come lookin' at the tobacca fields this time."

"You suppose Bernard had a hand in that?"

"No doubt 'bout it. You be hard put to get new contracts, you bein' a colored an' all."

"That may be the case this year, but that'll change next year. Buyers want good tobacco for their cigars. Our tobacco is a darned good quality blend. We can beat the competition."

"That soun' mighty fine, Massa. Mighty fine." Ebenezer moved out of the way as several dock loaders moved past them with large bales of tobacco on their shoulders. "I best check on the stacking in the hold."

"Go ahead. I'll talk to you later." Denzel went to the main deck in search of the captain. On his way, he glanced over the rail at the group of men standing before the tavern. Somehow, he didn't think he and Kindra would be invited to the tobacco convention. Maybe that would have to wait till next year too.

Kindra sat by old Rhea's bed with a white enamel bowl of cool water and a clean cloth bathing the elderly woman's forehead and face. The doctor had come and gone, promising to come back to look in on Rhea again in a few hours.

Kindra's back ached from sitting in the same position, leaning over the sick patient, but she refused to leave Rhea's side as long as she was awake tossing and turning. By midmorning, the doctor had given Rhea a sedative to help her sleep, promising to look in on her again in a few hours.

An hour later, Mayme tapped on the door and entered without waiting for a reply. "How is she, Miz Kindra?"

"She hasn't improved. In fact, I think she's getting worse," she whispered.

"Can she sip some broth?" Mayme held out a hot mug containing the clear liquid.

"No. She isn't awake. You might try later." Kindra leaned sideways and twisted, trying to get the kinks out of her back.

"Miz Kindra." Mayme stopped Kindra's hand as Kindra lifted the wet cloth from the tepid water. "I don't believe you should be down here with the maid sick as she is."

That was the second warning this morning, but Kindra only said, "Nonsense." and she continued to gently press the cloth to Rhea's burning skin.

"I've come to relieve you. You need to rest, ma'am."

Kindra clamped her mouth shut and dropped the hot cloth into the pan of lukewarm water.

"All right." She stood and bent sideways again, feeling stiff from head to toe. "I'll send down a pitcher of cold water."

"Ma'am." Mayme touched her arm softly. "Don't come back. I fear for the baby." Mayme glanced at Kindra's swollen tummy. "You have someone beside yourself to think about."

Deep down, Kindra knew the young girl was right. She laid a hand on Mayme's shoulder and said, "Thank you. I will send someone to relieve you in a while."

"Good." Mayme smiled. She leaned to where Rhea moaned in the bed.

Kindra gave Rhea one last glance, moved out of the dim room, and shut the door. When she climbed the servant's stairs and reached the main floor, she noticed the house was filled with a delightful confectionary scent coming from the kitchen. What a difference from the offensive odor and gloom from the room below.

She had barely set foot at the end of the hall when Clara, the cook came looking for her. "There you are," Clara said and stopped. "Are you under the weather, Miz Kindra?"

"No, Clara. I'm just tired from sitting with Rhea."

"You should leave that work for one of us."

"I know, and I will. You needed to see me?"

"Yes'm. Up till now our food deliveries be comin' from a ship at the harbor. Will you want to continue with their provisions? And might you have anythin' you'd be wantin' to add to the list?"

"Let's sit down in the dining room. We'll discuss the supplies needed. When we're done we'll give the list to Captain Kincade. He will be our new supplier."

"Duncan be the one who takes the list to the ship. He be glad to know he won't have to come face-to-face with that Scoot Sweeny no more."

"Why is that?"

"That man have no manners. He be such an angry sort that Duncan say he worse than an old weasel fightin' over a dead rat."

"Goodness." Kindra shook her head. "He'll like Barnabas just fine. The man is big and strong as an ox, but he's gentle as a lamb."

Kindra had now been at Kindra Hall longer than she'd been out to sea. And though she missed Grace dreadfully, and Cooper's Landing, she had no desire to go back to Jamaica. She found she enjoyed exploring each new aspect of this exotic island, and was thrilled each time she found something she hadn't known before. Colorful parrots and popinjays squawked in trees, making it difficult to ignore them. Though they were loud, she enjoyed watching their antics as they turned their heads every which way as if listening to the humans below.

The trees on the island were exotic, many with trunks that looked tangled and twisted. And there were tall palms and palmettoes that graced the land, ever beautiful. She especially loved the splash of color from the large variety of flowers that perfumed the island at every turn.

Though the lay of the land was breathtaking, the people were another matter. She had a tall hill to climb if she were to gain the respect of these islanders, for they had never seen a black man or woman own a plantation. The business proprietors looked down on her when she visited their shops. The scowls on their faces told her how the people felt about her, and their scathing remarks stung. All because she was black and did not dress as a pauper. Or more so, because she was black and wealthy, and owned a prosperous plantation. The white people didn't think kindly of this and had no desire to treat her or Denzel with respect.

Word traveled fast and she suspected the Bernards were at the core of it. It seemed the townspeople knew who she and Denzel were before they set foot inside an establishment. How long it would take to gain the town's respect, she didn't know, but this was her home now and she wasn't leaving.

Ten days later, a carriage sent dust flying up the long drive as a visitor neared the Great House. Kindra had just arisen from her writing desk when she peered out the window and observed a horse trotting up the lane.

Boaz opened the carriage door and waited as an old woman climbed down and headed toward the wide porch. Kindra recognized her at once and flew out the door.

"Missus Cavendish, how are you!" Kindra brushed past Boaz and hooked her arms with those of the genteel woman.

"I'm doing well," she said, taking the steep steps slow, her cane tapping the stone with each step. When they reached the porch, Agnes Cavendish stopped and glanced at Kindra from head to toe, her eyes slowing a moment at the swell in her midriff. "You look the picture of health I must say."

"It's so good to see you." Kindra couldn't stop herself. She gave the older woman a hug and pulled her into the house.

Netty, the house maid stopped to observe the commotion with her usual disdain. "Netty, tell Louiza to set up a tray of island punch and cookies, and please bring them into the sitting room," Kindra ordered.

"Right away, Miz Kindra." She frowned, but stepped through the dining room and disappeared into the kitchen without comment.

"Come. Have a seat," Kindra said as she guided her family friend to an armchair.

"I've wanted to come long before now, but I've been so busy in Charleston, I couldn't get away. But now I'm here and anxious to see how you're getting along."

Netty appeared with a silver tray and set it on a table between them. She poured a glass of island juice for both women and set the iced pitcher on the tray. Once done, her eyes lowered to the floor, her lips formed a thin line.

"Thank you, Netty. That will be all."

"Yes, ma'am." Netty nodded slightly and left the room.

"Grace told me you have a tobacco plantation here in Barbados," Kindra said. "Is that the reason you've come?"

"Yes and no. To be exact, I'm here for the tobacco convention that is held annually on the island."

"Denzel mentioned the convention. Apparently, we're not invited to the party."

"Fiddlesticks. All of the plantation owners are expected to attend this event. An invitation isn't always extended. It's expected."

"Really?" asked Kindra.

"Yes, of course. I didn't receive a personal invitation. I just show up like everyone else."

"Goodness. The party is in three days and I've done nothing to prepare for it." Kindra scooted to the edge of her seat.

"I've seen your gowns, my dear. You're always prepared," Agnes said with an encouraging smile.

"Truth to tell, Missus Cavendish, I'm not certain the plantation owners will welcome Denzel and me to the festivities, being black, I mean."

"Hogwash! You're a plantation owner. You should go. I'll be there. You can sit with me." Agnes patted Kindra's hand. "I can introduce you to some of the ladies on the island."

"Then it's settled. We'll come." Yet somehow, Kindra felt they shouldn't go. *Can any good come of it?*

NINETEEN

LONG BEFORE KINDRA reached the Rumball house, she noticed a glimmer over the long drive that bathed the area in the golden fires of torch and candle. Cattails and reeds, bound together and soaked in pitch, were staked at arms-length intervals along the wide drive. She watched as the flames burned slowly, providing a thick, smoky illumination.

The sound of carriage wheels and horses prancing toward the house echoed loudly as a continuous line of plantation owners arrived at Shelton Rumball's large estate. The lane leading to the grandiose hall was covered with bits and pieces of abalone shells, crushed and ground in hopes of keeping the ever-troubling dust down. They sparkled, glinting in light of the torches.

Kindra's stomach was in knots as she glanced out the window at the endless line of open carriages, elegant buggies and fancy prams. Drivers in white starched shirts and black jackets guided the horses to the front entrance where butlers and maids waited to retrieve hats and outer apparel from men who were dressed exquisitely in suits too thick for the island's humidity and heat; and women dressed in lavish gowns.

Kindra glanced down at her pale green gown with its modest ivy pattern edging the underskirt and overskirt. Double layers of pink eyelet embroidery set off the low, dropped-shoulder neckline and pink eyelet bows trimmed the short sleeves. She fingered the semi-precious gemstone necklace that hung in double rows, one near her throat and the other just above the lace neckline of her dress. Pearl-drop earrings with tiny green gemstones sparkled at her ears.

A pale green and pearl-colored shell comb held her mass of black hair off her neck. Mayme had fussed and worked to style Kindra's hair in the latest fashion, piling it high with tendrils curling at the nape of her neck, before her ears, and at her forehead.

Kindra was grateful for the white gloves she wore. Her palms were sweaty from the attack of nerves that assaulted her at this moment. Even at Cooper's Landing, she could not recall so many people congregating in one place at one time, though she knew that her father, Phillip Cooper, had held many such events to gather the planters together to celebrate the crop's harvest.

The difference was that *before* no one *cared* if she made an appearance. But tonight she and Denzel not only needed to make their debut as new plantation owners to Barbados, they also needed to join the planters in celebrating the mutual yield of tobacco crops. The carriage driver opened the door and held out his hand. Kindra glanced back at Denzel for reassurance before she stepped outside and waited for him.

"You are the most beautiful woman at the ball," Denzel whispered in her ear as he came to stand by her.

"Thank you, my love." Try as she might, she could not settle the flutter of butterflies that had taken residence in her stomach.

Denzel pulled her gloved hand through the crook of his arm and led her up the flowered pathway to the bricked steps.

The house butler nearly gasped when the couple before them went up the steps leaving Denzel and Kindra in full view for him to see.

"Uh-umm," the butler cleared his throat. Though he was a black man himself, he stared at the couple in disdain while he watched them pass by, for neither Denzel nor Kindra had anything to leave in his care, no hat, no shawl.

"Dis be a pawty for plantation owners. I believe you be at the wrong place." He took a step to block them from going any farther and his eyes dared them to step around him.

"Then we must be at the *right* place." Denzel smiled, but a slight storm brewed in his dark eyes. He put his hand at the small of Kindra's back, guiding her forward. "We are the new owners of Kindra Hall, one of the largest plantations on this island. Now if you'll excuse us." Denzel's hand gently touched the butler's arm moving him aside as he escorted Kindra forward.

The man's mouth dropped open, and the white of his eyes shone wide in his ebony face.

Kindra felt as if she were floating in a bubble toward the entrance to the house. She heard the hum of voices, and the tinkle of glasses that filled the hot evening air. When they entered the large foyer shimmering lights from a chandelier high above them lit up the area. They followed the other guests who inched their way toward the grand hall from where the sound of voices came.

An elder couple moved slowly in front of them, the woman's shoulders held high as she whispered into her husband's ear. He turned and looked over his shoulder, eyes wide. His bushy brows slanted inward, his lips pursed. "Say there. You two have come to the wrong party. You don't belong here." He waved his fingers in the air as if to brush them away.

"Right jolly of you to put these darkies in their place," said a man behind Denzel and Kindra. He looked at Denzel. "Have you lost your way, boy?" Restless commotion stirred behind him as guests shook their heads and made lewd comments about darkies at a white man's party.

Kindra loosened her hand on Denzel's arm as if to flee. But he tightened his hold on her. "Relax gentlemen." His teeth shone as he smiled. "We are at the right place." To Kindra he said, "Come darling."

Men and women gathered in small circles, some by the refreshment table, others along the sidelines of the ballroom. When Denzel and Kindra entered the spacious room, heads turned to stare. People retreated as if the newcomers were lepers and not simply black people. The party guests glanced at each other, then back to Denzel and Kindra. Kindra saw the look in their eyes, appalled at the darkies who had just arrived. Though the room was exceedingly warm, Kindra felt an inner heat radiate up her neck and over her scalp. The urge to leave overtook her. Resisting, she held her back straight and head high as she quickly searched the room for Mrs. Cavendish.

Numerous guests continued to stare as she and Denzel navigated to the side of the room to observe the many plantation owners who lived on the island.

Servants wearing stiff black coats carried silver trays laden with finely etched crystal glasses filled to the brim with red wine, rum, or island punch. Other house servants carried silver and china vessels across the polished floor, offering tea and coffee. It wasn't long, however, before Kindra realized that none of the refreshments were offered to her or Denzel.

She began to feel they had made a terrible mistake in coming to this event. As she looked out across the room she spotted plantation wives huddled together and pointing at her and Denzel, looking haughty and contemptuous as their hands concealed their mouths while they spoke.

Wanting to run, she felt Denzel's hand tighten on her arm. "Patience, my dear," he said. "We just got here."

"We shouldn't have come." She heard the quiver in her voice and tried to still the tumult in her stomach.

A tall bearded man, looking to be in his fifties, crossed the floor, a cigar in hand. "I don't believe I have met you two before. Are you at the right party?"

Denzel smiled. "If this is the event for tobacco plantation owners, I believe we are at the right place." He didn't extend his hand to the man. Everybody knew that would have been highly inappropriate. White men didn't shake hands with blacks.

The man's bushy gray eyebrows shot up. "Might you own a plantation?"

"Kindra Hall," Denzel said, proudly, tipping his head forward in a gesture.

"Kindra Hall, you say? But isn't that run by Stanley Bernard and his missus?"

"That has been the case in the past. My wife inherited the estate only recently and we have moved to the Hall."

"And what of Stanley Bernard?" The man's walrus mustache shook as he glanced around the room.

"He is seeking employment elsewhere. His services were no longer needed."

"I daresay that is quite a story. Quite a story indeed." He stared at Denzel taking in his fine clothes and then glanced to Kindra, who did all she could not to flinch under his daring gaze.

"And you are . . .?"

"Kindra Talmaze, sir."

"Wasn't Phillip Cooper the original owner of that estate?"

"Yes, sir. My father, Phillip Cooper, built the plantation for me." Her voice sounded cool, but the battle to stay put or to run waged within her.

"Well, I'll be," the man said. "I'm Shelton Rumball. This is my estate. I have to admit I was just about to run you two off my property. But in regard to Phillip Cooper, a long-time friend, and seeing you are a plantation owner, you have arrived at the right place. Though I should warn you . . . that doesn't mean one of the others won't try his hand at booting you off the grounds." He winked and glanced back to the men who congregated at the far end of the room.

Just then, Kindra spied Agnes Cavendish coming into the grand hall. She wanted to withdraw from this man and run to the old woman. Neither would be necessary as Mrs. Cavendish saw them and waved a lace handkerchief their way. She slowly crossed the floor with the help of her cane until she reached them. She stopped and said, "Well now, Mr. Rumball. I see you have met my good friends." Then she turned to admire Kindra's gown.

"You look exquisite, my dear. The color suits you well and you can barely tell you're . . . that you're . . . ."

"Thank you, Agnes," Kindra said, saving her friend from bringing up her sensitive condition at a place like this. "I've been watching for you. Shall we have a seat?"

Not until now did Denzel release Kindra's arm. With the old gal at Kindra's side, he let her go. Kindra followed Agnes to a line of chairs at one side of the ballroom. As they sat down on two of the polished wooden seats, the women around them gasped and promptly stood as if overtaken by mice. They fled to the other side of the room, putting distance between them and the black woman, parking themselves in new chairs, facing Kindra, their eyes glaring at her audacity.

"Hmmm," Agnes said. "Persnickety old women if you ask me."

"I was just about to ask Denzel if we might leave. Mr. Rumball is the only person who has spoken to us. His original intent was to make us leave at once."

Agnes surveyed the crowd in the hall and the women across the floor. "Humph! A bunch of biddies if ever I've seen one."

"Oh, Agnes we shouldn't have come." Kindra bit her lower lip.

"Maybe I misspoke when I told you to come. I should have known these ninnies would carry on like this. But don't worry, not a one of them has anything over on you."

Kindra followed Agnes' gaze to the group of women who could not remove their eyes from her. Fortunately the music soon started, which changed the atmosphere in the room. Men and women left their seats and spilled out onto the dance floor.

Mr. Rumball left Denzel's side and hurried off to the group of planters standing by the open veranda doors where a slight breeze wafted into the suffocating room. Denzel stood nearby watching the activity.

A moment later, Stanley and Ava Bernard entered the ballroom. Some of the women left their seats and greeted Ava, while Stanley, cigar in hand, sauntered across the floor to join the men.

Kindra bristled, her eyes jumping to where Denzel stood near the refreshment table speaking to a man in a suit that was not as shiny and new as most of the men's who attended the celebration. *Who is he speaking with?* she wondered.

"Well, young lady, you'll not meet a one of these uppity women sitting over here on the sidelines," Agnes frowned. "Come with me and I'll introduce you to the prominent ones that are married to owners of some of the largest estates on the island. Though I must say, not a one of them compare to the acreage you have at Kindra Hall. " She clucked her tongue and continued, "Even my plantation pales compared to yours. But I don't mind. With the cotton plantation I own in Charleston, my hands are full. It's all I can do to keep up with them, seeing as how they're at opposite ends of the globe."

"Goodness, Mrs. Cavendish, I had no idea you owned a plantation in America, as well. I would love to visit it someday."

"Oh, you will, I'm sure. Word gets around mighty fast these days. I've learned Cameron and Grace are fixing to move back to the Charleston area themselves. Likely you'll be seeing them from time to time. I will have to invite both of you women to my estate," she smiled brightly.

"Now you can judge for yourself if any of these women are worth their salt after you've made their acquaintance."

Agnes started to rise, but Kindra's hand gently clamped her frail arm. "Mrs. Cavendish! I'm not ready!" she gulped. She felt like a frightened rabbit ready to bolt and find a hole to burrow in. Never had she felt so at odds with herself. The band of women across the floor with their blatant stares unnerved her, and she would just as soon stay right where she was.

"Come, dear. You mustn't procrastinate. It'll do you more harm than good."

"All right."

On shaky legs, Kindra stood. She took a moment to brush the wrinkles from her gown and then let the old woman take the lead. As they crossed the room, threading their way between guests who had taken to the floor, she felt her ears ringing. Never before had she experienced such a feeling of helplessness. She wished she could rid her stomach of the jitters.

They neared a group of women in a dining area, sitting at round tables covered with lace cloths, topped with floral bouquets in crystal vases. The floor in that area was raised a good six inches and made for a pleasant backdrop to where the plantation wives were sitting.

By now, Kindra's heart was pounding in her chest and she had to force herself to breathe.

"Good evening, ladies," Agnes said, as she reached a frail hand around Kindra's waist to draw her up level with her. "May I introduce you to the new owner of Kindra Hall." Agnes smiled graciously at Kindra, and then to the women who stared at them.

At first, none of the women spoke, but they wasted no time in giving Kindra the once over. They glanced sternly from her coifed hairstyle to her white satin boots that peeked out at the hem of her pale green gown.

"Uh-umm," one woman cleared her throat, the feather on her wide stylish hat bobbing as she looked to the left, then to the right. Her flaming red hair was piled high, and balanced a hat precariously as she looked again at the tongue-tied women.

"My name's Rita Pickler," she said, nodding to the other plantation wives. "And this here is Flora." She laid a hand on an older, gray-haired woman sitting next to her in a dark purple gown with sequins studding the neckline. Although she was being introduced, Flora made no move toward Kindra. Rather, she leaned back and frowned her stark disapproval.

"You say you own Kindra Hall?" Mrs. Pickler asked, seemingly aghast at such a notion. "I was under the impression the estate belonged to Stanley and Ava Bernard. Now I am completely confused." She craned her neck to glance at Ava, who sat at the end of the row of chairs glaring at Kindra.

Kindra could not take her eyes off Ava Bernard. Something in her stiffened, and she found the backbone she lacked only moments earlier to brace herself. She wouldn't let the blonde-haired woman intimidate her. After all, she had done all that was expected of her when she first arrived at Kindra Hall, only to be humiliated daily by Ava looking down her nose at her. Nothing Kindra did had kept the snooty woman from treating her as nothing more than an outcast slave. Now that the tables had turned, and Ava was not the mistress of Kindra Hall, Kindra realized that she must steel herself and step up to her entitled position. After all, only she could do that.

At Mrs. Pickler's remark that Ava was still the owner of the estate, Kindra glanced at Ava once more, expecting the former mistress of Kindra Hall to make a comment. To Kindra's surprise, not a word came from Ava's mouth. Instead, astonishingly, she lowered her eyes, her face a scarlet hue. Might she and Stanley have declined to make an appearance had they known she and Denzel were coming to the event?

Kindra waited a beat before she said, "An easy mistake, Mrs. Pickler. Ava's husband was the foreman on the plantation for my father, the late Phillip Cooper. Might you know of him?"

Rita Pickler's eyes grew wide as saucers, as did those of the other women seated along the line of chairs. It seemed most of them needed to take a second look at the mistress of Kindra Hall before they turned to each other in hushed voices, their hands once again over their mouths as they spoke.

Kindra could not help but overhear a few strands of comments . . . "Well, I never!" . . . "That can't be his daughter!" . . . and . . . "Who would have thought?"

"Well, I, . . . uh . . . I surely did know your father," Rita Pickler stammered.

Kindra's cheeks burned. "The Bernards were caretakers of my father's estate. But once he passed, he left the plantation to me." She unconsciously laid a hand on her stomach, to quell the buzz of butterflies. "We have only been on the island a short while. We've been eager to meet the people of Bridgetown and especially those who share in growing tobacco." Kindra stopped. She could think of nothing else to say.

Agnes filled the void. "Phillip Cooper was a dear friend of mine. His ships have sailed the seas with my tobacco exports as well as most of yours for many years," she said. "He was a noble man and esteemed by most plantation owners on this island. I was certain you would want to meet his daughter."

Kindra nearly coughed at that, thinking Mrs. Cavendish had pushed a bit too far. From the looks on the faces of the women who glanced uncomfortably at the black woman dressed as a white woman, Agnes was far from being right. Surely they all had slaves. It was common knowledge that the treatment of slaves was harsh and cruel on any given day. If the slave didn't comply as expected, then the mistress of the house sat and watched the servant be flogged mercilessly for the simplest of mistakes.

To have a black woman stand before them now—as an equal, was unheard of. And from the looks on the women's faces, they despised it.

"How good of you to attend the gala once again," Flora said to Ava. Then she turned to Kindra. "And do the Bernards still work your plantation?"

"No," Kindra said, her throat closing in on her, choking off the words. "My husband has made changes on the grounds. The Bernards have recently moved on." She swallowed.

All eyes flew to Ava, whose cheeks were inflamed.

"Oh, dear! You poor thing," said one woman.

"What will the two of you do now?" said another. The women rushed to Ava and flocked around her, soothing and sympathizing with her, leaving Kindra alone with Agnes. A tear fell from Kindra's eye; and trailed down her cheek. She quickly wiped it away.

Denzel broke away from the small party of men encircled about Shelton Rumball, and strode over to the refreshment table. A bounty of desserts lay spread out in an assortment of cookies, cakes, custards and pies, as well as breads, jellies and hard cheese. He filled a small china plate with a couple of cookies, a thin slice of chocolate cake and a piece of hard cheese. He was reaching for a crystal glass of island punch when a familiar voice from behind stopped him.

"Hey, boy! Those refreshments are for the plantation owners."

Denzel half turned when he caught sight of Stanley Bernard glaring at him with a smirk on his face.

Denzel's tongue found the inside of his cheek and massaged the area while he gazed at the insolent man. He steadied himself before he spoke. "You and I both know I have a right to be here. Do me a favor and don't start anything you can't finish." Denzel inwardly flinched at his own remark, knowing full well he was instigating a fight. But he'd seen the way Bernard had pinned his gaze on him throughout the evening, and knew beyond a doubt, the foreman was itching to humiliate him as soon as the chance came his way.

Denzel clamped his jaw tight and decided not to egg the man on any further. Instead he said, "I'm done here. The table's all yours." He lifted his glass and strolled back to where the planters gathered, huddled together talking about the good yield of crops and what they'd do to improve the yields next year.

Upon glancing back at the refreshment table, Denzel saw Bernard was not there. He searched the room and spotted Kindra, standing before a group of women with Agnes Cavendish by her side. As his eyes continued to scan the large ballroom, he spotted Bernard stepping out a side door where private pathways led to an expansive garden with stone benches for guests who sought fresh air.

Thinking the ballroom was too small for the two of them, Denzel moved away from the table with a small plate in his hand. He kept a level gaze on the door that led to the gardens. Something told him Bernard was up to something. He didn't know what it was, but it was worth his time to stay alert.

TWENTY

WHEN STANLEY BERNARD stepped out from the brightly lit ballroom, he stopped long enough to let his eyes adjust to the muted darkness outside. Torches had been lit to illuminate the narrow pathways that led off in different directions. Stanley carried a rum cookie as he perused the garden path. Walking slowly, he deliberately strode farther away from the planter's house and moved toward a long row of hedges that stood a good twelve feet high. They walled in the garden grounds boxing in the delightful paths, ponds and benches.

When he reached an arched trellis with flowers blooming overhead and trailing down its sides, he unlatched the iron gate that could only be opened from the inside. The hairs on his neck bristled as he waited. Soon one man stepped inside the private garden and looked nervously about himself.

"What took you so long?" the man asked.

"Easy, Lee," Bernard said, recognizing his former overseer despite the darkness of their surroundings. "I told you I had to find out first if that darkie was going to show his face at the party."

"So is he here?" Lee growled.

Ignoring his question, Bernard glanced beyond his broad shoulders.

"Scoot Sweeny with you?"

"Yeah. He's comin.'"

No sooner had Lee affirmed Scoot was out there somewhere in the dark when he stepped into view from behind the bushes. Coming through the gate, a wariness was plainly written on his face. He pulled his collar up and shoved a lock of brown hair off his forehead. He furrowed his brows as he zeroed his gaze on Bernard.

"I believe the darkie you want us to rough up is Tia's son-in-law. This is going to be a pleasure."

Bernard was tall and built well, but Scoot Sweeny was a good two inches taller, broad shouldered and thick. He had a face on him that made a man question whether to mess with him: fierce, with a quiet stony gaze. His sleek dark brows intertwined across the long, aristocratic bridge of his nose. With the shadows surrounding him, the man appeared mysterious. Cold and remote. Bernard wasn't sure he could trust the man, but he'd already confided in him and was in too deep to back out now.

"Who's Tia?" Bernard asked.

"Never mind," Sweeny shook his head. "It's not important. Just someone I've done business with in the past."

Bernard paused, then said, "That prissy little darkie's mother?"

"Yeah. That and more." Sweeny said, his voice stiff.

"So did Talmaze show up?" asked Lee.

"He's here," Bernard told his henchman in a low voice. "He's walking around like he owns the estate."

"High time we put that blackie in his place," Lee said. The moon had risen and Bernard could see Lee's expression. He was ready to get on with what he'd come to do.

Zane Lee had worked alongside him the last five years. He too was tall. Only he was thin as a matchstick and his nose drooped like the beak of a great bird. His dark eyes gazed toward the lights of the house as if he were chomping at the bit to get even with Denzel Talmaze.

"Now here's the plan," Bernard said, going over what they'd rehearsed several days earlier. Once they'd cinched down his part, Bernard said, "Now, I'm going back inside. Stay out of sight, but watch for me. When I give the signal, the coast will be clear. That's when you make your move."

The two men nodded and waited as Bernard sauntered back toward the hall. When he neared the French doors, he unbuttoned his coat and flexed his shoulders. He glanced in both directions to see if he'd been missed. Nothing had changed. He crossed the floor to where Shelton Rumball and the planters were talking.

Denzel glanced his way, his eyes holding Bernard's. A moment later, Denzel stepped away from the conversation to lean against the jamb of the French doors. He gazed into the dark, enjoyed the night breeze.

Bernard grinned to himself. Fate was in his favor. He walked past Denzel, bumping his shoulder as he stepped through the doors, and glanced sideways, nodding to the men hidden in the shadows.

Denzel clamped his jaw tightly and watched Bernard fade into the darkness. He glanced at the moon and took a long swallow of his island punch. When he brought his hand down, two men jumped from beyond the portico's low bushes. Each man grabbed an arm and pinned Denzel against the wall.

Bernard stepped out of the shadow and eyed Denzel with an evil grin. "My, my. What have we here?"

Denzel tried to pull his arms out of the men's stronghold. At a glance, he recognized Zane Lee, his former overseer. The second man he didn't know.

"We're fixin' to show you that coloreds don't belong at the party. And you sure don't belong on this island. Maybe what you need is a good ole whuppin' to show you that you ain't any better than the rest of the blackies!"

Denzel had heard enough. He flexed his muscles and yanked his arm loose and threw a blow at Lee, punching him square in the nose.

"Ooww!" Lee howled as blood spurted from his nose. His hands flew to his face to stem the flow.

Bernard covered the ground between them, his fists flying. Denzel deflected each blow as if the man were hitting a wall. Stanley Bernard stumbling back into the bushes, crumpling to the ground.

The man on Denzel's left jumped onto Denzel's back, pummeling his head with his fists. Denzel swung the man off with such force that the man was jettisoned from Denzel's back and slammed to the ground.

The torches lit up the expanse of ground before them, causing the men's shadows to dance in the night. Denzel's adversaries found their footing and walked shoulder to shoulder toward him, their eyes blazing with evil intent.

"Grab him, boys!" Bernard barked.

By now a few men stood on the portico, watching the fight. None seemed intent on stopping the blows to Denzel. Dazed from the attack, Denzel took a step back and tripped on an uneven brick. He stumbled precariously, taking an awkward step backward before he fell through the closed French doors and inside the bright ballroom. When he did, his assailants rushed forward. Scoot and Zane Lee grabbed his arms and pinned him to the floor, while Bernard moved to stand over him.

Ava raised her eyes to Kindra, amber fire flaming in them. "We've got everything under control, ladies. My husband is very proficient when it comes to matters such as starting up a plantation. After all, mind you, it was *he* who built Kindra Hall from the ground up to the place it is today." A wry smile formed on her face. "He has already contacted a real estate firm in Bridgetown. We plan to buy property and grow our own tobacco. He may even try his hand at sugarcane. It, too, grows well on the island. Until then, we have found a residence in town where we will stay until the plantation house is built and the crops are planted." She raised her eyes to Kindra once more. "And to think, we will be your competition someday."

Kindra's back became rigid and she steadied her voice before she spoke. "One more planter won't make such a difference, I don't suppose." She looked at the haughty women who smirked at her. "Don't you agree?"

Agnes nudged her gently, and Kindra knew her friend was giving her the hint not to push her luck. But after weeks of living in the same house with Ava Bernard and her snooty attitude, it was all Kindra could do to remember herself and her own precarious position as the new girl in town. Not to mention the new *black girl* in town.

A ruckus in the background drew Kindra's attention away from the ladies. She heard the shouts of men and the sound of crashing doors and shards of glass shattering on the polished floor. A great silence filled the room as all eyes were averted to the far end of the hall where Stanley Bernard raised his fist to land another blow on Denzel's left cheek.

Kindra's heart stopped when she saw her husband laid out on the floor, two men holding him down with Stanley straddling him, pummeling his face. She broke away from the women and shoved her way past curious onlookers. "Stop!" she cried. "Stop it right now!" She raced across the floor and threw her hands on Stanley Bernard's shoulders, and with all the strength her tiny body could muster, tried to pull him off her husband.

Bernard elbowed her hard against her abdomen and sent her tumbling backwards. White, hot pain shot through her. As she fell to the floor, her head struck a chair.

She saw the foreman stand up, his fists clenched as he spat on Denzel, then drawing his leg back, he kicked him viciously in the ribs.

Then all went black.

TWENTY-ONE

FLASHES OF THE night before jolted through her mind as soon as Kindra awakened. The room bright, she knew it was mid-morning. She was not alone. Mrs. Cavendish sat in a chair next to her bed. "I hope you don't mind, dear girl, but I took charge after last evening's mishap."

Pushing both palms on the bed to rise to a sitting position, Kindra stopped. The pounding at the back of her skull felt dreadful, and a second ache came from her abdomen. All at once, she remembered that Stanley Bernard had elbowed her hard enough to send her flying backward into an abyss. Her hands flew to her midriff and she touched the slight swell of her stomach. At that same moment, she felt the baby flutter within her. "Oh, Agnes, I thought— "

"You did *not* lose the child if that's what you're worried about." Agnes said as she rose to hover over Kindra. "You're fortunate that terrible man did not give you a concussion." She laid a gentle hand on Kindra's arm.

"But will the baby be all right?" Kindra's lips quivered.

Agnes paused. "I should think so. Of course, only time will tell."

"I couldn't bear it if there's anything wrong with my baby!" Kindra massaged her stomach, her brows gathered in a worried frown.

"If there is, that man will get his just reward. Denzel will see to that."

At mention of Denzel, Kindra glanced toward the door. "Where is he? Is he all right?"

"Bernard lit into him pretty bad, I must say. From what I understand, he'll be laid up a while."

"How did you get us home?"

"Mister Rumball's servants carried your husband to your carriage. Abner brought him home. You rode in my carriage where I could keep an eye on you. When the two carriages arrived at Kindra Hall, I had your overseer help your husband up the stairs where he is now, sleeping in a guest room across the hall. Then Ebenezer carried you to your bedchamber."

"Oh, Agnes. This is all so terrible."

"I agree, dear girl. But I'll have you know your chambermaid has been in attendance nearly non-stop. I daresay you could not have found a better personal maid to care for you."

"Where is she now?" Kindra asked.

"I sent her downstairs to get a bite of food and then ordered her to rest before she shows her face in this room again." Agnes smiled kindly and brushed tendrils from Kindra's forehead. "Now you must get some sleep. I've seen that the rest of your servants will keep the house running smoothly. I'll not leave this place until I know that you're out of the woods and feeling your normal self."

"Thank you, Agnes. You're a godsend." Kindra's lids felt heavy and her hand went to her tummy again.

"Sleep. That is the best medicine right now." Agnes sat in her chair and picked up a thin novel. She removed a satin bookmarker and peered at the page, then looked at Kindra. The old woman's eyes seemed troubled. But then of course, why wouldn't they? She had witnessed last night's fiasco and then taken it upon herself to care for Kindra and Denzel. Their eyes met fleetingly before the warmth of the bed drew Kindra into a deep slumber.

The following afternoon, Kindra leaned against the fluffy pillows with a thick black Bible propped on her small mound. When she dozed her fingers relaxed. The Bible slipped to her side. She pulled it up again to perch on her stomach and read the words from Chapter 139 in the book of Psalms. The first three verses read: *O Lord, Thou hast searched me, and known me. Thou knowest my downsitting and mine up-rising, Thou understandest my thought afar off. Thou compassest my path and my lying down, and art acquainted with all my ways.*

Kindra read on, searching the words she needed after last night's terrible ordeal. *You know everything about me, Lord. And you know everything about this child in my womb,* she thought. She came to verse thirteen and read on through seventeen, catching phrases that ministered to her soul. *For Thou hast possessed my reins: Thou has covered me in my mother's womb. I will praise Thee; for I am fearfully and wonderfully made: marvelous are Thy works; and that my soul knoweth right well. My substance was not hid from Thee, when I was made in secret . . .* Kindra spread her hand over her stomach and read the last sentence: *How precious also are Thy thoughts unto me, O God!* This passage of scripture had always been her favorite. She let the words wash over her.

It was later that week when sitting there, resting her body as Doctor Coby had instructed, and being watched like a hawk by Corrie, the midwife, that Kindra's mind slipped back to the days when she and Cameron Bartholomew were children. How many times did Laulie, their nanny at Cooper's Landing, teach them to hide the word of God in their hearts?

In her mind she could hear Laulie's voice as though she just spoke: *You never know when the day will come when you'll have to pull God's promises from your hidin' place. You never know if you be in a place where you can't read God's words. Dem words need t' be hidin' and growin' in your heart. You need to remember the good Lawd's words. They be a restin' place for your soul and give you faith to git through the day. Dem's mighty powerful words in that big ole book. Give you hope when you be needin' it most.*

Kindra gazed at the Scripture now. Try as she might, she couldn't concentrate with Denzel lying in the other room, his face bruised and his ribs broken. He had hobbled into her room yesterday without the help of a walking stick and nearly fallen headlong before he reached her bed.

Mayme and Corrie had been coming down the long hallway when Denzel fell against the chair and gasped at the pain that had wrenched through him. He'd paled noticeably and Mayme had sent Corrie to fetch Duncan to help Denzel back to bed.

Now, Denzel again entered her room and allowed Mayme to help him into the chair beside the bed. Then she stepped away as if to give the two of them privacy.

Denzel's hand shook as he laid it on the coverlet. "How are you?" he asked, his eyes going to the small mound beneath the quilt.

"I'm fine, my love. The question is, how are you?"

He ignored her question. "The baby?"

"So far all seems well. Doctor Coby and Corrie have had my feet elevated. It looks as though the baby and I cheated death."

Denzel's eyes narrowed before he leveled them on her. "They won't get away with what they've done."

Kindra knew who *they* were. Stanley Bernard and his cohorts. "Leave them be for now, Denzel. I need you to be here for me and the baby."

"I know. And I will. But they haven't seen the last of me."

As he talked it seemed as if every breath, and every move hurt him, though she knew he would never admit it. "You should go back to the guest bed." She touched his hand. She wanted him by her side, but she could see it was all he could do to keep from wincing in pain.

As if on cue, Duncan showed up at the chamber door and stopped when he saw Denzel lean close to Kindra's side to kiss her.

Kindra placed both hands on her husband's face and gazed into his dark eyes. "I love you."

Denzel's hand went from her chin to the swell of her stomach and he spread his long fingers widely. He bowed his head and said, "Please Lord, be with my wife and child. Keep them safe always."

With his head bent in prayer, she caressed the crown of his dark head and softly ran her fingers through his hair.

Denzel looked up and the two of them gazed at each other, saying nothing, their hearts beating as one. Then he glanced over his shoulder. "Duncan."

"Yes, suh!" Duncan sprang forward to help Denzel to his feet. Kindra could see the act brought new pain to Denzel's eyes.

"I'll come see you next time," she said softly.

"No. Stay where you are," Denzel said.

"All right," Kindra agreed, but she knew she was on the mend and nothing could keep her away.

Two mornings later, Agnes breezed into the bedchamber. She wore a wide-brimmed flouncy hat with feathers and roses atop her head. She pulled a pair of gloves up to her elbows as she crossed the floor, her cane hooked in the crook of her arm. "I'm leaving," she announced as she came to stand by the bed. "I have eyes, and I can see you're doing much better." She grabbed her cane with her gloved hand and sat on the edge of the chair. "My ship sails this afternoon. I want you to promise me that you will continue to rest a few more days."

"I will, Agnes. And yes, it's true I am feeling better. Don't feel you are abandoning us. We'll do fine."

"I believe you will, which is why I think it's time I go. Promise me that when you come to America, you'll visit me in Charleston. I have plenty of room to put you up."

"Thank you for the invitation. I look forward to it."

Agnes Cavendish patted Kindra's hand, then walked out of the room. Kindra could hear the cane thumping down the hall. She would miss the older woman.

After she was sure Mrs. Cavendish was truly gone, Kindra climbed out of bed and pulled on a robe. She was going to see Denzel. She was happy to find strength in her legs again, the dull ache in her head easing and not a sign of pain in her abdomen. *Might I be on the mend, sooner than I anticipated?*

The door across the hall stood ajar and low voices could be heard. Kindra pushed the door open to find Ebenezer standing by the bed speaking to Denzel.

Denzel's brows went up at the sight of his wife at the same time Ebenezer turned around to see who had entered the room. Ebenezer left his place by the bed and crossed the floor to where Kindra stood gazing at Denzel.

"Miz Kindra, did Doctor Coby gib you permission to be out of bed?"

"No, Ebenezer. I did." She smiled. "I feel fine. How is our patient?" Kindra drew away from Ebenezer, walked to the bed, and gazed at Denzel. The doctor had put a tight bandage around his bare chest and waist. From the look in his dark eyes, Denzel wasn't going anywhere just yet.

His gaze traveled over her and she felt a warm glow inside. "The color has come back into your cheeks. You look beautiful," Denzel said.

"The rest did me good. I really do feel fine. So much so, I'm ready to get back into my old routine."

He clamped his fingers over her hand. "I understand you're ready to be up and around, but I don't want you leaving the estate or going to town by yourself anymore."

Kindra leaned down and kissed his forehead. "I'm not going anywhere." Her brows furrowed. "How long will you be in these bindings?"

"Five weeks. Doctor Coby said I have two broken ribs."

"Oh, Denzel! You must be in a lot of pain."

"I am. I'm willing to do as Doc says if it means getting back on my feet and back to work."

"Don't forget you have Ebenezer to keep things going here."

"As far as I know, Miz Kindra, all be well heah. Folks done heah wot happen to you and the Massa. Ain't gonna say there ain't no mixed feelin's. But I seein' some of the folks who say they feelin' bad fer you and they be askin' how y'all farin'."

Kindra stepped to the window and gazed out at the workers in the fields. It felt wonderful to know that maybe the tide had turned. Could it be true that the slaves had come to terms with their masters being black?

"I'm going to get dressed and go downstairs." Kindra kissed Denzel's forehead again and hurried back to her bedchamber. She pulled the tapestry cord and heard the bell clang. Mayme would be here in a moment. She was eager to get on with this day.

As Mayme brushed the wrinkles out of Kindra's rose-colored gown, Kindra asked, "How is Rhea doing? I've not heard a word about her the past few days."

Mayme kept her eyes lowered and stalled before she spoke.

"Mayme?"

"Miz Kindra. The news not be good. Rhea passed on the first mornin' you come back from that party."

"What? Rhea's gone?"

"Yes'm, Miz Kindra. She took fever real bad. More than it be while we be tendin' her. It seemed her skin lit up on fire. The next thing we know, she gone."

Kindra stepped away from the mirror, her joy for the morning deflated. "Is . . . is she still in her room?"

"No, ma'am. Doctor Coby say it be best she be in the ground in a hurry. That so nobody else get the sickness."

"Oh, Mayme." Kindra had to sit in the chair to take it all in.

"She be more'n jist your slave, Miz Kindra. That be plain to see. Doctor Coby and Miz Agnes say to keep quiet about it 'til you be on your feet." Mayme looked crestfallen having to be the bearer of bad news.

"Where is she now?" Kindra stood, her fingers entwined, her knuckles white.

"She be in the graveyard behind the slave town." Mayme bit her lip and shrugged. "I can take you there if you like."

"Yes . . . Mayme. I would like that very much."

Ten minutes later, Mayme stood back while Kindra took a moment to grieve by herself. Rhea's new grave was piled high with fresh soil. Time would compact the dirt and it would settle, but right now it was dark, a stark reminder that it had merely been a few days since her servant and friend had been laid to rest. It would be many days before the sun-drenched air would fade the earth.

Kindra set her small bouquet of flowers at the base of the cross that simply bore the name, 'Rhea.' An emerald-colored hummingbird flew down and swiftly jabbed its long, thin beak into the opening of an orange and yellow cou cou blossom, its wings whirring so fast she could barely see them move. Then just as swiftly as the tiny humming bird had made its appearance, it flew away, almost as if she had imagined it.

As Kindra stood by the grave of the women she'd known since childhood, she shed no tears, yet a heaviness hung in her heart. She hated the finality of death. When she looked up, there were field hands in the distance watching her. It seemed they had stopped their hoeing long enough to give the mistress the solemn respect she needed. Kindra nodded her head to them and turned back to where Mayme stood.

Together, the two women walked back to the house. "You have served me well during Rhea's illness. So, now, I'd like you to be my chambermaid."

"Yes, Miz Kindra," Mayme said as the two walked slowly away from the graveyard.

That afternoon, Kindra decided it was time to have a good talk with Corrie, the nanny and midwife. She was only four months into her time, but not too soon to pick out a room for the nursery and to move Corrie into the room next door. Chin up, Kindra went in search of the nanny. She wanted nothing more than to put doom and gloom behind her.

Five weeks had passed and the day was warm and humid after an early drizzle. Kindra had waited far too long to go to the corrals and visit her white Arabian mare, Angel. The horse snorted and pranced over to Kindra. Her nose, prickled with a few stiff hairs, was soft as velvet, and on her forehead the short, fine hair was silky smooth. Angel arched her neck proudly and the white mane fell over like heavy fringe.

"Did you think I'd forgotten about you?" Kindra's fingers splayed through the horse's mane. "Never would I do such a thing, beautiful girl. And if this child were born, I'd take you out for a run." She giggled.

Angel arched her neck and bent her head low and pawed the ground. Then just as quickly, she raised her head and her ears pricked forward as if she saw something beyond. She stepped back and snorted again.

Kindra looked over her shoulder in time to see Denzel in the distance. He walked with long, sure steps.

Denzel stopped his stride long enough to take in the scene before him. He looked up at the clouds that seemed to stair-step right into heaven. The billowing softness piled one on top of the other. That alone was breathtaking. Yet, below them stood Kindra with her satin-smooth bronze skin, dressed in a lavender day dress, her long, black, shiny hair pulled back in a matching bow. The sight of her standing at the corral with her snow-white horse nearly sucked his breath away. He heaved a long contented sigh and continued to where Kindra waited.

"You're up!" She grinned, one hand poking through the corral fence with a handful of oats. Angel munched at the treat, her eyes watching Denzel.

"I decided I couldn't stay in bed another minute in that blasted room. I told the maid to change the sheets and that I was moving back into the room with you."

"Umm . . . that's good." A gleam came to her eyes.

"I be moving faster if I wasn't tied up in these bandages." Denzel rubbed a hand over his shirt front.

Kindra dusted her hands together and gave Angel one last pat on her neck. She turned to Denzel. "Come with me. I've wanted to explore the grounds and familiarize myself with the workers and the crop."

"Sounds good." Denzel steered her to the lane that led to the tobacco fields. "We can start here and work our way back." His arm went over her shoulder.

Field hands glanced up as the two walked down the wagon road that led to the acres of green tobacco fields. Jasper was among the workers, and his hand went up to wave. White teeth shone in his dark face.

"He's a good man," Denzel said as he waved back.

"Is he married?" asked Kindra.

"I don't think so." He looked down at Kindra and chuckled. "Why? Are you thinking of becoming a matchmaker?"

"I don't know. Mayme's a nice girl."

"Whoa, little lady. You best let these folks work these things out for themselves."

Kindra smiled up at him. "We did, didn't we? And with all odds against us, too."

Denzel didn't answer. Instead, he pulled her closer, thanking God that she belonged to him. Maybe the worst was behind them. If not, he had the right woman beside him.

TWENTY-TWO

River Oak, Fields Landing

SEPTEMBER CAME UPON River Oak with a threat of colder days to come. In truth, Cameron welcomed the thought that the hot and humid days would finally be behind them. He had survived the heat of summer and the yellow fever that usually followed, though a few of his slaves had not. Still, most of his workers fared well, and the first year's rice crop made it through the summer rains. All in all, they were off to a good start.

Cameron removed his wide-brimmed straw hat, pulled a handkerchief from his pocket and mopped his brow. His gaze lingered on his project of the moment—the Great House. The contractor, Gilbert Griggs, had promised the cellars would be dug and the house framed before winter arrived. True to his word, the sound of hammers echoed through the air as a crew of men worked on all four sides of the structure. The house was framed and sturdy clapboard had been nailed to the sides. The roof had been completed a week before. The windows and doors would be next. The speed at which the men worked encouaged him.

A house so enormous sometimes took years to complete, yet they had constructed much of it in less than six months. True, it would take months before the inside of the house would be finished, with the lathe and plaster, flooring, and fine details that would make the Great House one of the finest in the Lowcountry.

Cameron replaced his hat and ambled down the sloped lawn to the second project at hand. Since it would be months before the Great

House was ready, he would need a place for Grace and the baby as soon as she arrived.

Sawdust floated his way as he neared the workmen who sawed floor boards the length needed for the front porch. He had hired a second contractor to build the small cottage that would serve as accommodations for guest when he and Grace moved into the Great House.

The sound of saws, hammers, and men calling out to each other as they worked filled the air and Cameron grinned. "If only you could be here to see this!" he said, thinking of Grace as he stood and watched the construction going on.

"What you say?" Tungo loped up to stand beside Cameron.

"Nothing, Tungo. I'm talking to myself."

"You be doin' a lotta that lately." Tungo's dark eyes lit up. "You be talkin' to yer lady again?"

"I'm afraid so," Cameron said.

"I hear you plannin' to sail out 'fore too long," Tungo said.

"You heard right. I need to get back to Jamaica before my wife delivers our first child. I'm afraid if I don't get out of here, I won't make it in time."

"How long you be on that ship, Massa Camp?"

"If all goes well, it'll take a month . . . one way. Two after we board the *Valiant* and sail back." Cameron glanced at the cottage house, seeing it was nearly completed. "I hope the house will be ready when we return."

"It be a mighty fine house, Massa."

"I agree." The noise from the construction was a sound he would never get tired of hearing. Every day he noticed changes being made, and his heart quickened at the thought of bringing his wife home.

Tungo's gaze traveled to the wagon that rode up the lane to the house. "You got comp'ny," he said.

Cameron squinted toward the horse and wagon coming to a stop just shy of the cottage house.

"I best be gettin' back to the village, Massa Camp. I jist wanted you to know we be ready to load some of that rice on the next steamship comin' this way."

"Sounds good. I'll stop by after my company leaves. I want to walk the fields and we'll talk about it then."

"Yes, suh." Tungo walked with purposeful strides as he headed back toward the direction of the rice fields and his people.

Newt, Cameron's brother, helped his wife Mary down from the wagon. The fourteen-year-old twins, Jenny and James, and young Donald, twelve, climbed out of the back of the wagon. The three waved 'hello,' before they ran off down the lane toward the river.

"Good to see you again," Cameron stretched out his hand.

Newt took it then clapped Cameron on the back. "I promised Mary I'd bring her out to see the place."

"I'm glad you did. I was just going to inspect the work the men are doing on the bridge." Cameron's gaze went over his shoulder. "Come take a look."

The three adults walked through the grass toward the pond and Mary's hand went to her mouth. "My goodness, Camp, this is utterly breathtaking." Her eyes lit up.

The workers gathered their tools and strode off the bridge. "See you in the morning," said one carpenter as the crew filed past them.

"Tomorrow." Cameron waved.

"I haven't crossed to the other side yet. Would you like to give it a try?" asked Cameron.

"Oh, could we?" Newton's wife looked at the arched span with eagerness.

"Be my guests," Cameron said with a chuckle.

The two men followed as Mary tentatively stepped onto the wooden bridge. She kept going until she reached the center, where the bridge arched high enough for a rowboat to float beneath. There, the three of them stopped to admire the view, while mindful of the fact that they stood a good ways above the water.

Cameron felt proud to find his project nearing completion. It had been a difficult feat of engineering due to the width and depth of the water way, but now the structure spanned the full distance to the other side.

"Your wife is going to love this," Mary said longingly. "I certainly would if this were mine."

"Now, Mary . . ." Newton said.

"Oh, don't give me that look, Newt. I'm not envying these folks one bit. I just know any woman would be a fool if she didn't appreciate the planning and workmanship that has gone into this."

Below, the water shimmered in the sun and a couple of lily pads floated out from beneath the bridge.

Cameron took in a breath of fresh cool air. "I'm ready for fall. The summer's been long and hard. And truth be told, I'm anxious to get home to my wife."

The three walked down the far side of the bridge and around to the wagon. "Which brings me to why we came by," Newt said. Cameron's head went up. "We're having a fall potluck at father's place. He asked me to invite you to the party," Newton continued.

"Do come, won't you?" Mary said.

"Why didn't Dad come out and ask me himself?" Cameron asked, disappointment shooting through him. He didn't need an answer. He knew why. The last time he'd joined the family for Sunday lunch, the two men still found it difficult to talk. Cameron held up an invisible guard toward his father. He didn't mean to. It surprised him as much as it did anyone else.

His father took the cue and held back, seeming unsure of their relationship. The two men talked, but it was all surface talk. Neither broached the subject of the past and for good reason. For now, Cameron wanted to keep it that way.

He'd left Charleston a wounded young boy, fending for himself. Phillip Cooper had become the father he had always wanted. How could he reveal such a truth to his real father? Time and hurt had created a breach between them. How they would close the gap he didn't know. He would let it be. He'd heard time healed all wounds. If that were true, he'd find out soon enough.

Standing by the wagon, Newton said, "I reckon he didn't feel right comin' out here uninvited. You'll have to decide whether you're up for it or not. We'd sure like for you to come."

"When is it?" Cameron asked.

"Two weeks from today," Mary cut in. "You don't have to bring anything but yourself."

"I won't be here in two weeks." Cameron breathed a relieved sigh. "I'll be sailing for Jamaica in the next few days. Tell Dad, thanks for the invitation."

"Too bad, Camp. The rest of the family was looking forward to seeing you," Newt said.

"I know. But I have to get back to Grace. If I don't go now, I might not make it in time before the baby comes. I'll never forgive myself if I miss being there."

"Understood." Newton clapped Cameron's shoulder and assisted Mary into the wagon. "Bring Grace out to see the family when you get back," Newt said.

"Or maybe we should all come out to River Oak," Mary said.

Cameron gazed at the wagon. "You rode in the wagon instead of taking the steamship? It would have been faster coming up river on the paddle boat."

"Yeah. I wanted to give the missus a nice Sunday ride."

"Well, I'll tell you what," Cameron said. "When we return, I'll send a post. You can all come on the *River Belle*. I'll notify the steamship captain. You'll enjoy the ride up river."

Mary's eyes lit up. "Thank you, Camp. We'll tell the others."

Newton put his thumb and index finger inside the corners of his mouth and blew a shrill whistle that split the air. A moment later the twins and Donald came running and clambered into the back of the wagon, laughing and shoving.

"Goodbye, Camp." Newton waved and flicked the reins.

Cameron raised his hat at the family as they turned back toward Fields Landing. He replaced his straw hat, fetched his horse and rode out to the rice paddies where bags of rice waited for shipment. He still had to have that talk with Tungo.

Cameron dismounted at the rice fields. As far as the eye could see, the land stretched in front of him. Darkies were busy, their steady work a necessity that made the plantation hum. Standing by the side of the road, Cameron watched the men and women in the fields. Workers were on the road and donkey carts were loaded with rice grass.

An uneasy feeling washed through him, as it often did when he stopped long enough to ponder the process that made a rice plantation possible. The workers were trapped. He could come and go as he pleased, but not the darkies. They were bound here, all of them, their lives not their own. And the result of all their work did not profit them, but the plantation owner. He often pushed his thoughts a measure further. Why did he deserve freedom, but the coloreds didn't? He hated the system, yet it was the way of the land.

His horse stomped its hooves and snorted. Cameron looked up to see Tungo riding his way through the tall grass. Cameron mounted his steed and reined his horse to fall in beside Tungo's and the two men rode up a narrow lane where a shed housed the finished bags of rice. The sun would be going down in another hour. He'd inspect the rice sacks and then call it a day. He needed to take the steamship down river to Fields Landing. Butler Wilder, the captain of the *Valiant,* would be waiting for him. They'd eat a meal and then make plans to sail to Jamaica.

His friend Sid Sparrow was supposed to be in town tonight. They'd discuss last minute details of his taking over River Oak in Cameron's absence. He trusted the man. He hoped to return the favor someday.

The shed held stacks of the Carolina Gold rice. Piles upon piles lined the wooden walls, with a narrow path in between. Cameron opened a bag and inspected the rice. He sifted a few grains through his fingers and let it fall into his palm. He cupped his hand and shook the rice. "How many bags are going out this shipment?" He tilted his head at Tungo.

"Hundred-fifty bags, suh." Tungo said.

"Good. We sent out that much last week."

"And we be getting ready to bag that many again." Tungo smiled.

The shed smelled of rice. Cameron ran his hand over a gunny sack filled to the brim. He thought of Dell Seward and his taunt about being the only plantation owner to win the annual trophy for bringing in the largest volume of rice. Cameron wouldn't enter the competition this year. He wasn't ready. But he looked at the healthy crop that had been harvested and filled the shed. He'd enter next year.

"Good job, Tungo." Cameron returned the man's smile. "You haven't let me down."

"I told you I would be first overseer, suh. I work hard for you. I make you see I be good overseer."

"That you did, Tungo. Just so you know, I'm still bringing Mingo back with me. But I'll see what we can work out." Cameron touched Tungo's shoulder. "I want to come back and find everything in order. Show me your worth while I'm gone."

"Yes, suh." Tungo stood tall. "I show you can trust me."

"Good." Cameron mounted his horse again and rode toward the village, where he continued to live until his house was done.

Cameron slid out of the saddle and started toward the cabin. He looked up in time to see a stranger ride in on his horse that kicked up dirt as it galloped toward the circular drive in front of the house. He turned and strode toward the horse and rider.

"Hullo," said the young man who stopped his horse in front of Cameron. "Are you Cameron Bartholomew?"

"Yes, I am."

"I've a letter for you, sir."

Cameron shaded his eyes as his head tipped back to face the postal carrier. "Where's the letter from?"

"Jamaica, sir."

Cameron reached out and took the small envelope. He sniffed it, then looked at the handwriting. "Grace," he murmured, smiling. He reached into his pants pocket and fished out a coin. He tossed it up to the courier. "A tip, for the long ride out."

"Thank you, sir. Do you have any outgoing mail?"

"No, I don't."

"Then I best be goin'. I've still got a satchel of mail to deliver." He turned his horse and headed back the way he came. He turned down the lane that led to other plantations along the river.

Cameron raised the small envelope to his nose again. He thought he smelled a faint scent of perfume.

Grace.

He lifted the seal and pulled out a thin sheet of paper. To his disappointment the letter was brief.

Dearest Cameron,

You must come home right away. Our lives depend on it.

Please do not delay. Drop everything and come!

I await your arrival, my dearest love,

Your loving wife, Grace

Our lives depend on it. The words echoed in his mind. *Gosh darn dingit! Why had he waited too long to leave!* Cameron shoved the letter back into the envelope. He walked back and mounted his horse again. He would ride as far downriver as he could until he met up with the steamship. He didn't have any time to waste. Grace needed him.

Oh, God! he prayed. *If you have an ear to hear . . . I ask that you keep my family safe. Make a way for me to get there in time!*

He dug his heels into the side of his horse and flew down the lane. Dust rose leaving a trail behind horse and rider. Cameron's heart pounded to the rhythm of his horse's hooves.

Hang on, Grace. I'm coming!

TWENTY-THREE

JUST BEFORE THE noon meal, out on a walk, Grace overheard one of the colored women speaking to another slave. They didn't know Grace had gone for her daily walk and was near enough to the shanty to hear the two women talking.

One of the woman said, "It won't be long now. There be a rebellion boiling in the pot. My Jimmy say the African people done had their fill o' workin' for the white man."

"You hear 'bout the latest news?" a second woman responded. "Some o' those men been givin' their massa a taste o' their own lashin's. They be whippin an' beatin' them snooty white folks to a pulp and they even be stringin' them up in their own trees!"

"Where this be happenin'?" the first woman asked.

"Down yonder on the coast. But I be hearin' they stirring the pot all right, and they be workin' their way to us. 'Fore too long, they be here. Then we's got to decide what to do with the mistress here."

Grace's hand flew to her mouth and her blood ran cold. Would the slaves really turn on her? On shaky legs, Grace crept away from the side of the building and made her way back to the Great House. Her heart pounding in her ears, she went through the kitchen door where Dinah, Gemma and Penny were busy making the noon meal.

"What's wrong, little missy? You be white as a ghost." Dinah set a bowl down on the counter and swept across the floor to Grace's side. "Is your baby trying to come?"

"No, Dinah. It's not the baby that has me turned inside-out."

"What, then?" Dinah threw her arms around Grace's bulky waist and led her to the kitchen table. "You best sit before you fall." Dinah laid a gentle hand on Grace's shoulder and pushed her into the chair. Then her chubby fists went to her waist while her brows puckered. "What be troubling you, chile?"

Grace searched Dinah's eyes, and then she gazed at Gemma and Penny. Were they for her or against her? Was she safe under her own roof? But all she saw was concern in their dark eyes. A tremor began to flow through her body and hot tears blurred her eyes.

"Have . . . have . . . you heard . . ." All at once she lost control of her emotions and the tears flowed.

"Gemma," Dinah said. "Put some tea on for this poor girl. I do believe she's gonna have this babe before the day's gone."

"No . . . no. It isn't that." Grace's hand went up to stop their talk.

"Then what be troubling you?" Dinah raised her apron to use it as a hand towel. When she finished wiping her hands, she sat across the table from Grace.

Gemma moved to the sink and pumped water into a tea kettle to boil. All the while she kept her eyes on Grace. "This won't take long, honey. A cup of Gemma's tea will settle your nerves right down." All the while, Penny stood speechless, watching the two older cooks calm the mistress of the house.

"Now tell old Dinah what be upsetting you."

Grace wiped away the tears on her cheeks and stared at the three women. With quivering lips, she tried to speak again.

"Do you know what's going on with the field hands?"

"Well, we know they been lollygaggin' more'n they should these days if that's what's botherin' you," Dinah said, her eyes glaring. "If Mastah Camp were here, they wouldn't be takin' advantage of you."

"It's worse than that," Grace said.

"What you talkin' about?" Dinah sat up straight.

"I went for my walk like I always do. Sometimes I like to watch the women in the colored district. I've always thought I should know what they're doing and if they need anything."

"Go on," Dinah said.

"I overheard two women talking about a slave revolt. They said African slaves are leaving their plantations, beating and whipping their masters . . . and . . . and . . ." Grace covered her face with her hands. "And hanging them in trees." A shiver ran the length of her body.

"That won't be happenin' here, you can be sure of that." Dinah thumped the table with her fists, and Grace jumped.

"I'm not so sure," Grace said. "They talked about what to do with me, as if they knew something was afoot here."

Dinah jumped up. "Which one of those ninnies say that? I have a mind to give them a piece of my– "

"Sit down, Dinah. It doesn't matter which one said it. The way they were talking, this has been going on for some time."

Dinah sat down, but it was evident she was fuming. The room grew silent.

Dinah looked at Gemma, who looked at Penny. The three cooks looked as if they were stumped at the frightful news. The teakettle whistled, breaking the silence. Gemma fetched a cup, filled a brewing spoon with tea leaves, and set it in the mug. Then she poured hot water over it.

Penny, wide-eyed, set a sugar bowl in front of Grace. It appeared all this talk of rebellion had snagged her tongue. Penny stepped back and wrung a towel around her hand.

Grace stirred the tea. "Have you heard any of this, Penny?"

"Well . . . Cato say there be some talk. But he don't want nothin' to do with it."

"And you didn't think I needed to know?" Grace raised her brow.

"Cato say it might not happen here. I . . . I didn't want to worry you."

Grace let out an exasperated sigh. "I always want to know everything that's going on. Fetch Cato for me."

Penny dropped the hand towel on the counter and slipped out the kitchen door. Before she returned, Aunt Katy and Josie entered the kitchen.

"What's taking you so long to get dinner on?" Aunt Katy glanced toward the table. "What's wrong, Grace? You've been crying."

Josie flew to Grace's side. "Is it the baby?"

"No, it's not the baby." She rose from her chair and said, "Let's go to the dining room." Grace glanced at Gemma. "Is the meal ready?"

"Yes, Miz Grace. We'll bring it right away."

Just then Cato and Penny flew in the back door and stopped to catch their breaths.

"Good you're here," Grace said to Cato. "Dinah, after the food is served, bring Nate up to the house. We're going to have a meeting."

"What's going on, Grace?" Aunt Katy followed her into the dining room.

After the three were seated, Grace paused before replying. "I believe it's time for us to go home to Charleston."

Once Aunt Katy and Josie were brought up to the current state of affairs, the three women began making plans to leave Cooper's Landing and Jamaica. Grace brought all the servants she believed were loyal to her into the drawing room and told them what was planned and what she would need from them. Leaving Cooper's Landing would not be an easy feat and there would be a great deal of work needed in order to accomplish it within a short period of time. She feared that once they left the plantation, there would be no house to return to. There were heirlooms she would take, but she had to think it through and make the best of their escape.

Grace rolled out of bed and stood for a moment trying to get her bearings. She looked down for the umpteenth time at the large swell of her belly and wondered what it would be like to see her feet again. She glanced out the window wistfully. She was in her seventh month and Cameron still had not come home. She hoped her urgent letter reached him in time. If he didn't come soon, she would do the unthinkable . . . board one of their ships and sail to Charleston without him.

The idea had been nagging at her for months. She had hoped the workers in the fields would settle down and stop their threats to revolt. But instead, things had gotten worse.

Today, she, Josie and her best friend and neighbor, Camille would go to the harbor and find out if any of the ships belonging to Grace were in port. She hoped to find Cameron coming to shore, sailing on the *Valiant*, or with Captain Drew Harding, Camille's husband, on the *Savannah Rose*. If not, they'd make do with another one of the vessels she'd inherited from her father.

The sound of horses' hooves came through the open window and Grace peeked outside in time to see Camille's yellow open carriage pull up in front of the house with her driver perched up front.

"Oh, goodness." Grace glanced down at her nightgown. "I'm late." She pulled on the cord for Hedy. She didn't have to wait long. The young black girl quickly appeared, a pleasant smile on her lips.

"I be lookin' in on you, Missy. You be sleepin' like a kitten."

"I'm up now and Camille is waiting for me."

Hedy went to the wardrobe and chose an outing dress. Within a half hour Grace was ready to descend the stairs.

Smitty, Grace's orange and white cat, waited at the bottom. "Meoww!"

"You poor soul. Are you feeling neglected?" Grace started to pick him up, but Hedy came down behind her and scooped up the forlorn cat. "Here you go, Missy. Will he be going to America too?"

Grace snuggled Smitty close to her neck and felt his body go into a loud purr. "Yes, he's coming with me. I wouldn't dream of leaving him behind."

Hedy looked wistfully at the cat then her eyes returned to Grace. "And me?"

"Oh, Hedy! Of course you're coming too. I wouldn't know what to do without you."

That brought a shine to Hedy's face. "Here, let me take him."

Grace heard voices in the drawing room and headed that way. She found Camille sitting next to Josie chatting away. Camille's stomach was rounded into a little bump, indicating her second child was on the way.

Aunt Katy turned when Grace entered the room. From the looks of her, she hadn't slept a wink the previous night.

"Aunt Katy, you look frazzled." Grace observed.

"And why wouldn't I, with these Africans scheming to take our lives? We'll not leave this island too soon for me."

"I was beginning to think you were going to sleep the morning away," Josie said.

"And make you wait to go to town?" Grace smiled.

"Josie kissed her mother's cheek, then turned to Grace. "Shall we go?"

"I'm ready," Grace replied.

"You are *not* going." Aunt Katy's eyes traveled to Grace's round stomach. "You ought not to bounce in the carriage on these hideous roads."

"Wild horses couldn't keep me away, Aunt Katy. I'm dying to have a look at the harbor. Maybe Camp will arrive today."

"And what if the ride sends you into labor?"

"We'll go slow . . . won't we, Camille?"

Camille and Josie grinned. "We'll look after her," Camille said. "She's been cooped up far too long, don't you agree?"

"Far be it from me to have a say in anything she does. Grace has always marched to the beat of her own drum," Aunt Katy said. "I learned that early on after her mother passed away. If she says she's going to do a thing, you best believe it."

Camille and Josie exchanged looks but remained silent.

"Oh, fiddlesticks!" Katy said. "Just be home before it gets dark. I won't sleep a wink until you do."

The three women climbed into the carriage and were off to Riverbend. Grace leaned against the leather seat, happy to be out of the house and on an important mission. And who knew, maybe Camp would be at the harbor when they arrived.

The air smelled of fish and sea when the carriage pulled into the congested traffic at the wharf. Grace scanned each of the ships hoping to see the *Valiant*. That was not to be, nor was the *Savannah Rose* in port. Grace and Camille exchanged disappointed looks.

"One of your other ships should be in port, shouldn't it?" asked Camille. "Have you traveled in any of the ships your father left you?"

"Of course not," Grace said. "They are merchant ships. I rarely give them any thought since Cameron does the books for them." She looked over the line of vessels docked near the pier. "Though I must say, should I find one of our merchant vessels in the harbor today, it will have to serve as a passenger ship in order to get all our people to Charleston."

The three women glanced ahead at the long line of sloops, schooners, and merchant ships. "I see one of my ships, the *Regale*," Grace said. And straining to inspect the names of the other ships, she spied another vessel that belonged to her, the *Intrepid*.

The street was crammed with wagons, pedestrians, dogs, and street sellers. "Do you think we can get a little closer to the ships?" Grace asked.

Camille's driver must have heard Grace's request, for he immediately guided the carriage through the mix of traffic and pulled up just past the gangplank of the *Regale*.

"It's anybody's guess if Captain Gifford is even aboard the ship," Grace said as she stood. The driver jumped down and assisted her to the ground. "Thank you, sir." She watched as he helped Camille and Josie climb down. Then he stood at attention.

"Burton, we shan't be long. Wait for us," Camille instructed. The three women wove their way up the gangplank.

"Can I help you, ladies?" came the voice of a crewman, his eyes searching the women.

Grace stepped forward. "Is Captain Jackson Gifford aboard the ship?"

"Wait here, please. I'll fetch him for you." He strode away, disappearing among the sailors shouting and moving about the main deck. Men worked on rigging and patched holes in a large mast. It wasn't long before the women were aware of the sailors staring at them, some with half grins on their faces.

A moment later, a tall dark-haired man with a broad-brimmed hat appeared. The man looked too clean-cut for a captain. His beard and mustache were neatly trimmed, and in spite of the heat, he wore a dark jacket. His hand went to his chest, and recognition showed in his eyes as they settled on Grace.

"Mrs. Bartholomew," he said. "The last time I had the pleasure of your company was at the celebration of your arrival to Cooper's Landing. You honored me with a dance." His grin deepened the creases in his face. "What brings you to my ship?" His eyes traveled over her face and down her dress until it reached the swell of her stomach. He cleared his throat.

"Is there someplace we can talk, Captain Gifford?" Grace lifted a hand over her brows to block the sun as she looked up at him.

"Follow me, ladies." He led the way to his cabin and pulled out a chair for each of them. He turned to the seaman who'd followed them. "Go to the galley and bring back fresh water for my guests."

"Aye, Cap'n!" The sailor disappeared out the cabin door.

Captain Gifford glanced at the three women and stopped when they came to Grace. He eyed her appreciatively. "I have to wonder what would bring three beautiful women to my not-so-comely ship."

"Are you aware of the slave rebellion raging through the islands, Mister Gifford?"

His brows rose. "As a matter of fact, I am. There's been a lot of talk in the taverns about these gruesome savages who have attacked several plantations west of us."

"That's why we're here. We need the use of your ship to sail to Charleston."

Gifford frowned. "We've only just arrived in port."

"I need a couple of days to finish last minute business," Grace said. "Will that give you time to prepare for our voyage?"

"How many passengers are we talking about?"

"The best I can guess is twenty-five to thirty, and my cat, Smitty."

"Thirty people and a cat," Gifford tapped his lip with his index finger. "This is not a passenger ship."

She leveled her gaze at him. "You will have to make it one for this trip."

His eyes fell to her stomach again, and he cocked his head. "I have to answer to Cameron. Does he know of this outrageous venture?"

"He isn't here and we are in danger if we stay."

"The sea is rough on the best of days."

"I sailed all the way from Charleston to Barbados and to this island a year and a half ago. I'm familiar with the antics of the sea."

Grace and the captain stared at each other, neither wavering.

Finally, Captain Gifford lifted his shoulders and dropped them, heaving a heavy sigh. "I'll see what I can do, Mrs. Bartholomew."

"I want decent bedding for all the passengers. Spare no expense to see that is done."

His eye narrowed. "It'll be tight quarters."

"Of course."

Captain Gifford strode to the cabin door and opened it. He stared out at the wharf as if giving her demand some thought. After a moment he said, "I'll give you this cabin." He shrugged and turned to face her.

"I don't need special accommodations, sir."

"Yes . . . you do. As I said, I have to answer to Cameron."

"Very well. Can an extra bed be brought in?"

Gifford glanced around the semi-spacious cabin. "I can arrange for another bed."

"For my midwife," Grace said, as if to clarify her request.

"Of course." He nodded.

Grace stood and heaved a sigh of relief. "That's settled. We will begin sending trunks and crates of personal supplies in the next two days. I'd like to leave Thursday."

His lips thinned. "Today is Monday." Grace waited without speaking. "We'll be ready Thursday morning at daybreak." Gifford's jaw tightened and she saw a flicker in his eye.

"Thank you, Captain. Until then."

Josie and Camille rose from their chairs. The sailor who'd gone for water held a tray of mugs outside the cabin door as the women filed out into the sea air.

"Your drinks?"

They each sipped the refreshing water and set their cups on the tray. "Thank you," the trio said as they made their way to the main deck and the gangplank. Once they were back on the street, Josie turned to Grace. "It's not often I see you in command of things. I'm impressed."

"Don't be, Josie. I'm quite a mess at the moment."

"You sure could have fooled me," Josie grinned.

"Yes, well . . ." A grin crept up her face. "I was half afraid the captain would refuse my request."

"You gave him no room to refuse and don't forget, you're his employer."

"I know, but I'm asking the impossible to get all my people on board his ship."

"He'll make it work," Camille assured her.

"He doesn't have a choice!" The three women glanced at each other and bubbles of laughter sailed through the air.

"Where to now?" asked Camille.

"The *Intrepid.*" Grace pointed to the vessel up the road on the wharf. "I need to see Captain Picoult. He'll be carrying the crates of supplies, furniture, horses and my father's carriage."

Camille and Josie stopped walking and stared at Grace.

"I'm not leaving them behind." Grace's chin jutted out.

"Lead the way," Josie said as they continued on. "This ought to be interesting."

TWENTY-FOUR

IT WAS LATE afternoon by the time the women finished their business, ate their noon meal at the Poppy Cock hotel café, and stopped at the new dressmaker's shop. By the time Camille's carriage headed back to Cooper's Landing, the sun was sinking below the horizon, its orange glow casting flames beneath the clouds. As they rode along the narrow lane, the orange changed to fiery red, and then to dark purple. In Jamaica, evening came fast. It wouldn't be long before the sky was black.

Grace was aware of the danger of three women being out on the lonely road with only Burton, the driver, for protection. Did he carry a musket? She tried to listen as Josie and Camille talked on the way back from the pier. They rode on for nearly an hour. This was the *longest* road at night.

"I do wish Drew had been in port," Camille said, wistfully.

"You're not alone," Grace said. "I'd give anything to travel to Charleston with Cameron. It appears that is not to be. You must alert your family to prepare to leave the island with us Thursday morning."

"Thank you, Grace. I'm sure Father will repay the favor some way."

"We must get home and get a good night's rest. Tomorrow we'll begin the process of packing and preparing for the journey."

As the carriage rounded the bend in the road, all at once Burton gasped and pulled on the reins. They had nearly careened into an overturned cart that lay on its side. Burton guided the horse to the left, missing the wreckage by a mere foot. He glanced back at the women, a stricken look on his face, then raised the whip to go on.

"Stop!" Grace called.

"Missus Bartholomew we should keep going," Burton called over his shoulder. "There might be slaves hiding in the bushes!"

"And leave these people stranded on the road?"

"Ma'am . . ."

"Stop the carriage!"

The driver pulled on the reins, jumped down, and ran to see if anyone was hurt. Supplies were scattered on the ground, and he wove around the items with only a sliver of moonlight to show the way.

Grace's curiosity got the better of her and she climbed down. As she neared the wooden cart, a young servant girl peeked out at her from around the corner.

All at once a blood-curdling scream ripped the air.

Camille ran up to Grace before the sound died away. "Who was that?" she asked, hugging herself and glancing about.

"I don't know, but it sounds like a woman in pain." Grace peered in the darkness, groping along the cart until she heard panting. She could only see the silhouettes of tree trunks in the dark. Where the woman was, she couldn't tell.

"It be my mother, Miz Grace," the young girl said. "She gonna have that baby."

Grace took a second look at the young girl and realized who she was. "You're Cuffee's daughter, aren't you?"

"Yes'm, Miz Grace. I'm Lilly."

"Lord have mercy! Where's your mama?"

"Down there." She pointed to the ditch. "We be goin' to the harbor to see if my papa comin' back, when she hollered somethin' awful bad and she lost control. The cart toppled over and threw both of us out. Mama rolled down into the ditch."

Camille moved past Grace. "I see her. She's over there." The horse, still hitched to the cart, stood precariously near the pregnant woman's head, stomping his hooves.

"Josie, come help me," Camille said.

Josie moved to the other side of the cart where the horse's reins stretched taut. "We need to tilt the cart back up on its wheels."

Burton grumbled something under his breath, but he moved over to the horse and held him still as the women dragged Cuffee's wife away from the horse and onto the mossy ground.

Grace bent over the woman. "Tabitha, we're going to help you. Just hold on." Behind her Burton struggled to right the cart. The horse snorted and side-stepped up the bank.

Grace leaned down and watched Tabitha squirm, obviously in pain. Great puffs of air blew through her mouth as she strained and pushed. The woman let out another blood curdling cry that pierced the night.

"We have to go," Camille said, her voice quivering.

"We can't leave them." Grace stood. "Let's put their supplies back into the cart, then we'll try to get her into the seat."

They all scurried around picking up supplies by the light of the moon. Grace sensed someone hiding in the jungle beyond the road. Was that a rustle of leaves in the bushes? A chill ran up her spine as she tried to see into the darkness. Was it her imagination, or did she hear feet running in the distance?

"The baby be comin'!" Tabitha wailed.

"What do we do?" Grace whirled around. "I've never delivered a baby before."

Lilly stared wide-eyed at the three women. "Can't you help my mama?"

Tabitha wailed again and Grace thought she was going to faint.

"Get back." Camille took charge. She knelt down and pushed up the slave woman's skirts. She called back to Josie and Grace. "This baby is about to be born!"

An hour later, they were all on the road again. Josie rode behind in the cart with Tabitha, the newborn and Lilly, as Camille's driver led the way. The ride back to Cooper's Landing seemed like the longest ride Grace could ever remember. She was aware of the tense silence between her and Camille. Neither spoke, their eyes on the road, aware of the danger that lurked beyond them. And Grace fretted about Aunt Katy as well. Would her aunt be pacing the floor wondering where they were? They turned from the main road to ride up the carriageway lined with fringed palms black against the starry night. Ahead, the Great House came into view. Kerosene lamps lit up the front rooms. But the windows were pitch dark upstairs. She had expected the whole house to be lit up like a Christmas Tree. Grace heaved a relieved sigh. Aunt Katy must have gone to bed.

"Finally," Grace breathed. When they arrived in the circular drive, she climbed down and said goodbye to Camille. "I'm glad you don't have far to go," she said.

"If I tried hard enough, I could see the lights on my front porch," Camille said. "Still, my parents will wonder why our outing took so long." Camille leaned against the leather seat. "Good night."

Grace blew Camille a kiss and turned to the small cart in the drive. "Josie, let's get Tabitha and her newborn to their shanty."

Lilly's eyes shone white in the darkness. "Thank you for helpin' my mama."

Grace slipped her arm over the young girl's shoulders as they followed Josie and Tabitha. "I'm glad we came when we did, Lilly. But your mama shouldn't have been out on the road with one of our carts."

"We were lookin' for Papa."

"I know." Grace held her irritation in check. That Cuffee had left his family enraged her. She wanted to promise they'd find him somehow. But truth be told, she didn't know if they'd ever see him again. He had run off just weeks before Tia had been arrested. He had been her right-hand man, while she smuggled slaves for Morgan

Blissmore. Tia never dirtied her own hands. She left that up to Cuffee. He had led a double life: he worked in the wee hours of the night for Tia, and during the day, he worked the fields for Phillip Cooper. It was a shame he was gone. He had worked well with the field hands. At one time, Phillip had even considered making him an overseer. None of that mattered now, Cuffee had disappeared like a mole in the ground.

When they reached Tabitha's door, it creaked open and a young boy peered out at them.

"That my boy seein' to the rest of the children," Tabitha said, cradling the newborn in her arms. She pushed Lilly past the boy and climbed up the step into the shanty doorway.

Grace nodded and entwined her fingers at her chest. "Get your things together. We'll be leaving for a long journey in two days."

"Where we goin'?" Tabitha asked.

"America."

"I don't believe I wanna go there," Tabitha said.

"You do if you want to see your husband again," Grace said, hoping to find him in the states.

Tabitha stared at Grace and then closed the door.

Grace and Josie stood outside in the vast darkness. Fear crept up Grace's neck and she instinctively encircled her stomach with both hands. Are *eyes watching us?* "Let's get back to the house," she said softly.

They quickened their steps until they made it to the kitchen door. Once inside, she whispered, "Goodnight, Josie."

"Aren't' you coming upstairs?"

"In a moment. Go on."

Josie slipped from the room, leaving Grace to stand alone in the dark kitchen. Grace leaned over the sink and tried to see out the window to the shanties and fields beyond. Cooper's Landing didn't feel safe any longer. Her eyes adjusted to the blackness and she pushed away from the counter. Weary, she headed upstairs.

She had only been in her room a moment before Hedy appeared, eyes heavy from sleep.

"We was worried about you, Missy." She started the task of unfastening the row of buttons in the back of Grace's dress. "Miz Johnson done went to bed, but not before she nearly wore a hole in the parlor rug. Is everything all right?"

"Yes, Hedy. We came upon an overturned cart in the road, that's all." Grace didn't think it wise to fill the help in on what really happened.

"Cuz of the rebellion, was it?"

"No. An accident. But everything turned out okay."

"I sure be worryin' a bit myself. That's why I came so quick. I be listenin' to every noise there be outside, wonderin' if you be comin' home tonight."

"Well I'm here, Hedy." Grace stepped out of her dress and bent down for her servant to slip a nightgown over her head. Hedy bent and pulled on the hem to straighten it. Grace laid a hand on the colored girl's arm. "Go to bed and get some rest. We have a busy day ahead of us tomorrow."

"Yes'm, Miz Grace. I'll be able to sleep real good now." She smiled, backed out the door, and shut it softly.

As was her custom, Grace went to the French doors and opened them. She stepped out onto the veranda and let her eyes take in the view in front of her. Beyond the outbuildings and cane fields lay a tropical jungle, and beyond them, the ocean. The trade winds began to blow in from the sea, rustling the surface of the bay into little waves, while in the distance tiny ships rested at anchor, their lantern lights blinking like lightning bugs. The moon cast shivering silhouettes over the palm trees. In the garden below, jasmine grew in profusion. A waft of aromatic scent sailed with the breeze. The fragrance reminded her of Tia and their past. Though the woman was gone, trouble still broiled at the estate. It was time to leave this island. She must go before it was too late.

TWENTY-FIVE

Princeton Harbor, Jamaica
10 September, 1831

IF THERE WAS one thing the prison guards wouldn't allow, it was a bunch of angry women sitting around with nothing to do but plan a way to escape the confines of the filthy place. An idle mind was fuel for fire and discontent. They wouldn't be sitting around for long, the guards would make sure of that. Beyond the walls of the prison fortress lay vast fields of pineapples, ripe and ready to pick.

Tia sulked most of the morning as she and the other prison women worked. The day was scorching hot after the early morning mist. It had drizzled enough to cover the plants with a thin layer of moisture. And now an ominous rise of steam hovered over them as the sun burned off the water.

Tia glanced down at the dirty rags covering her thin frame. Her garment had once been a lovely white gown with tiny jungle animals printed in browns and blacks, the hem lined with gold trim. The bottoms of her feet were cracked from months of walking barefoot over rough terrain. And her once soft hands were now dry and scratched and felt like leather. Her fingernails, no longer manicured, were chipped and ugly.

She had long since stopped looking into the well at her reflection in the water. When she did, what she saw sent a chill up her spine. She didn't recognize that woman looking back at her whose hair hung in tangles and whose face was so dry that a pale layer of dust hid the color of her skin and her identity.

Gone were the days of primping before a mirror fixing her hair and nails. Gone were the days of languishing in a warm bath, the water perfumed with flowered scents. And gone were the days of rubbing age-defying oils into her skin, her face, arms and legs to make her dark skin shine. What she would give to go to her wardrobe and pull out a shimmering gown and her gold slippers.

A sharp pain slid down her back and returned her to the present; every bone in her body ached. Tia sighed. Now all she could do was pin a sprig of white jasmine in her hair and remember the woman she once was.

Bending over the spindly pineapple plants day in and day out took a toll on her. And at the end of the day, being chained to the rough brick wall and sitting on the hard coarse floor only added to her discomfort.

"You best quit yer daydreamin' and get to pickin' this fruit, or you be wishin' yer mind had stopped its wanderin'," said an old gray-haired woman beside her. She pulled a large straw basket of pineapples along as she spoke.

"Mind your own business," Tia said. But she looked to see where the guard stood with his ever-present whip. She never thought she'd become a victim of that leather strap. But she was wrong. Not too many mornings ago, she had slowed her step, her mind wandering as it often did. The guard found her staring at the acres of pineapple plants, her mind a thousand miles away. A lash sliced across her back, sending her toppling over the row of pineapples, the stinging pain searing her skin.

"Back to work!" the guard shouted.

There hadn't been time to soothe the pain. The guard had yanked her to her feet and shoved her back in place. "Get back in line and pluck them fruits afore I give you a second lash!"

Tia had glanced down. She had picked up her thin knife that had dropped to the ground and, holding the top of the plant with her left hand, she sliced the stalk below with her right hand, and lifted the fruit out of the bed of greens. She tossed the heavy fruit into the waiting basket and moved to the next plant. As she worked, she felt blood trickle down her back, drying as it went, and sticking to her ragged dress.

The memory of that miserable day was not why she sulked this morning. Rather, it was the knowledge that Morgan Blissmore, a free man, had darkened the door of this prison in hopes of having a word with her. And what could the blasted man have to say of interest anyway? Her days of smuggling slaves were over.

A wry smile split her dry lips. Imagine the shock she'd see in his evil brown eyes if he saw her in her filthy garments covering her wretched skin. Never! And how was it that the man who had smuggled slaves long before she came along, was still roaming the sea? How had he dodged the authority of the British Empire? Yet he had! No, she wouldn't see him. Not now, not ever.

Tia sliced more fruit from the stalk, and threw it into the tall straw basket, then stood to stretch her back. The fields were dotted with a mixture of women, young and old, black and white. Some bent over the never-ending plants slicing the fruit from the thin stalks. Others helped heft full baskets of pineapples onto their coworkers' backs, who pulled a long leather strap attached to the basket over their foreheads to carry the weight. This balanced the baskets as the women carried them to the waiting donkey carts in the lane at the end of the rows.

Tia hefted her own basket, half full, and lifted the strap to settle across her forehead. "Throw in a few more pineapples," she said to the old woman as sweat escaped the bandana tied over her head.

The woman reached into her own basket and removed several fruits from her supply. "Thank you, Tia. I don't know why you be helpin' me. But I surely do thank you."

"Here," said Tia. She lifted the woman's straw basket as the short woman turned her back to receive the heavy load. "You go first." The two women worked their way past long stems that poked out into the path between the rows of plants. They usually stopped harvesting halfway through one row. By then the baskets were two-thirds full and too heavy to carry if they didn't empty them.

Once they reached the donkey cart, another woman lifted the baskets off their backs and dumped their load into the waiting cart. They would repeat this process throughout the day until the scorching sun reached the other side of the horizon. Then the prisoners would file past a guard who held a large wooden box collecting their work knives. One by one, the knives would clink into the box. The tired women would then be herded back to the dark hole in the ground where they would spend the rest of the night.

The evening meal was a bowl of slop; which consisted of stale water, a tiny morsel of meat–it was anyone's guess where that meat came from–and onions. Tia rested her weary head against the brick wall. She let her mind ramble to earlier days at Cooper's Landing. She imagined sitting on the beautiful brocade sofa, her feet resting on a matching ottoman. Gemma, the house servant, would enter the room and offer Tia a glass of cold island punch and a sweet biscuit. The tropical breeze from the trade winds of that long-ago paradise would be scented with jasmines, her favorite flower.

She had never appreciated the plantation as she did now. And to think it would be nine years and three months before she would set foot outside the doors of this prison. Would she ever see Kindra again after she had sent her away refusing to see her? She'd give anything to rest her weary eyes on her beloved daughter--to gaze at Kindra's silky smooth skin and emerald green eyes. Would that day ever come? Could she stay alive long enough for that day to arrive? She had to. She had to get out of here!

Shifting her back against the rough bricks, Tia shook her head. Of course she would leave this wretched place. She had a secret stash of emeralds waiting for her in the *Savannah Rose* ship. Her heart skipped a beat. Once she got out, she'd retrieve the pouch of stones she'd hidden in the vessel's first cabin. No one knew they were there except her. No one knew that behind the drawer, lying on the floor, lay a vast fortune.

The first thing she would do when she got back to Riverbend was to find the jewels and cash them in for British pounds. She wouldn't risk being found with the gems on her person. Jule Spade would probably be released from prison soon after she was out. Once she had the money, he couldn't prove she had stolen the emeralds. If she planned her moves just right, she might even be able to convince Jule to rekindle their relationship.

Together, with their nightmare behind them, they could build the fortress they had talked about. She would live in luxury once again, away from the perils of this compound. She would exchange her rags for riches.

Tia smiled inwardly. The guards thought they owned her soul and her every waking moment. But they didn't. They wouldn't wear her down. She had too much waiting for her beyond the confines of this horrid place.

She relaxed as best she could, letting her resolve wash over her. Eyes closed, she tried to sleep. Moments later, she felt a sting on her left toe and her eyes snapped open. "Get out of here you little devils!" She kicked a rat and sent him flying. She heard it shriek, then skitter away. She squinted her eyes in the pitch dark. She trained her vision on the tiny red eyes that pierced through the blackness. A half dozen rodents were nearby.

"Get off me!" another woman howled.

Tonight was going to be a long one. She and the other women would take turns chasing off the rats and hoping for sound sleep.

Nine years and three months, Tia thought. She'd get through this. She had to.

TWENTY-SIX

Cooper's Landing, Jamaica

THE SEPTEMBER BREEZE swirled around Grace's skirts as she entered the dining room to find Aunt Katy and Josie waiting for her. She sucked in a breath, ready to be scolded for coming home so late the night before.

Aunt Katy had bags under her eyes, a sure sign that she hadn't managed to get much sleep. Still, she waved a hand. "Don't worry, Grace. Josie told me what happened last night. I'm just glad the two of you made it home safe."

Grace let out the breath she'd been holding. "That's good to know. I wouldn't have blamed you a bit had you felt differently."

"All I want now is to help you pack so we can all go home," Aunt Katy said.

"You're not alone. Let's eat and we'll get started." Instead of seating herself at the table, Grace grabbed a biscuit and watched as Penny set a dish of scrambled eggs and salt fish on the table.

"Penny . . . please tell Dinah I need to see her, and then send Cato and Amos to see me."

"Yes, Miz Grace." Penny went through the swinging door of the kitchen and disappeared. A moment later Dinah came through, carrying a bowl of hot mush. She set it on the sideboard.

"You be needin' me, Miz Grace?"

"Yes, Dinah. Do you know where all the wooden crates are stored? We've got work to do."

"I do at that, Missy. I'll set Amos and Cato to bringing them up to the house."

"Where are all the trunks I brought?"

"They be in the same place," Dinah said her dark eyes round.

"Good. Then have the men bring them up to the house too. We need to start packing. We have no time to waste." Grace bit into the sweet biscuit.

"You gonna want all your mothah's china?" Dinah asked.

"Yes. She was particularly fond of the set. Father purchased them as a gift for her."Grace's gaze moved to the portrait of her mother over the sideboard. "I want Mother's picture wrapped up securely, and my father's as well."

"Course you do, honey girl. That be all you got left of them."

The house was in full steam as servants scurried from room to room packing items in crates per Grace's instructions. She could count on one hand the things she didn't want to forget and she kept checking to make sure they were wrapped or packed and waiting to be delivered to the *Intrepid*. She'd already set aside her rapier she'd brought from Charleston, and her father's heavy sword. She had Cato bring the weighty saber, encased in its royal blue shield with the Cooper seal on it, down from the master bedroom on the second floor.

As the morning progressed, Grace watched the servants carry crates of dishes and supplies out of the house to the waiting wagons in the circular drive. Thunder rumbled in the distance. September rains were normal. She hoped to get a load off to the harbor before everything got soaked.

While she stood on the front porch, a half-dozen of her workers walked up to the front yard from the northwest cane fields. Their dark eyes lanced her. What were they doing here? Why weren't they out in the field working as they should be? And where was Mingo that he didn't know the men were gone from the fields? A shaft of fear slithered down her back.

Lightning crackled overhead; its long sinewy veins of ghostly light streaked the grey sky. Every hair on Grace's arms stood straight. A million thoughts raced through her mind. She stared at the slaves and wondered, had they come to attack those of us who live in the house?

Within seconds, thunder rolled like a drumbeat, and with the rumble came a cool breeze giving Grace a chill . . . or was it from the threatening glances of the darkies?

One man stopped at the base of the porch stairs. He squared his shoulders. "What you be doin', Miz Grace?"

"Excuse me?" She'd never had a field hand question her actions. This surprised and alarmed her.

"Why you be leavin'?" the man asked.

"I might ask why you and these men are roaming the grounds instead of working? Where's Mingo?"

"He in the east field with the gang workers. They hoeing and planting the new crop. He only have two eyes. And he be only one man," the darky said, a curl to his lips.

A chill ripped up her back. She understood his meaning. She steeled herself. "So what is it you want?"

"We be warnin' you to go. There be a lotta our people comin' this way. They tired o' workin' for the likes o' you. They not patient. They not give you a warnin'. They jist kill you." He jabbed the machete he held in the air, pointing it at her, his black eyes fierce.

Grace took a step back, her resolve taking flight.

The darky gazed at his companions and they nodded, flints of fire in their eyes. It wasn't until now that she noticed they each had machetes in their hands. One black man bent and hacked at the tall grass in front of him, sending green blades flying in all directions. He stopped and looked at her, and then ran an index finger over the blade. He smiled wickedly.

Grace swallowed. She wouldn't run. She wouldn't show fear. That's what they were looking for. Her knees felt like jelly, but she faced the men nonetheless. She dragged her glance away from the man who toyed with the machete and swerved to look at the one who stood in front of the porch. She squared her shoulders. "Thank you for the warning."

"You go now!" he said.

"We leave in two days," she shot back.

The field hand jabbed his machete into the ground with such force that the handle wobbled in the air. He stared at the long knife and then his gaze narrowed at her. "Two days! No more!" He yanked the blade from the ground and his hand went up as he waved the men to follow him. The five men stared at her for what seemed an eternity before they started to walk away, single file, behind the first man.

"Wait," Grace called. The men stopped and glanced back. "Send Mingo to the house."

The first man nodded, then they all left. None of them looked back.

Grace's heart thundered in her chest. She'd been warned. Dare she trust them? On shaky legs, she turned to go back into the house. Aunty Katy and Josie were staring out the window, fear written all over their faces. When she stepped through the door, both women sped forward. "What was that all about, Grace?" Aunt Katy asked. Josie stood behind her wringing her hands.

"It isn't good, Aunt Katy. They warned us to go."

"It looked more like they were ready to attack you with their machetes!"

"But they didn't. We've got to get the packing done and go. I don't trust them."

All of the house servants stood in the room, wide-eyed. Then they began to whisper to each other or talk in low tones. Panic engulfed Grace. They had no time to waste. "Move!" Grace called emphatically. "You mustn't dawdle!" Within moments, tension and frenzy in the house was in full bloom.

Beyond the front door dark clouds covered the land and rain began to pour. Men ran to cover the wagons with canvas tarp while the women clamped lids on the crates and passed them off to Cato and Amos who nailed them closed for the ocean voyage.

Every now and then, Grace touched her stomach with a firm caress, as if to promise her little one they'd be safe. *I wish Camp were here.*

Servants moved in every direction, going up and down the stairs, and going in and out of rooms. They pushed the crates and trunks out to the porch while the male servants loaded them onto the soaking wet wagons. When they were full, the wagons would leave for the harbor, where dock loaders waited to carry the supplies onto the waiting ships.

"Grace, one of the field hands is on the porch," Josie said, her voice quivering.

Grace glanced over her shoulder and recognized Mingo. "Keep packing," she said and went to the door.

"Come in, Mingo." Grace held the door open.

He glanced awkwardly toward the foyer. "My feet be dirty, ma'am."

Grace stepped out onto the porch feeling the cool rain lessening the stifling heat.

"Mingo," she said, her eyes penetrating his. "Some workers came to the house. They carried machetes and warned us to leave."

Mingo nodded as if he knew.

"Did you send them to talk to me?"

"No, Miz Grace. We've been planting the east fields."

Grace felt rattled. "Why did they come to the house to warn me to leave? As you can see, we're working at full steam to do just that."

Mingo nodded again. "Things be bad, Miz Grace. Things be real bad."

"But you keep working as though nothing is going on."

"Mingo do what Massa Camp say to do. He say to keep the sugarcane growing. I be doin' just that."

Grace stared at him. "I don't think it matters anymore. I want you to pack your personal things. You're going with us."

Mingo stumbled backward as if her words stunned him.

"Massa Camp say I wait for him."

"There's no time and Camp wants you at River Oak."

Mingo stared at his large feet as if he'd find answers there.

"Mingo . . ."

All at once the rain stopped as if a spout had been turned off. They both looked out at the wet world beyond them.

"Mingo . . ."

"All right, Miz Grace. I get ready to go."

"Good. We leave early Thursday morning."

"Yes, ma'am."

"Be ready to travel before daybreak."

"Yes, ma'am."

"And for now, say nothing to the field hands. I don't want them to know you are going."

"Yes, ma'am."

"Who is your second-in-command out in the fields?"

"Abram, ma'am."

Grace paused. "I don't know him."

Mingo walked off the porch but looked back, his feet in the squishy mud. "I be ready Thursday mornin', ma'am."

Grace nodded and went back into the house. In all the time she'd lived at Cooper's Landing, she'd never seen it buzzing with activity like it was today.

Dinah strode up to her. "Miz Grace, you best sit and have a bite to eat before you get light-headed."

"Thank you, Dinah. I will." She found Aunt Katy and Josie at the table.

"What was that all about?" Josie asked, her eyes round.

"Mingo's going with us."

Aunt Katy nearly dropped her fork on the table. "Will there be enough room on the ship for all these people?"

"There has to be. Camp intended to take Mingo to Charleston. If he doesn't go now, I'm afraid he never will."

"Let Camp take him back," Aunt Katy said.

"No. He's going with us."

"Well, this is a fine kettle of fish." Aunt Katy shook her head. "You better eat; your food's getting cold."

Grace sat down and looked at the baked chicken, her appetite gone. She'd passed the morning with a frightful lump in her throat. She didn't think she could get anything past it now. *How had things gotten so bad?*

"Grace?" Aunt Katy said.

Grace picked up her knife and fork and started cutting the chicken into bite-sized portions.

Dinah moved the sweet potatoes and mango salad near her dish.

"Missy, I know your nerves be all twisted up. But you got a little bitty baby that needs nourishment."

"I know." Grace forked a bite. The chicken had been cooked in a honey glaze, and after the first bite her appetite returned. "Ummm," she said. "I'm glad I'm taking the cooks with us. They've spoiled me with their good cooking."

Later that evening Laulie, the midwife, stopped Grace in the upstairs hallway. "Miz Grace, may I have a word with you?"

"Of course. Right this way." Grace led the nanny into the sitting room adjoined to her bedchamber. "What's on your mind?"

"Miz Grace, I know I don't got no choice, but I don' wanna go on no boat away from heah."

"Why not?"

"I'm too old to be sailin' across the ocean. And to be truthful, I don't want to leave this place. It's been my home a lotta years."

"Laulie." Grace took the old woman's hands in hers. "I need you." She touched her stomach. "And the baby needs you. Things won't be like they were in the past. We'll all be gone."

238

"But Miz Grace– "

"You are family to Cameron, Laulie. You should be with us. And besides, you're the one who'll be delivering my baby."

Laulie shook her head. "All that sound good to me. But I have a bad feelin' 'bout goin'."

"Why?"

"Don't know, Missy. This feelin' been eggin' me all day."

"Don't worry. We're all going to be together. Nobody's going to let anything happen to you." Grace touched Laulie's hand.

"All right, Miz Grace. But these old bones ain't nevah been off dis island. I'm sure gonna miss dis place."

Thursday morning the candles and kerosene lamps burned in the wee hours. Everyone in the house was up and dressed and looking around to see if they'd missed anything they should take.

Out in front of the house, a large gathering of slaves climbed into the back of the wagons, some holding baskets of food. Tabitha and her six children sat among the travelers. She clung to her newborn, both of them crammed in amongst the rest of the darkies.

As she came from the house one last time, Grace saw smoke on the horizon beyond the fields. She stopped and stared at the dark grey smoke and red flames that seemed to be eating up acres of sugarcane in a far off field. Then she heard a faint roar of voices in the distance; slaves were running up the main road beyond the Borjeaus' plantation. Many of them waved machetes in the air while others carried torches.

Grace ran to the gate of the colored town. "Mingo! Come quick!"

Mingo popped his head out of his shanty and his eyes grew round. Flinging a sack over his shoulder, he stepped out of his cabin and rushed to her side. When they reached the long drive, they saw four wagons were loaded with servants and last minute crates to be hauled to the wharf. Coming headlong down the road, Grace saw a cloud of dust as the lead Borjeau wagon nearly tipped over when it flew into the drive and rounded the yard.

Camille's family were crammed into the wagon. Camille's mother, her face pale, sat tensely beside Camille, a shawl wrapped around her shoulder. All told, there were seven of them with her. They all looked over their shoulders up the main road toward their plantation. A trail of smoke spiraled into the sky from the direction of their home.

"Get out of here!" John Borjeau called out. "You've got to go now!" He climbed down and helped the last of Grace's servants into the wagons. Aunt Katy and Josie were already sitting up front on the first wagon.

"There's an army of slaves coming up the road. We have to go!" John said.

Grace could see the terror in Camille's eyes as she held little Jackson close.

Mingo looked back, then climbed into the wagon. He sat in the back, his large feet dangling over the edge.

The horses took off with a jerk, and the wagons bounced down the long drive. Aunt Katy's face was ashen as she sat facing the road. All she could say was, "Lord have mercy!"

Grace sat up front with her aunt and Josie. When she looked back at the fields, she saw they were all ablaze. As she watched, the fire rushed toward the house. Her hand flew to her mouth and she looked away. "This is all too terrible!"

She glanced back again and watched slaves who did not belong to them fling torches inside the front door, the windows and onto the porch. "No!" She started to stand.

"Sit down, Grace." Her aunt grabbed her arm and held on tight.

"I can't bear it," Grace sobbed. She watched the flames shoot up the draperies in the front rooms. "My father's home is going to go up in flames. Oh, God," she cried.

Up ahead, an army of British soldiers on horses flew down the narrow road. The wagons pulled to the side and stopped long enough to let the military thunder past them.

"They're too late," Grace sobbed.

"Don't look back, Grace. It won't do you any good. It's all gone, honey."

Grace fell into her aunt's arms and cried as the wagons picked up speed and headed to the harbor. "It's all going up in flames!" she wailed.

Even racing at full speed, it took nearly an hour for the wagons to reach the wharf. By then, Grace had collected her wits enough to prepare for boarding the ship. She and Josie had worked out a manifest of each person who'd board the ship, and who would be kept together on the voyage.

She watched Hedy climb down from the wagon carrying the cat in his cane carrier. "Hedy, can you keep him with you until we're settled?"

"Yes, ma'am. I'll keep an eye on Smitty."

Grace looked around. The servants moved up the gangplank, some looking unsure, as they'd never sailed before. Others kept looking back as if they feared for their lives.

Nerves were frayed.

Grace held her midriff as she started up the gangplank. *Lord God,* she prayed, *Give me the strength and wisdom to get these people aboard the ship and free from the rebellion behind us.*

Darkies stood and wailed in front of the burning Great House at Cooper's Landing. Slaves who'd been a part of the rebellion were gone. They had done their damage and fled to other plantations to burn and pillage and continue the revolt. Up ahead, British soldiers had captured some of the slaves and had bound them in neck harnesses before leading them down the road to waiting ships.

A lone horse and rider rode up the long drive towards the Great House. One of the women from the colored district turned to watch him. The rider continued up the drive and then dismounted. "I'm a mail courier and I'm looking for Grace Bartholomew," he said, his gaze on the horrific sight of flames licking through the windows and eating through the walls of the estate. "I've a letter for her." He held up a small envelope.

"Miz Grace be gone, suh." The black woman held a dirty cloth to her nose. "You best get dat lettah to de harbor, mistah. She be gone from heah. She be boardin' one o' dose big ol' ships."

"Where's she going?" he asked as he shoved the envelope back inside his breast pocket.

"She be goin' to her new home 'cross de water. I hear her say she be goin' to de River Oak. Dat be in America. I know cuz dat be all she be talkin' about dese days."

"How long ago did she leave?"

The colored woman shook her head. "Don' know 'zactly. Sometime dis mornin'."

"Did she say which ship she's sailing on?"

"No, suh. But I be knowin' it be sailin' out today. You might be tryin' to catch her before de ship leave de port."

The courier mounted his horse and circled his ride toward the main road. The horse snorted, skittish with the acrid smoke that filled the air. The young man nudged the steed toward the harbor. The horse flew down the narrow road.

The courier didn't have trouble locating which ship Grace was on. The dock loaders were still bringing trunks up to the main deck where the mistress paced.

"Ma'am," he called waving an envelope in the air. "Missus Bartholomew . . ." he said, reaching his arm forward, letter in hand. "I've a post for you."

"Thank you, sir." Grace took the letter and glanced at the address in the upper left-hand corner. "Barbados. It's from my sister!" A smile lit her face. "I shall read it once we've set sail and we're all settled."

"Well," said the young man, backing away as he noticed the gangplank was ready to rise. "I best get off this ship or I'll be sailing with you." He raised his cap. "Good day."

Grace looked at the script on the envelope again and hugged it to her chest. She hoped the letter brought good news. She needed something to cheer her up. She wanted to tear the seal open right then and there, but it would have to wait. She still had things to see to before she could relax in the privacy of her cabin. She slipped the envelope into her skirt pocket and turned back to the business at hand.

Right now, even with all these people who surrounded her, she still felt very much alone. She needed Cameron more than ever. She'd give anything to relinquish being in control and put it all into his strong competent hands. As it was, the ship was sailing away from the harbor. Tears stung her eyes and she swallowed. The shore grew smaller and smaller as they moved out into the ocean. She lifted her chin. She was going home. Cameron would be there. They were going to start a new life. With that thought in mind, she moved toward the captain's cabin. Once inside, she would give herself permission to have a good cry.

TWENTY-SEVEN

The Regale, Caribbean Coast

STUNNED BY THE morning's events, Grace took a deep breath and tried to calm the frantic beating of her heart. The beautiful Great House her father had built was gone, just like her mother and father were gone. She felt her world slipping away. She touched the envelope in her pocket, thankful the post-boy had found her in time. The letter was a lifeline to her sister.

The *Regale* sailed far enough out into the waters that Jamaica was only a glimmer on the horizon. She stood a moment longer, wanting to see the last of the land before it, too, was gone.

She should find Aunt Katy and Josie and see that they were settled into their cabins. Turning, she nearly bumped into Captain Gifford. "Oh!" she said, as the captain's hand flew out to steady her.

"Pardon me, Missus Bartholomew. I came to deliver you to your new quarters."

One hand flew to her stomach, as Grace looked up at the dark-haired man, whose brown eyes studied hers. "I've yet to get my sea legs, Captain Gifford." She brushed his hand from her shoulder and stepped back.

"Of course."

"Before I settle into my cabin, I'd like to make sure my aunt and cousin have found theirs and are comfortable."

"They are one step ahead of you, Grace." He paused. "May I call you Grace?"

"Certainly. We will be on this voyage for several weeks. I think we can drop formalities."

"Good. Then as your employee, you may call me Jackson."

"Uh . . . no. I prefer to use your title . . . for the sake of the passengers, Captain Gifford."

A smile spread across his face. "As you wish."

Grace cleared her throat and cast a glance behind him. "You say my family is already settled in their rooms?"

"Your cousin insisted we take your aunt to their cabin. It seems she had a trying morning."

"The word *trying* is putting it lightly, Captain. We've all had a ghastly morning. We nearly lost our lives as the Africans raided the house and fields with torches. I saved the people I could, but many of our workers were left behind. How they'll survive, I don't know."

Tears stung her eyes, and she strayed from looking at the handsome captain to the jade waters beyond.

"Come. Our crew will see to the passengers getting settled in their quarters. You should rest."

Grace sniffled and let him guide her to the captain's cabin that she and Laulie would share. "I was never cut out for such devastation," she said, wiping her eyes with the back of her hand.

"No one is, Grace. I commend you for the enormous task set before you. Watching the wagons come and go the past couple of days, and seeing the host of people you brought aboard this ship, I think for such a tiny woman, you've done an excellent job of saving a great many people."

When they reached the cabin, Grace breathed in deeply and looked up. "Thank you, Captain. I do wish you'd have given me another room, though. I hate to put you out of your personal living quarters."

"Nonsense. None of the other cabins would be fitting for you. I'll manage quite well with the crew. It'll be a good reminder of how good I have it when you no longer have need of it."

A quiver ran through her as she stepped into the lovely room. She set her reticule on the round table, and glanced about the small space. It wasn't as large as the cabin she'd had on the *Savannah Rose,* but it was more than sufficient. Being the captain's cabin, it was warm and plush unlike the crew's quarters with mere hammocks where she was certain many of the servants would sleep. This room boasted a real bed, writing desk, two plush chairs, and a bathtub.

Her brows raised. "I don't recall the tub, Captain Gifford."

"It is the one luxury I've afforded myself." He crossed the floor and stood at the head of the brass tub. "Don't worry. You didn't pay for this. I did." He grinned.

"I never gave it a thought. But I'm glad you did." Grace bent to look at the brass legs.

"It's bolted to the floor. No matter how the ship sails, the tub isn't going anywhere."

"Good." The extra bed was in the room as she requested. The cot was narrow but it would do.

"The midwife will share my room. Might you find Laulie, so she can bring her personal belongings in, too?"

"Right away." Captain Gifford stepped out and shut the cabin door behind him.

Grace went to the plush bed and sat down, remembering what it had been like when she sailed over a year ago to the island of Jamaica. It would be three, maybe four weeks before she saw dry land again. She might as well get comfortable. She reached into her pocket and drew out the envelope from Kindra.

What news do you have, sister?

Grace awoke hours later. At first she forgot where she was. The swaying of the ship brought her back to the present. She was going to her new home at River Oak. She hoped Cameron would be there waiting for her. Exhilaration filled her at the prospect that they'd be reunited soon. Then her eyes settled on Kindra's letter on the desk. She rose from the bed and held the vellum paper in her hand. Before reading it again, she glanced at Laulie's cot. It looked as though the woman hadn't come to claim her place in the cabin.

"Hmmm," Grace murmured as she re-read the short letter. When done, her eyes circled taking in the contents of the room, but her mind was still on Kindra. She had brought Grace up to date on all the news that had happened since she and Denzel had arrived at Kindra Hall.

It seemed there was no easy solution for getting rid of the former managers to her estate, and being black plantation owners had been a trial for both of them. Still, Kindra wrote of the beautiful mansion Phillip had built for her and their determination to make it all work. She'd even had a visit from Agnes Cavendish. Grace loved the old woman all the more for checking up on her sister.

The darkest part of the letter was the news that Kindra and Denzel were laid up in bed for a few days after a nasty ordeal at a tobacco festival.

We're strong. Grace concluded. For both she and Kindra had been through unthinkable hardships and neither had lost their baby. She rubbed a hand over her stomach. "Now to get through the ocean voyage and home to your father," she said to the baby.

A knock at the door brought her head up. "Come in," she said.

"There you are," Aunt Katy said as she entered the room. "Well, look at this, Josie. A room fit for a queen." She took in every nook and cranny before she said, "We've come to take you to supper."

Grace leaned against the rail of the ship as she gazed at the *Intrepid,* the sister ship a distance ahead. As they slid across the swells of water, the ship looked ghostly against the starlight. Grace thought of Cameron. *Won't he be surprised to see me?* She expected him to be angry too, that she had sailed in her condition. She would have to remind him that she and the baby had made it in one piece, for she was certain they would pull into port in good shape, seeing how they were halfway there and nothing contrary had threatened the baby's health.

A shiver ran through Grace and she hugged herself. Other than the muted creaks and groans that came naturally for a seasoned ship, a deathly silence hovered over the murky waters. An array of stars twinkled from an ebony sky into a dark world. Was she following the right course? She had prayed for guidance, and she felt she'd done the right thing leaving Cooper's Landing. Only their home had gone up in flames; they could have lost much more had she stayed. Her thoughts were in turmoil as she looked out at the black water, unable to discern much of anything. If it weren't for the lanterns on the *Intrepid*, she wouldn't have seen it.

"You're enjoying the night air," Captain Gifford said.

Grace didn't turn. Rather she leaned in a little more against the ship's rail.

"Yes. It's so quiet."

"I wish you wouldn't come out here alone. Anything can happen."

"I've been careful, Captain."

"It's late. You should go back to your cabin."

"Am I to assume you'll not retire to your room unless I retire to mine?" Grace kept her eyes on the inky waters, a small smile curving her lips in the silence that ensued.

Black clouds slid over and covered the moon and stars as if the expanse of sky were swallowed up, leaving an ominous threat over the sea. A rush of wind followed and she heard the groan of the ropes against the yardarms, then the noisy snap of canvas filled with the winds. The water began to roll higher and the splash of waves could be heard against the hull.

"The winds are picking up. To bed with you," Captain Gifford clamped his fingers on her arm. "That's an order."

"Yes, Captain. As you wish." She let him escort her to her cabin, where she said, "Good night." When she stepped inside, she found Laulie fast asleep on the small cot.

Grace tiptoed to her bed and pulled off her shoes and slipped out of her dress into her nightgown. After she blew out the lantern and crawled under the covers, she turned on her side and listened to the sounds of the water. Slap . . . slap . . . slap . . . was the constant rhythm of waves hitting the hull to form a never-ending beat that lulled her to sleep.

Grace didn't know how long she'd slept, but as she awoke, a low rumble of thunder shook the sea. Boots pounded the deck outside her cabin door. The *Regale* swooped over a wave, jarring the bed.

The next thing she heard was Captain Gifford's booming voice bellowing to the crew, "Tighten the rigging!"

Grace sat up and swung her legs over the side of the bed. She glanced toward Laulie's cot and found the bed empty. "Laulie?" Only silence.

Lightning illuminated the small cabin through the porthole. In that split second, Grace could see that Laulie was not in the room. The vessel tottered and a roll of thunder clapped overhead. "Where's Laulie?" Grace mumbled as she pulled on her robe and opened the cabin door.

A fierce wind snatched the door out of her hand and stinging rain smote her face. Grace strained to grab hold of the door and step back into the cabin. Holding on to the door handle for support, she closed it. The vessel rocked and swayed. She felt the ship rise over a large swell, then sink as if in a valley.

Where is Laulie? I have to find her!

Grace pushed open the door again and stepped out into the biting rain. The wind slammed her back, but she pressed on. It was as if the wind were a huge invisible force that was trying to keep her from taking another step. She clamped her fingers on the slippery rail and swayed, her bare feet on the slick deck unable to find solid footing.

She pushed forward, clasping to the rail as her life line. Up ahead sailors worked to tighten the rigging that had torn loose. In the murky night Grace searched for Laulie on the main deck. Slowly, she inched forward, her nightgown drenched and clinging to her body.

Someone shouted, "Get that darky off the main deck!"

Laulie!

Grace tried to see where Laulie was, but the onslaught of rain obscured her vision. A gust of wind slammed into her and she lost her grip on the rail, falling to her knees on the slippery plank floor. The ship slanted to the left and water washed over the deck. Men tumbled and rolled reaching out for anything to grab on to. Grace struggled to her feet. She had to get back to her cabin; her unborn child was in danger.

A foot of water covered Grace's feet as she scrambled again to get a firmer grip on the wet rail, determined to turn back. Then she heard Laulie's scream and froze. She had hoped the nanny had gone to the hold to be with the other servants, but now she knew for certain the old woman was on the main deck and in trouble, fighting for her life.

"Laulie!" she screamed.

Grace inched her way forward where experienced crewmen fought to get a foothold to pull on the rigging and tighten the mast. Sailors scrambled to and fro working furiously to stay the ship, but Grace could see Laulie clinging onto a ratline that dangled precariously from a wayward mast. Laulie looked terrified as the ship tilted dangerously this way and that.

"Hang on Laulie!"

Crewmen craned their necks to see where the voice had come from. When they spied Grace, their faces changed to a look of horror. Two men stopped what they were doing and slid to where Grace clung to the rigging.

"What are you doin' out here, Missy!" called one sailor.

"Get her back to the cabin!" cried another.

Across the deck, Grace saw Captain Gifford inching his way to Laulie, but the force of the wind and the tilt of the ship made it impossible. Lightning etched a ragged line across the sky, and the thunder that followed shook the ship so violently that crewmen lost their footing and slammed against the opposite side of the main deck, moaning and groaning in pain.

Grace slid forward to a wooden pole, banging her forehead against the beam. Her arms outstretched, she managed to keep her body from slamming into the wood, and hung on. She hugged the pole and slid to the rough deck, her legs wrapped around the post. She leaned her face against the coarse oak, panting, then she ran a hand over her stomach which had tightened. Salt-water stung her eyes as she tried to see where Laulie was.

The last time she'd looked, Laulie was clinging to a lifeline on the far side of the deck. But now . . . she was gone!

The ship tilted again. This time Grace used the leverage to get to her bare feet. Still hanging on, she glanced frantically over the deck. "Laulie!"

Captain Gifford shot her a glance as he struggled to his feet.

"Get back to your cabin!" he bellowed.

"I can't!" Grace clung to the pole. "I need to find Laulie! Where is she?"

The wind howled and the waves crashed into the sides of the ship. It was all she could do to hear him above the cacophony of wind and waves.

Captain Gifford started to make his way to where Grace clung to the pole. A wave crashed against the ship and he rolled and smashed into a large wooden box that was part of the main deck. He leaned against it for support and pointed to Grace. "Go back!"

Grace glanced behind her. The ship had tilted so far that the ocean water was nearly level with the rail. She couldn't go now. She feared the wind and rain would wash her over the rail and into the inky black sea. She clung to the pole, shivering, her nightgown clinging to her wet body. *Oh, God. Help me! I ask that you stop this storm and calm the seas!* Her teeth chattered as she hugged the wooden pole. She looked again for Laulie, but the woman was nowhere to be found. A wave of grief consumed her. Laulie was gone. She knew it. The waves had washed her into the sea!

A moment later, the wind eased and the rain became a drizzle. Crewmen worked frantically to right the ship.

Captain Gifford scrambled to his feet and trudged through the water to where Grace clamped her fingers in a vise grip around the post. "You've got to get back to the cabin," he said.

"Where's Laulie?"

"She's gone."

Grace felt a chill run through her body.

"Grace . . . let go of the pole." Gifford hovered over her.

Her hands went limp. She let Captain Gifford scoop her up and carry her to the cabin. She felt the salty breeze whip around them and the swaying of his steps as he moved alongside the rail. Once inside, he set her on the bed.

Grace's teeth continued to chatter. She couldn't speak, but her mind screamed--No! A moan came from her throat and she began to sob. She fell against the pillow and drew her knees up to her abdomen. "When is it going to stop?" Her shoulders shuddered as the tears flowed. She buried her face in the pillow, her wet body drenching the coverlets.

She was aware of the captain standing in the room, but she didn't care. Her heart was filled with anguish, and grief filled her soul. She needed to be left alone. Sobs wrenched from the depth of her being. Visions of the torment on the main deck flew through her mind. One moment the servant woman was clinging for dear life . . . and the next . . . she was gone. Poor Laulie . . . she cried. She buried her face deeper into the sodden pillow and cried her heart out.

A crewman came to the cabin. "Captain?"

"Morris. Bring Grace's aunt to the cabin. Be quick about it."

"Aye, Cap'n!" The crewman disappeared.

The sobs stopped, but Grace's breath stuttered in her chest and a heaviness consumed her. She felt the coverlets being dropped over her wet body. And she felt the captain standing, hovering over her, as if a sentry. But she couldn't look up. She didn't want to open her eyes. All she wanted was to go into an abyss and wake up to find this was all a bad dream.

Late the next morning, Grace awoke to the sun streaming into the small cabin. Someone lay on the cot that belonged to Laulie. At first, her hopes rose. She leaned on her elbow to see the nanny. Had it all been a dream? Was Laulie all right? But it wasn't Laulie. Hedy stirred and looked up. When she saw Grace was awake, she quickly crawled out from beneath the blanket.

"Miz Grace. You're awake."

Grace just stared at the young black girl. Her heart heavy, she had no words to say.

"You be tossin' and turnin' all night long. I be thinkin' you ain't never gonna fall asleep. But I be checkin' on you this mornin' and you be sleepin' like a baby."

"Yes, Hedy, I finally slept." She realized the coverlets were warm and cozy and peeked beneath the blanket.

"We changed your clothes and bedding," Hedy said.

"I see." A thick lump filled her throat and her eyes felt puffy. She burrowed farther under the blanket pulling it up to her neck. "I just don't understand why this happened to Laulie." When she spoke her throat felt raw and her voice sounded scratchy to her ears.

"I know, Missy. We all be wonderin' the same thing. Why she outside in the rain?"

"I woke up and she was gone. I went to find her. I was too late."

"Captain say there ain't nuthin' anybody could've done. The storm be too fierce."

Grace paused, then said, "She had a bad feeling about coming. She was right."

TWENTY-EIGHT

GRACE PRESSED HER nose against the porthole and felt the heat of the sunshine stream across her face. Excited voices beyond her cabin alerted her that something had changed. When she peeked out, she saw they were approaching the port. Charleston! She heard commands to lower the sails and the *Regale* slowed to a steady pace.

Grace flung open the door and stepped out into the passageway as the captain called out, "Bring her in easy."

She stepped back into their cabin and closed the door. "Hedy, we're here. Get me dressed."

"Yes, Missy. Things gonna be better now."

Two weeks had passed since the awful loss of their nanny. The day before, Grace had had a meeting with Mingo. They planned what they'd do when the ships pulled into port. Today, she would get off the vessel and let him deal with the details.

She found Josie and Aunt Katy, Camille and her family all waited for the gangplank to be lowered. Grace crossed the deck to the small party.

"Have you any idea what you'll do now that you're here?" Grace asked Camille.

"I'll look for Drew and the *Savannah Rose*. If he's not here, then I'll find a hotel and we'll wait for his return. Father has a friend who can help us too, should we need it."

"Good." Grace watched as the ship moved near the wharf. "For now, I'll go to Aunt Katy's home. From there I'll go to Fields Landing to find Cameron. He's been here long enough that people should know something about him."

The two women hugged. "Good luck," Camille said, tears shining in her eyes. "Thank you for bringing us to Charleston."

"I couldn't leave you behind. You are all such good people," Grace said.

Captain Gifford held out a hand to her. "I'm glad you made it to your destination with minimal loss."

She refused his hand at this remark. "Losing my midwife to the sea is not minimal loss, sir." Grace lifted her chin a tad.

"I understand your grief, but a storm like the one you experienced can take many lives in a matter of minutes. I lost two of my men in that same storm."

"You never mentioned you lost sailors, Captain Gifford." She lowered her chin. "I'm sorry to hear that."

"Thank you." He held out his hand again.

She took his hand this time. "And thank you for getting me and my people here. It was quite an experience to be sure."

The captain touched the brim of his hat and Grace picked up a small valise.

The gangplank lowered and the group moved to the opening. A mix of fragrance and smells met her as she followed her aunt and cousin. The scent of flowers tickled her nose, but just as quickly, strong odors replaced it. She smelled sea salt and seaweed, the acrid odor of burning oil, and smelly fish. Stevedores were thick among the crowd and their sweat nearly gagged her. But she didn't care. They were in Charleston, and she would see Cameron soon.

It wasn't long before Grace learned where River Oak could be found. And yes, the locals in Fields Landing knew her husband. Folks spoke favorably of him. Today she would see Cameron after seven long months. At the steamship office, she checked in her baggage, then glimpsed the red-and-white steamship rocking gently on the Cooper River. She and her servants would be taking the *River Belle* up the Taney River and if the information she'd been given was correct, the paddle boat would stop at a dock right in front of River Oak.

"Missus Bartholomew?" A porter approached her, wearing a yellow straw hat with a colorful band around the crown. "You best go aboard now and get settled. We'll be leaving soon."

Grace's heart beat against her chest. She had lived in Charleston all of her life until she went in search of her father and landed in Jamaica. Now, she was home. In fact, she was home for good. She swallowed. But it wouldn't feel like it until she saw Cameron.

The *River Belle* was over-filled with passengers since Grace brought all her servants, too. It steamed northward along the winding path of the Lowcountry. Standing on the deck, Grace couldn't drag her eyes from the scenery along the banks. She hadn't experienced the cypress swamps, or the brown marshlands, having always lived in the city of Charleston. But she delighted in the stands of magnolia and oaks that lined the river. She shaded her eyes and followed birds that swooped into trees or into the river and flew back up into the sky as if putting on a show for the spectators.

The steamer chugged on and followed a sharp bend in the water. Trees grew thicker here, and the marshy banks were more dense. If she watched carefully, she could see through the branches of trees where plantations lined the river, their lawns manicured and spreading uphill to magnificent mansions.

The air was hot and sticky. Grace pulled her handkerchief from her reticule and dabbed at her cheeks, forehead and the back of her neck. She stood at the rail, not wanting to miss the view as the steamer paddled upriver.

An old woman wearing a gray day dress and simple straw hat came to stand beside Grace at the rail. Several other passengers appeared on deck, as well. "You new in these parts?" the newcomer asked.

"Yes, I am. I'm Grace Bartholomew." She extended her hand.

"I'm Maggie Stowe." She accepted Grace's hand and nodded her head toward the riverbanks. "What brings you here?"

"My home is here. My husband has been building our new home and getting the estate in order," Grace said and smiled mischievously. "He doesn't know I'm coming."

The old woman stared at Grace's round tummy and raised her eyebrows.

"Oh," said Grace as her hand flew to her growing mound. "He's come to Jamaica to visit, but has spent the majority of his time here getting the house ready for our family."

"You best hope he's here and not on his way back to Jamaica," the old woman said. "Especially if this is a surprise." She glanced at the servants huddled together behind them. "These your darkies?"

"Yes. They sailed with me across the Atlantic Ocean."

"You got somewhere to put them when you get to your estate?"

Grace eyed the old woman who was full of questions. "I'm sure my husband has made arrangements for their shelter." Her chin lifted a tad.

The steamer slowed and bumped into a pier. Passengers gathered their belongings and lined up near the ship's rails.

"This is where I get off. I came to visit my daughter and grandchildren." Mrs. Stowe clutched a bag close to her side. "Perhaps I'll see you again."

Grace watched the passengers waiting to disembark. From the instructions the agent had given her, she wouldn't get off until they rounded a couple more bends. But she needn't worry. The captain would tell her when they arrived at the right landing.

After the steamer got underway, it was only another ten minutes before the paddle boat slowed to a stop. "This is your dock, Missus Bartholomew," said the captain.

Grace looked out across the rolling lawn and up the hill where a large house was under construction. She could see men working, coming and going from inside the Great House. Oaks lined a long drive leading up to the mansion. To the right, a small house sat on the lower ground, magnolia trees surrounding it. Beyond were the rice fields. She couldn't take it all in at once. There was too much to see.

"Well, Miss?"

"Oh, I have trunks and boxes that need to be unloaded."

"Right away, Miss." He held out his hand. "Your ticket?"

"Here you go." Grace handed him the ticket and turned to her servants who waited together on the back half of the deck. Zeek and Dinah leaned into each other, Dinah's arm around Zeek's waist.

It took Grace a moment to take this in and remember they were husband and wife. Nate and Gemma stood beside them. They, too, stood close together, Nate's arm protectively over Gemma's shoulder. Grace smiled to herself. There was a certain satisfaction she felt knowing she and Cameron did not split up the families.

"Follow me," Grace said, and she fell in step behind the agent to the gangplank that led to the small dock at the river bank. Soon her luggage and boxes were piled on the pier, along with the slaves' belongings. The servants had walked down the gangplank, and one by one they stepped onto the small dock and moved onto the ground beyond, standing in the shade of the old oaks and magnolias along the embankment. Within ten minutes, they were all off the steamer and on dry land, the children sitting on the green grass.

Three loud blasts from the ship's whistle signaled its departure. The *River Belle* belched a black cloud of smoke and steam and moved away from the landing.

A tall man strode down the lawn, coming toward her. He walked like a man who was in charge. But that couldn't be, because Cameron would be that man. Still the stranger who looked to be in his mid-thirties sauntered toward her, a smile creasing his cheeks. He had sandy hair and nice features.

He stopped several feet in front of her, his brows furrowing. He glanced at the coloreds under the shade trees and then to her, her midriff, then back to her face.

"Hello," Grace said. "I'm Grace Bartholomew. Is my husband, Cameron here?"

The man seemed at a loss for words. He took another step toward her, then glanced up river at the steamer that had just left.

"I . . . I don't know what to say . . ."

Grace felt heat rising up her neck and over her scalp. Had they gotten off at the wrong place? "We are at River Oak, are we not?"

"Yes, ma'am, you are."

"Then where is Cameron?"

"You just missed him . . . he's sailing to Jamaica to bring you home."

TWENTY-NINE

The Valiant , Atlantic Ocean

CAPTAIN BUTLER WILDER left the taffrail and crossed the deck. Cameron glanced over his shoulder in time to watch the bearded seaman stride lazily to his side. Neither man spoke. In the silence that held them, Cameron heard the rigging creak and groan in the wind.

A multitude of stars twinkled from an ebony sky like diamonds, God's handiwork in a dark world. Cameron prayed he would make it to Jamaica in time to save his wife and child and the people who depended upon him. But save them from what? Grace hadn't said in her letter what danger they were in. He could only surmise the slave rebellion had begun. *God help them!* his mind cried.

It had been three weeks since they'd sailed from Charleston. Three weeks while his gut twisted in anticipation to get to the island and save his people. Three weeks that he hoped to arrive in time to pull Grace into his arms to protect her from all harm.

"You're awake," Captain Wilder said.

"I couldn't sleep."

"Have you slept at all since we've started the voyage?"

"Not much. Catnaps. My mind is racing too much. Sleep evades me," Cameron said.

"Cook has a tea that could remedy that."

Cameron stared out into the waters. Glimmers of an occasional wave caught in the lantern light. His jaw tightened as a salty breeze danced over him. "What if we don't get there in time?"

"Don't go there, Camp. You have to believe we'll arrive in time to save your people." Captain Wilder threw an arm over Cameron's shoulder as if to give reassurance, and then he let go and clamped the rail with strong hands.

Cameron straightened and wiped his face. "Maybe I'll take you up on the cook's tea."

"There you go. I'll wake him and set him to work."

"No. Don't do that. I thought he was awake. I'll go to my cabin and try to get some sleep."

"You sure?"

"Absolutely."

"Good night then." Captain Wilder slapped Cameron's back as he straightened again.

"What about you? You staying up?" Cameron asked.

"I've got to make my rounds before I retire."

A waning moon cast its silver light on the wooden planks of the ship. Cameron headed for his cabin with a heavy heart. *Let me get there in time, Lord. We have to save Grace.* He opened his cabin door and eyed the bunk across the floor. Sinking on the bed, he leaned back, neglecting to remove his boots. Fading off to sleep, he hoped to wake up in the morning instead of the wee hours of the night. He needed his strength for when he reached the island.

One week later, Cameron stood on the deck of the *Valiant*, his eyes intent on the shoreline beyond.

"We'll be docking soon," Captain Wilder said.

Home at last! Cameron sighed to himself, eager to rent a horse and ride out to Cooper's Landing. He heard the commands to lower the sails and the ship heaved to and slowed on its tack. They were approaching the port of Riverbend, the town he'd called home for the past twenty-four years.

Sailors scrambled to ready the ship as it came into harbor. Topsails were reefed and the mainsails trimmed.

"Bring her in easy!" Captain Wilder called out.

Twenty minutes later, Cameron walked down the gangplank searching the area for telltale signs of a slave revolt. His heart sank. The initial buildings at the wharf were intact. But glancing beyond, he could see that a few buildings had been burned to the ground. Smoke still lifted lazily into the sky, but it looked as if the fires were about to die out.

People walked about with numb expressions, white eyes against smudged faces. Their skin and clothes were black from the acrid smoke that filled the air.

Men and women arriving on land from the ships for the first time since the slave rebellion milled about the harbor staying close to the vessels as if they weren't sure they should venture any farther. Others passed through the crowds in a hurry to get to their homes to see if there was anything left to come home to.

Cameron's heart lurched in his chest. He strode to the wharf's tavern and flung the door open wide. He glanced into the dim room and stopped short of walking into the center of the smoke-filled barroom. "Has anyone seen my wife, Grace Bartholomew?"

The noise of the bawdy house ceased to a low hum. It appeared the fishermen, sailors and bar maids stared at him with half interest.

"You jist get off the boat?" asked a sailor.

Cameron nodded and waited.

"I've not seen the missus." He glanced at his comrades. "How 'bout you? You see Camp's lady?"

"Nay!" said another man. "You best look fer her out at the Landin'."

A barmaid sauntered up to Cameron and swayed, her hands on her hips. "Don't get your hopes up, mister. This island's never seen the likes of it, as it's been this last month. If the plantation owners didn't leave when the gettin' was good–"

"Sit down, Sadie!" A sailor grabbed the barmaid's waist. "Don't listen to her. Your missus might be waitin' fer you."

Cameron turned around and pushed the heavy door to the tavern open and stumbled outside. He breathed in the fresh sea air and blinked away the bright sunlight. He picked up his gait and made his way to the office of the harbor master. Albert Brumley occupied a small, squalid office with windows that looked out over the entire harbor. A cluttered table served as his narrow desk, stacked with a mix of ledgers and sea charts. Cameron poked his head inside the open doorway.

"Mister Bartholomew," Albert said.

"Hello, Brumley. I'm looking for my wife, Grace. Did she leave the island before the rebellion broke out?" Cameron yanked off his wide-brimmed straw hat and scratched his sweaty head.

"Can't say, Bartholomew. This harbor has been like the great exodus for a month now."

Cameron glanced down the road from the harbor office. Brumley had a perfect view of everything going on. "She could have left before the others. She would have taken some of the servants." Cameron stared hard at the man's sea-battered face looking for recollection in the man's eyes.

Brumley shook his head. "Sorry, Camp. I don't recall seein' yer lady at the harbor. Like I said, too many folks been scramblin' to get off the island." He clucked his tongue. "If she were smart, she'd have followed suit."

Cameron jammed his hat back on his head. "All right. I best get on out to Cooper's Landing." Cameron edged away from the harbor master's office and picked up his pace. The road was crowded as usual. He wove through the mass of sweaty stevedores and carts pulled by baying donkeys. He wanted nothing more than to get out of town and find his wife. He wondered if Captain Drew Harding was in port. He might know something about Grace. He looked up to scrutinize the ships lined up at the dock.

"You're here alone?"

Cameron wheeled around at the sound of a familiar voice.

Jacqueline Moore, a woman he'd courted before he met Grace, fidgeted with her parasol as she stood at the side of the road next to him. She looked him over, unabashedly.

"Not for long," Cameron said. He glanced across the road and found Ruby Moore, Jacky's mother, and Jacky's sister, Violet, sitting on a bench, their trunks waiting near them.

"We're leaving," Jacqueline said, matter-of-factly. "There's nothing left to keep us here."

"What happened?" Cameron asked, disappointed that the river town lay in ruins.

"Slave rebellion. The slaves took over most of the plantations on the island." She tipped her parasol outward. "And they tried to take over the town."

"Is the *Savannah Rose* here?" Cameron shot a glance up the wharf looking for the ship.

"Yes. Captain Harding rode out to his wife's family's plantation. We're waiting for his return so we can board the ship." She gazed up wistfully. Her red hair aflame in the afternoon sun. She looked as if she'd lost weight. Cameron didn't have time to scrutinize the devious woman. His heart hammered in his chest. He needed to find Grace.

Putting two fingers into his mouth he blew a piercing whistle toward the livery stable. He needed to rent a horse. A liveryman stepped outside the building. He looked up in recognition at Cameron.

"I thought that was you," Mr. Bailey said.

"I need a horse . . . and I need it fast."

"Yes, sir!" The stableman ran back inside the barn and, moments later, led a horse out onto the busy road. "That'll be twenty pence."

Cameron fished a coin out of his pocket and tossed it to the man. "I'm riding out to Cooper's Landing. I might need this horse more than today."

"That's fine, Mister Bartholomew. I know where you'll be. Can't say you have much to see when you get there, though." The man hung his head and shook it. "Most folks come back with bad news."

Cameron mounted the steed and pulled the reins to circle around toward the main road. He kicked the stallion's side and the horse jumped forward. Soon they were galloping down the narrow road that led to Cooper's Landing. Every mile they passed, his mind raced farther ahead. What would he find when he got to the Great House?

His hopes sagged as he rode on. Most of the plantations he passed looked a sorry lot. Some of the mansions were burned to the ground. And if not, there wasn't a soul in sight. Others showed the aftermath of the horrendous revolt. Windows were smashed and front doors stood open like dark holes. Furniture lay strewn in the yards, and the stock strayed on the estates as if no one cared for them. Cows mooed a mournful cry, and pigs, sheep, and goats wandered around.

His mind continued to race as feverishly as did his horse, whose hooves kicked up dust on the narrow lane. The words that always brought dreaded images to the white planters were *slave uprising*. Except by the intervention of God's hand, every planter's Great House would have at least one person with his throat cut!

The horse's hooves beat the ground as if beating drums as Cameron urged his mount to keep going. Another plantation came into view. Dazed, he stared ahead. The bodies of ten African men swayed lightly in the afternoon breeze, each hanging from a noose from the tall oaks, their arms tied behind them, their necks broken. Likely an overseer had seen to it that the ugly execution had taken place at once as a warning.

The farther he rode, the bleaker it got. The next bend would bring him to Cooper's Landing. He held his breath as the horse galloped on. At last he came to the carriage road that led to the Great House. He pulled on the reins to slow his mount. The horse snorted and side-stepped, his sides heaving. Cameron stared with disbelief at the ruins.

Cooper's Landing hadn't been spared. It looked like all the other plantations he'd passed. His heart pounded in his ears as he nudged the horse's side and reined in to ride up the circular drive to the house.

Fear gripped him to the core.

The house was gutted and charred. It was too quiet. Not a soul walked about the estate. Numb, Cameron dismounted and tethered the horse to a burned post.

"Grace!" he called and heard his voice echo back to him.

"Grace!" He scrambled up the brick steps to what remained of the wide porch and slid on broken glass to a large gaping hole that once was the front entrance. Charred wood crunched under his boots. The second story to the structure had caved in and fallen to the first floor. All that remained were crumbled chunks of burned wood piled onto the charred floor of the Great House.

"Ah, Grace!" he cried, and fell to his knees. "No! Please God, no!" A cry leaped from the pit of his belly and consumed him with great gasps. He crawled on his hands and knees and shoved burned pieces of debris aside. "No!" He fell to his elbows, his head on the floor. "God, no!"

He stayed that way for a long time, the smell of acrid charred wood filling his lungs. When he lifted his face to look around, he spotted his reflection in a sooty broken window pane. His cheeks were black and tear streaked.

He rose to his feet and began pushing debris aside. Was there any sign of life? Might anyone have survived? He blinked away tears and wiped at his smudged face with black hands. He could only go a few feet. The blackened remains of the rubble stood in the way. He glanced out at the blackened fields where lush green sugarcane once grew. The outbuildings were burned to the ground. The only buildings that stood untouched were three slave shacks in the colored town. He squinted in the bright sunlight. Not a soul stirred.

He stumbled down the brick steps to the scorched lawn. He was going to be sick. He bent over, retching, and let himself vomit the taste of death. He gagged and spit. And vomited some more.

"No!" He lifted his face to the sky and cried out again with all his might, "Why, Lord?" He clamped his hands to his head and he cried, all the while spinning around, slowly taking in all the ruins. Angry, he kicked a wooden bucket and stumbled backward. The horse snorted and whinnied.

Cameron tore at his shirt as he walked to the side of the house and began to slowly move down the lane, the lane Grace walked every morning she was here. He saw her in his mind's eye; so beautiful and full of life, so friendly with the slaves, always seeking to help them. He gulped and tried to swallow the hot tears that clogged his throat.

So warm and lovely to hold . . . he remembered how she smelled . . . of fresh lavender. He stumbled past the slave district. Out of the dozens of cabins that used to house the field hands, he found it odd that three remained. They were fully intact as if the tragedy had never happened.

Then he saw them. There must have been at least a dozen Africans laying on the ground, lined up as if for exhibition. Their necks broken, deep welts tearing their flesh below their jaws. Two were women. Cameron gritted his teeth.

A growl worked its way from the pit of his innermost being. His heart kicked as if jungle drums beat in his chest. *Why? Why am I here and you are not? I don't understand!* He grit his teeth and his stomach roiled. "God! Why am I here and Grace is not?"

"Cameron?"

Cameron whirled around to see Captain Drew Harding standing in the lane. The man looked terrible. His face was pale and gritty with soot, and his eyes held a haunted look to them.

The two men stared at each other. Words not needed. From the look on Drew's face, Cameron could only believe that he suffered the same tragedy at his father-in-law's plantation as Cameron had found here.

Tears flooded Drew's eyes. "Did . . . did . . . you find anyone alive?"

"No." The word was barely a whisper. Cameron straightened. "No, Drew. I've not found anyone alive. Not a soul to be seen."

Drew nodded, a stark hollow gaze in his eyes. "What are we going to do?"

"I don't know. Right now, I don't want to do anything. Nothing matters anymore."

Silence filled the air. The two men stood, gazing at the charred remains of what used to be Cameron and Grace's home.

Cameron walked toward the structure, a great black mound of rubble. He stared at it for a long time. Drew stood by his side, a solitary friend who'd suffered the same.

"Where is everybody?" Drew looked out at the field and the three shanties.

"Gone," Cameron said. "If anybody lived, they're gone. No reason to stay here."

"What if . . ." Drew glanced up hopefully.

"What if they're in town?" Cameron finished the thought. Could Grace and the others have somehow escaped this nightmare? He wouldn't allow his mind to believe anything less.

"What if they are?" Drew said.

Cameron wiped his black hands on his breeches. "They sure aren't here . . ." He stared at the charred remains of the house and gulped.

Drew crossed his arms over his chest and stepped backward. "I refuse to believe they died in this rubble. Not at my house, either." He drew in a deep breath. "What do you say we go back to town and ask about our families?"

Cameron kicked another wooden bucket. A spark of hope flashed through him. "She's alive, Drew. I don't know where she is, but she's alive."

"My sentiments exactly. Somehow they got out of this hell hole."

"Let's go," Cameron said.

The two men mounted their horses and sat on their saddles taking in the burned ruins. Without a word, they nudged their horses and rode down the carriage lane one last time.

That evening, exhausted and discouraged, Cameron and Drew sat at a tavern. They had spent the afternoon questioning family after family, and they had visited multiple businesses that had survived the rebellion. Not one person recalled having seen either of their families. Frustrated, the two men were torn with disbelief. How could it be that their families had vanished without notice? Now they sat across from each other, staring at their hands.

"What are you going to do now?" Drew asked, his tone quiet.

"There's nothing left here. I'll sail back to Charleston. And you?"

"The same. My family's from Charleston, my parents and siblings," Drew said. "I can't even think what to do, truth be told. Camille's my life, my world. My son too. I'll find them." His eyes flooded with tears again.

"Grace." Cameron said, but he couldn't go on. His mind screamed that this nightmare be just that, a nightmare. He wanted to wake up and find out it was all a bad dream. He swallowed and looked up at Drew. "I've got to find her and my child. How can I leave here without knowing whether they survived or not?"

Drew nodded while a heaviness hung over them.

The door to the tavern opened and Captain Wilder entered the dim room. He nodded at the two men and stepped up to their table.

"From the looks of you two, things aren't good. I'm sorry." He touched Cameron's shoulder and then Drew's. He pulled out a chair to join them.

The waitress came to their table, holding a pitcher of rum. She filled their tankards to the brim.

Cameron tipped his tankard to his lips and allowed a large gulp of the dark, strong liquid to slide down his throat, radiating warmth to everything it touched. He leaned his head back and closed his eyes.

"I'll be bringin' some grub fer you too. Looks like y'all be needin' it." She slipped away before they could refuse. A moment later she was back with three plates piled high with rice, beef and vegetables all mixed together, and drowned in brown gravy.

The door opened to the tavern once more, and Jacqueline Moore stepped inside. She stayed by the door, but looked around the room. "There you are." She hurried over to Cameron's side and looked askance at Drew. "Captain, the passengers have been waiting all afternoon at the wharf. With the sun going down, a mist has gathered and it's quite uncomfortable." A scowl formed on her narrow brows. "How much longer will we be required to sit amongst those awful men working along the road?"

Drew glanced up, cutting his gaze from her to Cameron and then Captain Wilder.

"Why are you sitting alongside the road instead of inside the hotel where it's warm and dry? My ship has only arrived this morning and I don't know when I will sail," Captain Harding said.

Jacqueline frowned. "But we thought you were sailing out today."

"You thought wrong." Drew touched his lips with his napkin and then stared at Cameron. "Now if you don't mind, madam, we have our own troubles to deal with and need to be left alone."

"When will you sail?" Jacqueline asked.

"Tomorrow or the day after. Get a room and bring your mother and sister in from out of the drafty air."

Jacqueline turned away from the captain and stepped up to Cameron. Her lips pouted. "The trip would have been quite delightful with the two of us on the voyage. Unfortunately, I shall be traveling with my boorish sister, Violet, and my demanding mother. Your presence could have alleviated that." She tossed her burnished hair over her shoulder.

Cameron glared at her. "You seem to forget that I'm married."

"Of course, there is the handsome captain." She flitted a look at Harding. "But he's quite devoted to his wife." She gathered her full skirt in her hands and frowned at the three men. "This is quite a new adventure for me, traveling to America knowing I'm available to court someone when I reach Charleston. I understand there is a wide range of prominent suitors who are very well to do." She shot Cameron a venomous gaze.

"It appears, Miss Moore, that you have forgotten your audience. This is not a topic to be carried on in the company of men," Captain Wilder said.

"Well, Captain, maybe when Cameron sees my new suitors, he'll think twice about rushing into that silly marriage with Grace Cooper."

Cameron scooted his chair back and nearly stood, daggers in his eyes. Captain Wilder grabbed his arm and stood, pressing his palms to Cameron's shoulder. "Sit, my man. Don't let this silly wench goad you. She quite runs at the mouth!"

Jacqueline's chin jutted up and she marched out of the tavern.

The three men stared at each other with disbelief.

"And she'll be traveling on the *Savannah Rose,* I gather?" Cameron said.

"Sad, but true." Drew scowled.

"Better you than me." Cameron growled.

Captain Wilder stood and threw his napkin on the table. "I've quite lost my appetite. If you need me, you'll find me on the ship."

He started to walk away and thought better of it. "And for your information, Camp, Grace Bartholomew is one of the finest women I've ever met. This earth is a better place with her on it."

A young man sitting at a table next to them, bobbed his head toward Cameron. "Excuse me, sir, but I couldn't help but overhear what the captain just said about Missus Bartholomew."

The captain wheeled around and glanced at the young man. "Why don't you mind your own business?"

"I'm sorry, sir. I didn't mean to interfere. It's just that havin' met her on the ship only a month ago, that even in her condition," he cleared his throat, "she was quite a beautiful woman." His ears turned beet red.

All three of the men stared at the man. Cameron scooted his chair back and took a step to the man's side. "What did you say? What do you mean you saw her on a ship?"

The young man cleared his throat again and leaned away from Cameron. "I only meant that, as a postal carrier, I had a letter to deliver to Grace Bartholomew from Barbados. I went out to the estate, but . . ." He stopped wide-eyed. "The big house was in flames. One of the darkies was standing outside watching it burn when I rode up. She told me Grace Bartholomew was at the wharf getting ready to board a ship."

Cameron slid into the chair across from him. "Go on, lad. What do you know about my wife?"

"All I know is that I raced back to town and had no trouble finding the ship she was on. There was a host of people boarding the ship, prominent and colored."

"Well, don't stop there!" Cameron demanded. "Did you see Grace?"

"That's what I've been tryin' to tell you, sir. I had to deliver a letter to her. I handed the envelope into her very hands just before the gangplank went up. I had to hurry to get off or I'd have been one of the passengers." He smiled a cheeky grin. "She's a mighty pretty lady and was happy to get her letter. That's the best part of my job, sir, is seein' the looks on people's faces when they get their mail." He shrugged and crossed his arms over his chest proudly.

Drew stared at the man. "You didn't by any chance see my wife, Camille, did you? We have a small son, by the name of Jackson."

"That I did, sir. The little tike was tryin' to crawl all over the main deck and I remember a lady chasing him and callin' that little guy, 'Jackson, Jackson!'"

Tears flooded Drew's eyes.

Cameron considered this surprising news, trying to decide if he believed it or not. But a rush of relief welled up inside of him. The same with Drew from the looks of him. The two men stood and hugged each other, clapping each other's back. Then they looked at the astonished postal carrier and leaned down and pulled the young man to his feet.

"You just made the two of us the happiest men on earth!" Cameron said.

Drew called out to the waitress, "His meal is on us. He flipped a coin to the lady. "Make sure he eats good."

Captain Wilder was standing by now and his eyes lit up. "Guess I best be headin' back to the ship."

Cameron whirled around and stopped the young man before he sat down. "Did she say where she was going?"

"Charleston, sir."

"I best be telling the Moore women we'll be sailing first thing in the morning!"

"Excuse me, sir," the young man said. "Does that mean Grace Bartholomew is still in the land of the living?"

Cameron drew himself to full height. "Yes. I believe my wife will be waiting for me when I get back to Charleston."

"Good," said the postal carrier.

"Yes, that's good indeed," Cameron said. "But I shall have another sleepless night tonight," he said to the captain. "I won't be able to sleep a wink thinking of all the ways to tell my wife how much I love her. For that matter, I think I should put it all down in a journal."

When the three men stepped out into the dank air, Cameron heaved a sigh of relief and looked up into the heavens. *Forgive me, Father. I should never have doubted you would take care of my wife and family.* He noticed the stars were especially bright tonight, twinkling at each other.

I've said it once, but I'm going to say it again. Hang on Grace, I'm coming!

THIRTY

River Oak, Fields Landing
17 October, 1831

"WHAT?" GRACE FELT the color drain from her face. She took a step back and stared at the blond-haired stranger. Meeting him for the first time, she was wary. However, his southern charm, his intelligent grey eyes, had caught her off-balance. Her reserve toward him melted until she remembered what he'd said. "My husband isn't here?" She swallowed and then swayed dizzily.

Zeek, her butler, had been standing not ten feet away. His eyes stayed on her. Grace glanced at him and back to the stranger, feeling her world swirling hazily before her.

Zeek jumped forward and said, "Mistuh, my mistress 'bout ready to faint!"

The stranger lunged forward and reached out to grab Grace's arm.

"No," Grace said, pulling her arm away. "I'm fine." But she wasn't fine. In fact, after four weeks out to sea in her delicate condition, and having suffered the grief of losing Laulie in the thunderstorm amidst the challenge of keeping tabs on all the servants, she felt her world crushing in on her. As Grace's legs gave way, strong arms closed around her. She was lifted, then carried away from the water's edge. Feeling the sway of the stranger's walk, she sank into an abyss.

Sid Sparrow stood with Grace in his arms and glanced out at all the darkies who watched him. "I'll take her up to the cottage." He turned and carried Cameron's wife up the sloped lawn. Two older women picked up their skirts and followed him. When they reached the front porch, a Negro man brushed past them and opened the door, holding it wide for Sparrow and the two women to step through. Sparrow entered the master bedchamber and carefully laid the woman on the soft bed.

The older of the two rotund colored women who'd followed him took charge.

"Gemma, go fetch a glass of water for Miz Grace and I'll see if I can bring her to."

Gemma stepped out of the room and looked around for the kitchen. Sparrow led the way to a spacious room complete with all the amenities they would need to feed their masters. "The pump's by the sink and the glasses are on the shelves."

"Camp pretty near has this place ready for the two of 'em," Gemma said, glancing quickly around as she pumped water into a glass.

When they strode back to the bedchamber, Gemma said, "We's the house staff. Me and Dinah here, we be the cooks."

"Can you bring your mistress around?" he asked.

"Sure we can. Miz Grace just been through a heap o' trouble before we left the island and seein' as how Camp's not here, that just be more than the poor girl can handle. But she'll be right fine."

Sidney Sparrow nodded and watched as the cook bent over the bed and tended to her mistress.

Dinah wedged the edge of the glass between Grace's lips, allowing the fresh water to flow into her mouth, a few drops at a time.

Dinah straightened when Grace groaned and her eyes fluttered open. "Miz Grace?" Dinah said.

"Where's Cameron?" Grace asked.

"We're right sorry you havin' to go through this disappointment," Dinah said. "But like the man said, Cameron be on his way."

275

An hour later, and refreshed, Grace stepped out onto the porch of the cottage to find the stranger sitting in a wooden chair holding Smitty, her orange and white cat. Smitty sat languidly purring as the man stroked his fur. The stranger appeared to be watching the goings on in the slave district. To the left and down the sloped lawn was a narrow road that divided the slave cabins. A row of white-washed buildings, each building looking about fifteen-feet square, lined both sides of the lane. Two-hundred-year-old oaks towered over the road, providing welcoming shade. The oaks' black crooked arms reached for the heavens and green moss carpeted each limb, the leaves casting shadows on the ground.

At the entrance to the colored district, Mingo stood talking to another blackie who was waving his arms toward the rice fields and the workers' shacks.

"What's going on?" Grace asked.

The man jerked out of the chair dropping the cat to the porch floor and faced Grace. "You're up." He fumbled with his straw hat. "Are you going to be all right?"

"Yes, thank you." Grace's chin went up a notch. "I'm fine now."

"I think introductions are in order, ma'am."

"So do I. Who might you be?"

"My name's Sidney Sparrow. Most folks call me Sid. I'm a friend of your husband. He asked me to watch the plantation while he was gone. You must be Grace Bartholomew."

"I am. Nice to meet you." She strode to a slim pillar by the porch steps and gazed out across the lawn. She continued to watch Mingo and the other black man talk animatedly. "Who's the darky talking to my overseer?"

"That's Tungo. He's been the temporary overseer here. He's done a great job keeping the village people under control and seeing to the rice fields."

"Oh, dear." She gazed at the two men. "That could be a problem for them."

276

"No doubt."

"Mister Sparrow, I've brought my house servants, the overseer and the family of one of my missing field hands. The day is getting on. We should find a place for everyone to sleep for the night." Grace stepped down to the walkway and waited.

"Let's take a walk. Your husband has built new houses for the field hands, but there's a section of cabins behind them that were here when he bought the land."

"Lead the way, sir." Grace eyed the grounds expectantly.

Grace and Sid Sparrow spent the next hour getting the servants she'd brought to the plantation settled into their temporary dwellings. The shanties behind the new white-washed cabins were in sad repair. The servants avoided giving Grace eye contact, something she didn't miss.

"These cabins are no better than chicken coops," Grace bristled as she spun around and shook her head.

"The cabins be fine, Miz Grace," Nate said.

Grace stared at him. The cabins weren't fine. But her loyal stableman would never complain.

"I'll find out who's in charge of building the new cabins. You *will* have better living arrangements."

"Thank you, Miz Grace. You always do us good," Nate said.

The rest of the colored servants nodded. "We be jist fine, Miz Grace. You got alla us folks across that big ole ocean. We trust you, ma'am," said Tabitha.

Grace noticed Tabitha's brood clung to her. She held her newborn in her arms. There were more of them to be crammed into a small shanty than some of the other families.

"Can you find more cots for Tabitha's cabin?" Grace asked, turning to Mingo.

Mingo turned to Tungo. "There be more cots hidin' someplace?"

"Come this way," Tungo replied and waved at Mingo to follow him. "I show you where we keep the extra stuff."

Grace and Sid Sparrow exchanged a glance. The best they could hope for was that the two overseers would continue to get along until Camp returned to River Oak.

Grace gazed out past the old shanties to see a multitude of slaves and field hands grouped together near their cabins watching the new coloreds with curiosity. She breathed in deeply. These new slaves were her and Cameron's people, too. She had yet to meet them and learn their names. Was it possible there would be a midwife among them?

Sparrow glanced up the lawn. "Would you like to see the Great House?"

"Yes, I would." Grace cast a look back at the servants settling in and realized she'd need to do the same before evening came on. She and Mister Sparrow walked past the cottage house. She gazed at it as they strode past.

"I'm glad Cameron had the foresight to give us a place to live while waiting for the Great House to be built."

"He's talked of nothing more than getting your home ready. He didn't want the two of you living down-river, nor in one of the slave cabins. Although that's where he's been living in your absence"

"A slave cabin?"

"Yes. The first one on the lane. I've been staying there while he's gone."

"Do you have a home in Fields Landing?"

"I do. As a matter of fact, after I show you the house, I'll need to row upriver and check in on my family and my estate, Cherry Hill."

"Goodness, Mister Sparrow. So many lives are disrupted at the moment, and all because Cameron and I have been apart far too long."

They walked up the sloped path to the house as they talked until they were only a half-dozen feet from the red-bricked steps that led up to the grand home.

Grace took in the twin steps that led to the entrance. There were stairs from the left and right of the porch with a landing in between. The banisters had been painted a stark white, as well as all of the clapboard on the two-story structure, and chimneys peeked out of the roof here and there. Men crawled about the building installing windows and doors.

"This place has been like a beehive," Sparrow said. "Besides building the mansion and the cottage, he's seen to the shanties for the field hands and still planted your first rice crop."

Grace felt nearly dizzy seeing all that had been accomplished in her absence. "It's incredible, isn't it?" she said. "It has been difficult for the two of us to be apart, but it's obviously the only way he could have gotten all of this done."

Sid stopped and stared at her. "It must have been difficult running your plantation at Cooper's Landing while he was gone."

"Cooper's Landing is gone, Mister Sparrow." Grace felt hot tears well up as she clenched her jaw.

"What?" Sid jerked his head to pin his gaze on her.

"That's why I'm here. The slave rebellion has been raging in the Caribbean for some time, especially Jamaica.

"There was talk of it working its way to Riverbend, where we lived. I couldn't wait for Cameron any longer. The morning we drove away from my father's home . . . it was in flames. We barely left in time to save ourselves."

Sid stared at her as if he'd lost his tongue.

A single tear slid down Grace's cheek and she wiped it away. "I and my people have had quite a time of it getting here to safety. I must say . . . it is good to see life blooming here, healthy and secure."

"You're quite a woman, Missus Bartholomew. You've led all these people here to safety and have lost none of them."

"That's not so, Mister Sparrow," she swallowed. "I lost a good servant to the sea."

"I'm sorry to hear that." His gray eyes softened. "Some things happen in life that we have no control over. Don't beat yourself up over it."

"I try not to," Grace breathed softly. "The rest of us are here on solid ground. I mean to make the most of it and help my husband finish this project so that we can get on with the business of living."

"That's very commendable, Missus Bartholomew." Sid Sparrow beamed at her.

The next few days were full of productivity. Grace found the men who'd built the white-washed cabins and set them to work building houses for the new servants. Three houses would go up near the Great House next to the outer kitchen. That would be where the cooks lived, as well as the domestic servants who'd keep the house in good working order.

Grace sat with quill pen and paper jotting notes to herself. She had a running list of things needing to be completed. One of the first things Grace would need to do was interview the servants already at River Oak to see if one would be suitable to serve as head housekeeper. Since she'd lost Rhea to Kindra, Grace had yet to find a servant who would replace her. Gemma's kind face flashed in her mind. Could the cook maintain the house and still cook meals?

As she sat with one hand over her swollen stomach and felt the baby push out against it, she couldn't help but smile. If only Camp were here to feel this little one too. Just then, the cook appeared in the parlor doorway and interrupted her thoughts. "How are things going?" Grace asked, glancing up at Gemma.

"Fine, Miz Grace. There's a couple of wagons out front loaded with furniture. The driver say it be the furniture you brung on the other ship. I see the nursery furniture be peeking out on the second wagon. Maybe we can set up the nursery today."

"It's here." Grace clapped her hands to her chest and peered out the window at the two waiting wagons. "The house is far too sparse with only a sofa in the parlor and that old table in the dining room. Let's go look."

"Mister Sparrow be right," Gemma said as they descended the steps. "Master Cameron been purchasin' furniture for the Big House. The barn be loaded. You may want to walk down that old road and see fo' yourself."

"I'd love to. First I need to get some men to unload the furniture and get it into the house" Grace looked appreciative at the older women who led the way. "And Gemma, your duties have changed." Grace touched her servant's arm when they reached the ground. "You'll continue as cook, as I don't trust anyone else to fill your shoes in that capacity. But I'm giving you the title of Domestic Headmistress as well."

"Oh my, Miz Grace. You sure you wanna do that?" Gemma brought her apron up and fanned her face.

"I'm certain of it. There's not much to be done here, but when we move into the Great House and I bring in new house servants, I want you to train them and see to it that everything runs smoothly."

"Thank you, Miz Grace. I be honored."

Grace checked that item off her list and tucked it into her pocket. "Is the noon meal ready?"

"Yes'm, Miz Grace. I be about to make that announcement 'fore you swept me off my train of thought. Never can tell what's gonna be happen 'round heah."

THIRTY-ONE

AFTER THE NOON meal, Grace wandered down to the barn to have a look at the new furniture. The building was quiet and musty-smelling. She stepped past the rows of carts and tables that held the exquisite furniture of cherry, walnut or rich mahogany. She found ornamental lamps wrapped in soft blankets, as well as a myriad of other items that would make the Great House elegant and comfortable. Grace felt as if she were shopping in a warehouse.

The sound of footsteps behind her stopped Grace in her tracks. She wheeled around to find the temporary overseer standing behind her.

"You startled me!" she cried and stepped back, touching her midriff protectively.

"I didn't mean to scare you, ma'am."

"Well, you did. May I help you?"

"I been wantin' to meet you since you arrived at River Oak. But it not my place to go up to the house."

Grace waited, watching the muscular black man standing before her.

"You be in my territory, ma'am. It give me a chance to come forward."

"I see. You must be Tungo."

"Yes'm. I be Mastah Camp's overseer. I be seein' to the rice fields and the people in this village."

"I'm Grace Bartholomew. I'm glad we've met. You've met Mingo as well?" She knew he had, but asked just the same.

Tungo's brows furrowed, but he nodded. "I meet Mingo first day he arrived. We wait for Mastah Camp to tell us our rightful position."

"What is Mingo doing while you wait?"

"I show him the grounds. I show him how we plant the rice. I tell him how we harvest. I teach him how to drain the fields."

Grace watched as Tungo talked animatedly. She could tell the man was proud of his knowledge on how to grow the Carolina Gold, and how to harvest it. Camp had his work cut out for him when he got home. Tungo and Mingo both were strong men who were proud of the work they put into their respective jobs.

"You sound like you certainly know what you're doing," Grace said.

"I be in charge here." He pointed to himself.

"At least until my husband returns. Maybe you can help me with something else."

Tungo straightened. "I help if I can."

"I need a midwife." She touched her growing mound.

Tungo's eyes did not slide to her stomach. His jaws worked but a gleam came to his eyes. "We have three midwives in the colored district. You meet them." He waved her to come.

The colored district looked much homier than that of Cooper's Landing. The houses were spread apart, each with a small front porch. Some already had fences built around the yards. There was the lawn by the road under the great oaks, but she noticed there was no grass in the front yards of the cabins. It looked as if the ground had been smoothed with a rake.

"Your people," Grace turned to Tungo, "don't they like grass in their yards?"

"No grass for us, Missus. That be too dangerous. We live too close to the rice fields."

"What difference does that make?" She glanced at the stark yards.

"There be snakes that come up from the river. They visit our homes. If our people be out in the field working, we don't know we got company. If we go inside the house, the snake strike and kill us. So each morning we smooth the ground with our garden rakes. When we come home we stand at the gate and look at the dirt. If there be no sign of a snake wiggling through the soft dirt, we know it safe to go into our houses. But if we see sign of a snake on the ground, we keep our family out until we find snake and kill it."

A shiver ran down Grace's spine as she listened to Tungo. "But what if the family is home? Are they not in danger too?"

"They be in danger. But snake go where it's cool and quiet, not house where there be noise."

Grace looked around and pulled up her skirts and drew the hem close to her ankles. When she looked up, she found Tungo smiling at her, his white teeth shining and his eyes bright.

"You safe with Tungo, Missus."

"Thank you." Still a shiver licked up her spine.

Tungo led Grace to a white-washed cabin where a heavy-set Negro woman sat in a rocking chair snapping beans. Her kinky hair was hidden beneath a colorful bandana, neatly tied over her head, but a wisp of white hair escaped the head cloth.

"This be Ruby, Miz Grace."

Ruby nearly spilled the metal bowl of beans when she tried to stand. "Why you bring the missus heah before tellin' me you be comin'! I would'a been more presentable!"

"Please be seated," Grace said, laying a hand on the old woman's shoulder. "Don't mind me. I'm just looking for a midwife for when it's my time." Grace touched her stomach.

"You 'bout ready to have that chile fo' sure." Ruby smiled. The rocking chair creaked when she leaned back. "I be mighty pleased to be o' service, missus."

"Thank you," Grace said. "I want to meet the other midwives before I make a choice."

Two little black boys scampered past them and continued toward the river.

"I bring dem boys into the world." Ruby looked pleased with herself.

"The village is fortunate to have you at their service." Grace nodded toward the old woman and glanced up at Tungo. "I'd like to meet the other women." She waved goodbye to the old woman as they walked away.

In the next hour, Grace met the other midwives. They seemed wise, and told of their experience delivering babies. After observing the three midwives, Grace chose the youngest woman. She guessed the woman to be in her mid-forties. Beatrice shared a shanty with an older woman, as she had no family of her own. Grace learned that many years ago, a ship's captain, a slave trader, had separated her from her husband and children. Recently she'd been on the ship with the lot of slaves that Cameron had bought.

Beatrice seemed gentle though she bore a sad smile. A distant look filled her eyes. This was a woman who had likely faced many trials in her life, a woman who had learned to keep her head up in the face of adversity.

Grace hoped that bringing Beatrice to the Great House would give her life new meaning. But for now, they would be living in the cottage.

"Pack your personal things, Beatrice. You are moving into the house with me."

The woman glanced warily at the older midwife, but set to work packing her meager belongings into a coarse pillow slip. Together Grace and Beatrice left the colored district and walked to the cottage.

Once inside, Grace showed the midwife the nursery and room where Beatrice would sleep. "My baby is due in about six weeks. You are free to visit your friends in the quarters , but I want you here in the evenings. Is that understood?"

"Yes'm, Miz Bartholomew."

"Call me Miss Grace."

"Yes'm, Miz Grace. You want me to stay, seein' dat ev'nin' comin' on?"

"Yes, I do." Grace turned. "These trunks over here have items for the baby. You can unpack them and set up the nursery."

"Yes'm Miz Grace. I be doin' dat right away."

Grace stood in the doorway and watched her new midwife and soon-to-be-nanny. The woman stood in the middle of the room staring at the crib and dresser, a longing in her eyes.

"How old were your children?" Grace asked.

Beatrice turned glistening eyes to Grace. "I had four youngins' ma'am, when we started out to America on de ship. Two girls and two boys. My littlest un' be Abby. She be two. Den dere be Samson, we call him, Sammy, he be four. Celeste be six and Toby ten. They be de best children in all de world and made my heart sing ev'ry day. My husband, Willim, he be so strong. We be a good family. We don't do nuthin' to deserve dat evil captain tearin' us away from each other. But my baby girl, Abby, she die on de ship. She be too little for all de sickness goin' on. I nearly lost little Sammy, too. It be de grace o' God he live." Beatrice shook her head. "But maybe not. My little Sammy tore at my skirts somethin' fierce when de slave trader took him away. I can still hear him cryin' for me."

"Oh, Beatrice." Grace couldn't help herself. She went to the woman's side and touched her arm. "I'm so sorry."

"My Sammy be Samson now. He be a man if he live. Twenty-four. Ev'ry year I keep a calendar and I mark how old my babies be."

"Of course you do," Grace said smoothing the woman's sleeve, and nearly crying herself.

"Why you be so kind to me, Miz Grace?"

Grace's mouth flew open and she paused. "There's no reason not to be. Truth is, we want all our help to be happy."

"Dat be real good, Miz Grace. Alla us folks seen bad times. It be good to see a little bit o' heaven dis side of the River Jordan."

"River Jordan?"

"Dat what we call heaven on de other side o' the silver linin' in de clouds."

Grace turned around and left the room, her heart heavy. She never understood why the slave traders had to be so hateful and mean to the slaves. Why must they separate families?

Boom! Boom! Three weeks later, Grace awoke to a lot of noise.

Hedy ran into Grace's room, her brown eyes wide. "What be all that noise, Missy?"

"I don't know. Get me dressed."

Twenty minutes later, Grace stepped out onto the cottage porch with Hedy close behind. Overhead, thousands of blackbirds flew toward the rice fields. *Boom! Boom!*

"Goodness!" Grace lifted her skirts and hurried to the edge of the colored district. Birds flew into the oak trees, the rice fields, and everywhere else!

Sid Sparrow strode up to her and said, "I've instructed some of your field hands to shoot as many birds as they can."

"Why so many birds? Where did they come from?" Grace asked.

"This happens twice a year, ma'am. These nuisances are rice birds. As soon as the fields are planted, they come to steal the seeds."

"I've never seen anything like this."

"It's quite a sight to see, not to mention a planter's worse enemy."

"What do you do with the birds after you kill them?"

"We eat them." Sid Sparrow smiled. "It takes a half dozen birds to fill one plate, but leave it up to your slaves to cook them. They know how to make them tender and tasty."

Grace's brows went up as she eyed the thousands of birds flying overhead.

"Your two overseers have the muskets. The rest of the workers are chasing them away with hoes and rakes. They have become masters at clobbering the birds with the tools. They'll kill the pesky birds. Don't worry," Sparrow said. "This'll only last a few days--nothing you can do about it."

"Well, forever more!" Grace didn't know what else to say.

She entered the house with Hedy on her heels. Beatrice and the cooks all stared at her with raised brows.

"What you find out, Miz Grace?" asked Dinah.

"You're going to be baking birds for supper for a while. You best visit Mama Jezelee and find out how to bake them. That's what Mister Sparrow tells me. We'll be filling our tummies with rice birds until they fly the coop!"

THIRTY-TWO

"WHO IS MAMA Jezelee?" Dinah asked.

"She's one of the cooks in the village. I met her the other day. She's been cooking Cameron's meals," Grace said.

"Camp's cook? There ain't nobody who's Camp's cook but me!" Grace saw fire in Dinah's eyes.

"He had to have someone cook for him while he was away from Cooper's Landing."

"Well, she best be knowin' I'm here. I be his cook when he get home."

"Nobody can replace your cooking, Dinah."

"Just so she know that." Dinah glanced out the dining room window which was shadowed by a flock of birds flying overhead.

"And you best calm down, Dinah, or you'll be makin' yourself a heart attack," laughed Gemma, her shoulders shaking.

"Humph!" Dinah disappeared into the kitchen where she started whipping up some savory smelling food.

Grace stood on the bridge overlooking the pond. She couldn't get her mind off Cameron. Goldfish swam to the surface, nipping at water bugs and algae, the sunlight reflecting off their scales, only to disappear just as quickly. Sometimes it felt like this with her and Cameron these days. Hide and seek. She'd seen little of her husband this past year. *I'd give anything to be with you now*, Grace thought.

She would have preferred Camp show her the Great House, the grounds, the rice fields. But he wasn't here.

Knowing her child could be born any day, Grace became anxious. *I need Camp to be home when the hour is near. Please God, don't let him miss his child being born.*

A sharp stitch in her midsection brought a gasp. Stunned, Grace put a hand on the guard rail for support. *No! Not now!* Because the pain surprised her, she hurried off the bridge and sat on a bench in the garden, catching her breath. *The baby can't come yet. Camp's not here!*

Her fingers clenched the stone bench, her knuckles near white from the pressure. No one heard the single word she managed to utter, the sound like a whisper in the vast garden.

"Help . . ." The first pain came on strong. Where were the warning signs that should have alerted her today was the day her child would be born? Had she missed them somehow? She stumbled to her feet and started up the garden path, away from the pond.

Nate, the stableman, was walking Grace's horse along the oak-lined drive and looked up at the sound of her approach. Seeing her bent over from the pain, he hollered something to one of the carpenters in the Great House, then dropped the rope to the horse and scrambled up the lawn to where she stood panting.

"Miz Grace!" He stopped in front of her and held her elbow to help her stand. "Is it your time?"

"I'm afraid so, Nate. Get me to the house."

They walked slowly on the uneven ground as Nate supported her weight across the sloped lawn.

Up ahead, Penny was shaking a rug over the porch rail. She looked up at them, dropped the rug and hurried down the steps. "Missy, you gonna have your baby?"

"Penny, is Beatrice in the house?" Grace panted.

"No, Miz Grace. She gone to the village to visit her friends."

"Go fetch her," Grace said. "Hurry!"

Penny hefted her skirt and ran up the lane to the colored district. Grace could hear her calling, "Beatrice, come quick!"

Grace and Nate made it to the porch before she had to pause again. "I have to stop," Grace said. Sweat slicked her brow as another pain shot through her. "Oh!" she cried as she hugged her belly.

"Let me git you into the house, Miz Grace."

Grace looked back in time to see a carpenter standing in the circular drive holding the reins to Dandy. Behind him, Penny and Beatrice came running toward the house, their skirts hiked to keep from tripping.

"Good, they're coming." Grace took a deep breath and, with Nate's help, made her way up the steps. She leaned into him as he pushed open the door.

"Right this way, little Missy," he crooned.

Gemma and Dinah came out of the kitchen just as Nate pushed open the front door. "We best git the mistress to bed," he said.

The cooks stopped dead in their tracks, brows raised. "Is it her time?" asked Dinah. They followed as Nate lowered Grace onto the bed.

Beatrice squeezed through the two women and shooed Nate out the door before returning to examine Grace. She turned around and said, "All right, it look like our mistress 'bout to have a baby. You're gonna have to clear de room."

Before Dinah and Gemma turned to leave, Beatrice stopped them. "Boil some watah and bring clean rags."

"Right away," said Dinah.

"Penny, come help me," Beatrice said. "Pull de bedcovers down on de other side of de bed."

Hedy stepped into the room, her brown eyes wide. "I'll get Miz Grace's nightgown." Hedy sped around the room as if the place were on fire. She helped remove Grace's day dress and slipped a fresh nightgown over her head.

"Oh," Grace groaned, her vision growing hazy and unfocused. "The baby's coming." Beads of sweat formed on her brow. She winced, her eyes closed tightly and panted until the pain eased.

"You doin' real good, Miz Grace," said Beatrice. She dipped a cloth in cool water and dabbed Grace's brow.

A moment later, Grace cried out softly, her hands clenching and unclenching.

"You'll be fine, Miz Grace," Beatrice said, her voice soothing as she spoke.

Hours passed with no relief. Grace squirmed under the coverlets. "It hurts so much."

A knock came at the door. Beatrice cracked the door open. Sid Sparrow standing on the other side. "It be Mister Sparrow, ma'am," the midwife said.

"See what he wants."

"Ma'am?"

"Do as I say."

"Miz Grace can't be seein' you, sir. What you be needin'? And be quick about it. I gots to get back to her."

Grace listened to the midwife's hasty words and strained to hear what Mister Sparrow said.

"Sorry to bother you at a time like this . . . but one of the workers thought the lady of the house was in . . . labor."

"Dat she is, Mister. Ev'rybody know dat by now."

Grace closed her eyes and wriggled in pain. She clenched her teeth at the white-hot agony searing through her body. The pain lengthened. Slowly, ever so slowly, relief washed over her and the torment ebbed. She opened her eyes to find Beatrice standing over her.

"Did he leave?" she asked.

"He's pacing de floor," Beatrice said.

"Maybe he has news of Cameron."

Beatrice scowled. "Dis ain't a good time for the gent to be here." She cracked the door open once more. "What's your business?"

"Ask him if he has news of Cameron," Grace said.

"You got news of Massa Camp?"

"No. He should have been here by now. Tell your mistress I'm going to Charleston to look for him."

"You do dat and I tell the Missus."

Grace heard. *God speed,* she whispered before another contraction crept into her abdomen. She grabbed a handful of blankets and squeezed. *Oh, God, let Cameron make it home in time to see his child born.*

Grace licked at her lips, parched and dry from her labor. She felt pain curling up her spine and she cried out again. She puffed through her mouth and arched her back.

Beatrice wiped at the sweat gathering on Grace's forehead and brushed back the wet curls. Another wave of pain broke over Grace, and she cried out, grasping Beatrice's hand.

"I should have had the baby by now" Grace wailed.

"Dis be your first chile. It be normal if your labor be long."

"How can one live through such affliction?" Grace asked, gripping Beatrice's hand tightly. Hours had passed. "It must be nearly midnight and I have no child, only pain!"

"As I say, Mistress, dis be your first chile. Lie back and breathe slowly."

When the next wave of pain had passed, Grace glanced at the clock on the night stand. It was past one o'clock in the morning. Her first pain had started just after the noon hour. Could a woman endure such pain this long? She felt as if she would die if there was much more of this.

Beatrice cooled her brow with a wet rag and brushed tendrils away. "You be doing good, Miz Grace. Don't be lettin' fear have its way with you. You be doin' good."

Beatrice pulled back the blanket and took a look. She felt for the baby's head. "It be fine. Keep pushin'. But I be tellin' you. Dis chile goin' to come when it be good and ready."

The room grew quiet except for the labored breathing as Grace bore through the pain.

"Keep breathin'," Beatrice crooned.

Grace gritted her teeth and nodded, then gasped as another wave of pain tightened her body like a strained cord. She panted a few times and licked her lips again. "I'm scared. Am I going to live through this?"

Beatrice took her hand and held it firm. "You will live through dis, and more babies in de future."

As Grace lay there drenched in sweat, Beatrice continued to murmur to her. Grace closed her eyes as tears slid and pooled in her ears. The pain had been picking up steadily. The brief respites between contractions were growing shorter and shorter. She did not hear the door creak open as another pain ripped through her.

Grace's eyes fluttered and in her hazy swirl of delirium, she saw the love of her life slip into the room and stand beside her bed. His black hair was mussed and his face strained. He bent down. "Grace." He spoke through a choked voice. Tears spilled from his eyes and he knelt down by the bed, his rough hand resting on her brow. "I'm here."

Grace swallowed the tears that flowed unchecked. She pulled him to her, his head resting on her chest. "You're home!" she cried and laughed, and then another pain pierced through her. She propped herself up on her elbows as Cameron pulled back and watched her with horror-filled eyes. Her hair, tangled and wet with sweat, clung to her forehead. She felt weak.

Beatrice pulled on Cameron's shoulder. "You must leave de room now. Dis be over soon."

Cameron looked at the midwife with wild eyes and he shook his head. "I cannot leave her again. I will remain in the room."

"Dis no place for a man, Massa Camp."

"I'm not leaving."

Beatrice looked as though she didn't know what to do. Men didn't stay in the room during a delivery. But he was her master.

"Den stand back!" Beatrice commanded.

Cameron stumbled back a few feet. His eyes stayed on Grace.

Grace began to pant. Bending her head toward her belly, her shoulders arching off the bed, she let out a scream as she pushed.

Beatrice went to the foot of the bed and tossed the blankets out of the way. "Again!" Beatrice coached her.

And once again, Grace bent into the pain and pushed, a great gasp of air exploding from her lungs as she could push no further.

"Once more, Mistress! It be near! Once more!"

Grace opened her eyes. The room swirled, and the candles flickered and swayed before her. Cameron looked on in stunned silence. He wrung his hands as he paced the floor. For a brief moment, Grace was not sure she had the strength to push anymore.

"Again, Mistress. You can do it. You must!" Beatrice commanded.

Grace clamped her eyes shut. She clutched the linen in a tight grip, and fought the fear. She gritted her teeth, bent forward, and screamed out one more time.

A painful silence filled the room. Grace could hear her own heartbeat. She strained to hear that sweet sound every mother wanted to hear. And from someplace far away came a tiny cry and then whispering and excited laughter. To Grace's ears, the sounds were a heady mixture of relief and joy.

After a long moment, Cameron's weeping laughter mingled with that of a sharp new cry. It was the angry, excited cry of a soul just entering the cold world, upset that it had suddenly gone from warm and safe to drafty and coarse.

"You have a daughter! It be a girl!" Beatrice cried out.

Grace looked up and saw Beatrice wrap a clean linen about a tiny bloody bundle. She couldn't keep the smile from her face.

"A daughter," Grace whispered, as she let her elbows drop to the bed. She looked over at Cameron. "You wanted a boy."

"She's beautiful." Cameron smiled and he looked on at the baby as if he could never take his eyes off her. "I'm so proud."

Grace smiled softly while the tears slipped down her cheeks. She felt detached, as if the pain had never happened. This was the miracle of birth. One moment the searing pain and, then, when the babe was born, it was over. She felt as if she were afloat. Sleep wanted to consume her.

Grace and Cameron looked down at the wrinkled baby girl. "She's so tiny," Cameron said, rubbing the back of his finger against the downy softness of the baby's head.

"She be perfectly normal in size," Beatrice said. "Now let me clean her up." She took the baby and set about washing her with a soapy cloth. Moments later she set the baby back in Grace's arms.

Grace pulled her daughter close to keep her from chilling. "She has your black hair."

"I hope she has your emerald eyes."

The two gazed at the infant lovingly.

"The baby need to nurse, Massa Camp."

"I want to hold her first, if I may?" Cameron said.

Beatrice glanced at Grace who nodded. "Of course."

Grace pulled the bedding back and Cameron scooped the tiny linen-wrapped bundle from her arms. He centered the babe in his strong arms and instinctively started swaying. She listened to him hum to his baby girl. He looked over at Grace with love in his eyes. His smile said it all. He was the happiest man on earth.

"She looks like you," he said. The baby nudged her father and wriggled in his arms. Soon her eyelids closed and her lips moved in a sucking motion. All at once the baby scrunched up her tiny legs and a sharp wail carried through the room.

"All right, little one." Cameron kissed her black, downy hair, walked softly to the side of the bed, and leaned down to tuck the infant into her mother's arm. "Here you go, kitten. Mama has you now." He kissed the baby's forehead again and then Grace's brow.

"What'll we name her?" he asked.

"Katherine Olivia?" Grace said, her brows raised questioningly.

"And Kitten for short?"

Grace giggled. "Until she gets a little older, and then you can call her Kit for short."

"I like it." Cameron sighed.

"But I want to call her Katie," Grace said. "She can have a nickname from each of us." She positioned the squirming baby to her breast and watched as she began rooting. She startled when the baby latched on and began to suckle.

The room grew quiet as the two of them watched the baby fall asleep in the crook of her mother's arm.

"I'll leave you two be," Beatrice said as she gathered the bloody linen and left the room. The door clicked silently behind her.

Cameron knelt by the bed and encircled one arm over Grace's head and the other arm over the baby. "I thought I'd lost you," he choked. Tears brimmed his eyes. "I thought my whole world had gone up in ashes when I came to the burned ruins of the Great House. I knew then, I could never live without you."

Grace felt her heart swell. "You don't have to. I'm here."

"I will never let you out of my sight again, dear Grace."

"I'm going to hold you to that."

Cameron lowered his lips onto hers, tasting her sweetness. "Beautiful Grace."

"Hmmm . . ." she crooned softly.

"I hope our house is big enough for the family I intend to fill it with." He grazed her cheek with his scruffy beard.

Grace laughed softy. "If it's not, we'll just have to add more rooms." Grace smiled down at baby Katherine. "We'll have a house full of these, Lord willing."

"You need to rest. I'll be back later to check in on you and little Kitten."

"Don't go too far," Grace teased.

"Help! Help!" Outside the window, a shrill call pierced the night air. Grace looked up at Cameron, wide-eyed.

"What was that?"

"Peacocks," Cameron said, with a pleased grin.

"You brought peacocks home?"

"They were supposed to be a surprise." Cameron glanced toward the window as the peacocks pierced the night air with their cries.

"I'm surprised," she said.

"Not as surprised as I am coming home to our new baby." Cameron ran his palm over the baby's head. "I'm going to let the two of you sleep." He started to leave the room, but turned around, a questioning look on his face.

"Where's Laulie?"

Grace closed her eyes. Regret and guilt sliced through her. But he had to know. She opened her eyes and stared at him. "She's gone."

THIRTY-THREE

Bridgetown, Barbados
10 November, 1831

STANLEY BERNARD SAT upon his stallion and looked about the expanse of acreage before him, not for the first time. He had a keen interest in the land. To the left, the terrain was filled with tall sea oats, interspersed with palmettos and mangrove trees. He kneed his mount to take a few steps forward and when he did the horse snorted and looked to the right. Bernard glanced in that direction hoping to see a rider coming. He squinted in the bright sunlight. No one. He was alone.

He glanced to the left again, beyond the section of land that held his interest. The surf pounded onto the reefs and rocks below. The water shimmered and blinked beyond the shore. When he'd first visited this property, excitement flowed through his veins. He would soon realize his dreams and plant his own tobacco crops. But he wouldn't stop there, he'd plant sugarcane too. He'd be his own man with his own crops and his own income. Never mind that he'd come this far by skimming funds off Phillip Cooper's tobacco income, above and beyond the salary he received as foreman to Kindra Hall. If he hadn't, he would have fallen short of having the investment needed to buy this land. But once this land was his, he'd make his own money . . . and he planned to make a lot of it.

The horse swung his head down and chomped on the sea grass. Bernard glanced out at the exceptional view of the bay. The Big House would be built right here. He would spend his evenings on the front porch gazing out at the ocean, with fields of agriculture bringing him in a fine livelihood.

He rarely got a good night's sleep these days. His mind reeled with plans for the house and land. His and Ava's future looked bright, almost. But his patience was wearing thin, and suspicion sliced through him. Something wasn't right about his solicitor. Mister Bane, who'd been handling the sale of the land, had disappeared. Irritation gnawed on his mind to no end. He should have signed his name on the deed by now. But every time he went to the land office, Mister Bane was nowhere to be seen. Bernard found it odd that the man had up and disappeared into thin air, and his fellow employees knew nothing of his whereabouts.

There was no question his money was good, so what was the holdup? But that's not what kept Bernard from sleeping. What kept him awake at night was Ava. He didn't dare tell her he was suspicious. For some reason, the agent had led Bernard to believe the land was nearly theirs, but up and left him hung out to dry. His wife was in her element. She was ecstatic they would finally build their own house. She peppered him with questions every day. She wanted to know when the groundbreaking would begin. She counted on their new beginnings as a means to save face after being booted out on their hind ends by the owners of Kindra Hall.

Bernard turned his mount toward town. He came to a section of the road where the path narrowed. He could still see the ocean. He wouldn't go home, he decided. Instead, he would ride into town and stop at the Lazy Crab tavern. A tall tankard of rum would calm his nerves.

He hoped to find Mister Bane in the barroom. It was there that he'd met with the solicitor before they rode out to the property. Something told him this wouldn't be the last time he'd visit the tavern before going home each night. This was the fourth night this week that he'd visited the establishment. "Bane better be there tonight," Stanley muttered.

Bernard pulled open the rough heavy door and stepped into the dark room filled with a haze of smoke. A low hum met his ears as his eyes adjusted to the dimness.

"Evenin' Mr. Bernard." A woman approached him, her bare shoulders white as milk.

"Good evening," Bernard replied, uninterested in the female.

Although it was early evening, some of the women roamed the interior of the saloon dressed as if they were ready for bed. They wore gauzy robes that fluttered open revealing satin nightgowns. The painted-faced women roamed about the room, sometimes dropping onto the laps of patrons.

Not all of the females who worked for the Lazy Crab wore night clothes, just those who made frequent trips upstairs with a man in tow. The waitresses wore gaudy gowns in splashes of colors, and their hair was tinted in oranges and reds and worn loosely over their shoulders in long curls. But when they took orders for drinks, their eyes stayed on the men just as brazenly. All too often, the soiled doves did their best to encourage Bernard to make a trip upstairs. He might have taken them up on it had it not been that he was on a mission to find Banes. He wouldn't be deterred.

Maude, the waitress who'd seated him the last three nights, elbowed her way through the crowded room and called out to him. "Come on, Mister. The house is full tonight, but I found you a table against the wall."

Bernard followed her around the tables to the far side of the tavern where two empty mugs sat on the table. She snatched them up and said, "Have a seat." She gestured toward an empty chair.

Bernard slid into the vacant seat and looked around. For now he had the table to himself.

"What'll you have, Mister Bernard?"

"Same as yesterday," he said, leaning his elbows on the scarred table.

"Tankard of rum," she said, with a wink. "I'll be right back." She scurried off toward the long wooden bar.

Stanley panned the throng of faces for Mister Bane. He scratched his palm nervously, as he scrutinized the room. It was impossible to see everyone with all the movement and jostling going on, and men with their backs to him. The flouncy robes on the ladies of the night blocked his view. Still, he tried to find the solicitor in the candlelight and smoke-filled air.

The front door opened, a shaft of light filling the entrance. All eyes looked that way, including Bernard's. A rugged man nearly as big as the opening stood in the doorway. His clothes were dirty and his long beard and hair, both rust-colored, unkempt.

Maude hurried up to him and spoke animatedly. Soon, she was leading the robust man to Bernard's table. Stanley grunted to himself but scooted his chair back giving the large man ample room at the table.

"What'll you have, mister?" Maude asked the foul-smelling stranger.

"Give me a bottle of ale!" he bellowed.

"Right away," she said and headed to the bar.

Bernard had yet to receive his order, but it wasn't long before Maude wove her way to their table, a bottle in one hand and a tankard in the other. "Anything else?" she asked as she set the drinks on the table. "We got hot biscuits and beef stew tonight if ya wants."

"This'll do for now," the man said in a gravelly voice and eyed Bernard.

"I'll stick with the drink," Bernard said. "Supper's waiting for me at home."

Maude scurried away as if she'd already forgotten about them. The two men sat awkwardly facing each other. Bernard broke the silence.

"I'm Stanley Bernard." he stretched out his hand.

"Blissmore," the craggy man said, ignoring Bernard's hand. He picked up the bottle of ale. He guzzled half the contents before he set it down. "Morgan Blissmore." He belched.

Bernard took a long swallow from his mug, the liquid radiating warmth down his throat.

"So . . . what do you do?" Blissmore asked, peering at Bernard. Despite the question, it was apparent he had little interest in the answer.

Surprised the unrefined man asked a civil question, Bernard answered, "I've been a foreman to a tobacco plantation until recently."

Blissmore nodded, closing one eye as if narrowing his gaze on Bernard with the other. "Until recently? Har! What happened?"

Bernard raised a brow and took another long draw from the tankard.

"You ain't talkin'. That's all right."

Bernard leaned back. "What about you?"

"I'm Morgan Blissmore, I am. Captain of the Bloody Mary." He bellowed and raised his bottle to the patrons, then turned back to the table and took another swig. "This be my first night off the ship in a month."

Bernard surveyed the crowded room. "You alone?"

"You betcha!" he laughed. "Can only take so much of the crew. A man's gotta get away by himself sometimes."

Bernard smiled thinly. "What brings you to Barbados?"

"A little wench."

Bernard glanced up and stared at the rough scallywag.

"She ain't a wench like one o' these fillies in here." He slapped his knee and howled out a throaty laugh. He picked up the bottle and finished it off then held it high. "Barkeep! Bring us another bottle of ale!"

Maude showed up with two bottles. She leaned her elbow on Blissmore's shoulder. "Need anything else, Mister?" She gave him a knowing look.

"Maybe I do, maybe I don't. Har! We'll have to see!" He threw his arm around Maude's thick waist and drew her near. "Whatcha' got fer me?" He laughed, holding her captive for the moment. She threw her head back and giggled then whispered in his ear before quickly pulling out of his grip. "It's a busy night. I'll be back." She eyed him longer than necessary.

Bernard watched the exchange, thinking they suited each other.

"Where were we?" Blissmore asked, tipping the bottle to his mouth.

"You came to the island for a little wench," Bernard said.

"Oh, har! That ain't really so," he stopped and swayed in his seat a bit. "Only partly so," he burped.

Bernard was losing patience with the captain. He tipped the bottle of rum and took a long drink.

"The wench ain't *really* a wench," the captain said, with a sly smile. "She be just a slip of a girl. But not just any girl." Blissmore's eyes glazed over. "She be a girl who'll bring me what I'm lookin' fer."

"And what would that be?" Bernard was beginning to think this rusty bucket was wasting his time making up a string of yarn.

"Her mother."

Is he looking for his daughter in order to find his wife? From the looks of the captain, that seemed highly unlikely. But then, what did he know?

"Is she missing?" Bernard asked.

"No, she ain't missing, but she could come up missing if I don't keep a close watch on her daughter."

"This daughter . . . is she in Barbados?"

"That's what I be told. Like I said, I just pulled into port. But I'll be asking for her around town in the next couple o' days. From what I'm told, she ain't been here very long herself. She shouldn't be too hard to find."

"Maybe I can be of help. I've lived on this island for seven years. There aren't too many people I don't know."

"Maybe you can at that." The captain dangled the bottle in his hand. "Ever hear of a young lady by the name of Kindra . . . er . . . she used to be a Cooper, but I hear she done got married." Blissmore cocked his head sideways and stared at Bernard.

Stunned, Stanley Bernard felt his blood rush to his face. He clenched his fists under the table. "Phillip Cooper's half-breed daughter, Kindra?" Bernard cleared his throat. "She married a darky named Denzel Talmaze."

"That be the girl all right! You know where I can find her?"

"What connection do you have to her mother?" Bernard asked, curious how she fit in the scheme of things.

"Er . . . her mother and I have worked together a good long while. She owes me something." Fire shone in Blissmore's eyes.

"Like mother, like daughter," Bernard groaned.

"What's that?"

"Nothing. I can show you where to find the woman," Bernard said. "But I want something in return."

THIRTY-FOUR

Kindra Hall, Barbados
15 November, 1831

THE SHUTTER, LOOSENED by the island winds, banged loudly against the office window. Denzel looked up with a start and pushed the log book away. He leaned back and stretched the kinks out of his neck. It was only mid-morning, but he'd sat far too long going over the account books.

Just when he stood to inspect the banging shutter, the office door creaked open. Denzel cut a glance over his shoulder in the dim light. Hagar, the house maid, stood with a silver tray with a cup of hot tea and sweet biscuits.

Denzel let out a deep sigh. "Where's Louiza? She generally brings my tea."

"She's elbow deep in flour," Hagar said in a thick honey tone. "She and Clara are baking bread today." Hagar slanted him a coy smile. "I be certain you'd appreciate it if you didn't have to wait fo' yer afternoon tea." Her eyes roamed over him, then lowered to the tray she held in her hands. She stepped back, closing the door with her elbow.

Denzel swallowed a gulp of regret. He'd meant to have this servant sent out to the fields by now, but running the tobacco plantation kept his mind too busy. Again, he was caught alone with the maid against his wishes.

He moved to the opposite side of his desk, putting the heavy table between them. The shutter continued to slam against the house with great force, and he glanced irritably at the commotion to his right.

306

Hagar glided across the floor and set the tray on the desk's mahogany surface. She looked up, her dark eyes willing him to gaze at her and not the annoying shutter.

By now, Denzel was fighting to keep from snapping altogether. He wouldn't allow this woman to jeopardize his relationship with Kindra. "Where's my wife?" he asked, his hands gripping the edge of the desk. "Tell her I'd like her to join me for a cup of tea."

He turned away and strode toward the fireplace, where the embers flickered and sputtered to nearly dying. Denzel picked up the poker and jabbed at the red-hot coals that matched how he felt at the moment. He tossed another log onto the fire, purposely keeping his back to the troublemaker in his office.

"I can't be summonin' yer wife, suh." Her tone laced with thick molasses. She stood close behind him, too close. Denzel stiffened. "She left the house . . . to the stable." She touched his upper arm and ran her talon-fingers down his biceps.

Denzel whirled and shoved past Hagar. "She's outdoors in this windstorm?"

He didn't wait for a reply. He swept out of the study into the grand hallway, calling, "Boaz! Bring my overcoat!"

Boaz appeared straightaway, a wool coat in his hands. "Here you go, Massa."

When Denzel reached the entry, the front door swung open, filling the great hall with the bluster of the storm. Kindra flew in, her long winter coat entwined about her, her black silky hair filled with the wind, her face wet with rain. Her eyes were full of fear and her hand cupped her belly.

The door swung wider, slapping against the wall, the storm swirling about Kindra and Denzel as they stood facing each other.

Kindra bent over, nearly stumbling before Denzel caught her. Boaz rushed past the couple and slammed the door shut.

"What's wrong?" Denzel asked, fear paralyzing him.

"The baby's coming!" Kindra stumbled forward.

Denzel scooped her into his arms and headed up the stairs. "Boaz, send for the midwife." He took a few steps up the wide staircase and stopped. "And tell Mayme to meet me in Kindra's bedchamber!"

Hours passed and another wave of pain swept through Kindra's body. She shuddered as she tried to look at Corrie. Kindra nearly doubled in response to that pain, groaning and calling out. She grasped Corrie's hand and tried to steady her eyes on the midwife. Corrie wiped at the sweat gathering on Kindra's forehead like the dew on the petal of a flower.

"This birth is not right, I know it," Kindra said, her breath coming in fast gulps. "Don't lie to me, Corrie," she said, gripping the woman's hand tightly. "Hours have passed. It is nearly dawn, and I have no child. Only more pain."

"It be fine, Miz Kindra," Corrie crooned. "Each chile come into the world its own way. This baby not in a hurry, that's all."

Kindra wanted to believe Corrie. She tried with all her being to relax and let nature take its course. But soon her forehead and cheeks were drenched in sweat again and she twisted in pain.

"Mayme, dip de cloth in de cool water and lay it over her forehead." Corrie's words sounded as if they came from another room. But she felt the cool, wet cloth on her brow.

The room grew quiet save for the labored wheezing as Kindra bore through the agony. Her pain seemed to match the gusts of winds outside that banged the shutters against the windows. As the storm roared outside, a silent storm roared within her soul. She believed with all her heart that this baby didn't want to come, that something was terribly wrong.

Denzel paced the hallway outside their bedchamber. Every muscle in his body tensed. And against his will, in the wee hours, his body sought sleep. If he sat, his head lolled him awake. If he paced, that kept him from drifting. His ears were trained to the sounds coming from behind the closed door, where agonized cries made him shudder. How could his wife endure so many hours of pain? She was a fragile woman. A strong man such as himself could not endure the hours of agony that he heard seeping through the door.

He tried to see her twice, but before he cracked the door open enough to step into the room, he was chased out, the door slammed in his face. He clenched his fists. He felt helpless. The grandfather clock chimed the hours, almost as if the death angel hung near to take his beloved away.

Pray!

That's what Denzel did. He prayed as he paced the floor, seeking God to let him keep his wife. For he felt something was desperately wrong. The baby should have come by now.

"It's coming again," Kindra cried.

"Squeeze my hand, and squeeze it hard if you must," Mayme said as she knelt by the bed.

Kindra felt her body fading, as if it would slip into an abyss. "I can't squeeze, but I need to hold your hand," she whispered.

Within moments, the knifing stab of pain filled her body again. She couldn't push. She had no strength left. She struggled to breathe until the pain ebbed once more.

This time, after Corrie checked for the baby's progress and felt to see if the head was close, she looked at Kindra and shook her head. "Your baby be positioned wrong." Corrie washed the blood from her hands. "I deliver many babies, ma'am. Dey come head first. Dis baby not going to enter de world dat way. Yer baby comin' feet first, 'breach', dey call it. I'm sorry, Mistress, de worst ain't over." Corrie visibly shuddered. "We have work to do. We's got to bring dis chile into de world." She looked at Mayme. "Help me!"

"What do you want me to do?" Mayme's eyes were big as saucers.

"You's goin' ta push down on de mistress's stomach when I tell you. I be on de othah side doin' de same thing." She glanced at Kindra. "Tell us when de next contraction be comin'."

"It is now!" Kindra winced, her muscles tensing, her palms pulling at the bedclothes. She bit hard as the pain curled its way to her back. Her teeth dug into her bottom lip, leaving a thin trickle of blood. Then she screamed, the sound coming from somewhere within as she felt she could not utter another breath. Moments later, the pain ebbed.

Mayme stroked Kindra's damp hair. When Kindra looked at her chambermaid through hazy eyes, the young woman was pale, and tears ran down her cheek.

"I'm all right, Mayme," she whispered, a raspy sound. "God's not through with me yet."

Corrie chuckled. "That be right. That be de spirit. You gonna do jist fine." She looked at Mayme. "Let's prop her up on her elbows. Shove dat pillow farther down her back."

Mayme leaned Kindra forward as she pushed the pillow to the base of Kindra's back.

"Miz Kindra, when your body next calls out fer you to push dis baby, you must do so with all your might. We be pushin' from here as well. We'll get dis chile born with de three of us."

Kindra nodded. "I need to wait a moment. The last wave just swept over me." Her breath was labored. All at once Kindra began to pant. "The contraction is on me! It is time!" she cried, bending her head toward her belly, her shoulders arching off the bed.

Mayme and Corrie pushed hard against Kindra's belly, harder than before.

Kindra screamed.

Corrie checked Kinda again and said, "Yes, it be near! Once again!"

Kindra bent into her pain and pushed, a great gasp of air exploding from her lungs. "I can't push any longer!"

"Once more, Miz Kindra! You can't stop now. Push!"

Kindra wanted to fall back against her pillow and let sleep simply wash over her and carry her to a softer place. She wanted the pain gone. But Corrie's voice cut through the fog of her thoughts.

"Once more, Miz Kindra! You got to push one more time!"

Kindra gritted her teeth and shut her eyes. She didn't know where the strength came from, but she grabbed the bedding in both her fists and she pushed with all her might. She screamed . . . just before the pain slipped away. It was gone, just like that.

For a moment, there was silence. So still. Her eyes clamped shut, Kindra listened. She waited to hear if she was still there or if she had slipped away from earth and gone to heaven. The pain was gone, but then she heard the gentle rain pitter-pattering in the distance as if it ran down the window. And from someplace in the distance came a tiny wail, mingled with that of giddy laughter.

Kindra's eyes opened to see her baby held high. "You have a daughter! Kindra. It's a girl!" Mayme's voice quavered and she went to the door of the bedchamber and poked her head out.

"Massa! It's a girl!"

The room was quiet as Denzel and Kindra admired their new daughter. Kindra kissed the infant's black curly hair, still damp from being washed. The babe smelled of fresh soap and was bundled in a soft blanket wrapped tightly around her tiny form.

Tiny eyes blinked in the dim room, seemingly at her parents who gazed lovingly at her.

"Does she have your green eyes?" Denzel asked, his rough thumb stroking the infant's downy cheek.

"It's too soon to tell," Kinda said, trying to get a good glimpse of their daughter's eyes as the baby squinted at them.

"She'll have dark skin like you," Kindra said, smiling up at Denzel.

"Have you settled on a name?"

"I like the name, 'Damaris.' It's a biblical name. And it has a feminine ring to it."

"Damaris," Denzel said aloud. "Damaris Rose?" He glanced at Kindra.

"A lovely name," Kindra said tiredly.

The baby scrunched herself and wiggled beneath the blanket. Her little lips puckered then smoothed. A tiny hand worked its way from the blanket with three little fingers clamped to her thumb and a pinky standing straight up.

Kindra kissed her daughter's hand, love for this child filling a void she hadn't known existed. Her heart felt as if it would swell to overflowing. Nothing could have prepared her for the love she already felt for this tiny little life. And from the look in Denzel's eyes, she wasn't alone.

All at once Damaris scrunched up again and her little face turned red. A sharp wail pierced the room.

Denzel's smile broadened. "She has healthy lungs."

"Yes, and a healthy appetite. I've already fed her once, but I believe she's ready for another feeding."

"I'll leave you two alone for now. I'll be back." Denzel kissed Kindra on the top of her head.

Seeing the storm had passed over the island, Denzel wandered out to the curing barn in search of Ebenezer. He felt ten feet tall as he sauntered out to the building.

"Congratulations, Massa!" came several calls from the workers. News always spread quickly through the slave population.

"We hear it be a girl!" said another.

"You heard right," Denzel smiled.

At the sound of voices, Ebenezer came out of the barn and extended his hand to Denzel. "Congratulations, Massa. I be up all night, prayin' for your missus."

Denzel gazed into the black man's eyes. "Are you a praying man?"

"Yes, suh. I believe the Lawd hears our prayers." He brushed at his shirt and glanced at the Great House. "Word be spreadin' that your missus be havin' a bad time of it. I couldn't sleep. So I stayed up and prayed."

Denzel was touched. He laid a hand on Ebenezer's shoulder. "You're a good man, Eb. I was right to put my trust in you to run things around here."

"Thank you, Massa."

"Now let's talk business. It's about time to plant the fields again, am I right?"

"Yes, Denzel. Let's take a walk to the fields." When they'd walked far enough to be out of earshot from the other workers, Ebenezer's smile turned into a frown.

"Uh-oh, what's up?" asked Denzel.

"I told you I was up all night prayin' for your missus. What I didn't tell you was there was two men on horseback who come down the lane 'bout three o'clock in the mor'nin'."

Denzel swung a look at him.

"Couldn't tell who thoose men be, but they sat on the horses at the end o' the lane talkin' an' lookin' this way fo' a long time." He raised his chin toward the driveway. "I thought maybe it be best iffen I lit my lantern and walked around a bit." He nodded. "It worked. Those men turned their horses back toward town."

"Lord have mercy," Denzel said. "We best keep an eye out. No telling what those two were up to or what they wanted. But I sure don't want to be blindsided. Pick a couple of workers to start a night watch shift. Have them report to me if they see anything out of line." Denzel kicked a clod of dirt. "And don't hesitate to wake me in the middle of the night if they show up again."

"Yes, suh."

"You got a musket?"

"No, suh."

"You know how to shoot one?"

"No, suh."

"We'll look at the fields after a while. For now, come with me. It's time you learned how to shoot a gun."

"Why would I want to do that?"

"Because I don't want to fight the enemy by myself. Whoever's out there is likely thinkin' we're unable to defend ourselves. We have to show them we can handle anyone who wants to trespass onto my land. But I can't do it alone."

"Well, then, you best be showin' me how to shoot a gun, Massa Denzel. I think the feel o' metal in my hands is gonna feel mighty fine."

THIRTY-FIVE

LEAVING BABY KATHERINE with Beatrice, Cameron and Grace stepped out onto the porch of the cottage and looked up the sloped lawn toward the Great House. In the early morning sunlight the exterior of the mansion welcomed them. The white house with dark green shutters stood behind a great giant oak, its branches spread out over the lawn. The oak reached to the sky, all the while sending gray leaf shadows against the elaborate woodwork of the house.

Excitement leaped within Grace. The carpenters were gone this Sunday morning and she wanted to explore every inch of their new home with Cameron. He must have seen the gleam in her eye as he bent and kissed the tip of her nose.

"Come, darlin'. Let's see how much of the house is done. Hopefully, the three of us can move in soon." He touched her elbow as they descended the steps of the cottage and he led her up the small hill.

"The whole time you were gone and building our home, I never imagined it would be this beautiful," Grace said. She had to stop and take in the front of the house. The stairs to the wide porch were steep. She lifted her skirts and started up, Cameron at her side. When they reached the top and looked out over the plantation, the view was spectacular!

"Did you really know the plantation would be like this when you first set out to build?"

"I had an idea," Camp said. "I remember standing in the center of the ground where the house sits now and gazing out at the land and the oak lane in front of me . . ."

Grace glanced up to see a faraway look in his eyes. "And?"

Cameron pulled Grace against his side. "And I knew this had to be the place where you and I would stand one day starting our new life together."

"Hmmm." Grace leaned against him, loving the feel of his strong arms around her.

To the left was the cottage, beyond the slave quarters, and farther, lay the rice fields. In front of them lawn sloped down to the country lane that led to other plantations in both directions. She could see the river flowing lazily beyond the lane, the sun dappling the water. The long avenue to the house was lined with ancient oaks, moss growing on each tree bowing gracefully to the ground.

A parade of peacocks strutted across the lawn, their turquoise feathers fluttering as they cocked their heads to peer up at them.

"You thought of everything." She squeezed Cameron's arm. They watched the fowl continue on to the pond on the right. At this early hour, all the greenery of the trees and brush on the opposite side of the lake were mirrored in the water that was smooth as glass. The white bridge arched across the green image.

"Seen enough?" Cameron gave her a slight nudge and guided her to the front door. Within the next hour, she and Cameron covered every nook and cranny of the house. With no furniture in place, her mind was swirling with plans for each room.

When they reached the parlor, she was surprised to find a tapestry rug lying on the center of the floor all alone. She glanced up at Cameron. "Just a rug?"

"The warehouse down the lane has plenty of furniture to decorate our home." He smiled easily. "I don't pretend to think I could decide where to place the pieces the way you'd want them. I'll leave that to you." He winked at her.

"I want to start today!" Grace sailed across the floor and glanced out the window as a million ideas raced through her mind.

"Whoa! Not so fast, little lady. The construction workers have to finish the ceiling molding and then the place is all yours."

"Oh, Camp," she sighed, "it's more than I could ever have dreamed."

"Come here." Cameron pulled Grace into his arms and tipped her chin. He lowered his lips and kissed her soundly.

A delicious chill ran up her spine. "It's early, Mister Bartholomew, but I could easily lead you back to the cottage and lock us away for the day." She nibbled his lower lip and then eased away from him.

"I might take you up on that." Cameron pulled her back against him.

While they stood in each other's arms, Grace looked past his biceps to the colorful rug.

Cameron's eyes followed her gaze and she raised her brows.

"Wondering why the rug?" he asked.

"Um, yes."

"I thought you'd be curious about that, and rightly so." Cameron released her and bent over the rug. The next thing she knew he was rolling it up. Before he got halfway through the process she saw a peculiar thing.

"A trap door in the middle of the parlor?"

"Yes. Like you said earlier. I thought of everything."

"But why?"

The corners of Cameron's smokey gray eyes crinkled as he grinned.

"Well," she said. "I can understand having a cellar in the kitchen, and even one beyond the back of the house in case of a hurricane, but the parlor?"

"I saw this idea in one of the blue prints before having the house built. The builder gave me an explanation that made perfect sense."

"I'm dying to hear it." Grace stared at the trap door in the floor.

"For one, you wouldn't have to run outside to a cellar should a hurricane threaten us, but more importantly I think this would be a great place to hide should we ever need to."

Grace blinked. "Why would we ever need to hide?"

"I'm surprised you would ask me that after having just fled Jamaica and the slave revolt." He lifted his brows as if he'd made his case.

Grace swallowed the knot in her throat. "Surely we'll not face that challenge again."

"You never know. I thought it was a brilliant idea to have a cellar in the parlor. And besides–" Cameron leaned down and pulled the trap door open. "I'm just thinking ahead for safety reasons, that's all."

Grace leaned over the dark hole and gazed down into the blackness. She glanced back up at her husband.

"This could also be used to hide anything we feel is too valuable to be kept out with the rest of the things in the house," he added.

"And what might that be?" Grace folded her arms over her chest and tapped her foot.

"I haven't a clue at the moment." Cameron chucked her chin. "Does this frighten you?"

"Needing a place to hide . . . the idea that . . . um . . . yes, I suppose it does." She relented and felt a pout forming on her lips.

"Come on," Cameron said. "Let's go down. You'll see there's nothing to be afraid of."

She watched Cameron turn around and take the first step down into the darkness. He glanced up after he was halfway down the sturdy ladder.

"Wait before you come down. I've a kerosene lamp down here," he said.

Grace watched her husband continue his descent to the floor of the cellar. He stepped out of sight. It wasn't long before she heard him strike a match and a flicker of light appeared. A moment later the room lit up and she could see Cameron and the dirt floor of the cellar.

Cameron raised his hand toward her. "Come on. Take the rungs easy."

Grace peeked over the edge one more time before she turned around and let her right foot step onto the ladder. One by one, she lowered her feet feeling for the next rung until it wasn't long before she was looking up at the floor above.

"You're doing great, Grace. Keep going."

She climbed down another four steps and came to the bottom. She glanced up again, brushing her hands against her skirts, seeing they were quite a ways below the parlor.

A couple of trunks sat against one wall. "We can put things in here that we might need for emergency." He tapped the cover of a brown trunk.

Shelves lined another wall. Already a couple of kerosene lanterns sat on them along with a box of matches.

A shiver ran down Grace's spine. Even though the sun was shining bright outside, down here she felt a world away from everything. With the light flickering in the kerosene lamp it gave the illusion that the whole world was dark outside.

The cellar felt cool and damp. She hugged herself and looked about the small room. It was oblong and wide. A bench placed at the far end was the only furniture in the cellar besides the trunks.

Cameron went to the bench and sat down. "Have a seat." He patted the wooden bench.

Grace crossed the floor and sat next to him. From where she sat, she could peer up the ladder to the bright room above.

"What do you think?" Cameron raised his brows again.

A smile cracked her lips and she nudged him with her elbow. "You thought of everything. You're right. This is a perfect place to come should we need it."

"That-a-girl. When you're done putting the house together, you might want to bring down some pillows and blankets. Put them in the trunks."

"That's a good idea. I hope the day never comes that we'd need to hide down here. But I believe this cellar may be a blessing in disguise."

Two weeks later, Grace threw a shawl around her shoulders and bundled the baby tightly in her blanket. She stepped outside the cottage and looked around. A single wagon stood in the circular drive. It belonged to the carpenter who was finishing up the last details of the Great House. Only this morning Cameron had told her they'd be moving into the Great House in the next few days.

She gazed at baby Katie, whose button nose was peeking out of the blanket. She couldn't help herself. She lifted the bundle and kissed the baby. She waited for Beatrice who had taken to joining her on her daily walks. If Katie fussed, the nanny would take the baby back to the cottage.

"Here I am, Miz Grace."

"Good. It's a little nippy this morning." Grace glanced at the gathering clouds moving in from the north.

"Looks like a storm be brewing," Beatrice said.

"We won't go far," Grace said as the two women headed for the colored district. It was Grace's intent that the new slaves become as familiar with her as the slaves in Jamaica had been.

This morning she watched as the women stuffed mattresses with moss from the oak trees. There were several women tugging and pulling on the thick, coarse material, as other women shoved handfuls of moss into a gap in the bedding.

"I've heard of moss being used for mattresses, but I've never seen it done," Grace said.

"There be plenty o' moss on the plantation for the job," Beatrice said.

Grace slowed her steps as she watched the task at hand. A couple of darkies glanced over the shoulders of the other women and stared at her.

Grace raised a hand and waved.

The women did the same, curious eyes pinning hers.

The baby wriggled in the blanket and let out a sharp wail. "Oh, my," Grace said, lifting Katie to her shoulders. The women laughed and nodded their heads at the sound of the baby's cry.

"You best feed the little bitty baby. She be hungry!" one called out. They went back to work stuffing the mattress as they chuckled among themselves and peered at Grace with wide smiles.

Farther up ahead a few women sat on their porches weaving baskets from the long rice grass. It was gratifying to know that none of the crop went to waste.

While the women wove baskets, small children played in the dirt with sticks. They drew pictures on the ground and then covered them over with their bare feet, giggling and glancing over their shoulders at the white mistress.

The men were in the fields, hoeing weeds away from the green stems of the rice. Water filled another rice field across the road. The breeze carried the stagnant scent of the gray and muddy water.

Baby Katie wailed again.

"Are you hungry, my little one?" Grace kissed the baby's cheek and felt it was too cold. She pulled the blanket over Katie's face and turned to Beatrice. "She might just need her diaper changed. Let's go back to the house."

"You want me to take her?" Beatrice held out her hands.

"Yes, please." Grace handed her bundle of joy to the nanny.

"I'll be along shortly should Dinah or Gemma ask." Grace knew the cooks were busy preparing breakfast and would fuss if she took too long coming to the table. But she slowed her steps and gazed about her. She had fallen in love with River Oak and all its people. *God, keep us safe here. Give us the wisdom to do right by these people.*

The sound of wagon wheels rattling up the drive drew her attention and she spotted Cameron reining in the horse in front of the cottage. At second glance, she noticed a mischievous look on her husband's face.

What is he up to now? she wondered and picked up her steps. When she neared the buckboard she saw a bump beneath Cameron's overcoat.

"What do you have inside your coat?" she asked. No sooner were the words out of her mouth than she heard a tiny whimper. Something inside the coat began to jostle and squirm, and she looked at Cameron, curiosity getting the better of her.

"What have you got there?" she asked again.

He reached inside his coat and pulled out a black and white puppy.

"A puppy?"

"For Kitten," Cameron said.

"She's too little for a puppy," Grace laughed and reached up for the furry little creature.

"Not for long. The two of them can grow up together." Cameron set the brake and climbed down. He eyed the puppy in her arms.

Grace was already scratching behind the little dog's ears and the fluffy pup reached up and licked her face.

"Oh! Stop that," she giggled. "Do you have a name for him?"

"Jake. He'll make a fine family dog."

A gust of wind blew over them.

"Let's get inside," Cameron said, as the stable boy took the reins to the horse. The two of them started for the cottage just as the rain began to pelt the dry ground. He reached for the puppy and Grace grabbed for her skirts, lifting the hem as they raced to the house. Once they were on the porch they stopped and stomped the dirt from their shoes.

Grace didn't want to go in just yet. She gazed out over the plantation, her heart swelling just a bit. She knew every day wouldn't be as nice as today. But for now, she felt blessed.

THIRTY-SIX

Kindra Hall, Barbados
30 November, 1831

IT WAS MID-MORNING by the time Denzel corralled Ebenezer and Duncan in front of the house. Jasper was the last to hurry in from the tobacco fields.

"Got the housekeeper planted between two old coots who'll keep her in line, Massa." Jasper grinned in amusement.

"I should have sent Hagar out to the fields right after we moved in," Denzel said, cocking his head toward the green fields. "As far as I know, this is all new to her."

The she-cat reminded him too much of his mother-in-law. He wouldn't have the woman around him. He turned to Jasper. "Give her a couple of days to break into the job."

"Yes, suh. I watch her first couple o' days, but the sooner she pull her weight, the sooner life be better for her," Jasper said.

"Did she finish moving her personal belongings into Bitty's cabin?" Denzel asked.

"Yes, suh. Bitty not too fond o'sharin' her shanty with the likes o' Hagar. I 'spect there gonna be some noise comin' from dat place. That's fo' sure!" Jasper strode to Ebenezer's side. "We keep 'em under control." He slapped Ebenezer's shoulder.

"All right. Now that we've got the woman out of the house, I've called the three of you together for a purpose."

The men shuffled and waited.

"Follow me." Denzel led the men behind the curing barn where a row of canning jars sat on a makeshift table.

"I told Ebenezer I wanted him to learn how to shoot a musket." Denzel glanced at the two younger men. "You two ever shoot a gun?"

They shook their heads and stared at Denzel.

"That's what I thought." Denzel pulled a piece of canvas off an oblong wooden box. He pried open the lid. Inside lay four new long-barreled pistols, along with powder horns, powder and ramrods. He handed each of the men a pistol, and set the remaining contents on the table. For the next several minutes, the men took turns learning how to load the pistols with gunpowder and lead ball.

"All right, men," Denzel said. "It's plain to see you've all got the hang of loading your guns." Denzel raised his hand and signaled for Duncan and Jasper to step back.

"Ebenezer's going first." Denzel pointed at the row of canning jars. "The idea is to shoot those jars off the table." He glanced at the young men. "Pay close attention to what I tell Eb. After he takes a few shots, you're next." He smiled. "It's going to be noisy."

The men nodded, their eyes wide.

Denzel took the pistol and walked about twenty paces from the table. He raised his weapon and leveled it at a jar.

"Stand back," he said. "These pistols can give a fierce kick if you're not ready for it." Bracing himself, Denzel pulled the trigger.

Boom! The rank stench of gunpowder drifted back with the morning breeze.

The three men jumped at the crack of the shot, then laughed nervously. "Massa, that be a powerful weapon you got there," Ebenezer said.

Denzel stared at the spot where the jar once stood. The explosion had sent shards of glass everywhere.

"You think I can aim as well as you?" Ebenezer asked.

"You can do it, Eb. Maybe better."

The rest of the morning was filled with the sound of the guns' explosions piercing the air. By the time the men set their pistols on the rough surface of the table, Denzel felt pride for the three workers.

"You did well," he said. "Keep the guns. You'll need to hide them someplace where only you will know where to find them."

"Massa," Duncan interrupted. "Why you want us to keep the pistols? If the other field workers find them, maybe they steal them."

"Ebenezer spotted some men hanging around the plantation last week. It's my guess that Stanley Bernard is up to no good. He'd know that in the past, none of you had experience with a gun. I can't take the chance of a raid coming here and not being prepared." Denzel gripped the pistol in his hand. "You have my permission to keep doing target practice out behind the barn. Just make sure no one else is around. I don't want any accidents."

Duncan fingered the pistol in his large hand with pride. "I be careful, Massa. If I'm goin' to be any good at protectin' our people, I best practice some more."

"That's what I want to hear," Denzel said. He looked at Jasper.

"Me, too, Massa. We practice together."

"Good. Ebenezer, find a good place to hide the gunpowder and supplies. Think you can put them in the curing barn somewhere?"

"I know just the spot." The three men followed Ebenezer to the barn. He went to a small room off the large building and lifted the lid of what looked like a wooden tool chest. "We keep it here, boss."

"Perfect," Denzel said. He slapped the men's backs. "Let's get back to work."

An explosion reverberated through the air. Kindra set her quill pen down and hurried to the sitting-room window. Mayme entered the room and stopped.

"Did you hear that?" Kindra asked.

Clara and Louiza rushed out of the kitchen, and Netty, the downstairs housemaid, appeared in the entryway. All eyes went wide as the women scurried to the front room to find out what all the commotion was.

Boom!

"Are we bein' attacked?" Louiza asked, as she bounded into the room as fast as her plump frame would allow.

"No, we're not being attacked," Mayme said as she raised her hand in a gesture to calm the women down. "That's the master and some of our men shooting guns behind the barn."

"Whatever for?" asked Kindra, lifting her skirts and crossing the floor to where Mayme stood. She was surprised the chambermaid was privy to what was going on outside.

"I was fetching a bucket of water when I overheard Master Talmaze telling Jasper, Duncan and Ebenezer that they was goin' to have shooting lessons."

"But did Denzel say why?" Kindra circled in front of Mayme.

"Ma'am, I sure don't want to appear as if I've been eavesdroppin' or nothin' like that." A small smile crept into Mayme's cheeks. "I was lookin' for an excuse to be outside when I seen Jasper come traipsin' up the drive. I didn't have any idea he was meetin' up with the master or the overseer."

"You got your sights on that handsome Jasper, have you?" This came from Louiza, whose shoulders lifted as she chuckled and her eyes twinkled.

"Truth be told, I don't know what's come over me," Mayme admitted. "Jasper's been a part of this plantation about as long as anyone else around here. Up till now, it was as if I never knew that man existed." Mayme's cheeks grew rosy.

The women perked up at the news of Mayme's infatuation with the second-in-command field hand.

"Does he know you got eyes fo' him?" Louiza asked, her plump fist landing on her hips. She looked as if she were about to give Mayme a first-hand lesson on how to land a man.

"Of course not," Mayme frowned. "And don't none of you go sayin' nothin'. I only discovered he was handsome jist recent like." She brushed at her skirts. "Jasper probably don't even know I exist." Her hand went to her chin and she gazed out the window.

Boom! The women all jumped again.

Kindra placed her hand on Mayme's arm. "Did you hear my husband say why he's all fired up about shooting these guns?"

"No, ma'am. I didn't catch everythin' they said. I was afraid Jasper would see me hangin' around listenin'." Mayme looked at the women. "By the way, the bucket is still on the counter if you need it."

"Fool girl. We have the kitchen pump if we need water," Clara said, winking.

"I'll use it," Netty said. "I need water to scrub the floor in the library."

"See, you didn't make the trip out there for nothing." Kindra smiled at Mayme.

Crack! Another shot split the air. The women all stared at each other again.

"I don't think we have anything to worry about. You can all go back to work." Kindra watched the women disperse to their duties. She went back to the secretary and her letter to Grace.

She dipped the quill pen into the inkwell and scraped the nib against the bottle to rid the pen of extra ink. She stared at the vellum paper she wrote,

> I was just about to write that not much
> has happened around here since baby
> Damaris was born, but that was before
> I heard the explosion of a gunshot!

Seven days after the men took shooting lessons, Denzel and Kindra were awakened in the middle of the night from a sound sleep. They sat straight up in bed.

As she came to herself, Kindra realized she heard the ominous thunder of riders approaching. Denzel bailed out of bed, threw on his breeches and pulled on his boots. "Stay here!" He sprinted downstairs.

Kindra heard the kitchen door slam as she sprang from the covers and ran to the window. Denzel was shouting commands as the plantation came alive.

Boom! Boom! Boom!

Gunshots cracked through the night from the direction of the slave quarters.

Kindra ran from her room and across the hall to the nursery. Corrie was holding Damaris in her arms, her eyes wide and frightened.

"You must hide!" Kindra whispered. She rushed across the room and flung open a low cupboard door that stood about three feet high. When she opened the door, she pulled out the bedding that was piled inside. She flung the blankets and pillows across the floor. "Give me the baby."

The nanny understood what Kindra wanted her to do. Corrie got down on her knees, crawled into the open compartment, and raised her arms to take Damaris. By now the baby was wailing, her sharp cries piercing the darkness.

"Shhh!" Kindra whispered frantically.

The baby wriggled and squirmed in her arms. Kindra looked down at her daughter and felt a fear she'd never known. She'd do anything to protect her darling baby.

Damaris continued to shove and cry, the sharp wail carrying through the air.

"Shush, little one. Don't cry." Kindra crooned and kissed the top of her downy soft head. She handed the baby down into the hole where Corrie waited with outstretched arms. The nanny immediately cradled the infant, making a shushing sound.

"You should be the one hidin' in here, Miz Kindra," Corrie said.

"No. I need to help Denzel. Here, take a blanket and pillow. You might be in here a while."

Kindra closed the door and shoved a rocking chair in front of it. "I'll come for you when it's safe." She threw the extra blankets in the crib and closed the nursery door.

Back in her room she pulled on her night robe and glanced out the window again. An explosion shattered the thick night air, sending tremors through the plantation. Musket shots exploded like fireworks in the distance. The overpowering stench of gunpowder drifted into the house.

A barrage of gunfire cracked the darkness in the slave quarters, followed by a woman's strangled scream. Kindra flinched. She must do something. She couldn't just stand here helpless as a sow. She eyed the trunk that sat at the foot of her bed. She hadn't looked at the contents since she'd arrived at Kindra Hall. But she knew what lay at the bottom of it.

She knelt beside the trunk and tossed her frocks aside. She came across the letter her father had written her and lifted it out, feeling a surge of hope. She found the secret journal that belonged to her mother and frowned. Then her hand touched something else.

She lifted her father's pistol from its case and placed it on the floor beside her billowing robe. The long-barreled pistol with a walnut handle shone in the moonlight. The gun's breech and barrel were filigreed in Peruvian silver. A small coat of arms with the Cooper seal was engraved on the side of the barrel.

She drew in a small breath, staring at the weapon in her hand, remembering how Denzel had taught her to load. She snatched the powder flask and pulled back the trigger, holding the stop spring down hard with her thumb while inserting powder into the chamber. Next she pressed in the wadded balls and fastened the cap. She rose to her feet, and peered out the window again. A tortured scream rose above the tumult, followed by a crisp *pop! pop! pop!* of pistol and musket fire–louder this time.

She heard horses galloping toward the barns and around the shacks in the slave quarters. The thunder of riders was coming so fast she could feel the ground shaking under the house. With the shouts and horses and the dust and dirt flying, it looked as if a dozen men were bearing straight for the slaves' cabins, yelling and shouting. She heard screams from women and children. A shiver ran up her spine as she heard more gunfire and shouts. The sound of fear filled the air all around her and the terribleness of it all chilled Kindra to her bones. Horrible screams and loud explosions from the guns mingled together in an deafening roar.

Kindra shook from head to toe, feeling helpless as she watched the black-hooded riders fill the grounds below.

One rider slipped off his horse and ran up the steps of the house. She heard the front door slam against the wall as he charged into the entryway. Women screamed below. That could only be Clara and Louiza. *God, keep them safe!* she prayed. The stranger clomped his way up the stairs, the sound of heavy boots threatening all of them.

Kindra moved to the middle of her bedchamber, the heavy pistol in both hands. The gun shook as she pointed it toward the hallway, the hairs raised on the back of her neck as she waited for the vile man to appear at any moment.

Boots thudded on the top landing and her body shook. The gun wobbled in her hand, but she kept it pointed toward the door. The sound of footsteps stopped. Was that a silent shuffling of feet she heard just beyond the door? Her ears strained to hear the vicious snake who lingered near. He was there. She could feel his presence. She waited . . . the barrel of the gun raised and ready.

Then she saw him. The foul man wasn't coming to her chamber. He stood in front of the nursery door with his back to her. Ever so quietly, he turned the door knob and the door creaked open.

Kindra squeezed the trigger. *Boom!*

The man flew forward and sprawled on the floor with a thud. At the same time Corrie screamed inside the closet.

Kindra eyed the man's back for movement. He didn't appear to be breathing and blood thickened on the fabric of his shirt, creating a dark stain. She stealthily stepped over the body and watched him another few seconds. Was he dead? She grabbed a handful of his thick, black hair and looked at the man's hawk face. *Mister Lee*. The former overseer. She released her hold and turned to the closet door. "Corrie!"

"Yes, Miz Kindra?"

"Stay where you are. It's not safe to come out yet."

"Yes, Miz Kindra," said a shaky voice.

Kindra stepped over the body and went back to her bedchamber. She glanced out the window at the fury below. The moon shone bright, illuminating the mass destruction. The men in black hoods hollered and cursed. Marauders recklessly shot their guns in the air, and when darkies ran into the clearing from the slave district, the riders raised their muskets and shot them. The shouting and gunfire continued. The horses sidestepped and whinnied, kicking up dirt.

Then, before her very eyes, she watched Denzel run out in front of a horseman, pointing his pistol at the man. He raised his gun, but not before the rider shot him square in the chest.

"Denzel!"

Everything went cold inside of her as she watched her husband stagger back several steps before he fell to the ground, arms splayed at his sides.

"No!" Kindra cried. "No, God! No!"

THIRTY-SEVEN

KINDRA PICKED UP the hem of her night robe as she ran down the hall, flew down the stairs, and rushed out onto the porch. "Denzel!" she screamed.

The riders thundered down the long drive, their horses kicking up dust, leaving a trail of death behind.

"No!" Kindra cried. She ran out to the yard and slid in front of the deathly still form of her husband. "No!" she sobbed and crumpled to her knees. She leaned over his bloody chest and clamped her arms around him. "Denzel, don't die on me!" Kindra raised her head and searched his face. No movement. She shook him frantically. "Denzel, wake up!" A shudder ran through her body, and all at once her world felt hazy. She *couldn't* lose him.

Someone pulled her away and moved in front of her. It took a moment for her to realize it was Doctor Coby who'd come and now leaned over Denzel's body and listened for a heartbeat.

Chaotic shouting, wailing and gunshots rang out around them. Field hands grabbed their wounded and carried them to their shanties. Others ran down the long drive after the marauders, carrying clubs and shovels, threatening to kill them if they came back. Kindra hugged herself, her teeth chattering. Her world was careening out of control.

"He's not dead . . . yet." Came the doctor's low voice. "We need to get him into the house."

333

"He's alive?" Kindra clutched her robe and rose to her feet. She stared anxiously down at her husband. His chest barely moved; his breathing shallow.

"I need two men to carry him." Doctor Coby called out.

Out of the darkness, Duncan and Jasper came onto the scene. "We carry Massa," said Duncan.

Kindra ran ahead. "Clara! Louiza!" Her voice came hoarse, unfamiliar to her ears. "Light the lamps in the sitting room and be quick about it!"

The two cooks clambered for matches and lit the wicks to the kerosene lamps. The dark room came to life just as the two men carried Denzel into the entryway.

"Where can we lay him?" asked the doctor. The men struggled to hold Denzel's limp body.

"There's a sofa in the sitting room." Kindra said, her heart pounding in her ears. "He's still alive?" she asked, staring at her husband.

"Just barely," said the doctor. "He's hanging on by less than a thread. Step aside, Missus."

Kindra did as she was told. She stared at Denzel's blood-soaked shirt. *God, save him!* She trembled. He had to live!

"Over here," she said. By now the cooks had laid a large blanket on the sofa and a pillow nearby.

"You don't have a downstairs bedroom we could use?" the doctor asked as they eased Denzel on the couch.

"All the bedrooms are upstairs," she said.

"We shouldn't jostle him anymore than we have to," Doctor Coby advised.

"What are you going to do?" Kindra wrung her hands.

"I'm going to get that slug out of his chest," Coby said.

Kindra held her breath. "How?"

"How do you think? Dig it out with a knife, that's how. It'll probably kill him," he added, "but if I don't, close to his heart like that, it'll kill him anyway," Doctor Coby said.

Kindra felt faint. The thought of the doctor cutting into her husband's chest made her stomach roil. Mayme must have seen the change come over her, because she came to Kindra's side and touched her arm. "Miz Kindra, it be time we let the doctor do what he has to do. It's best if we wait in the kitchen."

"Boil some water while you're in there. I'm going to need plenty of it," Coby said. Jasper and Duncan stood back as if waiting for orders.

"You two stand by. I have to go to my cabin and get my black bag. Don't leave, whatever you do. I might need you to hold him down at some point." The doctor walked out of the room and left through the kitchen door.

Kindra had heard all she wanted to hear. If she didn't leave the parlor now, she was going to faint. Upon entering the kitchen, she found that Clara was already pumping water into the pot while Louiza stoked the fire.

"You jist sit down over there, Miz Kindra. We got this."

On shaky legs she folded herself into a chair at the kitchen table. Mayme sat across from her and reached out to take Kindra's trembling hands. Tears welled up in Kindra's eyes. The room blurred. Her heart hammered.

"This be a time we gots to have faith and believe in God, Miz Kindra," said Louiza.

"I . . . I don't know if I have that kind of faith right now. Denzel . . . he's my whole world."

"Don't you worry 'bout havin' enough faith, missus," Clara said. "That's where we come in. My mammy done tell us what the good book say. She say, 'if two or three come together believin' and they pray as one, for *anythin'*, that God hear our p'tition.' There be three of us right here. We best be prayin' for our massa to live and not die, " Clara said.

Mayme looked over her shoulder at Kindra. "That's right. The good Lord, he can hear our prayers all right."

Clara set the pot of water on the stove and then the two cooks came to the table where Kindra sat. "You jist sit tight and we do the prayin'."

The cooks and Mayme made their petitions over the next few moments and when done the three said, "Amen!"

Kindra let out a long sigh. "Thank you."

The cooks smiled and went back to the stove.

Kindra wished she felt better, but the truth was, she didn't. She slumped over the table, her forehead on one arm, and gave way to a torrent of tears. "I can't lose him," she sobbed. "My baby ne . . . needs her . . . father." She hiccupped.

"You go ahead and have a good cry, Miz Kindra. De man upstairs, he understand." Louiza laid a comforting hand on Kindra's head and smoothed her hair.

Kindra wiped her face and stood. "I'm going upstairs to check on the baby." She steeled herself as she climbed the stairs. The dead body would be in the nursery. Entering the room, the still form lay on the floor. Kindra raced to the closet. "Corrie." she called as she pulled the door open and found Corrie and the baby waiting inside. The nanny shrank back, her eyes wide, the baby fast asleep in the crook of her arm. "Oh, Corrie. I'm sorry you had to wait so long." Kindra stretched out her hands. "Give me Damaris."

Corrie leaned forward and handed the sleeping babe to her. Kindra clasped the wriggling baby to her chest. "Are you all right, little one?" A torrent of tears fell as she swayed and kissed the baby's downy head. Glancing down at Mr. Lee's body, she said, "Let's get out of here."

"Bring the baby to my chamber," Corrie said, leading the way.

Kindra followed Corrie to the room next door where she sat and rocked her baby ignoring the tears that streamed down her face. Tremors racked her body. "I have to go downstairs." Kindra said. "I'll send someone to remove the body next door."

"Miz Kindra. I done heard a lot of guns goin' off. Is everybody all right?"

"No, Corrie. Many slaves have been killed . . . and they shot Denzel."

"What?" Corrie moved to Kindra's side.

"He's not dead . . ." Kindra's voice shook as she handed Damaris to Corrie. "I must see how he's doing."

Doctor Coby returned from the slave quarters. He walked through the kitchen carrying a black bag and disappeared into the sitting room. Kindra didn't know what to do right then. She felt helpless. She stared at the stove where the water simmered in the pot. It didn't seem any too anxious to boil. She looked away, frustrated. 'A watched pot never boils', Dinah used to say. The kitchen grew quiet as the four women waited to hear the water bubble and hiss.

Doctor Coby reentered the kitchen, his sleeves rolled up. "He came to," he said to Kindra. "He's mighty weak. I'm not sure I can do him any good. But he's asking for you. Says he wants to talk before–"

Kindra ran to the sitting room, tears streaming down her cheeks.

Denzel lay there, eyes closed. Should she wake him? He must have sensed her standing over him because his eyes opened and he gave her a slight smile.

"Hey . . ." he said weakly.

"Denzel," she said. Her night robe rustled as she knelt beside him, her small hands clasping his large, callused one. He looked so pale and his breathing was raspy.

"Don't talk, honey. I'm here," she whispered.

"I . . . I." Just that much effort seemed to take everything out of him.

"Shhh." Kindra touched his lips softly with her fingertips.

He brushed her hand away and winced. "I . . . love . . . you," he finally said.

Tears sprang to her eyes again. Was he saying goodbye? "Denzel, stay with me. Don't you give up!"

"I . . . want to . . ." His eyes closed and his head fell to one side. Fear clutched her heart. Did he drop back into unconsciousness or was he . . .? She leaned her ear to his stained chest. She barely heard the sporadic rhythm of his heart, so faint was it. She leaned back on her heels and rested her head on his arm. A single tear escaped and trailed down her cheek. His heart was so faint, while hers beat hard and fast as if jungle drums warred within her.

Gentle hands pulled her away.

"I must work fast if I'm to save him."

Kindra rose and clamped her hands together, staring at the knife in the doctor's hands.

"Leave the room, please. I'll work better without you here." He glanced behind her, and she looked back to see Mayme standing by.

"I need your maid to assist me. You go."

Kindra picked up her skirts and fled to the bright kitchen again. Once seated at the table, she crossed her arms over her chest in an attempt to stop the tremors overtaking her. Time ticked slowly. She and the cooks waited in silence.

An eternity came and went before the doctor came back to the kitchen. Mayme followed. He held his surgical knife and wiped it with a white cloth. With so much blood, both the knife and cloth were stained crimson. Kindra's stomach lurched and she looked away.

Coby cleaned up in the sink then went back to get his bag. Ignoring the servants, he nodded to Kindra to follow him to the door. Desperate for good news, she stood on the back steps of the kitchen porch while her world stood still.

"I got the slug out," Coby said. He handed the lead ball to her. She took it, feeling the coarse bullet.

"It doesn't look good, Miz Kindra. He lost a lot of blood, but . . . that's not the worst of it."

She searched the doctor's eyes and waited.

"It was too close to his heart . . ."

Kindra swallowed.

"I did what I could, but I'm thinkin' it'd be best if you don't hold out much hope . . ." he said. "I gave him laudanum for the pain. That'll hold him for a few hours. I'll come back in the mornin' in the off chance that he survives the night."

"Th . . . thank you, Doctor Coby. Come early, will you?"

"I'll come first thing." He glanced out toward the slave quarters and sighed. "One of the men in the slave district said Bernard was one of the men in the raid. Said he shot your husband."

The news sent a jolt through her. "He got away?"

"No one's seen him since his henchmen left."

Kindra hugged herself.

"There're more folks who need my services tonight. I don't think I'm gonna get much sleep."

Kindra followed his gaze. Field hands were working in the dark, moving dead bodies to the side of the drive, and helping others to their cabins.

What would the morning bring? Death surrounded them.

"Thank you," Kindra stammered woodenly and watched the doctor disappear into the night.

Duncan and Jasper stepped out of the house and started past her.

"Wait." Kindra called to the men. "There's a dead body in the nursery. He needs to be removed from the room."

"Who killed him?" asked Duncan.

"I did. He was after my baby."

The two men stared at each other, then turned back toward the house. They quickly disappeared inside.

She walked back into the house. Mayme sat on a footstool next to Denzel. Kindra needed only to dart up the stairs to hold baby Damaris one more time before she spent the night in a vigil beside her wounded husband.

Kindra awakened sometime in the wee hours of the morning. A single candle flickered on a table near the sofa. It was dreadful seeing Denzel's pale face, his shirt torn away, a large bandage wrapped over his chest with stains of red showing through. She felt his forehead. Clammy and cold. His breathing, shallow. *God, spare his life!* She watched and prayed until slumber claimed her.

The doctor came at dawn. He changed Denzel's dressing and left again, his face grim. He offered no words of hope, saying only, "He not out of the woods yet. He'll bleed some more. Then we'll see if infection sets in. If not, he may live. Only the good Lord knows."

Kindra nodded and kept her eyes on her husband, her arms hugging her midsection.

"Talk to him and wipe his face with a damp cloth. It might revive him." The doctor shrugged and headed for the kitchen. "I got others fighting for their lives." Then he disappeared.

As the doctor instructed, she continued to sit beside Denzel. Sometimes Mayme joined her. Sometimes her chambermaid stayed with him while Kindra stretched her legs and went upstairs to hold the baby. Each time she sat beside him, she spoke softly of their days together, reminding him what he had to live for. Sometimes she sang to him. Sometimes she held his limp hand watching for signs that he would pull through. Always, she prayed.

Although everybody took turns sitting with Denzel, Kindra did the most. Day and night someone was assigned to stay by him. Fever came on him the fifth day. A raging heat that consumed his body, almost scorching to touch. He talked out of his head for almost a week after that, his words making no sense. Words about the foreman, Stanley Bernard, coming back. Words about Jamaica. Words about Kindra. Sometimes he whispered her name, and when he did, tears slid down his face. Every now and then he cried out to God. But more than anything, he slept. Kindra had begun to think her husband would never wake up.

Her mind flew to Stanley Bernard. No matter what happened to Denzel, the man would have to pay for what he'd done. One of the workers said Bernard shot her husband. How to make him pay, she didn't know, but Bernard would not get away with it. Justice would prevail for Denzel.

Kindra walked to the slave district. The dead bodies had been cleared away and buried. People roamed the grounds with numb expressions on their faces. Some had lost children during the awful raid. Some had lost spouses. It was a terrible thing to see, the loss of life and watching those who were left behind to pick up the pieces.

Helping the people gave Kindra renewed hope. She worked alongside the women, cleaning out their cabins, hoeing their gardens, bathing their infants. She wanted the women to know she cared. Something about working beside them gave life some meaning.

More than once in the past weeks she had looked death in the eye. If Denzel didn't pull through, could she stay here at Kindra Hall without him? Could she run the tobacco plantation without the help of her strong husband? And what of Damaris? Would it be safe to stay here with her daughter without her father to protect them?

She wouldn't allow her mind to dwell on the dark side too long. Denzel would pull through. She must be strong for him. She had to believe that one day soon, her husband would walk out of the house well and restored. This was only a test of her faith.

She carried a toddler on her hip, giving relief to a woman who'd spent much of her day nursing her own husband back to health. Kindra wandered out to the graveyard. Fresh mounds of dirt dotted the interior of the fenced-in area. Names were carved on crude stakes. Many of the names she didn't know. This saddened her. She and Denzel were still so new to the plantation; they hadn't learned who all these people were. The toddler clung to her neck as she roamed the rows of graves until she came to a name she recognized. Staring at the name, she remembered the strangled scream that had seared through the air that fateful night. Not only the men were attacked, so were the women and children. She closed her eyes. She didn't want to see the name on the stake. Had the scream she'd heard come from the body that lay here? *Hagar.* Just a name on the crude post. No date of birth or death. Just Hagar. *Why had Denzel been so adamant about sending her to the fields?*

Kindra hugged the little boy to her and wiped a tear from her eye. She glanced back at the house. Would she have better news today? Doctor Coby still didn't give much hope.

She walked back to the slave district and delivered the child to his mother. Then she picked up her gait and walked toward the Great House. Just this morning she read from the Good Book: *Have not I commanded thee? Be strong and of a good courage; be not afraid, neither be thou dismayed: for the Lord thy God is with thee withersoever thou goest.* A gust of wind stirred up and blew over her and she looked up at the vast blue sky. *Is that You, Lord? Is that the winds of courage washing over me?* She closed her eyes and lifted her face to the heavens. When she opened them, she felt renewed.

Kindra strode into the house and walked straight to the parlor. There Denzel was, with his eyes open. A little color had returned to his cheeks. The maid had gotten him into a clean shirt, and as she stared in disbelief, he tried to stand up. But he was too weak and lightheaded to last more than a few seconds. He quickly sank to the couch.

"What are you doing?" Kindra rushed to his side. She knelt on the floor before him. "It's good to see you awake. But you mustn't overdo." She pressed his shoulder gently, making him lean against the sofa for support.

"If I have to be in this room one more day, I think I'll explode," Denzel said in a raspy voice.

Kindra laughed and kissed his cheek. "You're sitting up and you're alive!"

Denzel pulled her carefully against him and stared into her eyes. "Looking at you gives me a reason to live. I knew every moment you sat by my side. I sensed when you were near and smelled the sweet fragrance of your perfume. It kept me breathing." He kissed her forehead. "I'm going to live," he laughed softly. "And I'm going to be here for years to come, to raise our family and grow old with you. Will you grow old with me, my sweet flower?"

"Yes," Kindra sighed. "That's my heart's desire."

He kissed her softly and ran his thumb over her bottom lip. "I know you will. I never doubted it for a moment."

She kissed him then. A kiss that would last them for a lifetime.

"Where's Damaris?" he asked.

"She's upstairs with the nanny."

"Bring her down to me, please."

Kindra started up the stairs, and then stopped. Looking down at her husband sitting up on the sofa, joy flooded her soul. He'd been given a second chance at life. She imagined many more years to come in which she and Denzel would raise their family together. Who knows what tomorrow might bring? She didn't know, and for now she didn't care. She would delight in today. Picking up her skirts she padded up the stairs to bring Denzel's child to him.

Weeping may last for a night, she thought, *but joy comes in the morning!*

EPILOGUE

KINDRA CARRIED THE letter from Grace to a bench under an oak tree. She had escaped the house to read her letter alone. She tore the seal loose and pulled out the vellum paper. A scent of lavender wafted in the air. *Grace and her lavender perfume.* Kindra smiled. Her eyes trailed over the words and she read:

My dearest Kindra,

I hope this post finds you, Denzel and baby Damaris doing well. This year has been quite an adventure for Cameron and me. We now live in Fields Landing on our new plantation, River Oak. And as you know, our darling baby Katherine fills our days with laughter and joy. We both have nicknames for her. Kit for Cameron, and Katie for me. For now she's too little to be confused with her names.

Most of the slaves made it on our voyage to South Carolina. But I regret to inform you that Laulie did not. I know you loved her as did Cameron. She not only raised both of you, but she taught you the Word of God. She was a wonderful woman. I have no doubt that she is roaming the streets of heaven now, and telling Father all about what is going on with us.

On a lighter note, River Oak is such a pleasant place to live. A pond graces the grounds with a bridge over it. And peacocks roam the plantation, often shrieking their raucous calls. Their colorful feathers fanning out more than make up for the noise they make. Taney River flows in front of our property and throughout the day, the *River Belle* steamboat paddles up and down the water, either picking up or delivering people along the way to or from their plantations. Steamboats loaded with cargos of rice are often seen on the river, too. Our rice has grown well and Cameron says we've had a good first year selling the Carolina Gold.

The carpenters are done building the Great House. It is a beautiful structure. Cameron said it's the loveliest of all the mansions in the Lowcountry. Now it's my turn to decorate the rooms. I will put Mother's and Father's portraits side-by-side in the sitting room. There is much to be done, but long days to do it in. I'm in no hurry as I want everything to be perfect.

Every day, I watch for a letter from you. I'm dying to hear all about your first year at Kindra Hall. You must send me a lengthy letter. I want to hear everything. You have always been good at writing word pictures. You must tell me about your darling, Damaris. Does she have your green eyes? Is she fair like you, or does she have her father's coloring?

I miss you so very much. Now that we are both settled, we must plan a visit. Either you come here to South Carolina, or we must find time and set sail for Barbados. We cannot let too much time go by for I could not stand not seeing you soon. Give Denzel our good wishes, and kiss your baby girl from her Aunty Grace.

Till we see each other again,

I send my fond love and affection,

Your sister, Grace

Kindra wiped the tears from her face, and held the letter to her heart. She swallowed the ache in her throat and stood. She agreed with Grace. They couldn't let too much time go by before they met again. She gathered her skirts and skipped back to the house. Her daughter would be waking up soon, and as Grace requested, she would kiss her little brow and tell her that was from her aunty.

Over all it had been a good year for her and Denzel, too. She lifted her chin. They would face whatever tomorrow brought. God had given them the courage to face their trials. He would give them the courage to face the future. And hopefully, she and Grace would be able to sit on the porch and share their dreams. God knows they had plenty of them!

Kindra lifted baby Damaris from her cradle and walked out onto the porch. Eyeing the porch swing, she slid onto the seat and set it moving into a gentle rhythm with her toe on the planked floor. Gazing at the green lawn her mind went to her mother, Tia. What did she mean when she wrote in her journal that she'd stolen the emerald stones? And who was Jule Spade?

Thank you for reading!

Dear Reader,

I hope you enjoyed The Winds of Courage, book two. I have to tell you I really love the characters Cameron and Grace, and Denzel and Kindra. Be sure to stay tuned because book three is in the works. Will the drama end? No! Will Grace and Kindra find a happy ending? I sure hope so.

As an author, I love feedback. Tell me what you liked, what you loved, even what you hated. I'd love to hear from you. You can write me at Authormarilynking@gmail.com and visit me on the web at www.marilynking.net.

Finally, I need to ask a favor. If you're so inclined, I'd love a review of The Winds of Courage. Loved it, hated it–I'd just enjoy your feedback. Reviews can be tough to come by these days, and you, the reader, have the power to make or break a book. If you have the time, here's the link to my author page, along with all my books on Amazon:
The Winds of Grace: http:goo.gl/tCmKTe
Isabel's Song: http:goo.gl/PZGCkv

Thank you so much for reading The Winds of Courage and for spending time with me.

Warm Regards,

Marilyn King

Made in the USA
San Bernardino, CA
19 November 2017